When you first meet Isaac Asimov, you get the impression that all the man is interested in is himself. It's all a put on. Beneath Isaac's public persona is a very intelligent and perceptive human being. Then you begin to read Asimov's writings. Your first impression is, "This is easy! Why, I could write like this." Try doing it. That simple, straightforward style hides depths of understanding and talent far deeper than almost anyone suspects. As you will see in the pages that follow, Asimov has chosen to write about scientists—those flawed and faulty humans who strive to create wonders. Perhaps that is the essence of true optimism, the belief that imperfect men can build toward perfection. That is certainly the message you will find in this book. That is the foundation of faith that has made Isaac Asimov who and what he is.

—Ben Bova, from the Introduction to *The Edge of Tomorrow*

THE EDGE OF TOMORROW

W9-BZW-728

ISAAC ASIMOV
THE EDGE OF TOMORROW

A TOM DOHERTY ASSOCIATES BOOK

This is a work of fiction. All the characters and events portrayed in this book are fictitious, and any resemblance to real people or events is purely coincidental.

THE EDGE OF TOMORROW

Copyright © 1985 by Nightfall, Inc.

All rights reserved, including the right to reproduce this book or portions thereof in any form.

A TOR Book
Published by Tom Doherty Associates, Inc.
49 West 24 Street
New York, NY 10010

Cover art by Boris Vallejo

ISBN: 0-812-53133-7   CAN. ISBN: 0-812-53134-5

Library of Congress Catalog Card Number: 85-52301

First edition: July 1985
First mass market printing: July 1986

Printed in the United States of America

0 9 8 7 6 5 4

ACKNOWLEDGMENTS

"Unique Is Where You Find It." © 1985 by Isaac Asimov.

"The Eureka Phenomenon." *Fantasy and Science Fiction*, June 1971; © 1971 by Mercury Press, Inc.

"The Feeling of Power." *Worlds of If Science Fiction*, February 1958; © 1957 by Quinn Publishing Co., Inc.

"The Comet That Wasn't." *Fantasy and Science Fiction*, November 1976; © 1976 by Mercury Press, Inc.

"Found!" *Omni*, October 1978; © 1978 Omni Publications International, Ltd.

"Twinkle, Twinkle, Microwaves." *Fantasy and Science Fiction*, May 1977; © 1977 by Mercury Press, Inc.

"Paté de Foie Gras." *Astounding Science Fiction*, September 1956; © 1956 by Street & Smith Publications, Inc. Copyright renewed 1984 by Isaac Asimov.

"The Bridge of the Gods." *Fantasy and Science Fiction*, March 1975; © 1975 by Mercury Press, Inc.

"Belief." *Astounding Science Fiction*, October 1953; © 1953 by Street & Smith Publications, Inc. Copyright renewed 1981 by Isaac Asimov.

"Euclid's Fifth." *Fantasy and Science Fiction*, March 1971; © 1971 by Mercury Press, Inc.

"The Plane Truth." *Fantasy and Science Fiction*, April 1971; © by Mercury Press, Inc.

"The Billiard Ball." *Worlds of If Science Fiction*, March 1967; © by Galaxy Publishing Corporation, 1967.

"The Winds of Change." *Speculations*, edited by Isaac Asimov and Alice Laurance (Houghton Mifflin, 1982); © 1982 by Laura W. Haywood and Isaac Asimov.

"The Figure of the Fastest." *Fantasy and Science Fiction*, November 1973; © 1973 by Mercury Press, Inc.

"The Dead Past." *Astounding Science Fiction*, April 1956; © 1956 by Street & Smith Publications, Inc. Copyright renewed 1984 by Isaac Asimov.

"The Fateful Lightning." *Fantasy and Science Fiction*, June 1969; © 1969 by Mercury Press, Inc.

"Breeds There a Man?" *Astounding Science Fiction*, June 1951; © 1951 by Street and Smith Publications, Inc. Copyright renewed 1979 by Isaac Asimov.

"The Man Who Massed the Earth." *Fantasy and Science Fiction*, September 1969; © 1969 by Mercury Press, Inc.

"Nightfall." *Astounding Science Fiction*, September 1941; © 1941 by Street & Smith Publications, Inc. Copyright renewed 1968 by Isaac Asimov.

"The Planet That Wasn't." *Fantasy and Science Fiction*, May 1975; ©
    1975 by Mercury Press, Inc.
"The Ugly Little Boy." *Galaxy*, September 1958 (under the title of
    "Lastborn"); © 1958 by Galaxy Publishing Corporation.
"The Three Who Died Too Soon." *Fantasy and Science Fiction*, July
    1982; © 1982 by Mercury Press, Inc.
"The Last Question." *Science Fiction Quarterly*, November 1956; © by
    Columbia Publications, Inc. Copyright renewed 1984 by Isaac
    Asimov.
"The Nobel Prize That Wasn't." *Fantasy and Science Fiction*, April
    1970; © 1970 by Mercury Press, Inc.

Dedicated to

the memory of Sally S. Greenberg
(1937-1984)

CONTENTS

FOREWORD

When you first meet Isaac Asimov, you get the impression that all the man is interested in is himself. After all, his favorite topics of conversation are (in order of frequency) the number of books he has written, the fact that he is a genius, the fact that he is sweetly dangerous among the women, and the fact that he enjoys immensely all of the above.

It isn't a lie, exactly. Isaac is proud of his accomplishments and has every right to be. And he certainly is heterosexual. But the brash, bragging public image he presents, the kid from the Brooklyn candy store who will compose a lecherous limerick at the drop of a hint—that's a *persona*, a disguise that Isaac wears, like the stingy millionaire that Jack Benny portrayed for so many decades, or the clumsy, pratfalling oaf played by Chevy Chase.

It's all a put-on. Beneath the cloak Isaac shows to the public is a thoughtful, kind and loving man; not only a friend, but a friend in need, a man who has been rather like a big brother to me for nearly thirty years. There is a great heart in Isaac, a heart as great as his mind.*

Let me tell you just one story to illustrate that point.

Shortly after I first met Isaac, when we both lived in the Boston area, he phoned to tell me that I would soon be receiving a call from the editor of *Amazing Science Fiction*

---

*Although Isaac's heart is truly great, its coronary arteries needed the help of triple bypass surgery in 1983. He is fully recovered now.

magazine, asking me to write a series of nonfiction articles about the possibilities of life on other worlds.

"She asked me to do the series," Isaac said, "but I told her I couldn't because I was too busy and that you were a better choice anyway, since you knew more about the subject than I did."

I damned near fainted. Here's the foremost writer in the field, a PhD biochemist and polymath, telling me—a writer with almost no credits and only a smattering of the basics of astronomy—that I knew more about extraterrestrial life than he did.

Sensing my consternation, Isaac explained, "Look, I'll tell you everything I know about the subject. And you must know some things I don't. So that way you'll know more than I do!"

He was as good as his word. I did the series, and it established me as a writer within the science-fiction community.

So much for Isaac's public *persona*.

Then you begin to read Asimov's writings. Fact or fiction, the first impression you get is, "This is *easy*! Why, I could write something like this."

Try doing it. I have, and it's far from easy. For that simple, straightforward Asimovian style hides depths of understanding and talent far deeper than almost anyone suspects.

Isaac loves numbers, as you will see in many of the essays in this book. And when he talks about his writing, he stresses the number of books he's written: more than three hundred as of this moment. Other writers talk about the pain of creation, the turmoil of their art, the struggle of overcoming writer's block. Isaac sits down and writes. He enjoys doing it; he's probably the only person I know who actually enjoys the physical task of writing.

Look beyond the numbers. Look at the breadth of subject matter he has written about: everything from the Bible to biochemistry, from poetry to paleontology, from history to science fiction.

He does make it look easy. His special genius is to take a subject, any subject, and present it so clearly and so well that the reader can understand it with hardly any effort at all.

Isaac writes in a way that has often been described as an

effortless style. (I once teased him that it was really a "style-less effort." It took him all of ten seconds to realize that I was kidding.) Because his style is so smooth, so clear, so logical and rational, there is some tendency among the more self-conscious literati to dismiss Isaac's nonfiction writings as "mere popularizations" and his science fiction as "old-fashioned pulp writing."

To paraphrase Shakespeare: They jest at scars, who never felt a wound. I have spent a fair part of my life as an editor, and let me tell you that finding essays about science (or any subject) that are as clear and cleanly written as Asimov's is rare to the vanishing point. And finding fiction as thought-provoking and haunting as "The Ugly Little Boy" or "Nightfall" is equally uncommon. If these be popularizations and old-fashioned, then let's have more of them! I dare the literati to produce them.

As you will see in the pages that follow, Isaac has chosen to write about scientists—real ones out of history and imaginary ones from the realm of science fiction.

You will find some marvelously curious things in these essays and stories. You will meet some fascinating people. Some of them you may already know; others will be new to you. There are many surprises in store, such as:

• Isaac Newton, revered as the greatest figure in science by *our* Isaac, was a moral coward.

• Two famous writers—Goethe and Omar Khayyam—were involved in the advancement of mathematics.

• The weight of the Earth is zero.

• Ben Franklin's lightning rod did more to shake the grip of religion on the mind of Western man than Darwin's theory of evolution.

• There was no Nobel Prize for physics given in 1916, and Isaac wants to mount a campaign to correct that injustice.

• Queen Victoria (of all people) struck one of the earliest and strongest blows for Women's Liberation.

All that is in the nonfiction essays of this book: the *Scientists Past*. In the fiction, the *Scientists Future*, you will meet:

• A goose that literally lays golden eggs, with an accurate scientific description of how it's done.

• A scientist who realizes that the human race is nothing more than an experiment created by a superior intelligence.

- A man who can walk on air.
- A homicide committed with a billiard ball.
- A man in the far future who can do arithmetic in his head . . . and pays the price for that talent.
- A Neanderthal baby snatched out of his own time and brought into ours.
- A world that periodically goes insane.
- And, in the story that Isaac has often claimed to be his personal favorite, a computer that puzzles for eons over "The Last Question."

A strange thing about these works of fiction. In each of these stories, Isaac Asimov—the eternal optimist, the rational enthusiast of science—shows what can only be described as the dark side of scientific research. These stories show scientists as the public never sees them, as the history books never portray them: scientists who doubt themselves, who worry about the moral implications of their work, who scheme against one another, and even commit murder.

Which proves the point I started with. Beneath Isaac's public *persona* is a very perceptive, extremely intelligent and sensitive human being. He knows, better than most of those who rail against scientific research and mushrooming technology, that science is a *human* activity, that research is conducted by fallible, emotional, imperfect men and women.

Yet despite the dark side, despite the schemings and shortcomings of the people in these stories, the work of science proceeds. These flawed and faulty human beings build marvelous creations for us: generators that deliver energy endlessly, machines that allow us to travel through time, computers and robots that free humankind from drudgery.

Perhaps that is the essence of true optimism, the belief that imperfect human beings can build toward perfection. That is certainly the message you will find among the scientists, past and future, in this book. That is the foundation of faith that has made Isaac Asimov who and what he is.

Ben Bova
West Hartford,
Connecticut

INTRODUCTION

I have put together a number of collections of my nonfiction essays (usually, but not always, on science). Then, too, I have also put together a number of collections of my fiction (usually, but not always, science fiction). Besides that, I have also published full-length nonfiction books and full-length novels.

This has made it possible for some readers to read my nonfiction and avoid my fiction—and vice versa. It is certainly their right to do this, but nevertheless, it doesn't please me to have them do so. It is not part of my policy to have people avoid any major part of my works. My idea of a properly run Universe is one in which everybody reads everything I write.

Consequently I was at once interested when my good friend, Ben Bova, suggested I put together a collection that contained *both* fiction and nonfiction.

Why not? For all I know, someone who would then read the book for the sake of one category might, simply because the other was so handy, read a bit of that, too. And, liking it (I can dream, can't I?), that reader would then go out and buy a light sampling of several dozen books of mine that earlier he would not have dreamed of touching.

Ben said there ought to be a unifying theme that would tie both halves of the book together, and he suggested that all the items in the book should deal, in one way or another, with scientists.

1

This was a very good thought (so I'm not surprised that Ben had it) since I am a professional chemist by training and a science historian by fascination.

"Why not," said Ben, "couple a science essay that details some particular point about a real scientist with a piece of science fiction that makes the same point about a fictional scientist?"

My heart bounded. That would be terrific.

Unfortunately, after considerable thought and after leafing through my works (not an easy task, considering the wordage), I saw this wouldn't do. I did not write my science-fiction with the intention of paralleling any of my nonfiction essays on science. It never occurred to me to do so. In fact, to be perfectly honest, I don't know that I ever thought of anything at all when I wrote a story—except, perhaps, that it would be nice if I sold it and made an honest dollar or two.

However, while I was convincing myself that the whole thing wouldn't work, a contract arrived from Tor Books (with whom Ben works as an advisor) for just such a hybrid collection.

As it happens, I have a constitutional aversion to not signing a book contract. I don't know why that should be, but it is partly the reason for the somewhat large number of books I have managed to turn out. Spending an hour each day signing contracts means, perforce, spending the other twenty-three hours writing. (I have long since abandoned any thought of eating or sleeping.)

So I signed the contract, and now I have to put together the book.

But I still can't present fiction and nonfiction in pairs, like a latter-day Plutarch. I can't say: "Note how the scientist of the future in this particular science-fiction story parallels the scientist of the past in this particular science essay." It just doesn't seem to me that I have any cases of this sort.

Instead, all I can do is present you with a group of essays and a group of stories, all of which feature scientists at work. It may be that *you* can see parallels and will write me letters that begin, "You idiot—." (I do get occasional letters that begin in that way.)

Don't start to analyze the book right away though. First read the essays and stories in a lighthearted, carefree manner and enjoy them thoroughly (I can still dream, can't I?), and then go over them again and see if you can obtain deep insights with which you can enlighten me.

The twelve essays contained in this book are taken from *The Magazine of Fantasy and Science Fiction*. I have been writing essays for this magazine for twenty-six years now, without missing an issue, and I have, throughout, been given a completely free hand.

The result is that I do anything I want to in these essays, and one of the things I seem to want to do is to start each essay with a personal anecdote. The main reason I do this is because it amuses me to do so, but a subsidiary reason (I have been told by those who investigate my techniques more closely than I myself care to do) is that it serves to slip the reader into the body of the essay in a more or less painless manner. In any case, you are warned.

In the fiction portions of the book you must remember that I don't deal with real scientists, although I do my best to make my scientists realistic. All the scientists exist in a possible future, near or far, and all deal with problems of a kind that don't involve real scientists today.

* * *

EDITOR'S NOTE:

Far be it from me to argue with The Good Doctor, but I think most readers will find some unifying themes that link these essays and stories.

3

1

Unique Is Where You Find It

This is not exactly "Scientists Future," and it is not exactly science fiction. It is "Scientists Present," and it is a puzzle story. What's more, this story has never appeared in any of my collections, for it is freshly written. It is a "Black Widower" story, one of a well-established series of stories I have written, of which this is the fiftieth. Parts of this story are quite authentic since I draw on my own experiences as a graduate student. I was a wise guy in those days, very much like Horace, and the Beilstein incident took place exactly as I say, complete (I believe) with damage to my grades. The puzzle, of course, is invented.

Emanuel Rubin would have fought to the death rather than admit that the smile on his face was a fatuous one. It was though. Try as he might, he could not conceal the pride in his voice or the pleased gleam in his eye.

"Fellow Widowers," he said, "now that even Tom Trumbull is here, let me introduce my guest of the evening. This is my nephew, Horace Rubin, eldest son of my younger brother and the shining light of the new generation."

Horace smiled weakly at this. He was a full head taller than his uncle and a bit thinner. He had dark, crisply curled hair, a prominent, well-beaked nose, and a wide mouth. He was definitely not handsome, and Mario Gonzalo, the artist of the

4

Black Widowers, was fighting hard not to exaggerate the features. Photographic accuracy was caricature enough. What didn't get into the drawing, of course, was the unmistakable light of quick intelligence in the young man's eyes.

"My nephew," said Rubin, "is working toward his PhD at Columbia. In chemistry. And he's doing it now, Jim, not in 1900 as you did."

James Drake, the only Black Widower with a legitimate doctorate (although all were entitled to be addressed as "Doctor" by the club rules), said, "Good for him—and my own degree was earned just before the war; World War II, that is." He smiled reminiscently through the thin column of smoke curling upward from his cigarette.

Thomas Trumbull, who had, as usual, arrived at the preprandial cocktail hour late, scowled over his drink and said, "Am I dreaming, Manny, or is it customary to elicit these details during the grilling session after dinner? Why are you jumping the gun?" He waved his hand petulantly at the cigarette smoke and stepped away from Drake in a marked manner.

"Just laying the foundation," said Rubin indignantly. "What I expect you to grill Horace about is the subject of his coming dissertation. There's no reason the Black Widowers can't gain a little education."

Gonzalo said, "Are you going to make us laugh, Manny, by telling us you understand what your nephew is doing in his laboratory?"

Rubin's scanty beard bristled. "I understand a lot more about chemistry than you think."

"You're bound to, because I think you understand zero." Gonzalo turned to Roger Halsted and said, "I happen to know that Manny majored in Babylonian pottery at some correspondence college."

"Not true," said Rubin, "but still a step above your major in beer and pretzels."

Geoffrey Avalon, who listened with disdain to this exchange, detached his attention and said to the young student, "How old are you, Mr. Rubin?"

"You'd better call me Horace," said the young man in an

5

unexpected baritone, "or Uncle Manny will answer and I'll never get a word in edgewise."

Avalon smiled grimly. "He is indeed our conversational monopolist when we allow him to be, but how old are you, Horace?"

"Twenty-two, sir."

"Isn't that rather on the young side for a doctoral candidate, or are you just beginning?"

"No. I should be starting my dissertation about now, and I expect to be through in half a year. I'm rather young, but not unusually so. Robert Woodward got his PhD in chemistry when he was twenty. Of course he nearly got kicked out of school at seventeen."

"Twenty-two isn't bad, though."

"I'll be twenty-three next month. I'll be getting it at that age—or never." He shrugged and looked despondent.

The soft voice of Henry, the perennial and irreplaceable waiter at all the Black Widower banquets, made itself heard. "Gentlemen, dinner is served. We are going to have curried lamb, and our chef, I'm afraid, believes that curry was made to be tasted, so if any of you would prefer something rather on the blander side, tell me now and I will see to it that you are obliged."

Halsted said, "If any faint-heart would rather have scrambled eggs, Henry, just bring me his helping of curried lamb in addition to my own. We must not waste it."

"Nor must we contribute to your overweight problem, Roger," growled Trumbull. "We'll all have the curry, Henry, and bring in the accompanying condiments, especially the chutney and coconut. I intend to be heavy-handed myself."

"And keep the bicarbonate handy, too, Henry," said Gonzalo. "Tom's eyes are more optimistic than his stomach lining."

Henry was serving the brandy when Rubin clattered his spoon against a water glass and said, "To business, gentlemen, to business. My nephew, I have observed, has wreaked havoc on the comestibles and it is time that he be made to pay for that in the grilling session. Jim, you'd be the natural grill-master since you're a chemist of sorts yourself, but I don't want you and Horace to get into a private discussion of chemical minutiae. Roger, you're a mere mathematician, which puts you sufficiently off the mark. Would you do the honors?"

"Gladly," said Halsted, sipping gently at his curacao. "Young Rubin—or Horace, if you prefer—how do you justify your existence?"

Horace said, "Once I get my degree and find myself a position on a decent faculty, I'm sure that the work I do will be ample justification. Otherwise—" He shrugged.

"You seem doubtful, young man. Do you expect to have trouble finding a job?"

"It's not something one can be certain about, sir, but I've been interviewed here and there, and if all goes well, it seems to me that something desirable should solidify."

"If all goes well, you say. Is there some hitch in your research?"

"No, not at all. I had enough good sense to pick a fail-safe problem. Yes, no, or maybe—any of the three possible answers—would earn me a degree. As it happens, the answer is yes, which is the best of the alternatives, and I consider myself set."

Drake said suddenly, "Who are you working for, Horace?"

"Dr. Kendall, sir."

"The kinetics man?"

"Yes, sir. I'm working on the kinetics of DNA replication. It's not something to which physical chemical techniques have hitherto been rigorously applied, and I am now able to build computerized graphics of the process, which—"

Halsted interrupted. "We'll get to that, Horace. Later. For now, I'm still trying to find out what's bugging you. You have the prospect of a job. Your research has gone well. What about your course work?"

"Never any problem there. Except—"

Halsted endured the pause for a moment, then said, "Except what?"

"I wasn't that good in my lab courses. Especially organic lab. I'm not . . . deft. I'm a theoretician."

"Did you fail?"

"No, of course not. I just didn't cover myself with glory."

7

"Well, then, what *is* bugging you? I overheard you tell Jeff that you'd be getting your PhD when you're twenty-three—or never. Why never? Where does that possibility come in?"

The young man hesitated. "It's not the sort of thing—"

Rubin, clearly flustered, frowned and said, "Horace, you've never told *me* you were having problems."

Horace looked about as though searching for a hole through which he could crawl. "Well, Uncle Manny, you've got *your* troubles and you don't come to *me* with them. I'll fight this out on my own—or not."

"Fight *what* out?" asked Rubin, his voice growing louder.

"It's not the sort of thing—" began Horace again.

"Number one," said Rubin vigorously, "anything you say here is completely, totally confidential. Number two, I told you that at the grilling session you would be expected to answer all questions. Number three, if you don't stop playing games, I'll kick your behind into raspberry gelatin."

Horace sighed. "Yes, Uncle Manny. I just want to say . . ." he looked about the table, "that he's threatened me like this since I was two and he's never laid a hand on me. My mother would take him apart if he did."

"There's always a first time, and I'm not afraid of your mother. I can handle *her*," said Rubin.

"Yes, Uncle Manny. All right then. My problem is Professor Richard Youngerlea."

"Uh-oh," said Drake softly.

"Do you know him, Dr. Drake?"

"Well, yes."

"Is he a friend of yours?"

"Well, no. He's a good chemist but, as a matter of fact, I despise him."

Horace's homely face broke into a wide smile, and he said, "Then may I speak freely?"

"You could anyway," said Drake.

"Here it is," said Horace. "I'm sure Youngerlea is going to be on my examining board. He wouldn't miss the chance, and he swings enough weight to get on it if he wants to."

Avalon said in his deep voice, "I take it, Horace, that you dislike him."

"Very much," said Horace in a heartfelt tone.

8

"And I imagine he dislikes you."

"I'm afraid so. I had my organic lab under him and, as I said, I didn't shine."

Avalon said, "I imagine a certain number of students don't shine. Does he dislike them all?"

"Well, he doesn't *like* them."

"I gather you suspect that he wants to be on your examining board in order to cut you down. Is that the way he reacts to every student who doesn't shine in his laboratory?"

"Well, he does seem to think that lab work is motherhood and apple pandowdy and everything that's good and noble, but no, it's not just that I didn't shine."

"Well, then," said Halsted, taking over the grilling again, "we're getting to it. I teach in a junior high school and I know all about obnoxious students. I am sure that the professor found *you* obnoxious. In what way?"

Horace frowned. "I am *not* obnoxious. Youngerlea is. Look, he's a bully. There are always some teachers who take advantage of the fact that they are in an unassailable position. They excoriate students; they brutalize them verbally; they hold them up to ridicule. They do this although they know full well that the students are reluctant to defend themselves for fear of getting a poor mark. Who's to argue with Youngerlea if he hands out a C, or, for that matter, an F? Who's to argue with him if he expresses his very influential opinion at a faculty conference that such and such a student doesn't have what it takes to make a good chemist?"

"Did he hold *you* up to ridicule?" asked Halsted.

"He held *everybody* up to ridicule. There was one poor guy who was British, and when he referred to aluminum chloride, which is used as a catalyst in the Friedel-Crafts reaction, he referred to it as aluminium chloride, with the accent on the third syllable and the first 'u' as 'yoo' instead of 'oo.' It was just the British pronunciation, after all, but Youngerlea chewed him out. He denounced all this crap—his expression—of having an unnecessary extra syllable, five instead of four, and so on, and the stupidity of making any chemical name longer than necessary. It was *nothing* and yet he *humiliated* the poor man, who didn't dare say a word in his

9

own defense. And all the damned sycophants in the class laughed."

"So what makes you worse than the rest?"

Horace flushed, but there was a note of pride in his voice. "I answer back. When he starts on me, I don't just sit there and take it. In fact, I interrupted him in this aluminum-aluminium business. I said in a good, loud voice, 'The name of an element is a human convention, Professor, and not a law of nature.' That stopped him, but he did say in his sneering way, 'Ah, Rubin, been dropping any beakers lately?' "

"And the class laughed, I suppose?" said Halsted.

"Sure they did, the pimple-heads. I dropped one beaker all course. One! And that was only because someone jostled me. And then once I came across Youngerlea in the chem library looking up some compound in Beilstein—"

Gonzalo asked, "What's Beilstein?"

"It's a reference book of about seventy-five volumes, listing many thousands of organic compounds, with references to the work done on each; all of them are listed in order according to some logical but very complicated system. Youngerlea had a couple of volumes on his desk and was leafing through first one and then the other. I was curious, and asked him what compound he was searching for. When he told me, I was overcome with ecstasy because I realized he was looking in the wrong volumes altogether. I moved quietly to the Beilstein shelves, took down a volume, found the compound Youngerlea wanted—it took me thirty seconds—went back to his table and put the volume in front of him, open to the correct page."

"I suppose he didn't thank you," said Drake.

"No, he didn't," said Horace, "but at that, he might have if I hadn't had the world's biggest grin on my face. At the moment, though, I would rather have had my revenge than my PhD. And that may be the way it will work out."

Rubin said, "I've never considered you the most tactful person in the world, Horace."

"No, Uncle Manny," said Horace sadly. "Mom says I take after you—but she only says that when she's really annoyed with me."

Even Avalon laughed at that, and Rubin muttered something under his breath.

Gonzalo said, "Well, what can he do to you? If your marks are all right, and your research is all right, and you do all right on the exam, they've *got* to pass you."

"It's not that easy, sir," said Horace. "In the first place, it's an oral exam and the pressures are intense. A guy like Youngerlea is a past master at intensifying the pressure, and he can just possibly reduce me to incoherence, or get me into a furious slanging match with him. Either way, he can maintain that I don't have the emotional stability to make a good chemist. He's a powerful figure in the department, and he might swing the committee. Even if I pass and get my degree, he has enough influence in chemical circles to blackball me in some very important places."

There was silence around the table.

Drake said, "What are you going to do?"

"Well— I tried to make peace with the old bastard. I thought about it and thought about it, and finally I asked for an appointment so that I could eat a little crow. I said I knew we had not gotten along but that I hoped he didn't think I would make a bad chemist. I said that, really, chemistry was my life. Well, you know what I mean."

Drake nodded. "What did *he* say?"

"He enjoyed himself. He had me where he wanted me. He did his best to make me crawl; told me I was a wise guy with an ungovernable temper, and a few other things designed to make me go out of control. I held on, though, and said, 'But granted I've got my peculiarities, would you say that necessarily makes me a bad chemist?'

"And he said, 'Well, let's see if you're a good chemist. I'm thinking of the name of a unique chemical element. You tell me what the element is, why it's unique and why I should think of it, and I'll admit you're a good chemist.'

"I said, 'But what would that have to do with my being a good chemist?' He said, 'The fact that you don't see that is a point against you. You ought to be able to reason it out, and reasoning is the prime tool of a chemist, or of any scientist. A person like you who talks about being a theoretical scientist and who therefore scorns little things like manual dexterity should have no trouble agreeing with this. Well, use your reason and tell me which element I am thinking of. You have one week from this moment; say 5 P.M. next Monday; and you only have one chance. If your choice of element is wrong, there's no second guess.'

"I said, 'Professor Youngerlea, there are a hundred and five elements. Are you going to give me any hints?'

" 'I already have,' he said. 'I told you it's unique, and that's all you're going to get.' And he gave me the kind of grin I gave him at the time of the Beilstein incident."

Avalon said, "Well, young man, what happened the next Monday? Did you work out the problem?"

"It isn't next Monday yet, sir. That's coming three days from now, and I'm stuck. There's no possible way of answering. One element out of a hundred and five, and the only hint is that it's unique."

Trumbull said, "Is the man honest? Granted that he is a bully and a rotter, do you suppose he is really thinking of an element and that he'll accept a right answer from you? He wouldn't declare you wrong no matter what you say, would he, and then use that as a weapon against you?"

Horace made a face. "Well, I can't read his mind, but as a scientist, he's the real thing. He's actually a great chemist and as far as I know, he's completely ethical in his profession. What's more, his papers are marvelously well-written—concise, clear. He uses no jargon, never a long word when a shorter one will do, never a complicated sentence when a simpler one will do. You have to admire him for that. So if he asks a scientific question, I think he will be honest about it."

"And you're really stuck?" asked Halsted. "Nothing comes to you?"

"On the contrary, a great deal comes to me, but too much is as bad as nothing. For instance, the first thought I had was that the element had to be hydrogen. It's the simplest atom, the lightest atom, atom number one. It's the only atom that has a nucleus made of a single particle—just a proton. It's the only atom with a nucleus that contains no neutrons, and *that* certainly makes it unique."

Drake said, "You're talking about hydrogen-1?"

"That's *right*," said Horace. "Hydrogen is found in nature in three varieties, or isotopes—hydrogen-1, hydrogen-2, and hydrogen-3. The nucleus of hydrogen-1 is just a proton, but hydrogen-2 has a nucleus composed of a proton and a neutron, and hydrogen-3 has one composed of a proton and two neutrons. Of course almost all hydrogen atoms are hydrogen-1, but Youngerlea asked for an element, not an isotope, and if I say that the *element* hydrogen is the only one with a nucleus containing no neutrons, I'd be wrong. Just wrong."

Drake said, "It's still the lightest and simplest element."

"Sure, but that's so obvious. And there are other possibilities. Helium, which is element number two, is the most inert of all the elements. It has the lowest boiling point and doesn't freeze solid even at absolute zero. At very low temperatures it becomes helium-2, which has properties like no other substance in the Universe."

"Does it come in different varieties?" asked Gonzalo.

"Two isotopes occur in nature, helium-3 and helium-4, but all those unique properties apply to both."

"Don't forget," said Drake, "that helium is the only element to be discovered in space before being discovered on Earth."

"I know, sir. It was discovered in the Sun. Helium can be considered unique in a number of different ways, but it's so obvious too. I don't think Youngerlea would have anything obvious in mind."

Drake said, after blowing a smoke ring and regarding it with some satisfaction, "I suppose if you're ingenious enough, you can think up something unique about each element."

"Absolutely," said Horace, "and I think I've just about done it. For instance, lithium, which is element number three, is the least dense of all the metals. Cesium, element fifty-five, is the most active of all the stable metals. Fluorine, element nine, is the most active of all the nonmetals. Carbon, element six, is the basis of all organic molecules, including those that make up living tissue. It is probably the only atom capable of playing such a role, so that it is the unique element of life."

"It seems to me," said Avalon, "that an element uniquely related to life is unique enough—"

"No," said Horace violently, "it's the answer least likely to be true. Youngerlea is an organic chemist, which means he deals with carbon compounds only. It would be impossibly obvious to him. Then there's mercury, element eighty—"

Gonzalo asked, "Do you know all the elements by number?"

"I didn't before last Monday. Since then I've been poring over the list of elements. See?" He pulled a sheet of paper from his inside jacket pocket. "This is the periodic table of elements. I've just about memorized it."

Trumbull said, "But it doesn't help, I gather."

"Not so far. As I was saying, mercury, element eighty, has the lowest melting point of any metal; it is the only metal that is a liquid at ordinary temperatures. That's certainly unique."

Rubin said, "Gold is the most beautiful element, if you want to get into aesthetics, and the most valued."

"Gold is element seventy-nine," said Horace. "It's possible to argue, though, that it's neither the most beautiful nor the most valued. Many people would say a properly cut diamond is more beautiful than gold, and weight for weight, it would certainly be worth more money—and diamond is pure carbon.

"The densest metal is osmium, element seventy-six, and the least active metal is iridium, element seventy-seven. The highest-melting metal is tungsten, element seventy-four, and the most magnetic metal is iron, element twenty-six. Technetium, element forty-three, is the lightest element that has no stable isotopes but is radioactive in all its varieties, and it is the first element to be produced in the laboratory. Uranium, element ninety-two, is the most complicated atom to occur in substantial quantities in the Earth's crust. Iodine, element fifty-three, is the most complicated of those elements essential to human life; while bismuth, element eighty-three, is the most complicated element that has at least one isotope that is stable and not radioactive.

"You can go on and on and on and, as Dr. Drake said, if you're ingenious enough, you can tag each and every element with a unique characteristic. The trouble is that there's nothing to say which one Youngerlea is thinking of, which uniqueness is *his* uniqueness, and if I don't come up with the right something, he's going to say it proves I don't have the capacity to think clearly."

Drake said, "If we put our minds together right now—"

Trumbull said, "Would that be legitimate? If the young man gets the answer from others—"

Avalon said, "What are the rules of the game, Horace? Did Professor Youngerlea tell you that you could not consult anyone else?"

Horace shook his head emphatically. "Nothing was said about that. I've been using this periodic table. I've been using reference books. I see no reason why I can't ask other human beings. Books are just the words of human beings, words that have been frozen into print. Besides, whatever you may suggest, it's I who will have to decide whether the suggestion is good or bad and take the risk on the basis of my own decision. But will you be able to help me?"

"We might," said Drake, "If Youngerlea is an honest scientist, he wouldn't give you a problem that contains within it no possibility of reaching a solution. There must be some way of reasoning out an answer. After all, if you can't solve the problem, you could challenge him to give you the right answer. If he can't do that, or if he makes use of an obviously ridiculous path of reasoning, you could complain loudly to everyone in the school. *I* would."

"I'm willing to try, then. Is there anyone here, besides, Dr. Drake, who is a chemist?"

Rubin said, "You don't have to be a professional chemist at the PhD level to know something about the elements."

"All right, Uncle Manny," said Horace. "What's the answer, then?"

Rubin said, "Personally, I'm stuck on carbon. It's the chemical of life, and in the form of diamond, it has another type of uniqueness. Is there any other element that, in its pure form, has an unusual aspect—"

"Allotrope it's called, Uncle."

"Don't fling your jargon at me, pipsqueak. Is there any other element that has an allotrope as unusual as diamond?"

"No. And aside from human judgments concerning its beauty and value, the diamond happens to be the hardest substance in existence under normal conditions."

"Well, then?"

"I've already said that it's too obvious for an organic chemist to set up carbon as a solution to the problem."

"Sure," said Rubin. "He chose the obvious because he thinks you'll dismiss it *because* it's obvious."

15

"There speaks the mystery writer," grumbled Trumbull.

"Just the same, I reject that solution," said Horace. "You can advise me, any of you, but I'm the one to make the decision to accept or reject. Any other ideas?"

There was complete silence around the table.

"In that case," said Horace, "I'd better tell you one of my thoughts. I'm getting desperate, you see. Youngerlea said, 'I'm thinking of the name of a unique chemical element,' He didn't say he was thinking of the element, but of the *name* of the element."

"Are you sure you remember that correctly?" asked Avalon. "You didn't tape the conversation, and memory can be a tricky thing."

"No, no. I remember it clearly. I'm not the least uncertain. Not the least. So yesterday I got to thinking that it's not the physical or chemical properties of the element that count. That's just a red herring. It's the *name* that counts."

"Have you got a unique name?" asked Halsted.

"Unfortunately," said Horace, "the names give you as much oversupply as the properties do. If you consider an alphabetical listing of the elements, actinium, element eighty-nine, is first on the list, and zirconium, element forty, is last on the list. Dysprosium, which is element sixty-six, is the only element with a name that begins with a D. Krypton, element thirty-six, is the only one with a name that begins with a K. Uranium, vanadium and xenon, elements ninety-two, twenty-three, and fifty-four respectively, are the only elements to begin with a U, V or X. How do I choose among these five? U is the only vowel, but that seems weak."

Gonzalo said, "Is there any letter that doesn't start the name of any element at all?"

"Three. There is no element that starts with J, Q or W—but what good is that? You can't claim an element is unique just because it doesn't exist. You can argue that there are an infinite number of elements that don't exist."

Drake said, "Mercury has, as an alternate name, 'quicksilver.' That starts with a Q."

"I know, but that's feeble," said Horace. "In German, I and J are not distinguished in print. The chemical symbol of iodine is I, but I've seen German papers in Latin print in which the symbol of the element is given as J, but that's even feebler.

"Speaking of the chemical symbols, there are thirteen elements with symbols that are single letters. Almost always that letter is the initial of the name of the element. Thus carbon has the symbol C; oxygen, O; nitrogen, N; phosphorus, P; sulfur, S; and so on. However, the element potassium has the symbol K."

"Why?" asked Gonzalo.

"Because that's the initial of the German name, *kalium*. If potassium were the only case, I might consider it, but tungsten has the symbol W, for the German name *wolfram*, so neither is unique. Strontium has a name that starts with three consonants, but so do chlorine and chromium. Iodine has a name that starts with two vowels, but so do einsteinium and europium. I'm stopped at every turn."

Gonzalo asked, "Is there anything about the spelling of the element names that is the same in almost all of them?"

"Almost all of them end in 'ium.'"

"Really?" said Gonzalo, snapping his fingers in an agony of thought. "How about the element the British pronounce differently? They call it 'aluminium' with the 'ium' ending, but we say 'aluminum' so that it has only an 'um' ending, and the professor made a fuss about it. Maybe it's aluminum that's unique then."

"A good thought," said Horace, "but there's lanthanum, molybdenum and platinum, each with an 'um' ending. There are also endings of 'ine,' 'en' and 'on,' but always more than one of each. Nothing unique. Nothing unique."

Avalon said, "And yet there must be something!"

"Then tell me what it is. Rhenium was the last stable element to be discovered in nature; promethium is the only radioactive rare earth metal; gadolinium is the only stable element to be named after a human being. Nothing works. Nothing is convincing."

Horace shook his head dolefully. "Well, it's not the end of the world. I'll go to Youngerlea with my best guess, and if it's wrong, let him do his worst. If I write a crackerjack dissertation, it may be so good they couldn't possibly flunk me, and if Youngerlea keeps me from getting a place at Cal

17

Tech or M.I.T., I'll get in somewhere else and work my way up. I'm not going to let him stop me."

Drake nodded. "That's the right attitude, son."

Henry said softly, "Mr. Rubin?"

Rubin said, "Yes, Henry."

"I beg your pardon, sir. I was addressing your nephew, the younger Mr. Rubin."

Horace looked up. "Yes, waiter. Is there something else to order?"

"No, sir. I wonder if I might discuss the matter of the unique element?"

Horace frowned, then said, "Are you a chemist, waiter?"

Gonzalo said, "He's not a chemist, but he's Henry and you had better listen to him. He's brighter than anyone in the room."

"Mr. Gonzalo," said Henry in soft deprecation.

"It's so, Henry," insisted Gonzalo. "Go ahead. What do you have to say?"

"Only that in weighing a question that seems to have no answer, it might help to consider the person asking the question. Perhaps Professor Youngerlea has some quirk that would lead him to attach importance to a particular uniqueness, which, to others, might be barely noticed."

"You mean," asked Halsted, "uniqueness is where you find it?"

"Exactly," said Henry, "as is almost everything that allows for an element of human judgment. If we consider Professor Youngerlea, we know this about him. He uses the English language carefully and concisely. He does not use a complicated sentence when a simpler one will do, or a long word where a shorter word will do. What's more, he was furious with a student for using a perfectly acceptable name for aluminum but a name which added a letter and a syllable. Am I correct in all this, Mr. Rubin?"

"Yes," said Horace. "I've said all that."

"Well, then, on the club's reference shelf there is the World Almanac, which lists all the elements, and we have the Unabridged, of course, which gives the pronunciations. I've taken the liberty of studying the material during the course of the discussion that has been taking place."

"And?"

"It occurs to me that the element 'praseodymium,' which is number fifty-nine is uniquely designed to rouse Professor Youngerlea's ire. Praseodymium is the only name with six syllables. All other names have five syllables or less. Surely, to Professor Youngerlea, praseodymium is bound to seem unbearably long and unwieldy—the most irritating name in all the list, and unique in that respect. If he had to use that element in his work, he would probably complain loudly and at length, and there would be no mistake in the matter. Perhaps, though, he does not use the element?"

Horace's eyes were gleaming. "No, it's a rare earth element, and I doubt that Youngerlea, as an organic chemist, has ever had to refer to it. That *would* be the only reason we haven't heard him on the subject. But you're right, Henry. Its mere existence would be a constant irritant to him. I accept that suggestion, and I'll go to him with it on Monday. If it's wrong, it's wrong, but," and he was suddenly jubilant, "I'll bet it's right. I'll bet *anything* it's right."

"If it should be wrong," said Henry, "I trust you will keep your resolve to work your way through in any case."

"Don't worry, I will, but praseodymium is the answer. I know it is. However, I wish I had gotten it on my own, Henry. *You* got it."

"That's a small item, sir," said Henry, smiling paternally. "You were considering names, and I'm sure the oddity of praseodymium would have struck you in a very short time. I got to it first only because your labors had already eliminated so many false trails."

2

The Eureka Phenomenon

This first essay considers the matter of "inspiration." Does enlightenment strike a scientist with the force and suddenness of a lightning bolt? Sometimes it seems to!

In the old days, when I was writing a great deal of fiction, there would come, once in a while, moments when I was stymied. Suddenly I would find I had written myself into a hole and could see no way out. To take care of that, I developed a technique that invariably worked.

It was simply this—I went to the movies. Not just any movie. I had to pick a movie which was loaded with action but which made no demands on the intellect. As I watched, I did my best to avoid any conscious thinking concerning my problem, and when I came out of the movie, I knew exactly what I would have to do to put the story back on the track.

It never failed.

In fact, when I was working on my doctoral dissertation, too many years ago, I suddenly came across a flaw in my logic that I had not noticed before and that knocked out everything I had done. In utter panic, I made my way to a Bob Hope movie— and came out with the necessary change in point of view.

It is my belief, you see, that thinking is a double phenomenon like breathing.

You can control breathing by deliberate voluntary action:

20

You can breathe deeply and quickly, or you can hold your breath altogether, regardless of the body's needs at the time. This, however, doesn't work well for very long. Your chest muscles grow tired, your body clamors for more oxygen, or less, and you relax. The automatic involuntary control of breathing takes over, adjusts it to the body's needs, and unless you have some respiratory disorder, you can forget about the whole thing.

Well, you can think by deliberate voluntary action too, and I don't think it is much more efficient on the whole than voluntary breath control is. You can deliberately force your mind through channels of deductions and associations in search of a solution to some problem and before long you have dug mental furrows for yourself and find yourself circling round and round the same limited pathways. If those pathways yield no solution, no amount of further conscious thought will help.

On the other hand, if you let go, then the thinking process comes under automatic involuntary control and is more apt to take new pathways and make erratic associations you would not think of consciously. The solution will then come while you *think* you are *not* thinking.

The trouble is, though, that conscious thought involves no muscular action and so there is no sensation of physical weariness that would force you to quit. What's more, the panic of necessity tends to force you to go on uselessly, with each added bit of useless effort adding to the panic in a vicious cycle.

It is my feeling that it helps to relax, deliberately, by subjecting your mind to material complicated enough to occupy the voluntary faculty of thought, but superficial enough not to engage the deeper involuntary one. In my case, it is an action movie; in your case, it might be something else.

I suspect it is the involuntary faculty of thought that gives rise to what we call "a flash of intuition," something that I imagine must be merely the result of unnoticed thinking.

Perhaps the most famous flash of intuition in the history of science took place in the city of Syracuse in third-century B.C. Sicily. Bear with me and I will tell you the story—

* * *

About 250 B.C., the city of Syracuse was experiencing a kind of Golden Age. It was under the protection of the rising power of Rome, but it retained a king of its own and considerable self-government; it was prosperous; and it had a flourishing intellectual life.

The King was Hieron II, and he had commissioned a new golden crown from a goldsmith, to whom he had given an ingot of gold as raw material. Hieron, being a practical man, had carefully weighed the ingot and then weighed the crown he received back. The two weights were precisely equal. Good deal!

But then he sat and thought for a while. Suppose the goldsmith had subtracted a little bit of the gold, not too much, and had substituted an equal weight of the considerably less valuable copper. The resulting alloy would still have the appearance of pure gold, but the goldsmith would be plus a quantity of gold over and above his fee. He would be buying gold with copper, so to speak, and Hieron would be neatly cheated.

Hieron didn't like the thought of being cheated any more than you or I would, but he didn't know how to find out for sure if he had been. He could scarcely punish the goldsmith on mere suspicion. What to do?

Fortunately Hieron had an advantage few rulers in the history of the world could boast. He had a relative of considerable talent. The relative was named Archimedes, and he probably had the greatest intellect the world was to see prior to the birth of Newton.

Archimedes was called in and was posed the problem. He had to determine whether the crown Hieron showed him was pure gold, or was gold to which a small but significant quantity of copper had been added.

If we were to reconstruct Archimedes' reasoning, it might go as follows. Gold was the densest known substance (at that time). Its density in modern terms is 19.3 grams per cubic centimeter. This means that a given weight of gold takes up less volume than the same weight of anything else! In fact, a given weight of pure gold takes up less volume than the same weight of *any* kind of impure gold.

The density of copper is 8.92 grams per cubic centimeter,

just about half that of gold. If we consider 100 grams of pure gold, for instance, it is easy to calculate it to have a volume of 5.18 cubic centimeters. But suppose that 100 grams of what looked like pure gold was really only 90 grams of gold and 10 grams of copper. The 90 grams of gold would have a volume of 4.66 cubic centimeters, while the 10 grams of copper would have a volume of 1.12 cubic centimeters, for a total value of 5.78 cubic centimeters.

The difference between 5.18 cubic centimeters and 5.78 cubic centimeters is quite a noticeable one and would instantly tell if the crown were of pure gold or if it contained 10 percent copper (with the missing 10 percent of gold tucked neatly in the goldsmith's strongbox).

All one had to do, then, was measure the volume of the crown and compare it with the volume of the same weight of pure gold.

The mathematics of the time made it easy to measure the volume of many simple shapes: a cube, a sphere, a cone, a cylinder, any flattened object of simple, regular shape and known thickness, and so on.

We can imagine Archimedes saying, "All that is necessary, sire, is to pound that crown flat, shape it into a square of uniform thickness, and then I can have the answer for you in a moment."

Whereupon Hieron must certainly have snatched the crown away and said, "No such thing. I can do that much without you; I've studied the principles of mathematics too. This crown is a highly satisfactory work of art, and I won't have it damaged. Just calculate its volume without in any way altering it."

But Greek mathematics had no way of determining the volume of anything with a shape as irregular as the crown, since integral calculus had not yet been invented (and wouldn't be for two thousand years, almost). Archimedes would have had to say, "There is no known way, sire, to carry through a nondestructive determination of volume."

"Then think of one," said Hieron testily.

And Archimedes must have set about thinking of one and gotten nowhere. Nobody knows how long he thought, or how hard, or what hypotheses he considered and discarded, or any of the details.

23

What we do know is that, worn out with thinking, Archimedes decided to visit the public baths and relax. I think we are quite safe in saying that Archimedes had no intention of taking his problem to the baths with him. It would be ridiculous to imagine he would, for the public baths of a Greek metropolis weren't intended for that sort of thing.

The Greek baths were a place for relaxation. Half the social aristocracy of the town would be there, and there was a great deal more to do than wash. One steamed one's self, got a massage, exercised, and engaged in general socializing. We can be sure that Archimedes intended to forget the stupid crown for a while.

One can envisage him engaging in light talk, discussing the latest news from Alexandria and Carthage, the latest scandals in town, the latest funny jokes at the expense of the country-squire Romans—and then he lowered himself into a nice hot bath which some bumbling attendant had filled too full.

The water in the bath slopped over as Archimedes got in. Did Archimedes notice that at once, or did he sigh, sink back, and paddle his feet awhile before noting the water-slop? I guess the latter. But whether soon or late, he noticed, and that one fact, added to all the chains of reasoning his brain had been working on during the period of relaxation when it was unhampered by the comparative stupidities (even in Archimedes) of voluntary thought, gave Archimedes his answer in one blinding flash of insight.

Jumping out of the bath, he proceeded to run home at top speed through the streets of Syracuse. He did *not* bother to put on his clothes. The thought of Archimedes running naked through Syracuse has titillated dozens of generations of youngsters who have heard this story, but I must explain that the ancient Greeks were quite lighthearted in their attitude toward nudity. They thought no more of seeing a naked man on the streets of Syracuse, than we would on the Broadway stage.

As he ran, Archimedes shouted over and over, "I've got it! I've got it!" Of course, knowing no English, he was compelled to shout it in Greek, so it came out, "*Eureka! Eureka!*"

Archimedes' solution was so simple that anyone could understand it—once Archimedes explained it.

If an object that is not affected by water in any way is immersed in water, it is bound to displace an amount of water equal to its own volume, since two objects cannot occupy the same space at the same time.

Suppose, then, you had a vessel large enough to hold the crown and suppose it had a small overflow spout set into the middle of its side. And suppose further that the vessel was filled with water exactly to the spout, so that if the water level were raised a bit higher, however slightly, some would overflow.

Next, suppose that you carefully lower the crown into the water. The water level would rise by an amount equal to the volume of the crown, and that volume of water would pour out the overflow and be caught in a small vessel. Next, a lump of gold, known to be pure and exactly equal in weight to the crown, is also immersed in the water, and again the level rises and the overflow is caught in a second vessel.

If the crown were pure gold, the overflow would be exactly the same in each case, and volumes of water caught in the two small vessels would be equal. If, however, the crown were of alloy, it would produce a larger overflow than the pure gold would and this would be easily noticeable.

What's more, the crown would in no way be harmed, defaced, or even as much as scratched. More important, Archimedes had discovered the "principle of buoyancy."

And was the crown pure gold? I've heard that it turned out to be alloy and that the goldsmith was executed, but I wouldn't swear to it.

How often does this "Eureka phenomenon" happen? How often is there this flash of deep insight during a moment of relaxation, this triumphant cry of "I've got it! I've got it!" which must surely be a moment of the purest ecstasy this sorry world can afford?

I wish there were some way we could tell. I suspect that in the history of science it happens *often;* I suspect that very few significant discoveries are made by the pure technique of voluntary thought; I suspect that voluntary thought may possibly prepare the ground (if even that), but that the final

25

touch, the real inspiration, comes when thinking is under involuntary control.

But the world is in a conspiracy to hide that fact. Scientists are wedded to reason, to the meticulous working out of consequences from assumptions, to the careful organization of experiments designed to check those consequences. If a certain line of experiments ends nowhere, it is omitted from the final report. If an inspired guess turns out to be correct, it is *not* reported as an inspired guess. Instead, a solid line of voluntary thought is invented after the fact to lead up to the thought, and that is what is inserted in the final report.

The result is that anyone reading scientific papers would swear that *nothing* took place but voluntary thought maintaining a steady, clumping stride from origin to destination, and that just can't be true.

It's such a shame. Not only does it deprive science of much of its glamour (how much of the dramatic story in Watson's *Double Helix* do you suppose got into the final reports announcing the great discovery of the structure of DNA?*), but it hands over the important process of "insight," "inspiration," "revelation" to the mystic.

The scientist actually becomes ashamed of having what we might call a revelation, as though to have one is to betray reason—when actually what we call revelation in a man who has devoted his life to reasoned thought is, after all, merely reasoned thought that is not under voluntary control.

Only once in a while in modern times do we ever get a glimpse into the workings of involuntary reasoning, and when we do, it is always fascinating. Consider, for instance, the case of Friedrich August Kekule von Stradonitz.

In Kekule's time, a century and a quarter ago, a subject of great interest to chemists was the structure of organic molecules (those associated with living tissue). Inorganic molecules were generally simple in the sense that they were made up of few atoms. Water molecules, for instance, are made up of two atoms of hydrogen and one of oxygen (H_2O). Molecules of ordinary salt are made up of one atom of sodium and one of chlorine (NaCl), and so on.

Organic molecules, on the other hand, often contain a large

*I'll tell you, in case you're curious. None!

26

number of atoms. Ethyl alcohol molecules have two carbon atoms, six hydrogen atoms, and an oxygen atom (C_2H_6O); the molecule of ordinary cane sugar is $C_{12}H_{22}O_{11}$, and other molecules are even more complex.

Then, too, it is sufficient in the case of inorganic molecules generally merely to know the kinds and numbers of atoms in the molecule; in organic molecules, more is necessary. Thus, dimethyl ether has the formula C_2H_6O, just as ethyl alcohol does, and yet the two are quite different in properties. Apparently the atoms are arranged differently within the molecules—but how to determine the arrangements?

In 1852 an English chemist, Edward Frankland, had noticed that the atoms of a particular element tended to combine with a fixed number of other atoms. This combining number was called "valence." Kekule in 1858 reduced this notion to a system. The carbon atom, he decided (on the basis of plenty of chemical evidence) had a valence of four; the hydrogen atom, a valence of one; and the oxygen atom, a valence of two (and so on).

Why not represent the atoms as their symbols plus a number of attached dashes, that number being equal to the valence. Such atoms could then be put together as though they were so many Tinker Toy units, and "structural formulas" could be built up.

It was possible to reason out that the structural formula

of ethyl alcohol was

$$
\begin{array}{c}
\ \ \ \ \text{H}\ \ \ \text{H} \\
\ \ \ \ |\ \ \ \ \ | \\
\text{H}-\text{C}-\text{C}-\text{O}-\text{H} \\
\ \ \ \ |\ \ \ \ \ | \\
\ \ \ \ \text{H}\ \ \ \text{H}
\end{array}
$$

, while that of

dimethyl ether was

$$
\begin{array}{c}
\ \ \ \ \text{H}\ \ \ \ \ \ \ \ \ \text{H} \\
\ \ \ \ |\ \ \ \ \ \ \ \ \ \ \ | \\
\text{H}-\text{C}-\text{O}-\text{C}-\text{H} \\
\ \ \ \ |\ \ \ \ \ \ \ \ \ \ \ | \\
\ \ \ \ \text{H}\ \ \ \ \ \ \ \ \ \text{H}
\end{array}
$$

.

In each case there were two carbon atoms, each with four dashes attached; six hydrogen atoms, each with one dash

27

attached; and an oxygen atom with two dashes attached. The molecules were built up of the same components, but in different arrangements.

Kekule's theory worked beautifully. It has been immensely deepened and elaborated since his day, but you can still find structures very much like Kekule's Tinker Toy formulas in any modern chemical textbook. They represent oversimplifications of the true situation, but they remain extremely useful in practice even so.

The Kekule structures were applied to many organic molecules in the years after 1858, and the similarities and contrasts in the structures neatly matched similarities and contrasts in properties. The key to the rationalization of organic chemistry had, it seemed, been found.

Yet there was one disturbing fact. The well-known chemical benzene wouldn't fit. It was known to have a molecule made up of equal numbers of carbon and hydrogen atoms. Its molecular weight was known to be seventy-eight, and a single carbon-hydrogen combination had a weight of thirteen. Therefore the benzene molecule had to contain six carbon-hydrogen combinations and its formula had to be C_6H_6.

But that meant trouble. By the Kekule formulas, the hydrocarbons (molecules made up of carbon and hydrogen atoms only) could easily be envisioned as chains of carbon atoms with hydrogen atoms attached. If all the valences of the carbon atoms were filled with hydrogen atoms, as in "hexane," whose molecule looks like this—

$$H-\overset{\overset{\displaystyle H}{|}}{\underset{\underset{\displaystyle H}{|}}{C}}-\overset{\overset{\displaystyle H}{|}}{\underset{\underset{\displaystyle H}{|}}{C}}-\overset{\overset{\displaystyle H}{|}}{\underset{\underset{\displaystyle H}{|}}{C}}-\overset{\overset{\displaystyle H}{|}}{\underset{\underset{\displaystyle H}{|}}{C}}-\overset{\overset{\displaystyle H}{|}}{\underset{\underset{\displaystyle H}{|}}{C}}-\overset{\overset{\displaystyle H}{|}}{\underset{\underset{\displaystyle H}{|}}{C}}-H.$$

the compound is said to be saturated. Such saturated hydrocarbons were found to have very little tendency to react with other substances.

If some of the valences were not filled, unused bonds were added to those connecting the carbon atoms. Double bonds were formed as in "hexene"—

28

$$\text{H—C—C—C} = \text{C—C—C—H}$$

Hexene is unsaturated, for that double bond has a tendency to open up and add other atoms. Hexene is chemically active.

When six carbons are present in a molecule, it takes fourteen hydrogen atoms to occupy all the valence bonds and make it inert—as in hexane. In hexene, on the other hand, there are only twelve hydrogens. If there were still fewer hydrogen atoms, there would be more than one double bond; there might even be triple bonds, and the compound would be still more active than hexene.

Yet benzene, which is C_6H_6 and has eight fewer hydrogen atoms than hexane, is *less* active than hexene, which has only two fewer hydrogen atoms than hexane. In fact, benzene is even less active than hexane itself. The six hydrogen atoms in the benzene molecule seem to satisfy the six carbon atoms to a greater extent than do the fourteen hydrogen atoms in hexane.

For heaven's sake, why?

This might seem unimportant. The Kekule formulas were so beautifully suitable in the case of so many compounds that one might simply dismiss benzene as an exception to the general rule.

Science, however, is not English grammar. You can't just categorize something as an exception. If the exception doesn't fit into the general system, then the general system must be wrong.

Or take the more positive approach. An exception can often be made to fit into a general system, provided the general system is broadened. Such broadening generally represents a great advance, and for this reason, exceptions ought to be paid great attention.

For some seven years Kekule faced the problem of benzene and tried to puzzle out how a chain of six carbon atoms could be completely satisfied with as few as six hydrogen atoms in benzene and yet be left unsatisfied with twelve hydrogen atoms in hexene.

Nothing came to him!

And then one day in 1865 (he tells the story himself), he was in Ghent, Belgium, and in order to get to some destination, he boarded a public bus. He was tired and, undoubtedly, the droning beat of the horses' hooves on the cobblestones lulled him. He fell into a comatose half-sleep.

In that sleep he seemed to see a vision of atoms attaching themselves to each other in chains that moved about. (Why not? It was the sort of thing that constantly occupied his waking thoughts.) But then one chain twisted in such a way that head and tail joined, forming a ring—and Kekule woke with a start.

To himself he must surely have shouted "Eureka!" for indeed he had it. The six carbon atoms of benzene formed a ring and not a chain, so that the structural formula looked like this:

$$
\begin{array}{c}
H \\
| \\
C \\
H-C \diagdown \diagup C-H \\
\| \quad \quad \| \\
H-C \diagup \diagdown C-H \\
C \\
| \\
H
\end{array}
$$

To be sure, there were still three double bonds, so you might think the molecule had to be very active—but now there was a difference. Atoms in a ring might be expected to have different properties from those in a chain, and double bonds in one case might not have the properties of those in the other. At least chemists could work on that assumption and see if it involved them in contradictions.

It didn't. The assumption worked excellently well. It turned out that organic molecules could be divided into two groups:

30

aromatic and aliphatic. The former had the benzene ring (or certain other similar rings) as part of the structure and the latter did not. Allowing for different properties within each group, the Kekule structures worked very well.

For nearly seventy years Kekule's vision held good in the hard field of actual chemical techniques, guiding the chemist through the jungle of reactions that led to the synthesis of more and more molecules. Then, in 1932, Linus Pauling applied quantum mechanics to chemical structure with sufficient subtlety to explain just why the benzene ring was so special, and what had proven correct in practice proved correct in theory as well.

Other cases? Certainly.

In 1764, the Scottish engineer James Watt was working as an instrument-maker for the University of Glasgow. The university gave him a model of a Newcomen steam engine that didn't work well and asked him to fix it. Watt fixed it without trouble, but even when it worked perfectly, it didn't work well. It was far too inefficient and consumed incredible quantities of fuel. Was there a way to improve that?

Thought didn't help; but a peaceful, relaxed walk on a Sunday afternoon did. Watt returned with the key notion in mind of using two separate chambers, one for steam only and one for cold water only, so that the same chamber did not have to be constantly cooled and reheated to the infinite waste of fuel.

The Irish mathematician William Rowan Hamilton worked up a theory of "quaternions" in 1843 but couldn't complete that theory until he grasped the fact that there were conditions under which $p \times q$ was *not* equal to $q \times p$. The necessary thought came to him in a flash one time when he was walking to town with his wife.

The German physiologist Otto Loewi was working on the mechanism of nerve action, in particular, on the chemicals produced by nerve endings. He woke at 3 A.M. one night in 1921 with a perfectly clear notion of the type of experiment he would have to run to settle a key point that was puzzling him. He wrote it down and went back to sleep. When he woke in the morning, he found he couldn't remember what his inspiration

31

had been. He remembered he had written it down, but he couldn't read his writing.

The next night he woke again at 3 A.M. with the clear thought once more in mind. This time he didn't fool around. He got up, dressed himself, went straight to the laboratory and began work. By 5 A.M. he had proved his point, and the consequences of his findings became important enough in later years so that in 1936 he received a share in the Nobel Prize in medicine and physiology.

How very often this sort of thing must happen, and what a shame that scientists are so devoted to their belief in conscious thought that they so consistently obscure the actual methods by which they obtain their results.

3

The Feeling of Power

Inspiration moves in strange paths. As we look farther and farther into the future, it becomes possible to ask stranger and stranger questions. If society grows more and more computerized, what happens if human beings forget how to do simple arithmetic? Questions of this sort are now being asked, but the following story was written in 1957, well before anyone (except perhaps a few science-fiction writers) was thinking of such things. It might be the job of scientists, someday, not to discover, but to re-discover.

Jehan Shuman was used to dealing with the men in authority on long-embattled Earth. He was only a civilian but he originated programming patterns that resulted in self-directing war computers of the highest sort. Generals consequently listened to him. Heads of congressional committees too.

There was one of each in the special lounge of New Pentagon. General Weider was space-burned and had a small mouth puckered almost into a cipher. Congressman Brant was smooth-cheeked and clear-eyed. He smoked Denebian tobacco with the air of one whose patriotism was so notorious, he could be allowed such liberties.

Shuman, tall, distinguished, and Programmer-first-class, faced them fearlessly.

He said, "This, gentlemen, is Myron Aub."

33

"The one with the unusual gift that you discovered quite by accident," said Congressman Brant placidly. "Ah." He inspected the little man with the egg-bald head with amiable curiosity.

The little man, in return, twisted the fingers of his hands anxiously. He had never been near such great men before. He was only an aging low-grade Technician who had long ago failed all tests designed to smoke out the gifted ones among mankind and had settled into the rut of unskilled labor. There was just this hobby of his that the great Programmer had found out about and was now making such a frightening fuss over.

General Weider said, "I find this atmosphere of mystery childish."

"You won't in a moment," said Shuman. "This is not something we can leak to the first comer. —Aub!" There was something imperative about his manner of biting off that one-syllable name, but then he was a great Programmer speaking to a mere Technician. "Aub! How much is nine times seven?"

Aub hesitated a moment. His pale eyes glimmered with a feeble anxiety. "Sixty-three," he said.

Congressman Brant lifted his eyebrows. "Is that right?"

"Check it for yourself, Congressman."

The congressman took out his pocket computer, nudged the milled edges twice, looked at its face as it lay there in the palm of his hand, and put it back. He said, "Is this the gift you brought us here to demonstrate. An illusionist?"

"More than that, sir. Aub has memorized a few operations and with them he computes on paper."

"A paper computer?" said the general. He looked pained.

"No, sir," said Shuman patiently. "Not a paper computer. Simply a sheet of paper. General, would you be so kind as to suggest a number?"

"Seventeen," said the general.

"And you, Congressman?"

"Twenty-three."

"Good! Aub, multiply those numbers and please show the gentlemen your manner of doing it."

"Yes, Programmer," said Aub, ducking his head. He fished a small pad out of one shirt pocket and an artist's hairline stylus out of the other. His forehead corrugated as he made painstaking marks on the paper.

34

General Weider interrupted him sharply. "Let's see that."

Aub passed him the paper, and Weider said, "Well, it looks like the figure seventeen."

Congressman Brant nodded and said, "So it does, but I suppose anyone can copy figures off a computer. I think I could make a passable seventeen myself, even without practice."

"If you will let Aub continue, gentlemen," said Shuman without heat.

Aub continued, his hand trembling a little. Finally he said in a low voice, "The answer is three hundred and ninety-one."

Congressman Brant took out his computer a second time and flicked it, "By Godfrey, so it is. How did he guess?"

"No guess, Congressman," said Shuman. "He computed that result. He did it on this sheet of paper."

"Humbug," said the general impatiently. "A computer is one thing and marks on paper are another."

"Explain, Aub," said Shuman.

"Yes, Programmer. Well, gentlemen, I write down seventeen and just underneath it I write twenty-three. Next I say to myself: seven times three—"

The congressman interrupted smoothly, "Now, Aub, the problem is seventeen times twenty-three."

"Yes, I know," said the little Technician earnestly, "but I *start* by saying seven times three because that's the way it works. Now seven times three is twenty-one."

"And how do you know that?" asked the congressman.

"I just remember it. It's always twenty-one on the computer. I've checked it any number of times."

"That doesn't mean it always will be, though, does it?" said the congressman.

"Maybe not," stammered Aub. "I'm not a mathematician. But I always get the right answers, you see."

"Go on."

"Seven times three is twenty-one, so I write down twenty-one. Then one times three is three, so I write down a three under the two of twenty-one."

"Why under the two?" asked Congressman Brant at once.

"Because—" Aub looked helplessly at his superior for support. "It's difficult to explain."

Shuman said, "If you will accept his work for the moment, we can leave the details for the mathematicians."

Brant subsided.

Aub said, "Three plus two makes five, you see, so the twenty-one becomes a fifty-one. Now you let that go for a while and start fresh. You multiply seven and two, that's fourteen, and one and two, that's two. Put them down like this and it adds up to thirty-four. Now if you put the thirty-four under the fifty-one this way and add them, you get three hundred and ninety-one, and that's the answer."

There was an instant's silence and then General Weider said, "I don't believe it. He goes through this rigmarole and makes up numbers and multiplies and adds them this way and that, but I don't believe it. It's too complicated to be anything but hornswoggling."

"Oh no, sir," said Aub in a sweat. "It only *seems* complicated because you're not used to it. Actually, the rules are quite simple and will work for any numbers."

"Any numbers, eh?" said the general. "Come then." He took out his own computer (a severely styled GI model) and struck it at random. "Make a five seven three eight on the paper. That's five thousand, seven hundred and thirty-eight."

"Yes, sir," said Aub, taking a new sheet of paper.

"Now," (more punching of his computer) "seven two three nine. Seven thousand, two hundred and thirty-nine."

"Yes, sir."

"And now multiply those two."

"It will take some time," quavered Aub.

"Take the time," said the general.

"Go ahead, Aub," said Shuman crisply.

Aub set to work, bending low. He took another sheet of paper and another. The general took out his watch finally and stared at it. "Are you through with your magic-making, Technician?"

"I'm almost done, sir. Here it is, sir. Forty-one million, five hundred and thirty-seven thousand, three hundred and eighty-two." He showed the scrawled figures of the result.

General Weider smiled bitterly. He pushed the multiplication contact on his computer and let the numbers whirl to a halt. And then he stared and said in a surprised squeak, "Great Galaxy, the fella's right."

36

The President of the Terrestrial Federation had grown haggard in office and, in private, he allowed a look of settled melancholy to appear on his sensitive features. The Denebian war, after its early start of vast movement and great popularity, had trickled down into a sordid matter of maneuver and counter-maneuver, the discontent rising steadily on Earth. Possibly it was rising on Deneb, too.

And now Congressman Brant, head of the important Committee on Military Appropriations, was cheerfully and smoothly spending his half-hour appointment spouting nonsense.

"Computing without a computer," said the President impatiently, "is a contradiction in terms."

"Computing," said the congressman, "is only a system for handling data. A machine might do it, or a human brain might. Let me give you an example." And using the new skills he had learned, he worked out sums and products until the president, despite himself, grew interested.

"Does this always work?"

"Every time, Mr. President. It is foolproof."

"Is it hard to learn?"

"It took me a week to get the real hang of it. I think you would do better."

"Well," said the President, considering, "it's an interesting parlor game, but what is the use of it?"

"What is the use of a newborn baby, Mr. President? At the moment there is no use, but don't you see that this points the way toward liberation from the machine? Consider, Mr. President," the congressman rose and his deep voice automatically took on some of the cadences he used in public debate, "that the Denebian war is a war of computer against computer. Their computers forge an impenetrable shield of counter-missiles against our missiles, and ours forge one against theirs. If we advance the efficiency of our computers, so do they theirs, and for five years a precarious and profitless balance has existed.

"Now, we have in our hands a method of going beyond the computer, leapfrogging it, passing through it. We will combine the mechanics of computation with human thought; we will have the equivalent of intelligent computers, billions of them. I can't predict what the consequences will be in detail, but they will be incalculable. And if Deneb beats us to the punch, they may be unimaginably catastrophic."

The President said, troubled, "What would you have me do?"

"Put the power of the administration behind the establishment of a secret project on human computation. Call it Project Number, if you like. I can vouch for my committee, but I will need the administration behind me."

"But how far can human computation go?"

"There is no limit. According to Programmer Shuman, who first introduced me to this discovery—"

"I've heard of Shuman, of course."

"Yes. Well, Dr. Shuman tells me that in theory there is nothing the computer can do that the human mind cannot do. The computer merely takes a finite amount of data and performs a finite number of operations upon them. The human mind can duplicate the process."

The President considered that. He said, "If Shuman says this, I am inclined to believe him—in theory. But in practice, how can anyone know how a computer works?"

Brant laughed genially. "Well, Mr. President, I asked the same question. It seems that at one time computers were designed directly by human beings. Those were simple computers, of course, this being before the time of the rational use of computers to design more advanced computers had been established."

"Yes, yes. Go on."

"Technician Aub apparently had, as his hobby, the reconstruction of some of these ancient devices, and in so doing, he studied the details of their workings and found he could imitate them. The multiplication I just performed for you is an imitation of the workings of a computer."

"Amazing!"

The congressman coughed gently. "If I may make another point, Mr. President—the further we can develop this thing, the more we can divert our federal effort from computer production and computer maintenance. As the human brain takes over, more of our energy can be directed into peacetime pursuits and the impingement of war on the ordinary man will be less. This will be most advantageous for the party in power, of course."

"Ah," said the President, "I see your point. Well, sit down, Congressman, sit down. I want some time to think about this. But meanwhile, show me that multiplication trick again. Let's see if I can't catch the point of it."

Programmer Shuman did not try to hurry matters. Loesser was conservative, very conservative, and liked to deal with computers as his father and grandfather had. Still, he controlled the West European computer combine, and if he could be persuaded to join Project Number in full enthusiasm, a great deal would be accomplished.

But Loesser was holding back. He said, "I'm not sure I like the idea of relaxing our hold on computers. The human mind is a capricious thing. The computer will give the same answer to the same problem each time. What guarantee have we that the human mind will do the same?"

"The human mind, Computer Loesser, only manipulates facts. It doesn't matter whether the human mind or a machine does it. They are just tools."

"Yes, yes. I've gone over your ingenious demonstration that the mind can duplicate the computer, but it seems to me a little in the air. I'll grant the theory but what reason have we for thinking that theory can be converted to practice?"

"I think we have reason, sir. After all, computers have not always existed. The cave men with their triremes, stone axes, and railroads had no computers."

"And possibly they did not compute."

"You know better than that. Even the building of a railroad or a ziggurat called for some computing, and that must have been without computers as we know them."

"Do you suggest they computed in the fashion you demonstrate?"

"Probably not. After all, this method—we call it 'graphitics,' by the way, from the old European word 'grapho,' meaning 'to write'—is developed from the computers themselves so it cannot have antedated them. Still, the cave men must have had *some* method, eh?"

"Lost arts! If you're going to talk about lost arts—"

"No, no. I'm not a lost-art enthusiast, though I don't say

39

there may not be some. After all, man was eating grain before hydroponics, and if the primitives ate grain, they must have grown it in soil. What else could they have done?"

"I don't know, but I'll believe in soil-growing when I see someone grow grain in soil. And I'll believe in making fire by rubbing two pieces of flint together when I see that too."

Shuman grew placative. "Well, let's stick to graphitics. It's just part of the process of etherealization. Transportation by means of bulky contrivances is giving way to direct mass-transference. Communications devices become less massive and more efficient constantly. For that matter, compare your pocket computer with the massive jobs of a thousand years ago. Why not, then, the last step of doing away with computers altogether? Come, sir, Project Number is a going concern; progress is already headlong. But we want your help. If patriotism doesn't move you, consider the intellectual adventure involved."

Loesser said skeptically, "What progress? What can you do beyond multiplication? Can you integrate a transcendental function?"

"In time, sir. In time. In the last month I have learned to handle division. I can determine, and correctly, integral quotients and decimal quotients."

"Decimal quotients? To how many places?"

Programmer Shuman tried to keep his tone casual. "Any number!"

Loesser's lower jaw dropped. "Without a computer?"

"Set me a problem."

"Divide twenty-seven by thirteen. Take it to six places."

Five minutes later Shuman said, "Two point zero seven nine six two three."

Loesser checked it. "Well, now, that's amazing. Multiplication didn't impress me too much because it involved integers after all, and I thought trick manipulation might do it. But decimals—"

"And that is not all. There is a new development that is, so far, top secret and which, strictly speaking, I ought not to mention. Still—we may have made a breakthrough on the square-root front."

"Square roots?"

"It involves some tricky points and we haven't licked the bugs yet, but Technician Aub, the man who invented the science and who has an amazing intuition in connection with it, maintains he has the problem almost solved. And he is only a Technician. A man like yourself, a trained and talented mathematician, ought to have no difficulty."

"Square roots," muttered Loesser, attracted.

"Cube roots too. Are you with us?"

Loesser's hand thrust out suddenly. "Count me in."

General Weider stumped his way back and forth at the head of the room and addressed his listeners after the fashion of a savage teacher facing a group of recalcitrant students. It made no difference to the general that they were the civilian scientists heading Project Number. The general was the overall head, and he so considered himself at every waking moment.

He said, "Now square roots are all fine. I can't do them myself and I don't understand the methods, but they're fine. Still, the Project will not be sidetracked into what some of you call the fundamentals. You can play with graphitics any way you want to after the war is over, but right now we have specific and very practical problems to solve."

In a far corner Technician Aub listened with painful attention. He was no longer a Technician of course, having been relieved of his duties and assigned to the Project with a fine-sounding title and good pay. But of course the social distinction remained and the highly placed scientific leaders could never bring themselves to admit him to their ranks on a footing of equality. Nor, to do Aub justice, did he himself wish it. He was as uncomfortable with them as they were with him.

The general was saying, "Our goal is a simple one, gentlemen: the replacement of the computer. A ship that can navigate space without a computer on board can be constructed in one-fifth the time and at one-tenth the expense of a computer-laden ship. We could build fleets five times, ten times, as great as Deneb could if we could but eliminate the computer.

"And I see something even beyond this. It may be fantastic now, a mere dream, but in the future I see the manned missile!"

There was an instant murmur from the audience.

The general drove on. "At the present time, our chief bottleneck is the fact that missiles are limited in intelligence. The computer controlling them can only be so large, and for that reason they can meet the changing nature of anti-missile defenses in an unsatisfactory way. Few missiles, if any, accomplish their goal, and missile warfare is coming to a dead end; for the enemy, fortunately, as well as for ourselves.

"On the other hand, a missile with a man or two within, controlling flight by graphitics, would be lighter, more mobile, more intelligent. It would give us a lead that might well mean the margin of victory. Besides which, gentlemen, the exigencies of war compel us to remember one thing. A man is much more dispensable than a computer. Manned missiles could be launched in numbers and under circumstances that no good general would care to undertake as far as computer-directed missiles are concerned—"

He said much more but Technician Aub did not wait.

Technician Aub, in the privacy of his quarters, labored long over the note he was leaving behind. It read finally as follows:

> *When I began the study of what is now called graphitics, it was no more than a hobby. I saw no more in it than an interesting amusement, an exercise of mind.*
>
> *When Project Number began, I thought that others were wiser than I; that graphitics might be put to practical use as a benefit to mankind, to aid in the production of really practical mass-transference devices perhaps. But now I see it is to be used only for death and destruction.*
>
> *I cannot face the responsibility involved in having invented graphitics.*

He then deliberately turned the focus of a protein-depolarizer on himself and fell instantly and painlessly dead.

They stood over the grave of the little Technician while tribute was paid to the greatness of his discovery.

Programmer Shuman bowed his head along with the rest of

them but remained unmoved. The Technician had done his share and was no longer needed, after all. He might have started graphitics, but now that it had started, it would carry on by itself overwhelmingly, triumphantly, until manned missiles were possible with who knew what else.

Nine times seven, thought Shuman with deep satisfaction, is sixty-three, and I don't need a computer to tell me so. The computer is in my own head.

And it was amazing the feeling of power that gave him.

4

The Comet That Wasn't

Often a scientist may not be dreaming of making a revolutionary study. He may simply be making methodical observations, one after the other, out of a sense of inner neatness or compulsiveness and then may stumble across something altogether unexpected and find himself suddenly immortal—as the next essay will show.

I have just received a phone call from a young woman who asked to speak to me about one of my books.

"Certainly," I said. And then, with sudden alarm at her tone, I asked, "Are you weeping?"

"Yes, I am," she said. "It's not really your fault, I suppose, but your book made me feel so sad."

I was astonished. My stories, while excellent, are chiefly noted for their cerebral atmosphere and tone and are not usually considered remarkable for their emotional content. Still, one or two of my stories might pluck at the heartstrings,* and there's something a little flattering about having your writing reduce someone to tears.

"Which book are you referring to, miss?" I asked.

"Your book about the Universe," she said.

If I had been astonished before, that was nothing compared to my confusion now. *The Universe* (Walker, 1966) is a

*See "The Ugly Little Boy," Chapter 21.

44

perfectly respectable volume, written in a logical and sprightly manner, and doesn't possess one word calculated to elicit tears. Or so I thought.

I said, "How could that book make you feel sad?"

"I was reading about the development of the Universe and about how it must come to an end. It just made me feel there was no *use* to anything. I just didn't want to live."

I said, "But, young woman, didn't you notice that I said our Sun had at least eight billion years to live and that the Universe might last hundreds of billions of years?"

"But that's not forever," she said. "Doesn't it make *you* despair? Doesn't it make astronomers just not want to live?"

"No, it doesn't," I said earnestly. "And you mustn't feel that way either. Each of us has to die in much less than billions of years, and we come to terms with that, don't we?"

"That's not the same thing. When we die, others will follow us, but when the Universe dies, there's nothing left."

Desperate to cheer her, I said, "Well, look, it may be that the Universe oscillates and that new universes are born when old ones die. It may even be that human beings may learn how to survive the death of a Universe in time to come."

The sobbing seemed to have diminished by the time I dared let her hang up.

For a while I just sat there staring at the telephone. I am myself a notoriously softhearted person and cry at movie listings, but I must admit it would never occur to me to cry over the end of the Universe billions of years hence. In fact, I wrote about the end of the Universe in my story, "The Last Question,"* and was very upbeat about it.

Yet as I sat there, I felt myself beginning to think that astronomy might be a dangerous subject and one from which sensitive young women ought to be shielded. Surely, I thought, I can't let myself fall into *that* trap, so the only thing I can do now is to sit down immediately at my typewriter and determinedly begin an astronomical essay.

Let's begin with the number seven, a notoriously lucky number. It is used in all sorts of connotations that make it seem

*See "The Last Question," Chapter 23.

like the natural number for important groups. There are the seven virtues, the seven deadly sins, the seven wonders of the world, and so on, and so on.

What makes seven so wonderful?

You could decide that it is because of some numerical property. Perhaps we might feel that there was something wonderful about its being the sum of the first odd number and the first square; or that there is something about the fact that it is the largest prime under ten that is significant.

I don't think so. I suspect that seven was lucky long before people grew sophisticated enough to become mystical about numbers.

My own feeling is that we have to go back in time to a point where there were seven objects that were clearly exactly seven, clearly important, and even clearly awe-inspiring. The impressive nature of those objects would then cast an aura of holiness or good fortune on the number itself.

Can there be any question that the objects I'm referring to must be the traditional seven planets of ancient times, the objects which we now call Sun, Moon, Mercury, Venus, Mars, Jupiter and Saturn?

It was the ancient Sumerians, some time in the third millennium B.C., who made the first systematic observations of these seven bodies and observed the manner in which each changed position from night to night relative to the fixed stars.*

The changing patterns of the planets against the constellations through which they passed in their more or less complicated movements were gradually assumed to have significance with respect to earthly affairs. Their influence in this respect was more than human power could account for, and they were naturally considered gods. The Sumerians named the planets for various gods in their pantheon, and this habit has never been broken in Western history. The names were changed, but only to those of other gods, and at this very time *we* call the planets by the names of Roman gods.

It was from the seven planets that the custom of the seven-

---

*It is this position change that gave rise to the word "planet," for that is from the Greek for "wandering."

day period we call the week arose in Sumeria, with each day presided over by a different one of them, and that is reflected in the names of those days.

The Jews picked up the notion of the week during the Babylonian Captivity but devised a Creation story that accounted for the seven days without reference to the seven planets—since planet-gods were not permitted in the strict monotheism of postexilic Judaism.

But if the number seven lost the holiness of the planets in the Judeo-Christian ethic, it gained the holiness of the Sabbath. The aura of inviolability seems, therefore, to have persisted about the seven planets. It was somehow unthinkable that there should be eight, for instance, and that feeling persisted through the first two centuries of modern science.

After the Polish astronomer Copernicus presented his heliocentric theory in 1543, the term "planet" came to be used for only those bodies that moved about the Sun. Mercury, Venus, Mars, Jupiter, and Saturn were still planets under the new dispensation, but the Sun itself was not, of course. Nor was the Moon, which came to be called a "satellite," a name given to those bodies that circled primarily about a planet as the Moon circled about the Earth. To counterbalance the loss of the Sun and Moon, the Earth itself came to be considered a planet in the Copernican theory.

Still, that was just nomenclature. Whatever one called the various wandering bodies in the sky visible to the unaided eye, there were exactly seven of them, and we shall still refer to them as the "seven traditional planets."

In 1609 the Pisan astronomer Galileo turned his telescope on the sky and discovered that there were myriads of fixed stars that were too faint to be seen by the unaided eye, but which existed just the same. Despite this, no one seems to have suggested that, in analogy, new planets might also be discovered. The inviolability of the traditional, and sacred, number seven seemed firm.

To be sure, there were also bodies, unseen by the unaided eye, in the solar system itself, for in 1610 Galileo discovered four smaller bodies circling Jupiter, satellites to that planet as Moon is satellite to Earth. Then, before the century was over, five satellites of Saturn were discovered, making a total of ten satellites in all that were known when our own Moon is included.

Nevertheless, even that didn't alter the sacred number of seven. By defiant illogic, our Moon retained its separate place, while the satellites of Jupiter and Saturn were lumped with the respective planets they circle. We can rationalize this by saying that there are still only seven *visible* wandering bodies in the sky—visible to the unaided eye, that is.

There were the comets, of course, which wandered among the stars too, but their appearance was so atypical and their comings and goings so unpredictable that they didn't count. Aristotle felt that they were atmospheric exhalations and part of the Earth rather than of the sky. Others suspected they were special creations, sent across the sky as one-shots, so to speak, in order to foretell catastrophe.

Even in 1758, when the English Astronomer Royal Edmund Halley's prediction that the comet of 1682 (now called "Halley's comet" in his honor) would return in that year was verified and it was understood that comets moved in fixed orbits about the Sun, they were *still* not included among the planets. The appearance remained too atypical and the cigar-shaped orbits too elongated for them to be allowed on the sacred precincts.

And yet the odd thing is that there is an additional wanderer that fulfills all the criteria of the traditional seven. It is visible to the unaided eye, and it moved relative to the fixed stars. It cannot be denied the right to be considered an additional planet, so just for a while let us call it "Additional."

Why was Additional never observed for all the centuries down to the eighteenth? To answer that, let's ask why the seven traditional planets *were* observed.

For one thing, they are bright. The Sun is the brightest object in the sky by far, and the Moon, thought a very poor second, is second. Even the remaining five traditional planets, which are starlike points far dimmer than the Sun and the Moon, are nevertheless brighter than almost anything else in the sky. In Table 1 the magnitude of the seven planets is given, along with that of Sirius and Canopus, the two brightest of the fixed stars—and Additional.

48

TABLE 1

Object	Magnitude at brightest	Brightness (Sirius = 1)
Sun	− 26.9	15,000,000
Moon	− 12.6	30,000
Venus	− 4.3	14
Mars	− 2.8	3.5
Jupiter	− 2.5	2.5
Sirius	− 1.4	1.0
Mercury	− 1.2	0.9
Canopus	− 0.7	0.5
Saturn	− 0.4	0.4
Additional	+ 5.7	0.0015

As you see, the five brightest of the traditional planets are also the five brightest objects in the sky. Even the two dimmest of the traditional planets are not far behind Sirius and Canopus. So it is clear that the seven traditional planets attract the eye, and anyone observing the sky in primitive times would see them even if he saw very little else.

Additional, on the other hand, is only 1/700 as bright as Sirius and only 1/270 as bright as Saturn. While it is visible to the unaided eye, it is just *barely* visible.

Of course, brightness isn't the only criterion. Sirius and Canopus are of planetary brightness, but no one ever mistook them for planets. A planet had to shift its position among the fixed stars, and the faster it shifted, the more readily it was noticed.

The Moon, for instance, shifts most rapidly—by an average of 48,100 seconds of arc per day, a distance which is nearly twenty-six times its own width. If one were to watch the Moon at night for a single hour under Sumerian conditions (clear skies and no city lights), that would be enough to show the shift unmistakably.

The rest of the planets move more slowly, and in Table 2 the average shift per day is given for each of them, with Additional included.

TABLE 2

Planet	Average shift (seconds of arc per day)	Days to move the width of the Moon
Moon	48,100	0.038
Mercury	14,900	0.125

49

Venus	5,840	0.319
Sun	3,550	0.525
Mars	1,910	0.976
Jupiter	302	6.17
Saturn	122	15.3
Additional	42.9	43.5

Of the seven traditional planets, you see that Jupiter and Saturn are the slow-shifting ones, with Saturn by far the slower of the two. It takes Saturn 29.5 years to accumulate shift enough to circle the entire sky. For that reason Saturn may have been the last planet to have been recognized in old days, since it was both the least bright and the least fast. (Mercury, which competes for that honor, is in some ways the hardest to see since it is always near the Sun, but once it is glimpsed at sunset or at dawn, its extraordinarily rapid motion may give it away at once.)

But what about Additional, which is only 1/270 as bright as Saturn and which shifts at only a little over one-third its speed? That combination of dimness and slowness is fatal. No observer in ancient times and very few even in early telescopic times were likely to look at that object from night to night. There was nothing that made it seem more remarkable than any of the remaining two or three thousand stars of the same brightness. Even if astronomers did actually look at it for a few nights in a row, its slow motion was not likely to make itself overwhelmingly obvious.

So Additional went unnoticed—at least as a planet. Anyone with 20/20 vision who looked in its direction would see it as a "star," of course, and anyone with a telescope certainly would.

In fact, an occasional astronomer with a telescope, plotting the position of the various stars in the sky, might have seen Additional, have plotted it as a star, and even given it a name. In 1690 the first Astronomer Royal, John Flamsteed, noted it in the constellation Taurus, recorded it, and called it "34 Tauri."

Afterward, some other astronomer might have seen Additional in a different place, plotted its new position, and even given it a different name. There would have been no reason to identify the new star with the old star. In fact, the same astronomer might have recorded it in slightly different posi-

tions on different nights—each time as a different star. The French astronomer Pierre Charles Lemonnier apparently recorded the position of Additional thirteen different times in thirteen different places in the middle 1700s, under the impression that he was recording thirteen different stars.

How was this possible? Two reasons.

The other planets were, first of all, clearly planets, even if one disregarded their motion and their brightness. Planets were not points of light as the stars were; they were round discs. The Sun and Moon appeared as discs to the unaided eye, while Mercury, Venus, Mars, Jupiter and Saturn all appeared as discs even through the primitive telescopes of the seventeenth and eighteenth centuries. Additional, however, did not show up as a disc in the telescopes of men like Flamsteed and Lemonnier, and in the absence of a disc, why should they think in terms of planets?

And the second reason is that the sevenness of the traditional planets was so well entrenched in the common thinking of man that Additional, as a planet, was unthinkable, and so astronomers didn't think of it. You might as well suddenly decide you had discovered an eighth day of the week.

But then upon the scene came Friedrich Wilhelm Herschel, born in Hannover on November 15, 1738. Hannover was a then-independent state in what is now West Germany, and for historical reasons its ruler happened to be King George II of Great Britain.

Herschel's father was a musician in the Hannoverian army and Herschel himself entered the same profession. In 1756, however, the Seven Years' War began (an odd coincidence that the number seven should figure crucially in Herschel's life in so completely nonplanetary a way), and the French, fighting Prussia and Great Britain, occupied the Hannoverian realm of the British monarch in 1757.

The young Herschel, unwilling to suffer the miseries of an enemy occupation, managed to wriggle out of Hannover, deserting the army in the process, and got to Great Britain, where he remained the rest of his life and where he anglicized his Christian names to a simple "William."

He continued his musical career, and by 1766 he was a well-known organist and music teacher at the resort city of Bath, tutoring up to thirty-five pupils a week.

Prosperity gave him a chance to gratify his fervent desire for learning. He taught himself Latin and Italian. The theory of musical sounds led him to mathematics and that, in turn, led him to optics. He read a book that dealt with Isaac Newton's discoveries in optics and he became filled with a fervent and lifelong desire to observe the heavens.

But for that he needed a telescope. He couldn't afford to buy one, and when he tried renting one, it turned out that its quality was poor and he was very disappointed at what he saw—or, rather, didn't see.

He came to the decision at last that there was nothing to do but to attempt to make his own telescopes and, in particular, to grind his own lenses and mirrors. He ground two hundred pieces of glass and metal without making anything that satisfied him.

Then, in 1772, he went back to Hannover to get his sister, Caroline, who, for the rest of her life, assisted first William, then his son John, in their astronomic labors with a single-minded intensity that precluded marriage or virtually any life for herself at all.*

With Caroline's help, Herschel had better luck. While he ground for hours at a time, Caroline would read to him and feed him. Eventually he got the trick of grinding and developed telescopes good enough to satisfy him. In fact, the musician who could not afford to buy a telescope ended by making for himself the best telescopes then in existence.

His first satisfactory telescope, completed in 1774, was a six-inch reflector, and with it he could see the Great Nebula in Orion and clearly make out the rings of Saturn. That was not bad for an amateur.

Much more was ahead, however. He began to use his telescope systematically, passing it from one object in the sky to another. He bombarded learned bodies with papers on the mountains on the Moon, on sunspots, on variable stars, and on

*She did make astronomic observations of her own eventually, with a telescope William made for her. She discovered eight comets, was the first woman astronomer of note, and died, at last, just ten weeks short of her ninety-eighth birthday.

the Martian poles. He was the first to note that Mars' axis was tilted to its plane of revolution at about the same angle as Earth's was, so that the Martian seasons were essentially like Earth's, except that they were twice as long and considerably colder.

Then, on the night of Tuesday, March 13, 1781, Herschel, in his methodical progress across the sky, suddenly found himself looking at Additional.

There was now an important difference. Herschel was looking at Additional with a telescope that was far superior to any of those used by earlier astronomers. Herschel's telescope magnified the object to the point where it appeared as a *disc*. Herschel, in other words, was looking at a disc where no disc was supposed to be.

Did Herschel jump at once to the notion that he had found a planet? Of course not! An additional planet was unthinkable. He accepted the only possible alternative and announced that he had discovered a comet.

But he kept on observing Additional, and by March 19 he could see that it was shifting position with respect to the fixed stars at a speed only about a third as great as that of Saturn's shift.

That was a troublesome thing. Ever since ancient Greek times it had been accepted that the more slowly a planet shifted against the stars, the farther it was likely to be from us, and the new telescopic astronomy had confirmed that, with the modification that it was distance from the Sun that counted.

Since Additional was shifting much more slowly than Saturn, it had to be more distant from the Sun than Saturn was. Of course comets moved in orbits that took them far beyond Saturn, but no comet could be seen out there. Comets had to be much closer to the Sun than Saturn was in order to become visible.

What's more, Additional's motion was clearly in such a direction as to indicate the object was making its way through the signs of the zodiac, as all the planets did, but as virtually none of the comets did.

Then, on April 6, 1781, he managed to get a good enough view of Additional to see that the little disc had sharp edges like a planet, not hazy ones like a comet. What's more, it showed no signs of a tail.

Finally, when he had enough observations to calculate an orbit, he found that orbit to be nearly circular, like that of a planet, and not very elongated, like that of a comet.

Reluctantly, he had to accept the unthinkable. His comet wasn't; it was a planet. What's more, from its slow shift, it lay far beyond Saturn; it was just twice as far from the Sun as Saturn was.

At one bound the diameter of the known planetary system was doubled. From 2,850,000,000 kilometers (1,770,000,000 miles), the diameter of Saturn's orbit, it had risen to 5,710,000,000 kilometers (3,570,000,000 miles), the diameter of Additional's orbit. It is Additional's great distance that is responsible for its dimness, its slow shift against the stars, its unusually small disc—in short, for its very belated recognition as a planet.

Now it was up to Herschel to name the planet. In a bit of excess diplomacy, he named it after the then-reigning sovereign of Great Britain, George III, and called it "Georgium Sidus" ("George's star"), an uncommonly poor name for a planet.

King George was, of course, flattered. He officially pardoned Herschel's youthful desertion from the Hannoverian army and appointed him his private court astronomer at a salary of three hundred guineas a year. As the discoverer of a new planet, the first new one in at least five thousand years, he at once became the most famous astronomer of the world, a position he retained (and *deserved*, for he made many other important discoveries) to the end of his life. Perhaps most comforting of all, he married a rich widow in 1788, and his financial problems were nonexistent thereafter.

Fortunately, for all Herschel's new-found prestige, the name he gave Additional was not accepted by the indignant intellectuals of Europe. They weren't going to abandon the time-honored practice of naming planets for the classical gods just in order to flatter a British king. When some British astronomers suggested "Herschel" as the name for the planet, that was rejected too.

It was German astronomer Johann Elert Bode who offered a

classical solution. The planets that are farther from the Sun than Earth is present a sequence of generations. Those planets, in order, are Mars, Jupiter, and Saturn. In the Greek mythology, Ares (the Roman Mars) was the son of Zeus (the Roman Jupiter), who was the son of Kronos (the Roman Saturn). For a planet beyond Saturn, it is only necessary to remember that Kronos was the son of Ouranos (the Roman Uranus). Why not, then, call the new planet "Uranus"?

The notion was accepted with a glad cry, and Uranus it was, and has remained ever since.

Oddly enough, the sacred seven was not really disturbed by the discovery of Uranus. Rather, it was restored! By the Copernican system, in which the Sun and Moon are *not* planets and Earth *is*, there were just six known planets prior to 1781. These, in order of increasing distance from the Sun, were Mercury, Venus, Earth, Mars, Jupiter and Saturn. Once Uranus was added, the number of Copernican planets became *seven!*

As Herschel's reputation and wealth grew, he built ever bigger and better telescopes. He returned to his planet Uranus in 1787 and found two satellites circling it, the eleventh and twelfth known to exist (counting our Moon).* These satellites were eventually named Titania and Oberon, after the queen and king of the fairies in Shakespeare's *A Midsummer Night's Dream*. It was the first time that classical mythology had been abandoned in naming the satellites.

These satellites introduced an interesting anomaly. The axes of several of the planets were tipped from the perpendicular to the plane of their orbital revolutions. Thus Saturn's axis was tipped twenty-seven degrees, Mars' was tipped twenty-four degrees, and Earth's 23.5 degrees. Jupiter's axis was a little unusual in being tipped only three degrees.

The planes of the orbital revolutions of the satellites of Jupiter and Saturn were tipped to the same extent that the axes of those planets were. The satellites revolved in the plane of the planetary equator.

But the satellites of Uranus moved in a plane that was tipped

_____

*In 1789 he discovered two more satellites of Saturn, making seven for that planet and fourteen altogether.

ninety-eight degrees from the perpendicular to the plane of Uranus' orbit. Could it be that Uranus' axis was tipped by that much and was very nearly in the plane of its orbital revolution? If so, Uranus would seem to be lying on its side, so to speak, as it moved around the Sun.

This extreme axial tip was eventually confirmed, and to this day astronomers have no adequate explanation as to why Uranus, alone of all the known planets, should be lying on its side.

5

Found!

Scientists don't always lead sedentary lives in laboratories. In their search for evidence, they may have to become world travelers and engage in mountain climbing, in plunges into the depths of the sea, in exploration of all kinds. Not all of them do so, of course, but some of them must.

Among the first to indulge in ballooning, for instance, were scientists interested in the characteristics of the atmosphere at great heights. A century later they went ballooning to study cosmic rays. And today, scientists are doing their work in space.

Computer-Two, like the other three that chased each others' tails in orbit round the Earth, was much larger than it had to be.

It might have been one-tenth its diameter and yet contained all the volume it needed to store the accumulated and accumulating data needed to control space flight.

They needed the extra space, however, so that Joe and I could get inside if we had to.

And we had to.

Computer-Two was perfectly capable of taking care of itself. Ordinarily, that is. It was redundant. It worked everything out three times in parallel, and all three programs had to mesh perfectly; all three answers had to match. If they did not, the answer was delayed for nano-seconds while Computer-Two checked itself, found the malfunctioning part and replaced it.

There was no sure way in which ordinary people would know how many times it caught itself. Perhaps never. Perhaps twice a day. Only Computer-Central could measure the time delay induced by error and only Computer-Central knew how many of the component spares had been used as replacements. And Computer-Central never talked about it. The only good public image is perfection.

And for all practical purposes, it's *been* perfection, for there was never any call for Joe and me.

We're the trouble-shooters. We go up there when something really goes wrong and Computer-Two or one of the others can't correct itself. It's never happened in the five years we've been on the job. It did happen now and again in the early days of their existence, but that was before our time.

We keep in practice. Don't get me wrong. There isn't a computer made that Joe and I can't diagnose. Show us the error and we'll show you the malfunction. Or Joe will, anyway. I'm not the kind who sings one's own praises.

Anyway, this time neither of us could make the diagnosis.

The first thing that happened was that Computer-Two lost internal pressure. That's not unprecedented and it's certainly not fatal. Computer-Two can work in a vacuum, after all. An internal atmosphere was established in the old days when it was expected there would be a steady flow of repairmen fiddling with it. And it's been kept up out of tradition. Who told you scientists aren't chained by tradition? In their spare time from being scientists, they're human too.

From the rate of pressure loss, it was deduced that a gravel-sized meteoroid had hit Computer-Two. Its exact radius, mass and energy were reported by Computer-Two itself, using that rate of pressure loss and a few other things as data.

The second thing that happened was that the break was not sealed and the atmosphere was not regenerated. After that came the errors, and they called us in.

It made no sense. Joe let a look of pain cross his homely face and said, "There must be a dozen things out of whack."

Someone at Computer-Central said, "The hunk of gravel ricocheted, very likely."

58

Joe said, "With that energy of entry, it would have passed right through the other side. No ricochets. Besides, even with ricochets, I figure it would have had to take some very unlikely strikes."

"Well, then, what do we do?"

Joe looked uncomfortable. I think it was at this point that he realized what was coming. He had made it sound peculiar enough to require the trouble-shooters on the spot—and Joe had never been up in space. If he had told me once that his chief reason for taking the job was that he knew it meant he would never have to go up in space, he had told it to me 2^x times, with x a pretty high number.

So I said it for him. I said, "We'll have to go up there."

Joe's only way out would have been to say he didn't think he could handle the job, and I watched his pride slowly come out ahead of his cowardice. Not by much, you understand—by a nose, let's say.

To those of you who haven't been on a spaceship in the last fifteen years—and I suppose Joe can't be the only one—let me emphasize that the initial acceleration is the only troublesome thing. You can't get away from that, of course.

After that it's nothing, unless you want to count possible boredom. You're just a spectator. The whole thing is automated and computerized. The old romantic days of space pilots are gone totally. I imagine they'll return briefly when our space settlements make the shift to the asteroid belt as they constantly threaten to do—but then only until additional Computers are placed in orbit to set up the necessary additional capacity.

Joe held his breath throughout the acceleration, or at least he seemed to. (I must admit that I wasn't very comfortable myself. It was only my third trip. I've taken a couple of vacations on Settlement-Rho with my husband, but I'm not exactly a seasoned hand.)

After that he was relieved for a while, but only for a while. He got despondent.

"I hope this thing knows where it's going," he said pettishly.

I extended my arms forward, palms up, and felt the rest of me sway backward a bit in the zero-gravity field. "You," I said, "are a computer specialist. Don't you *know* it knows?"

"Sure, but Computer-Two is off."

"We're not hooked into Computer-Two," I said. "There are three others. And even if only one were left functional, it could handle all the space flights undertaken on an average day."

"All four might go off. If Computer-Two is wrong, what's to stop the rest?"

"Then we'll run this thing manually."

"You'll do it, I suppose? You know how—I think not?"

"So they'll talk me in."

"For the love of Eniac," he groaned.

There was no problem, actually. We moved out to Computer-Two as smooth as vacuum, and less than two days after takeoff, we were placed into a parking orbit not ten meters behind it.

What was not so smooth was that, about twenty hours out, we got the news from Earth that Computer-Three was losing internal pressure. Whatever had hit Computer-Two was going to get the rest, and when all four were out, space flight would grind to a halt. It could be reorganized on a manual basis, surely, but that would take months at a minimum, possibly years, and there would be serious economic dislocation on Earth. Worse yet, several thousand people now out in space would surely die.

It wouldn't bear thinking of and neither Joe nor I talked about it, but it didn't make Joe's disposition sweeter and, let's face it, it didn't make me any happier.

Earth hung over 200,000 kilometers below us, but Joe didn't seem to be bothered by that. He was concentrating on his tether and was checking the cartridge in his reaction-gun. He wanted to make sure he could get to Computer-Two and back again.

You'd be surprised—if you've never tried it—how you can get your space legs if you absolutely have to. I wouldn't say there was nothing to it, and we did waste half the fuel we used, but we finally reached Computer-Two. We hardly made any bump at all when we struck Computer-Two. (You hear it, of course, even in vacuum, because the vibration travels through the metalloid fabric of your space suit—but there was hardly any bump, just a whisper.)

Of course, our contact and the addition of our momentum altered the orbit of Computer-Two slightly, but tiny expenditures of fuel compensated for that and we didn't have to worry about it. Computer-Two took care of it, for nothing had gone wrong with it, as far as we could tell, that affected any of its external workings.

We went over the outside first, naturally. The chances were pretty overwhelming that a small piece of gravel had whizzed through Computer-Two and that would leave an unmistakable ragged hole. Two of them in all probability; one going in and one coming out.

Chances of that happening are one in two million on any given day—even money that it will happen at least once in six thousand years. It's not likely, but it can, you know. The chances are one in not more than ten billion that, on any one day, it will be struck by a meteoroid large enough to demolish it.

I didn't mention that because Joe might realize that we were exposed to similar odds ourselves. In fact, any given strike on us would do far more damage to our soft and tender bodies than to the stoical and much-enduring machinery of the computer, and I didn't want Joe more nervous than he was.

The thing is, though, it wasn't a meteoroid.

"What's this?" said Joe finally.

It was a small cylinder stuck to the outer wall of Computer-Two, the first abnormality we had found in its outward appearance. It was about half a centimeter in diameter and perhaps six centimeters long. Just about cigarette-sized for any of you who've been caught up in the antique fad of smoking.

We brought our small flashlights into play.

I said, "That's not one of the external components."

"It sure isn't," muttered Joe.

There was a faint spiral marking running round the cylinder from one end to the other. Nothing else. For the rest, it was clearly metal, but of an odd, grainy texture—at least to the eye.

Joe said, "It's not tight."

He touched it gently with a fat and gauntleted finger, and it ·

61

gave. Where it had made contact with the surface of Computer-Two, it lifted and our flashes shone down on a visible gap.

"There's the reason gas pressure inside declined to zero," I said.

Joe grunted. He pushed a little harder and the cylinder dropped away and began to drift. We managed to snare it after a little trouble. Left behind was a perfectly round hole in the skin of Computer-Two, half a centimeter across.

Joe said, "This thing, whatever it is, isn't much more than foil."

It gave easily under his fingers, thin but springy. A little extra pressure and it dented. He put it inside his pouch, which he snapped shut, and said, "Go over the outside and see if there are any other items like that anywhere on it. I'll go inside."

It didn't take me very long. Then I went in. "It's clean," I said. "That's the only thing there is. The only hole."

"One is enough," said Joe gloomily. He looked at the smooth aluminum of the wall and, in the light of the flash, the perfect circle of black was beautifully evident.

It wasn't difficult to place a seal over the hole. It was a little more difficult to reconstitute the atmosphere. Computer-Two's reserve gas-forming supplies were low, and the controls required manual adjustment. The solar generator was limping but we managed to get the lights on.

Eventually we removed our gauntlets and helmets, but Joe carefully placed the gauntlets inside his helmet and secured them both to one of his suit loops.

"I want these handy if the air pressure begins to drop," he said sourly.

So I did the same. No use being devil-may-care.

There was a mark on the wall just next to the hole. I had noted it in the light of my flash when I was adjusting the seal. When the lights came on, it was obvious.

"You notice that, Joe?" I said.

"I notice."

There was a slight, narrow depression in the wall, not very noticeable at all, but it was there beyond doubt if you ran your finger over it, and it continued for nearly a meter. It was as

62

though someone had scooped out a very shallow sampling of the metal, and the surface where that had taken place was distinctly less smooth than elsewhere.

I said, "We'd better call Computer-Central downstairs."

"If you mean back on Earth, say so," said Joe. "I hate that phony space talk. In fact, I hate everything about space. That's why I took an Earth-side job—I mean a job on Earth, or what was supposed to be one."

I said patiently, "We'd better call Computer-Central back on Earth."

"What for?"

"To tell them we've found the trouble."

"Oh? What did we find?"

"The hole. Remember?"

"Oddly enough, I do. And what caused the hole? It wasn't a meteoroid. I never saw one that would leave a perfectly circular hole with no signs of buckling or melting. And I never saw one that left a cylinder behind." He took the cylinder out of his suit pocket and smoothed the dent out of its thin metal, thoughtfully. "Well, what caused the hole?"

I didn't hesitate. I said, "I don't know."

"If we report to Computer-Central, they'll ask the question and we'll say we don't know, and what will we have gained? Except hassle?"

"They'll call us, Joe, if we don't call them."

"Sure. And we won't answer, will we?"

"They'll assume something killed us, Joe, and they'll send up a relief party."

"You know Computer-Central. It will take them at least two days to decide on that. We'll have something before then and once we have something, we'll call them."

The internal structure of Computer-Two was not *really* designed for human occupancy. What was foreseen and allowed for was the occasional and temporary presence of trouble-shooters. That meant there was room for maneuvering and there were tools and supplies.

There weren't any armchairs, though. For that matter, there was no gravitational field, either, or any centrifugal imitation of one.

We both floated in midair, drifting very slowly this way or

that. Occasionally, one of us touched the wall and rebounded very slowly. Or else part of one of us overlapped part of the other.

"Keep your foot out of my mouth," said Joe and pushed it away violently. It was a mistake because we both began to turn. Of course, that's not how it looked to us. To us, it was the interior of Computer-Two that was turning, which was most unpleasant, and it took us a while to get relatively motionless again.

We had the theory perfectly worked out in our Earth-side training, but we were short on practice. A lot short.

By the time we had steadied ourselves, I felt unpleasantly nauseated. You can call it nausea, or astronausea, or space sickness, but whatever you call it, it's the heaves and it's worse in space than anywhere else because there's nothing to pull the stuff down. It floats around in a cloud of globules and you don't want to be floating around with it. —So I held it back, and so did Joe.

I said, "Joe, it's clearly the computer that's at fault. Let's get at its insides." Anything to get my mind off *my* insides and let them quiet down. Besides, things weren't moving fast enough. I kept thinking of Computer-Three on its way down the tube; maybe Computers-One and -Four by now, too; and thousands of people in space with their lives hanging on what we could do.

Joe looked a little greenish, too, but he said, "First I've got to think. Something got in. It wasn't a meteoroid, because whatever it was chewed a neat hole out of the hull. It wasn't cut out because I didn't find a circle of metal anywhere inside here. Did you?"

"No. But it hadn't occurred to me to look."

"*I* looked, and it's nowhere in here."

"It may have fallen outside."

"With the cylinder covering the hole till I pulled it away? A likely thing. Did you see anything come flying out?"

"No."

Joe said, "We may still find it in here, of course, but I doubt it. It was somehow dissolved and something got in."

"What something? Whose is it?"

Joe's grin was remarkably ill-natured. "Why do you bother

64

asking questions to which there is no answer? If this was last century, I'd say the Russians had somehow stuck that device onto the outside of Computer-Two. —No offense. If it were last century, you'd say it was the Americans."

I decided to be offended. I said, coldly, "We're trying to say something that makes sense *this* century, Iosif," giving it an exaggerated Russian pronunciation.

"We'll have to assume some dissident group."

"If so," I said, "we'll have to assume one with a capacity for space flight and with the ability to come up with an unusual device."

Joe said, "Space flight presents no difficulties if you can tap into the orbiting computers illegally—which has been done. As for the cylinder, that may make more sense when it is analyzed back on Earth—downstairs, as you space buffs would say."

"It doesn't make sense," I said. "Where's the point in trying to disable Computer-Two?"

"As part of a program to cripple space flight."

"Then everyone suffers. The dissidents, too."

"But it gets everyone's attention, doesn't it, and suddenly the cause of whatever-it-is makes news. Or the plan is to just knock out Computer-Two and then threaten to knock out the other three. No real damage, but lots of potential and lots of publicity."

"I don't believe it," I said. "It's too dramatic."

"On the contrary," said Joe. "I'm trying to be nondramatic." He was studying all parts of the interior closely, edging over it square centimeter by square centimeter. "I *might* suppose the thing was of nonhuman origin."

"Don't be silly."

"You want to make the case? The cylinder made contact, after which something inside ate away a circle of metal and entered Computer-Two. It crawled over the inside wall eating away a thin layer of metal for some reason. Does that sound like anything of human construction?"

"Not that I know of, but I don't know everything. Even you don't know everything."

Joe ignored that. "So the question is, how did it—whatever it is—get into the computer, which is, after all, reasonably

65

well-sealed. It did so quickly, since it knocked out the resealing and air-regeneration capacities almost at once."

"Is *that* what you're looking for?" I said, pointing.

He tried to stop too quickly and somersaulted backward, crying, "That's it! That's it!"

In his excitement he was thrashing his arms and legs which got him nowhere, of course. I grabbed him and for a while we were both trying to exert pushes in uncoordinated directions, and that got us nowhere either. Joe called me a few names, but I called him some back and I had the advantage of him there. I understand English perfectly, better than he does, in fact; but his knowledge of Russian is—well, fragmentary would be a kind way of putting it. Bad language in an ununderstood tongue always sounds very dramatic.

"Here it is," he said when we had finally sorted ourselves out.

Where the computer-shielding met the wall, there was a small circular hole left behind when Joe brushed aside a small cylinder. It was just like the other one on the outer hull, but it seemed even thinner. In fact, it seemed to disintegrate when Joe touched it.

"We'd better get into the computer," said Joe.

The computer was a shambles.

Not obviously. I don't mean to say it was like a beam of wood that had been riddled by termites.

In fact, if you looked at the computer casually, you might swear it was intact.

Look closely, though, and some of the chips would be gone. The more closely you looked, the more you realized were gone. Worse yet, the stores which Computer-Two used in self-repair had dwindled to almost nothing. We kept looking, and every once in a while one of us would discover something else was missing.

Joe took the cylinder out of his pouch again and turned it end for end. He said, "I suspect it's after high-grade silicon in particular. I can't say for sure, of course, but my guess is that the sides are mostly aluminum but that the flat end is mostly silicon."

I said, "Do you mean the thing is a solar battery?"

"Part of it is. That's how it gets its energy in space; energy to get to Computer-Two, energy to eat a hole into it, energy to—to—I don't know how else to put it. Energy to stay alive."

"You call it alive?"

"Why not? Look, Computer-Two can repair itself. It can reject faulty bits of equipment and replace them with working ones, but it needs a supply of spares to work with. Given enough spares of all kinds, it could build a Computer just like itself, when properly programmed—but it needs the supply, so we don't think of it as alive. This object that entered Computer-Two is apparently collecting its own supplies. That's suspiciously lifelike."

"What you're saying," I said, "is that we have here a microcomputer advanced enough to be considered alive."

"I don't honestly know what I'm saying," said Joe.

"Who on Earth could make such a thing?"

"Who *on Earth*?"

I made the next discovery. It looked like a stubby pen drifting through the air. I just caught it out of the corner of my eye and it registered as a pen.

In zero gravity things will drift out of pockets and float off. There's no way of keeping anything in place unless it is physically confined. You expect pens and coins and anything else that can find an opening to drift their way through the opening eventually and go wherever air currents and inertia lead them.

So my mind registered "pen" and I groped for it absently, but of course my fingers didn't close on it. Just reaching for something sets up an air current that pushes it away. You have to reach over it and sneak behind it with one hand, and then reach for it with the other. Picking up any small object in midair is a two-handed operation.

I know some people can do it one-handed, but they're space hounds and I'm not.

I turned to look at the object and pay a little more attention to retrieval, then realized that my pen was safely in its pouch. I felt for it and it was there.

"Did you lose a pen, Joe?" I called out.

"No."

"Anything like that? Key? Cigarette?"

"I don't smoke. You know that."

A stupid answer. "Anything?" I said in exasperation. "I'm seeing things here."

"No one ever said you were stable."

"Look, Joe. Over there. Over there."

He lunged for it. I could have told him it would do no good.

By now, though, our poking around in the Computer seemed to have stirred things up. We were seeing them wherever we looked. They were floating in the air currents.

I stopped one at last. Or rather it stopped itself, for it was on the elbow of Joe's suit. I snatched it off and shouted. Joe jumped in terror and nearly knocked it out of my hand.

I said, "Look!"

There was a shiny circle on Joe's suit where I had taken the thing off. It had begun to eat its way through.

"Give it to me," said Joe. He took it gingerly and put it against the wall to hold it steady. Then he shelled it, gently lifting the paper-thin metal.

There was something inside that looked like a line of cigarette ash. It caught the light and glinted, though, like lightly woven metal.

There was a moistness about it, too. It wriggled slowly, one end seeming to seek something blindly.

The end made contact with the wall and stuck. Joe's finger pushed it away. It seemed to require a small effort to do so. Joe rubbed his finger and thumb and said, "Feels oily."

The metal worm—I don't know what else I can call it— seemed limp now after Joe had touched it. It didn't move again.

I was twisting and turning, trying to look at myself.

"Joe," I said, "for heaven's sake, have I got one of them on me anywhere?"

"I don't see one," he said.

"Well, *look* at me. You've got to watch me, Joe, and I'll watch you. If our suits are wrecked we might not be able to get back to the ship."

Joe said, "Keep moving, then."

It was a grisly feeling, being surrounded by things hungry to dissolve your suit wherever they could touch it. When any showed up, we tried to catch them and stay out of their way at the same time, which made things almost impossible. A rather long one drifted close to my leg and I kicked at it, which was stupid, for if I had hit it, it might have stuck. As it was, the air current I set up brought it against the wall, where it stayed.

Joe reached hastily for it—too hastily. The rest of his body rebounded and as he somersaulted, one booted foot struck the wall near the cylinder lightly. When he finally managed to right himself, it was still there.

"I didn't smash it, did I?"

"No, you didn't," I said. "You missed it by a decimeter. It won't get away."

I had a hand on either side of it. It was twice as long as the other cylinder had been. In fact, it was like two cylinders stuck together lengthwise, with a constriction at the point of joining.

"Act of reproducing," said Joe as he peeled away the metal. This time what was inside was a line of dust. Two lines. One on either side of the constriction.

"It doesn't take much to kill them," said Joe. He relaxed visibly. "I think we're safe."

"They do seem alive," I said reluctantly.

"I think they seem more than that. They're viruses. Or the equivalent."

"What are you talking about?"

Joe said, "Granted I'm a computer technologist and not a virologist—but it's my understanding that viruses on Earth, or downstairs, as you would say, consist of a nucleic-acid molecule coated in a protein shell.

"When a virus invades a cell, it manages to dissolve a hole in the cell wall or membrane by the use of some appropriate enzyme and the nucleic acid slips inside, leaving the protein coat outside. Inside the cell it finds the material to make a new protein coat for itself. In fact, it manages to form replicas of itself and to form a new protein coat for each replica. Once it has stripped the cell of all it has, the cell dissolves and in place of the one invading virus there are several hundred daughter viruses. Sound familiar?"

"Yes. Very familiar. It's what's happening here. But where did it come from, Joe?"

"Not from Earth, obviously, or any Earth settlement. From

somewhere else, I suppose. They drift through space till they find something appropriate in which they can multiply. They look for sizable objects ready-made of metal. I don't imagine they can smelt ores."

"But large metal objects with pure silicon components and a few other succulent matters like that are the products of intelligent life only," I said.

"Right," said Joe, "which means we have the best evidence yet that intelligent life is common in the Universe, since objects like the one we're on must be quite common or it couldn't support these viruses. And it means that intelligent life is old, too, perhaps ten billion years old—long enough for a kind of metal evolution, forming a metal/silicon/oil life as we have formed a nucleic/protein/water life. Time to evolve a parasite on space-age artifacts."

I said, "You make it sound as though every time some intelligent life form develops a space culture, it is subjected before long to parasitic infestation."

"Right. And it must be controlled. Fortunately, these things are easy to kill, especially now when they're forming. Later on, when they're ready to burrow out of Computer-Two, I suppose they will grow, thicken their shells, stabilize their interiors, and prepare, as the equivalent of spores, to drift a million years before they find another home. They might not be so easy to kill, then."

"How are we going to kill them?"

"I already have. I touched that first one when it instinctively sought out metal to begin manufacturing a new shell after I had broken open the first one—and that touch finished it. I didn't touch the second, but I kicked the wall near it and the sound vibration in the metal shook its interior apart into metal dust. So they can't get us, now, or any more of the computer, if we just shake them apart now!"

He didn't have to explain further—or as much. He put on his gauntlets slowly and then banged at the wall with one. It pushed him away and he kicked at the wall where he next approached it.

"You do the same," he shouted.

I tried to, and for a while we both kept at it. You don't know how hard it is to hit a wall at zero gravity, at least on purpose, and do it hard enough to make it clang. We missed as often as not or just struck it a glancing blow that sent us whirling but made virtually no sound. We were panting with effort and aggravation in no time.

But we had acclimated ourselves (or at least I had), and the nausea didn't return. We kept it up and then when we gathered up some more of the viruses, there was nothing inside but dust in every case. They were clearly adapted to empty, automated space objects which, like modern Computers, were vibration-free. That's what made it possible, I suppose, to build up the exceedingly rickety complex metallic structures that possessed sufficient instability to produce the properties of simple life.

I said, "Do you think we got them all, Joe?"

"How can I say? If there's one left, it will cannibalize the others for metal supplies and start all over. Let's bang around some more."

We did until we were sufficiently worn out not to care whether one was still left alive.

"Of course," I said, panting, "the Planetary Association for the Advancement of Science isn't going to be pleased with our killing them all."

Joe's suggestion as to what the P.A.A.S. could do with itself was forceful, but impractical. He said, "Look, our mission is to save Computer-Two, a few thousand lives and, as it turned out, our own lives too. Now they can decide whether to renovate this Computer or rebuild it from scratch. It's their baby.

"The P.A.A.S. can get what they can out of these dead objects and that should be something. If they want live ones, I suspect they'll find them floating about in these regions. They can look for them if they want live specimens, but they'd better watch their suits at all times. I don't think they can vibrate them to death in open space."

I said, "All right. My suggestion is we tell Computer-Central we're going to jerry-rig this Computer and get it doing some work anyway, and we'll stay till a relief is up for main repairs or whatever in order to prevent any reinfestation. Meanwhile, they better get to each of the other Computers and set up a system that can set it to vibrating strongly as soon as the internal atmosphere shows a pressure drop."

71

"Simple enough," said Joe sardonically.

"It's lucky we found them when we did."

"Wait awhile," said Joe, and the look in his eye was one of deep trouble. "We didn't find them. *They* found *us*. If metal life has developed, do you suppose it's likely that this is the only form it takes? Just this fragile kind?

"What if such life forms communicate somehow and, across the vastness of space, others are now converging on us for the picking? Other species too; all of them after the lush new fodder of an as yet untouched space culture. *Other* species! Some that are sturdy enough to withstand vibration. Some that are large enough to be more versatile in their reactions to danger. Some that are equipped to invade our settlements in orbit. Some, for the sake of Univac, that may be able to invade the Earth for the metals of its cities.

"What I'm going to report, what I must report, is that we've been *found*!"

6

Twinkle, Twinkle, Microwaves

You might feel that it was easy to make an accidental discovery two hundred years ago when there was so much scientists didn't know and therefore so much more to come across. However, as time goes on and scientists discover more and more, the chances for coming across something unexpected and revolutionary when you're simply making a routine search must (you might feel) grow steadily smaller.

Not so. The search is made with subtler and subtler instruments, and the chance of chance (so to speak) does not diminish. Here is something that happened less than two decades ago.

When I look back over the essays that have appeared in my books and which have been written over the last eighteen and a half years, I'm not too surprised to find an occasional one of them that has become obsolete through the advance of science.

And when that happens, I suppose I am honor-bound, sooner or later, to say so and deal with the matter once again on a newer basis.

Years ago, for instance, I wrote an essay on pygmy stars of various kinds. I entitled it "Squ-u-u-ush," and it appeared in my book *From Earth to Heaven* (Doubleday, 1966).

In it I discussed, among other things, tiny stars called "neutron stars." I said that there was speculation that one

73

existed in the Crab Nebula, a cloud of very active gas known to be the remnants of a supernova that was seen on Earth just under a thousand years ago. X-rays were given off by the Crab Nebula, and neutron stars might be expected to give off X-rays.

If it were a neutron star, however, the X-rays would be emerging from a point source. The Moon, passing in front of the Crab Nebula, would in that case cut off the X-rays all at once. I went on to say:

"On July 7, 1964, the Moon crossed the Crab Nebula and a rocket was sent up to take measurements . . . Alas, the X-rays cut off gradually. The X-ray source is about a light-year across and is no neutron star.

". . . In early 1965, physicists at C.I.T. recalculated the cooling rate of a neutron star . . . They decided it would . . . radiate X-rays for only a matter of weeks."

The conclusion, apparently, was that it was not very likely that *any* X-ray source could be a neutron star and that these objects, even if they existed, could probably never be detected.

And yet just two years after I wrote the essay (and about eight months after the essay collection was published), neutron stars were discovered after all, and quite a few of them are now known. It's only reasonable that I explain how that came about—by going back a bit.

Let's begin by looking at white dwarfs—stars that have the mass of ordinary stars but the volume of planets. The first white dwarf to be discovered, Sirius B, has a mass equal to that of our Sun but a diameter less than that of the Earth.

How can that be?

A star like the Sun has a sufficiently intense gravitational field to pull its own matter inward with a force that will crush the atoms and reduce them to an electronic fluid within which the much tinier nuclei will move freely. Even if, under those circumstances, the Sun compressed itself to 1/780,000 of its present volume and 780,000 times its present density, so that it was a white dwarf the duplicate of Sirius B, it would still be—from the standpoint of the atomic nuclei—mostly empty space.

Yet the Sun does not so compress itself. Why not?

There is nuclear fusion going on at the stellar core which raises the temperature there to about 15,000,000° C. The expansive effect of that temperature balances the inward pull of gravity and keeps the Sun a large ball of incandescent gas with an overall density of only 1.4 times that of water.

Eventually, however, the nuclear fusion at the center of a star will run out of fuel. This is a complicated process which we don't have to go into here, but in the end there is nothing left to supply the necessary heat at the core—the heat that keeps the star expanded. Gravitation then has its way; there is a stellar collapse, and a white dwarf is formed.

The electronic fluid within which the nuclei of the white dwarf move can be viewed as a kind of spring that resists when it is compressed, and resists more strongly as it is compressed more tightly.

A white dwarf maintains its volume and resists further compression by the gravitational in-pull through this spring action and not by the expansive effect of heat. This means that a white dwarf doesn't have to be hot. It may be hot, to be sure, because of the conversion of gravitational energy into heat in the process of collapse, but this heat can very slowly be radiated away over the eons so that the white dwarf will become, eventually, a "black dwarf." Even so, it will still maintain its volume, the compressed electronic fluid remaining in equilibrium with the gravitational pull forever.

Stars, however, come in different masses. The larger the mass of a star, the more intense its gravitational field. When the nuclear fuel runs out and a star collapses, then the larger its mass and the more intense its gravitational field, the more tightly compressed the white dwarf that results, and the smaller.

Eventually, if the star is massive enough, the gravitational pull will be intense enough and the collapse energetic enough to shatter the spring of the electronic fluid, and no white dwarf will then be able to form or sustain its planetary volume.

An Indian-American astronomer, Subrahmanyan Chandrasekhar, considered the situation, made the necessary calculations, and in 1931 announced that the shattering would take place if the white dwarf had a mass more than 1.4 times that of the Sun. This mass is called "Chandrasekhar's limit."

Not very many stars have masses beyond that limit—not more than 2 percent of all the stars in existence do. However, it is precisely the massive stars that run out of nuclear fuel first. The more massive a star, the more quickly it runs out of nuclear fuel and the more drastically it collapses.

Collapse must, in the fifteen-billion-year life span of the Universe, have taken place to a disproportionate amount among the massive stars. Of all the stars that have consumed their nuclear fuel and collapsed, at least a quarter, possibly more, have had masses greater than Chandrasekhar's limit. What happened to them?

The problem did not bother most astronomers. As a star uses up its nuclear fuel, it expands, and it seems likely that in the ultimate collapse, only the inner regions would take part. The outer regions would linger behind to form a "planetary nebula," one in which a bright, collapsed star was surrounded by a vast volume of gas.

To be sure, the mass of the noncollapsed gas of a planetary nebula is not very great, so only stars slightly above the limit would lose enough mass in this way to be brought safely below the limit.

On the other hand, there are exploding stars, supernovas, that, in the course of explosion, lose anywhere from 10 to 90 percent of their total stellar masses. Each explosion spreads dust and gas in all directions, as in the Crab Nebula, leaving only a small inner region, sometimes only a *very* small inner region, to undergo collapse.

One could suppose, then, that whenever the mass of a star was beyond Chandrasekhar's limit, some natural process would remove enough of the mass to allow whatever portion collapsed to be below Chandrasekhar's limit.

But what if this were not always so? What if we could not trust the benevolence of the Universe that far, and what if sometimes a too-massive conglomeration of matter collapsed?

In 1934 the two American astronomers, Swiss-born Fritz Zwicky and German-born Walter Baade, considered this possibility and decided that the collapsing star would simply crash through the electron-fluid barrier. The electrons, compressed further and further, would be squeezed into the protons of the atomic nuclei moving about in the fluid, and the combination would form neutrons. The main bulk of the star would now consist only of the neutrons present in the nucleus to begin with, plus additional neutrons formed by way of electron-proton combinations.

The collapsing star would thus become virtually nothing but neutrons and it would continue to collapse until the neutrons were essentially in contact. It would then be a "neutron star." If the Sun collapsed into a neutron star, its diameter would be only 1/100,000 of what it is now. It would be only 14 kilometers (9 miles) across—but it would retain all its mass.

A couple of years later, the American physicist J. Robert Oppenheimer and a student of his, George M. Volkoff, worked out the theory of neutron stars in detail.

It would appear that white dwarfs were formed when relatively small stars reached their end in a reasonably quiet way. When a massive star explodes in a supernova (as only massive stars do), then the collapse is rapid enough to crash through the electronic-fluid barrier. Even if enough of the star is blown away to leave the collapsing remnant below Chandrasekhar's limit, the speed of collapse may carry it through the barrier. You could therefore end up with a neutron star that was less massive than some white dwarfs.

The question is, though, whether such neutron stars really exist. Theories are all very nice, but unless checked by observation or experiment, they remain only pleasant speculations that amuse scientists and science-fiction writers. Well, you can't very well experiment with collapsing stars, and how can you observe an object only a few kilometers across that happens to be at a distance of many light-years?

If you go by light only, it would be difficult indeed, but in forming a neutron star, enough gravitational energy is converted to heat to give the freshly formed object a surface temperature of some 10,000,000° C. That means it would radiate an enormous quantity of very energetic radiation—X-rays, to be exact.

That wouldn't help as far as observers on the Earth's surface were concerned, since X-rays from cosmic sources would not penetrate the atmosphere. Beginning in 1962, however, rockets equipped with instruments designed to detect X-rays were sent beyond the atmosphere. Cosmic X-ray sources were discovered and the question arose as to whether any of them might be neutron stars. By 1965, as I explained in "Squ-u-u-ush," the weight of the evidence seemed to imply they were not.

Meanwhile, however, astronomers were turning more and more to a study of radio-wave sources. In additional to visible light, some of the short-wave radio waves, called "microwaves," could penetrate the atmosphere, and in 1931 an American radio engineer, Karl Jansky, had detected such microwaves coming from the center of the galaxy.

Very little interest was aroused at the time because astronomers didn't really have appropriate devices for detecting and dealing with such radiation, but during World War II, radar was developed. Radar made use of the emission, reflection, and detection of microwaves, and by the end of the war, astronomers had a whole spectrum of devices they could now turn to the peaceful use of surveying the heavens.

"Radio astronomy" began and made enormous strides. In fact, astronomers learned how to use complex arrays of microwave-detecting devices ("radio telescopes") that were able to note objects at great distances and with more sharply defined locations than optical telescopes could.

As the technique improved, detection grew finer not only in space, but in time. Not only were radio astronomers detecting point sources, but they were also getting indications that the intensity of the waves being emitted could vary with time. In the early 1960s there was even some indication that the variation could be quite rapid, a kind of twinkle.

The radio telescopes weren't designed to handle very rapid fluctuations in intensity because no one had really foreseen the necessity for that. Now special devices were designed that would catch microwave twinkling. In the forefront of this work was the British astronomer Antony Hewish of Cambridge University Observatory. He supervised the construction of 2,048 separate receiving devices spread out in an array that covered an area of 18,000 square meters (or nearly three acres).

In July 1967 the new radio telescope was set to scanning the heavens in search of examples of twinkling.

Within a month a young British graduate student, Jocelyn Bell, who was at the controls of the telescope, was receiving bursts of microwaves from a place midway between the stars Vega and Altair—very rapid bursts, too. In fact, they were so rapid as to be completely unprecedented, and Bell could not believe they came from the sky. She thought she was detecting interference with the radio telescope's workings from electrical devices in the neighborhood. As she went back to the telescope night after night, however, she found the source of the microwaves moving regularly across the sky in time with the stars. Nothing on Earth could be imitating that motion and something in the sky had to be responsible for it. She reported the matter to Hewish.

Both zeroed in on the phenomenon and by the end of November, they were receiving the bursts in such detail that they were able to determine that they were both rapid and regular. Each burst of radio waves lasted only 1/20 of a second and the bursts came at intervals of 1.33 seconds, or about 45 times a minute.

This was not just the detection of a surprising twinkle in a radio source that had already been detected. That particular source had never been reported at all. Earlier radio telescopes were not designed to catch such very brief bursts and would have detected only the average intensity, including the dead period between bursts. The average was only 3 percent of the maximum burst intensity and that went unnoticed.

The regularity of the bursts proved almost unbelievably great. They came so regularly that they could be timed to 1/10,000,000,000 of a second without finding significant variations from pulse to pulse. The period was 1.3370109 seconds.

This was extremely important. If the source were some complex agglomeration of matter—a galaxy, a star cluster, a dust cloud—then parts of it would emit microwaves in a fashion that would differ somewhat from the way other parts did it. Even if each part varied regularly, the meshing together would result in a rather complex resultant. For the microwave bursts detected by Bell and Hewish to be so simple and regular, a very small number of objects, perhaps even a *single* object, had to be involved.

In fact, at first blush the regularity seemed too much to

79

expect of an inanimate object and there was a slightly scary suspicion that it might represent an artifact after all—but not one in the neighborhood or on Earth. Perhaps these bursts were the extraterrestrial signals some astronomers had been trying to detect. The phenomenon was given the name "LGM" just at first ("little green men").

The LGM notion could not be long maintained, however. The bursts involved total energies perhaps ten billion times that which could be produced by all Earth's sources working together, so they represented an enormous investment of energy if they were of intelligent origin. Furthermore, the bursts were so unvaryingly regular that they contained virtually no information. An advanced intelligence would have to be an advanced stupidity to spend so much energy on so little information.

Hewish could only think of the bursts as originating from some cosmic object—a star perhaps—that sent out pulses of microwaves. He therefore called the object a "pulsating star" and that was quickly shortened to "pulsar."

Hewish searched for suspicious signs of twinkles in other places in the records that his instrument had been accumulating, found them, went back to check, and in due course, was quite sure he had detected three more pulsars. On February 9, 1968, he announced the discovery to the world (and for that discovery eventually received a share of the 1974 Nobel Prize for physics).

Other astronomers around the world began to search the skies avidly and more pulsars were quickly discovered. Over a hundred pulsars are now known, and there may be as many as 100,000 in our galaxy altogether. The nearest known pulsar may be as close as 300 light-years or so.

All the pulsars are characterized by extreme regularity of pulsation, but the exact period varies from pulsar to pulsar. The one with the longest period has one of 3.75491 seconds (or 16 times a minute).

A pulsar with a particularly short period was discovered in October 1968 by astronomers at the National Radio Astronomy Observatory at Green Bank, West Virginia. It happens to be in the Crab Nebula, and this was the first clear link between pulsars and supernovas. The Crab Nebula pulsar has a period of only 0.033099 seconds. This is about 1,813 times a minute and about 113 times as rapid a pulsation as that of the longest-period pulsar known.

But what could produce such rapid and such regular pulsations?

Leaving intelligence out of account, it could only be produced by the very regular movement of one or possibly two objects. These movements could be either (1) the revolution of one object about another with a burst of microwaves at some one point in the revolution; (2) the rotation of a single body about its axis, with a burst at one point in the rotation; or (3) the pulsation, in and out, of a single body, with a burst at one point in the pulsation.

The revolution of one object about another could be that of a planet about its sun. This was the first fugitive thought of the astronomers when the suspicion existed for a while that the bursts were of intelligent origin. However, there is no reasonable way in which a planet could revolve or rotate at a rate that would account for such a rapid regularity in the absence of intelligence.

The fastest revolutions would come when the gravitational fields were most intense, and in 1968 that meant white dwarfs. Suppose you had two white dwarfs, each at the Chandrasekhar limit and revolving about the other in virtual contact. There could be no faster revolution, by 1968 thinking, and that was still not fast enough. The microwave twinkle could not be the result of revolution, therefore.

How about rotation? Suppose a white dwarf were rotating in a period of less than four seconds? No go. Even a white dwarf, despite the mighty gravitational field holding it together, would break up and tear apart if it were rotating that fast—and that went for pulsations as well.

If the microwave twinkle were to be explained at all, what was needed was a gravitational field much more intense than those of white dwarfs—and that left astronomers only one direction in which to go.

The Austrian-born American astronomer Thomas Gold said it first. The pulsars, he suggested, were the neutron stars that Zwicky, Baade, Oppenheimer, and Volkoff had talked about a generation before. Gold pointed out that a neutron star was small enough and had a gravitational field intense enough to be able to rotate about its axis in four seconds or less without tearing apart.

What's more, a neutron star should have a magnetic field as any ordinary star might have, but the magnetic field of a neutron star would be as compressed and concentrated as its matter was. For that reason, a neutron star's magnetic field would be enormously more intense than the fields about ordinary stars.

The neutron star, as it whirled on its axis, would give off electrons from its outermost layers (in which protons and electrons would still be existing), thanks to its enormous surface temperature. Those electrons would be trapped by the magnetic field and would be able to escape only at the magnetic poles at opposite sides of the neutron star.

The magnetic poles would not have to be at the actual rotational poles (they aren't in the case of the Earth, for instance). Each magnetic pole would sweep around the rotational pole in one second or in fractions of one second and would spray out electrons as it did so (just as a rotating water sprinkler jets out water). As the electrons were thrown off, they would curve in response to the neutron star's magnetic field and lose energy in the process. That energy emerged in the form of microwaves, which were not affected by magnetic fields and which went streaking off into space.

Every neutron star thus would end by shooting out two jets of radio waves from opposite sides of its tiny globe. If a neutron star happened to move one of those jets across our line of sight as it rotates, Earth would get a very brief pulse of microwaves at each rotation. Some astronomers estimate that only one neutron star out of a hundred would just happen to send microwaves in our direction, so that of the possibly 100,000 in our galaxy, we might never be able to detect more than a thousand.

Gold went on to point out that if his theory were correct the neutron star would be leaking energy at its magnetic poles and its rate of rotation would have to be slowing down. This meant that the faster the period of a pulsar, the younger it was likely to be and the more rapidly it might be losing energy and slowing down.

That fits the fact that the Crab Nebula neutron star has so short a period, since it is not quite a thousand years old and may easily be the youngest we can observe. At the moment of its formation, it might have been rotating one thousand times a second. The rotation would have slowed rapidly down to a mere 30 times a second now.

The Crab Nebula neutron star was studied carefully and it was indeed found to be lengthening its period. The period is increasing by 36.48 billionths of a second each day and, at that rate, its period of rotation will double in length in 1,200 years. The same phenomenon has been discovered in the other neutron stars whose periods are slower than that of the Crab Nebula and whose rate of rotational slowing is also slower. The first neutron star discovered by Bell, now called CP1919, is slowing its rotation at a rate that will double its period only after 16,000,000 years.

As a pulsar slows its rotation, its bursts of microwaves become less energetic. By the time the period has passed four seconds in length, the neutron star would no longer be detectable. Neutron stars probably endure as detectable objects for tens of millions of years, however.

As a result of the studies of the slowing of the microwave bursts, astronomers are now pretty well satisfied that the pulsars are neutron stars, and my old essay "Squ-u-u-ush" stands corrected.

Sometimes, by the way, a neutron star will suddenly speed its period very slightly, then resume the slowing trend. This was first detected in February 1969, when the period of the neutron star Vela X-1 was found to alter suddenly. The sudden shift was called, slangily, a "glitch," from a Yiddish word meaning "to slip," and that word is now part of the scientific vocabulary.

Some astronomers suspect glitches may be the result of a "starquake," a shifting of mass distribution within the neutron star that will result in its shrinking in diameter by one centimeter or less. Or perhaps it might be the result of the plunging of a sizable meteor into the neutron star so that the momentum of the meteor is added to that of the star.

There is, of course, no reason why the electrons emerging from a neutron star should lose energy only as microwaves.

They should produce waves all along the spectrum. They should, for instance, emit X-rays too, and the Crab Nebula neutron star does indeed emit them. About 10 to 15 percent of all the X-rays the Crab Nebula produces is from its neutron star. The other 85 percent or more, which came from the turbulent gases surrounding the neutron star, obscured this fact and disheartened those astronomers who had hunted for a neutron star there in 1964.

A neutron star should produce flashes of visible light too. In January 1969, it was noted that the light of a dim sixteenth-magnitude star within the Crab Nebula *did* flash on and off in precise time with the radio pulses. The flashes were so short and the period between them so brief that special equipment was required to catch those flashes. Under ordinary observation, the star seemed to have a steady light.

The Crab Nebula neutron star was the first "optical pulsar" discovered, the first *visible* neutron star. (After this essay was first published, a second visible neutron star was detected, also a pulsar that rotated in little more than a *thousandth* of a second.)

Paté de Foie Gras

This story also deals with an accidental discovery, of sorts. It is set in the present, and it actually pretends to be nonfiction. However, you won't read far before realizing that the problem is not realistic. —Or is it? I certainly do my best to make it sound plausible.

The story, which was written in 1956, ends with a puzzle presented to the reader for solution. There actually was a logical solution at the time, and a number of readers supplied me with it. As time went on, a second possible solution arose, and I began to get letters on that too. You're still welcome to send me a solution of your own if you haven't come across the story before, but I can't promise I'll be able to answer you.

I couldn't tell you my real name if I wanted to and, under the circumstances, I don't want to.

I'm not much of a writer myself, unless you count the kind of stuff that passes muster in a scientific paper, so I'm having Isaac Asimov write this up for me.

I've picked him for several reasons. First, he's a biochemist, so he understands what I tell him; some of it, anyway. Secondly, he can write: or at least he has published considerable fiction, which may not, of course, be the same thing.

But most important of all, he can get what he writes published in science-fiction magazines, and he has written two articles on thiotimoline, and that is exactly what I need for reasons that will become clear as we proceed.

I was not the first person to have the honor of meeting The Goose. That belongs to a Texas cotton farmer named Ian Angus MacGregor, who owned it before it became government property. (The names, places and dates I use are deliberately synthetic. None of you will be able to trace anything through them. Don't bother trying.)

MacGregor apparently kept geese about the place because they ate weeds but not cotton. In this way, he had automatic weeders that were self-fueling and, in addition, produced eggs, down, and, at judicious intervals, roast goose.

By summer of 1955, he had sent an even dozen of letters to the Department of Agriculture requesting information on the hatching of goose eggs. The Department sent him all the booklets on hand that were anywhere near the subject, but his letters simply got more impassioned and freer in their references to his "friend," the local congressman.

My connection with this is that I am in the employ of the Department of Agriculture. I have considerable training in agricultural chemistry, plus a smattering of vertebrate physiology. (This won't help you. If you think you can pin my identity out of this, you are mistaken.)

Since I was attending a convention at San Antonio in July of 1955, my boss asked me to stop off at MacGregor's place and see what I could do to help him. We're servants of the public, and besides, we had finally received a letter from MacGregor's congressman.

On July 17, 1955, I met The Goose.

I met MacGregor first. He was in his fifties, a tall man with a lined face full of suspicion. I went over all the information he had been given, explained about incubators, the values of trace minerals in the diet, plus some late information on vitamin E, the cobalamins and the use of antibiotic additives.

He shook his head. He had tried it all and still the eggs wouldn't hatch. He had tried every gander he could get as co-workers in the deal and that hadn't helped either.

What could I do? I'm a Civil Service employee and not the archangel Gabriel. I'd told him all I could and if the eggs still

86

wouldn't hatch, they wouldn't and that was that. I asked politely if I might see his geese, just so no one could say afterward I hadn't done all I possibly could.

He said, "It's not geese, mister; it's one goose."

I said, "May I see the one goose?"

"Rather not."

"Well, then, I can't help you any further. If it's only one goose, then there's just something wrong with it. Why worry about one goose? Eat it."

I got up and reached for my hat.

He said, "Wait!" and I stood there while his lips tightened and his eyes wrinkled and he had a quiet fight with himself.

He said, "If I show you something, will you keep it secret?"

He didn't seem like the type of man to rely on another's vow of secrecy, but it was as though he had reached such a pit of desperation that he had no other way out.

I said, "If it isn't anything criminal—"

"Nothing like that," he snapped.

And then I went out with him to a pen near the house, surrounded by barbed wire, with a locked gate to it, and holding one goose—The Goose.

"That's The Goose," he said. The way he said it, I could hear the capitals.

I stared at it. It looked like any other goose, heaven help me—fat, self-satisfied and short-tempered. I said, "Hmm" in my best professional manner.

MacGregor said, "And here's one of its eggs. It's been in the incubator. Nothing happens." He produced it from a capacious overall pocket. There was a queer strain about his manner of holding it.

I frowned. There was something wrong with the egg. It was smaller and more spherical than normal.

MacGregor said, "Take it."

I reached out and took it. Or tried to. I gave it the amount of heft an egg like that ought to deserve and it just sat where it was. I had to try harder and then up it came.

Now I knew what was queer about the way MacGregor held it. It weighed nearly two pounds. (To be exact, when we weighed it later, we found its mass to be 852.6 grams.)

I stared at it as it lay there, pressing down the palm of my hand, and MacGregor grinned sourly. "Drop it," he said.

I just looked at him, so he took it out of my hand and dropped it himself.

It hit soggy. It didn't smash. There was no spray of white and yolk. It just lay where it fell with the bottom caved in.

I picked it up again. The white eggshell had shattered where the egg had struck. Pieces of it had flaked away, and what shone through was a dull yellow in color.

My hands trembled. It was all I could do to make my fingers work, but I got some of the rest of the shell flaked away and stared at the yellow.

I didn't have to run any analyses. My heart told me.

I was face to face with The Goose!

The Goose That Laid the Golden Eggs!

You don't believe me. I'm sure of that. You've got this tabbed as another thiotimoline article.

Good! I'm *counting* on your thinking that. I'll explain later.

Meanwhile, my first problem was to get MacGregor to give up that golden egg. I was almost hysterical about it. I was almost ready to clobber him and make off with the egg by force if I had to.

I said, "I'll give you a receipt. I'll guarantee you payment. I'll do anything in reason. Look, Mr. MacGregor, they're no good to you anyway. You can't cash the gold unless you can explain how it came into your possession. Holding gold is illegal. And how do you expect to explain? If the government—"

"I don't want the government butting in," he said stubbornly.

But I was twice as stubborn. I followed him about. I pleaded. I yelled. I threatened. It took me hours. Literally. In the end I signed a receipt, and he dogged me out to my car and stood in the road as I drove away, following me with his eyes.

He never saw that egg again. Of course, he was compensated for the value of the gold ($656.47 after taxes had been subtracted), but that was a bargain for the government.

When one considers the potential value of that egg—

The *potential* value! That's the irony of it. That's the reason for this article.

The head of my section at the Department of Agriculture is Louis P. Bronstein. (Don't bother looking him up. The "P" stands for Pittfield if you want more misdirection.)

He and I are on good terms and I felt I could explain things without being placed under immediate observation. Even so, I took no chances. I had the egg with me and when I got to the tricky part, I just laid it on the desk between us.

Finally he touched it with his finger as though it were hot.

I said, "Pick it up."

It took him a long time, but he did, and I watched him take two tries at it as I had.

I said, "It's a yellow metal and it could be brass, only it isn't because it's inert to concentrated nitric acid. I've tried that already. There's only a shell of gold because it can be bent with moderate pressure. Besides, if it were solid gold, the egg would weigh over ten pounds."

Bronstein said, "It's some sort of hoax. It *must* be."

"A hoax that uses real gold? Remember, when I first saw this thing, it was covered completely with authentic unbroken eggshell. It's been easy to check a piece of the eggshell. Calcium carbonate. That's a hard thing to gimmick. And if we look inside the egg—(I didn't want to do that on my own, Chief)—and find real egg, then we've got it, because that would be impossible to gimmick. Surely this is worth an official project."

"How can I approach the secretary with—" He stared at the egg.

But he did in the end. He made phone calls and sweated out most of the day. One or two of the department brass came to look at the egg.

Project Goose was started. That was July 20, 1955.

I was the responsible investigator to begin with, and I remained in titular charge throughout, though matters quickly got beyond me.

We began with the one egg. Its average radius was 35 millimeters (major axis, 72 millimeters; minor axis, 68 millimeters.) The gold shell was 2.45 millimeters in thickness.

Studying other eggs later on, we found this value to be rather high. The average thickness turned out to be 2.1 millimeters.

Inside *was* egg. It looked like egg and it smelled like egg.

Aliquots were analyzed and the organic constituents were reasonably normal. The white was 9.7 percent albumin. The yolk had the normal complement of vitellin, cholesterol, phospholipid and carotenoid. We lacked enough material to test for trace constituents, but later on, with more eggs at our disposal, we did and nothing unusual showed up as far as the contents of vitamins, coenzymes, nucleotides, sulfhydryl groups, etc., etc., were concerned.

One important gross abnormality that showed was the egg's behavior on heating. A small portion of the yolk, heated, "hard-boiled" almost at once. We fed a portion of the hard-boiled egg to a mouse. It survived.

I nibbled at another bit of it. Too small a quantity to taste, really, but it made me sick. Purely psychosomatic, I'm sure.

Boris W. Finley of the Department of Biochemistry of Temple University (a Department Consultant) supervised these tests.

He said, referring to the hard-boiling, "The ease with which the egg proteins are heat-denatured indicates a partial denaturation to begin with, and, considering the nature of the shell, the obvious guilt would lie at the door of heavy-metal contamination."

So a portion of the yolk was analyzed for inorganic constituents, and it was found to be high in chloraurate ion, which is a singly-charged ion containing an atom of gold and four of chlorine, the symbol for which is $AuCl_4$. (The "Au" symbol for gold comes from the fact that the Latin word for gold is "aurum.") When I say the chloraurate ion content was high, I meant it was 3.2 parts per thousand, or 0.32 percent. That's high enough to form insoluble complexes of "gold-protein," which would coagulate easily.

Finley said, "It's obvious this egg cannot hatch. Nor can any other such egg. It is heavy-metal poisoned. Gold may be more glamorous than lead, but it is just as poisonous to proteins."

I agreed gloomily, "At least it's safe from decay too."

"Quite right. No self-respecting bug would live in this chlorauriferous soup."

The final spectrographic analysis of the gold of the shell came in. Virtually pure. The only detectable impurity was iron, which amounted to 0.23 percent of the whole. The iron content of the egg yolk had been twice normal also. At the moment, however, the matter of the iron was neglected.

One week after Project Goose was begun, an expedition was sent into Texas. Five biochemists went (the accent was still on biochemistry, you see) along with three truck-loads of equipment and a squadron of army personnel. I went along too, of course.

As soon as we arrived, we cut MacGregor's farm off from the world.

That was a lucky thing, you know—the security measures we took right from the start. The reasoning was wrong, at first, but the results were good.

The Department wanted Project Goose kept quiet at the start simply because there was always the thought that this might still be an elaborate hoax, and we couldn't risk the bad publicity if it were. And if it weren't a hoax, we couldn't risk the newspaper hounding that would definitely result for any goose-and-golden-egg story.

It was only well after the start of Project Goose, well after our arrival at MacGregor's farm, that the real implications of the matter became clear.

Naturally MacGregor didn't like the men and equipment settling down all about him. He didn't like being told The Goose was government property. He didn't like having his eggs impounded.

He didn't like it, but he agreed to it—if you can call it agreeing when negotiations are being carried on while a machine gun is being assembled in a man's barnyard and ten men, with bayonets fixed, are marching past while the arguing is going on.

He was compensated, of course. What's money to the government?

The Goose didn't like a few things either—like having blood samples taken. We didn't dare anesthetize it for fear of

91

doing anything to alter its metabolism, and it took two men to hold it each time. Ever try to hold an angry goose?

The Goose was put under a twenty-four-hour guard with the threat of summary court-martial to any man who let anything happen to it. If any of those soldiers read this article, they may get a sudden glimmering of what was going on. If so, they will probably have the sense to keep quiet about it. At least if they know what's good for them, they will.

The blood of the The Goose was put through every test conceivable.

It carried two parts per hundred thousand (0.002 percent) of chloraurate ion. Blood taken from the hepatic vein was richer than the rest, almost four parts per hundred thousand.

Finley grunted. "The liver," he said.

We took X-rays. On the X-ray negative the liver was a cloudy mass of light gray, lighter than the viscera in its neighborhood, because it stopped more of the X-rays, because it contained more gold. The blood vessels showed up lighter than the liver proper, and the ovaries were pure white. No X-rays got through the ovaries at all.

It made sense, and in an early report Finley stated it as bluntly as possible. Paraphrasing the report, it went, in part:

"The chloraurate ion is secreted by the liver into the bloodstream. The ovaries act as a trap for the ion, which is there reduced to metallic gold and deposited as a shell about the developing egg. Relatively high concentrations of unreduced chloraurate ion penetrate the contents of the developing egg.

"There is little doubt that The Goose finds this process useful as a means of getting rid of the gold atoms which, if allowed to accumulate, would undoubtedly poison it. Excretion by eggshell may be novel in the animal kingdom, even unique, but there is no denying that it is keeping The Goose alive.

"Unfortunately, however, the ovary is being locally poisoned to such an extent that few eggs are laid, probably not more than will suffice to get rid of the accumulating gold, and those few eggs are definitely unhatchable."

That was all he said in writing, but to the rest of us he said, "That leaves one peculiarly embarrassing question."

92

I knew what it was. We all did.

Where was the gold coming from?

No answer to that for a while, except for some negative evidence. There was no perceptible gold in The Goose's feed, nor were there any gold-bearing pebbles about that it might have swallowed. There was no trace of gold anywhere in the soil of the area, and a search of the house and grounds revealed nothing. There were no gold coins, gold jewelry, gold plate, gold watches, or gold anything. No one on the farm even had as much as gold fillings in his teeth.

There was Mrs. MacGregor's wedding ring, of course, but she had only had one in her life and she was wearing that one.

So where was the gold coming from?

The beginnings of the answer came on August 16, 1955.

Albert Nevis, of Purdue, was forcing gastric tubes into The Goose (another procedure to which the bird objected strenuously) with the idea of testing the contents of its alimentary canal. It was one of our routine searches for exogenous gold.

Gold *was* found, but only in traces, and there was every reason to suppose those traces had accompanied the digestive secretions and were therefore endogenous (from within, that is) in origin.

However, something else showed up, or the lack of it, anyway.

I was there when Nevis came into Finley's office in the temporary building we had put up overnight (almost) near the goosepen.

Nevis said, "The Goose is low in bile pigment. Duodenal contents show about none."

Finley frowned and said, "Liver function is probably knocked loop-the-loop because of its gold concentration. It probably isn't secreting bile at all."

"It *is* secreting bile," said Nevis. "Bile acids are present in normal quantity. Near normal, anyway. It's just the bile pigments that are missing. I did a fecal analysis and that was confirmed. No bile pigments."

Let me explain something at this point. Bile acids are steroids secreted by the liver into the bile and *via* that are poured into the upper end of the small intestine. These bile

93

acids are detergentlike molecules which help to emulsify the fat in our diet (or The Goose's) and distribute them in the form of tiny bubbles through the watery intestinal contents. This distribution, or homogenization, if you'd rather, makes it easier for the fat to be digested.

Bile pigments, the substance that was missing in The Goose, are something entirely different. The liver makes them out of hemoglobin, the red oxygen-carrying protein of the blood. Worn-out hemoglobin is broken up in the liver, the heme part being split away. The heme is made up of a ringlike molecule (called a "porphyrin") with an iron atom in the center. The liver takes the iron out and stores it for future use, then breaks the ringlike molecule that is left. This broken porphyrin is bile pigment. It is colored brownish or greenish (depending on further chemical changes) and is secreted into the bile.

The bile pigments are of no use to the body. They are poured into the bile as waste products. They pass through the intestines and come out with the feces. In fact, the bile pigments are responsible for the color of the feces.

Finley's eyes begin to glitter.

Nevis said, "It looks as though porphyrin catabolism isn't following the proper course in the liver. Doesn't it to you?"

It surely did. To me too.

There was tremendous excitement after that. This was the first metabolic abnormality, not directly involving gold, that had been found in The Goose!

We took a liver biopsy (which means we punched a cylindrical sliver out of The Goose, reaching down into the liver). It hurt The Goose but didn't harm it. We took more blood samples too.

This time we isolated hemoglobin from the blood and small quantities of the cytochromes from our liver samples. (The cytochromes are oxidizing enzymes that also contain heme.) We separated out the heme, and in acid solution some of it precipitated in the form of a brilliant orange substance. By August 22, 1955, we had five micrograms of the compound.

The orange compound was similar to heme, but it was not heme. The iron in heme can be in the form of a doubly charged ferrous ion (Fe^{++}) or a triply charged ferric ion (Fe^{+++}), in which latter case, the compound is called hematin. (Ferrous and ferric, by the way, come from the Latin word for iron, which is "ferrum.")

The orange compound we separated from heme had the porphyrin portion of the molecule all right, but the metal in the center was gold—to be specific, a triply charged auric ion (Au^{+++}). We called this compound "aureme," which is simply short for "auric heme."

Aureme was the first naturally occurring, gold-containing organic compound ever discovered. Ordinarily it would rate headline news in the world of biochemistry. But now it was nothing; nothing at all in comparison to the further horizons its mere existence opened up.

The liver, it seemed, was not breaking up the heme to bile pigment. Instead, it was converting it to aureme; it was replacing iron with gold. The aureme, in equilibrium with chloraurate ion, entered the bloodstream and was carried to the ovaries, where the gold was separated out and the porphyrin portion of the molecule disposed of by some as yet unidentified mechanism.

Further analyses showed that 29 percent of the gold in the blood of The Goose was carried in the plasma in the form of chloraurate ion. The remaining 71 percent was carried in the red blood corpuscles in the form of "auremoglobin." An attempt was made to feed The Goose traces of radioactive gold so that we could pick up radioactivity in plasma and corpuscles and see how readily the auremoglobin molecules were handled in the ovaries. It seemed to us the auremoglobin should be much more slowly disposed of than the dissolved chloraurate ion in the plasma.

The experiment failed, however, since we detected no radioactivity. We put it down to inexperience since none of us were isotopes men, and that was too bad since the failure was highly significant, really, and by not realizing it, we lost several days.

The auremoglobin was, of course, useless as far as carrying oxygen was concerned, but it only made up about 0.1 percent of the total hemoglobin of the red blood cells so there was no interference with the respiration of The Goose.

This still left us with the question of where the gold came from, and it was Nevis who first made the crucial suggestion.

"Maybe," he said at a meeting of the group held on the evening of August 25, 1955, "maybe The Goose doesn't replace the iron with gold. Maybe it *changes* the iron to gold."

Before I met Nevis personally that summer, I had known him through his publications (his field is bile chemistry and liver function) and had always considered him a cautious, clear-thinking person. Almost overcautious. One wouldn't consider him capable for a minute of making any such completely ridiculous statement.

It just shows the desperation and demoralization involved in Project Goose.

The desperation was the fact that there was nowhere, literally nowhere, that the gold could come from. The Goose was excreting gold at the rate of 38.9 grams a day, and had been doing it over a period of months. That gold had to come from somewhere and, failing that—absolutely failing that—it had to be made from something.

The demoralization that led us to consider the second alternative was due to the mere fact that we were face to face with The Goose That Laid the Golden Eggs; the undeniable GOOSE. With that, everything became possible. All of us were living in a fairy-tale world and all of us reacted to it by losing all sense of reality.

Finley considered the possibility seriously. "Hemoglobin," he said, "enters the liver and a bit of auremoglobin comes out. The gold shell of the eggs has iron as its only impurity. The egg yolk is high in only two things; in gold, of course, and also, somewhat, in iron. It all makes a horrible kind of distorted sense. We're going to need help, men."

We did, and it meant a third stage of the investigation. The first stage had consisted of myself alone. The second was the biochemical task force. The third, the greatest, the most important of all, involved the invasion of the nuclear physicists.

On September 5, 1955, John L. Billings of the University of California arrived. He had some equipment with him, and more arrived in the following weeks. More temporary structures were going up. I could see that within a year we would have a whole research institution built about The Goose.

Billings joined our conference the evening of the fifth.

Finley brought him up to date and said, "There are a great many serious problems involved in this iron-to-gold idea. For one thing, the total quantity of iron in The Goose can only be of the order of half a gram, yet nearly 40 grams of gold a day are being manufactured."

Billings had a clear, high-pitched voice. He said, "There's a worse problem than that. Iron is about at the bottom of the packing fraction curve. Gold is much higher up. To convert a gram of iron to a gram of gold takes just about as much energy as is produced by the fissioning of one gram of U-235."

Finley shrugged. "I'll leave the problem to you."

Billings said, "Let me think about it."

He did more than think. One of the things done was to isolate fresh samples of heme from The Goose, ash it and send the iron oxide to Brookhaven for isotopic analysis. There was no particular reason to do that particular thing. It was just one of a number of individual investigations, but it was the one that brought results.

When the figures came back, Billings choked on them. He said, "There's no Fe^{56}."

"What about the other isotopes?" asked Finley at once.

"All present," said Billings, "in the appropriate relative ratios, but no detectable Fe^{56}."

I'll have to explain again. Iron, as it occurs naturally, is made up of four different isotopes. These isotopes are varieties of atoms that differ from one another in atomic weight. Iron atoms with an atomic weight of 56, or Fe^{56}, make up to 91.6 percent of all atoms in iron. The other atoms have atomic weights of 54, 57 and 58.

The iron from the heme of The Goose was made up only of Fe^{54}, Fe^{57} and Fe^{58}. The implication was obvious. Fe^{56} was disappearing while the other isotopes weren't, and this meant a nuclear reaction was taking place. A nuclear reaction could take one isotope and leave others be. An ordinary chemical reaction, any chemical reaction at all, would have to dispose of all isotopes equally.

"But it's energically impossible," said Finley.

He was only saying that in mild sarcasm with Billings' initial remark in mind. As biochemists, we knew well enough

97

that many reactions went on in the body which required an input of energy and that this was taken care of by coupling the energy-demanding reaction with an energy-producing reaction.

However, chemical reactions gave off or took up a few kilocalories per mole. Nuclear reactions gave off or took up millions. To supply energy for an energy-demanding nuclear reaction required, therefore, a second and energy-producing nuclear reaction.

We didn't see Billings for two days.

When he did come back, it was to say, "See here, the energy-producing reaction must produce just as much energy per nucleon involved as the energy-demanding reaction uses up. If it produces even slightly less, then the overall reaction won't go. If it produces even slightly more, then considering the astronomical number of nucleons involved, the excess energy produced would vaporize The Goose in a fraction of a second."

"So?" said Finley.

"So the number of reactions possible is very limited. I have been able to find only one plausible system. Oxygen-18, if converted to iron-56, will produce enough energy to drive the iron-56 on to gold-197. It's like going down one side of a roller-coaster and then up the other. We'll have to test this."

"How?"

"First, suppose we check the isotopic composition of the oxygen in The Goose."

Oxygen is made up of three stable isotopes, almost all of it O^{16}. O^{18} makes up only one oxygen atom out of 250.

Another blood sample. The water content was distilled off in vacuum and some of it put through a mass spectrograph. There was O^{18} there but only one oxygen atom out of 1300. Fully 80 percent of the O^{18} we expected wasn't there.

Billings said, "That's corroborative evidence. Oxygen-18 is being used up. It is being supplied constantly in the food and water fed to The Goose, but it is still being used up. Gold-197 is being produced." Iron-56 is one intermediate and since the reaction that uses up iron-56 is faster than the one that produces it, it has no chance to reach significant concentration, and isotopic analysis shows its absence.

We weren't satisfied, so we tried again. We kept The Goose for a week on water that had been enriched with O^{18}. Gold production went up almost at once. At the end of a week, it was producing 45.8 grams, while the O^{18} content of its body water was no higher than before.

"There's no doubt about it," said Billings.

He snapped his pencil and stood up. "That Goose is a living nuclear reactor."

The Goose was obviously a mutation.

A mutation suggested radiation among other things, and radiation brought up the thought of nuclear tests conducted in 1952 and 1953 several hundred miles away from the site of MacGregor's farm. (If it occurs to you that no nuclear tests have been conducted in Texas, it just shows two things: I'm not telling you everything, and you don't know everything.)

I doubt that at any time in the history of the atomic era was background radiation so thoroughly analyzed and the radioactive content of the soil so rigidly sifted.

Back records were studied. It didn't matter how top-secret they were. By this time Project Goose had the highest priority that had ever existed.

Even weather records were checked in order to follow the behavior of the winds at the time of the nuclear tests.

Two things turned up.

One: The background radiation at the farm was a bit higher than normal. Nothing that could possibly do harm, I hasten to add. There were indications, however, that at the time of the birth of The Goose, the farm had been subjected to the drifting edge of at least two fallouts. Nothing really harmful, I again hasten to add.

Second: The Goose, alone of all geese on the farm; in fact, alone of all living creatures on the farm that could be tested, including the humans, showed no radioactivity at all. Look at it this way: *everything* shows traces of radioactivity; that's what is meant by background radiation. But The Goose showed none.

Finley sent one report on December 6, 1955, which I can paraphrase as follows:

"The goose is a most extraordinary mutation, born of a

99

high-level radioactivity environment which at once encouraged mutations in general and which made this particular mutation a beneficial one.

"The Goose has enzyme systems capable of catalyzing various nuclear reactions. Whether the enzyme system consists of one enzyme or more than one is not known. Nor is anything known of the nature of the enzymes in question. Nor can any theory be yet advanced as to how an enzyme can catalyze a nuclear reaction, since these involve particulate interactions with forces five orders of magnitude higher than those involved in the ordinary chemical reactions commonly catalyzed by enzymes.

"The overall nuclear change is from oxygen-18 to gold-197. The oxygen-18 is plentiful in its environment, being present in significant amounts in water and all organic foodstuffs. The gold-197 is excreted via the ovaries. One known intermediate is iron-56, and the fact that auremoglobin is formed in the process leads us to suspect that the enzyme or enzymes may have heme as a prosthetic group.

"There has been considerable thought devoted to the value this overall nuclear change might have to The Goose. The oxygen-18 does it no harm, and the gold-197 is troublesome to be rid of, potentially poisonous, and a cause of its sterility. Its formation might possibly be a means of avoiding greater danger. This danger—"

But just reading it in the report, friend, makes it all seem so quiet, almost pensive. Actually I never saw a man come closer to apoplexy and survive than Billings did when he found out about our own radioactive gold experiments which I told you about earlier—the ones in which we detected no radioactivity in The Goose, so that we discarded the results as meaningless.

Many times over he asked how we could possibly consider it unimportant that we had lost radioactivity.

"You're like the cub reporter," he said, "who was sent to cover a society wedding and returned saying there was no story because the groom hadn't shown up.

"You fed The Goose radioactive gold and lost it. Not only that, you failed to detect any natural radioactivity about The Goose. Any carbon-14. Any potassium-40. And you called it failure."

100

We started feeding The Goose radioactive isotopes. Cautiously, at first, but before the end of January of 1956, we were shoveling it in.

The Goose remained nonradioactive.

"What it amounts to," said Billings, "is that this enzyme-catalyzed nuclear process of The Goose manages to convert unstable isotope into a stable isotope."

"Useful," I said.

"Useful? It's a thing of beauty. It's the perfect defense against the atomic age. Listen, the conversion of oxygen-18 to gold-197 should liberate eight and a fraction positrons per oxygen atom. That means eight and a fraction gamma rays as soon as each positron combines with an electron. No gamma rays either. The Goose must be able to absorb gamma rays harmlessly."

We irradiated The Goose with gamma rays. As the level rose, The Goose developed a slight fever and we quit in panic. It was just fever, though, not radiation sickness. A day passed, the fever subsided, and The Goose was as good as new.

"Do you see what we've got?" demanded Billings.

"A scientific marvel," said Finley.

"Good Lord, don't you see the practical applications? If we can find out the mechanism and duplicate it in the test tube, we've got a perfect method of radioactive ash disposal. The most important gimmick preventing us from going ahead with a full-scale atomic economy is the thought of what to do with the radioactive isotopes manufactured in the process. Sift them through an enzyme preparation in large vats and that would be it.

"Find out the mechanism, gentlemen, and you can stop worrying about fallouts. We would find a protection against radiation sickness.

"Alter the mechanism somehow and we can have Geese excreting any element needed. How about uranium-235 eggshells?

"The mechanism! The mechanism!"

He could shout "Mechanism" all he wanted. It did no good.

We sat there, all of us, staring at The Goose and sitting on our hands.

If only the eggs would hatch. If only we could get a tribe of nuclear-reactor Geese.

"It must have happened before," said Finley. "The legends of such Geese must have started somehow."

"Do you want to wait?" asked Billings.

If we had a gaggle of such Geese, we could begin taking a few apart. We could study their ovaries. We could prepare tissue slices and tissue homogenates.

That might not do any good. The tissue of a liver biopsy did not react with oxygen-18 under any conditions we tried.

But then we might perfuse an intact liver. We might study intact embryos, watch for one to develop the mechanism.

But with only one Goose, we could do none of that.

We don't dare kill The Goose That Lays the Golden Eggs.

The secret was in the liver of that fat Goose.

Liver of fat goose! *Paté de foie gras!* No delicacy to us!

Nevis said thoughtfully, "We need an idea. Some radical departure. Some crucial thought."

"Saying it won't bring it," said Billings despondently.

And in a miserable attempt at a joke, I said, "We could advertise in the newspapers," and that gave *me* an idea.

"Science fiction!" I said.

"What?" said Finley.

"Look, science-fiction magazines print gag articles. The readers consider them fun. They're interested." I told them about the thiotimoline articles Asimov wrote and which I had once read.

The atmosphere ·was cold with disapproval.

"We won't even be breaking security regulations," I said, "because no one will believe it." I told them about the time in 1944 when Cleve Cartmill wrote a story describing the atom bomb one year early and the F.B.I. kept its temper.

They just stared at me.

"And science-fiction readers have ideas. Don't underrate them. Even if they think it's a gag article, they'll send their notions to the editor. And since we have no ideas of our own, since we're up a dead-end street, what can we lose?"

They still didn't buy it.

So I said, "And you know—The Goose won't live forever."

That did it, somehow.

102

* * *

We had to convince Washington; then I got in touch with John Campbell, the science-fiction editor, and he got in touch with Asimov.

Now the article is done. I've read it, I approve, and I urge you all not to believe it. Please don't.

Only—

Any ideas?

8

The Bridge of the Gods

Scientists sometimes have the pleasure (or the shock) of making a discovery that contravenes something that has been taken for granted for as long as human beings have thought about the matter. What can be as pure as the light from the blessed Sun? What can be as unmixed as clear, white light? Well, read on—

On June 6, 1974, my wife, Janet, and I were in the Forest of Dean, in southwestern England near the Welsh border. It was a day of showers interspersed with sunshine, and in the late afternoon Janet and I took a walk among the immemorial beeches.

A sprinkle of rain sent us under one of those beeches, but the Sun was out and a rainbow appeared in the sky. Not one rainbow, either, but *two*. For the only time in my life I saw both the primary and secondary bows, separated, as they should be, by about twenty times the diameter of the full Moon. Between them the sky was distinctly dark, so that, in effect, we saw a broad band of darkness crossing the eastern sky in a perfect circular arc, bounded on either side by a rainbow, with the red side of each bordering the darkness and the violet side fading into the blue.

It lasted several minutes and we watched in perfect silence. I am not a visual person, but that penetrated—and deeply.

Nine days later, on June 15, 1974, I visited Westminster Abbey in London and stood beside Isaac Newton's grave (I refused to step *on* it). From where I stood, I could also see the graves of Michael Faraday, Ernest Rutherford, James Clerk-Maxwell, and Charles Darwin; all told, five of the ten men whom I once listed as the greatest scientists of all time. It penetrated as deeply as the double rainbow.

I couldn't help thinking of the connection between the rainbow and Newton and decided at once to do an article on the subject when the occasion lent itself to the task—and here it is.

Suppose we begin with light itself. In ancient times, those we know of who speculated on the matter thought of light as preeminently the property of the heavenly bodies and, in particular, of the Sun. This heavenly light was not to be confused with earthly imitations such as the fire of burning wood or of a burning candle. Earthly light was imperfect. It flickered and died; or it could be fed and renewed. The heavenly light of the Sun was eternal and steady.

In Milton's *Paradise Lost* one gets the definite impression that the Sun is simply a container into which God has placed light. The light contained in the sun is forever undiminished, and by the light of that light (if you see what I mean) we can see. From that point of view, there is no puzzle in the fact that God created light on the first day and the Sun, Moon and stars on the fourth. Light is the thing itself, the heavenly bodies merely the containers.

Since sunlight was heavenly born, it would naturally have to be divinely pure, and its purity was best exemplified in the fact that it was perfectly white. Earthly "light," imperfect as it was, could have color. The flames of earthly fires were distinctly yellowish, sometimes reddish. Where certain chemicals were added, they could be any color.

Color, in fact, was an attribute, it seemed, of materials only, and when it intruded into light, it seemed invariably a sign of impurity. Light reflected from an opaque-colored object, or transmitted through a transparent colored object, took on the color and imperfection of matter just as clear water coursing over loose silt would grow muddy.

There was only one aspect of color that, to the eyes of the

ancients, did not seem to involve the kind of matter they were familiar with, and that was the rainbow. It appeared in the sky as a luminous arc of different colors: red, orange, yellow, green, blue and violet, in that order, with the red on the outer curve of the arc and the violet on the inner curve.*

The rainbow, high in the sky, insubstantial, evanescent, divorced from any obvious connection with matter, seemed as much an example of divine light as that of the Sun—and yet it was colored. There was no good explanation for that except to suppose that it was another creation of God or of the gods, produced in color for some definite purpose.

In the Bible, for instance, the rainbow was created after the Flood. God explained its purpose to Noah: "And it shall come to pass, when I bring a cloud over the earth, that the bow shall be seen in the cloud: And I will remember my covenant, which is between me and you and every living creature of all flesh; and the waters shall no more become a flood to destroy all flesh." (Genesis 9:14–15)

Presumably, though the Bible doesn't say so, the rainbow is colored so that it can the more easily be seen against the sky, and serve as a clearer reassurance to men trembling before the wrath of God.

The Greeks took a less dramatic view of the rainbow. Since it reached high in the sky and yet seemed to approach the Earth at either end, it seemed to be a connecting link between Heaven and Earth. It was the bridge of the gods (colored, perhaps, because it was a material object, even though of divine origin) whereby they could come down to Earth and return to Heaven.

In Homer's *Iliad*, the goddess Iris is the messenger of the gods and comes down from Olympus now and then to run some errand or other. But *iris* is the Greek word for "rainbow" (and because that portion of the eye immediately about the pupil comes in different colors, it too is called the iris). The genitive form of the word is *iridis*, and when there is a colored, rainbowlike shimmering on matter, as on a soap

---

*A seventh color is often added, "indigo." To my eyes, indigo is only a bluish-violet and does not deserve the dignity of a separate color of the rainbow. The presence of an indigo-colored component of the light emitted by a certain ore heated to incandescence revealed a new element, however, which was consequently named "indium."

106

bubble, it is said to be "iridescent." And because the compounds of a certain new element showed a surprising range of color, the element was named "iridium."

In the Norse myths, the rainbow was "Bifrost," and it was the bridge over which the gods could travel to Earth. Before the last battle, Ragnarok, it was one of the signs of the coming universal destruction that under the weight of the heroes charging from Valhalla, the rainbow bridge broke.

But what about rational explanations? Steps were made toward those too. In ancient times the Greek philosopher Aristotle, about 350 B.C., noted a rainbow effect seen through a spray of water—the same colors in the same arrangement and just as insubstantial. Perhaps the rainbow itself, appearing after rain, was produced in similar fashion by water droplets high in the air.

Nor was water the only transparent substance associated with the rainbow. About A.D. 10 or so, the Roman philosopher Seneca wrote of the rainbowlike effect of colors that showed on the broken edge of a piece of glass.

But what is there about light and transparent substances that can produce a rainbow? It is quite obvious that light passing through such substances in ordinary fashion produces no colors. There is, however, a certain peculiarity in the way light behaves when it crosses from one type of transparent substance to another—from air to water, for instance—that might offer a clue.

This peculiar behavior first entered the history of science when Aristotle pointed out what innumerable people must have casually noticed: that a stick placed into a bowl of water seems to be bent sharply at the water surface, almost as though it were broken back into an angle at that point. Aristotle attributed this to the bending of light as it passed from air into water, or from water into air. After all, the stick itself was not really bent, since it could be withdrawn from the water and shown to be as straight as ever—or felt while it was still in the water and experienced as still straight. The bending of light in passing from one medium to another is called "refraction" (from Latin words meaning "breaking back").

Could it be that the rather unusual event of color-formation by the water or glass could involve the rather unusual fact of the changing of direction of a beam of light?

The first person actually to suggest this was a Polish monk named Erazm Ciolek, in a book on optics which he wrote in 1269 under the partially Latinized name Erasmus Vitellio.

Merely to say that refraction was responsible for the rainbow is easy. To work out exactly how refraction could result in an arc of the precise curvature and in the precise position in the sky is an altogether more difficult thing to do, and it took three and a half centuries after the refraction suggestion was made for someone to dare work it out mathematically.

In 1611, Marco Antonio de Dominis, Archbishop of Spalato (who was imprisoned by the Inquisition toward the end of his life because he was a convert to Anglicanism and argued against Papal supremacy), was the first to try, but managed only a very imperfect job. Unfortunately, ever since Greek times people had had an inaccurate idea as to the precise manner in which light was refracted—and so did the Archbishop.

It was not until 1621 that refraction was finally understood. In that year a Dutch mathematician, Willebrord Snell, studied the angle which a beam of light made with the perpendicular to the water surface it was entering, and the different angle it made with the perpendicular once it was within the water. It had been thought for many centuries that as one angle changed, the other angle changed in proportion. Snell showed that it is the sines* of the angles that always bear the same ratio, and this constant ratio is called the "index of refraction."

Once the notion of an index of refraction was known, scientists could trace the path of light through spherical water droplets, allowing for both reflection and refraction, with considerable precision.

This was done by the French philosopher René Descartes in 1637. He used Snell's Law to work out the precise position

*I try to explain every concept I use as I come to it, but a line has to be drawn. Sines, and trigonometric functions generally, deserve an entire essay to themselves and someday I'll write one. Meanwhile, if you don't know what sines are, it doesn't matter. They play no further part in the present argument.

and curvature of the rainbow. However, he did not give the proper credit to Snell for the law but tried to leave the impression, without actually saying so, that he had worked it out himself.

Snell's Law, however, did not, in itself, properly explain the *colors* of the rainbow.

There seemed only two alternatives. First, it was possible that the color arose, somehow, out of the colorless water (or glass) through which the light passed. Second, it was possible that the color arose, somehow, out of the colorless light as it passed through the water (or glass).

Both alternatives seemed very unlikely since, in either case, color had to derive from colorlessness, but there was a tendency to choose the first alternative since it was better to tamper with water and glass than with the holy light of the Sun.

The Sun and its light had so often been touted as a symbol of deity (not only in Christian times, but in pre-Christian times, dating back to the Egyptian pharaoh Ikhnaton in 1360 B.C., and who knows how much further back to what dim speculations of prehistoric time?) that it had come to seem, rather foolishly, that to impute imperfection to the Sun and sunlight was to deny the perfection of God.

Consider what happened to Galileo, for instance. There were a number of reasons why he got into trouble with the Inquisition, the chief of them being that he could never conceal his contempt for those less intelligent than himself, even when they were in a position to do him great harm. But it helped that he gave them weapons with which to attack him, and perhaps the chief of these was his discovery of dark spots on the Sun.

He had noted sunspots first toward the end of 1610, but made his official announcement in 1612, and presented a copy of his book on the subject to Cardinal Maffeo Barberini, who was then a friend of his but who from that time (for various reasons) slowly began to cool toward him, and who was Pope Urban VIII and an outright enemy when, twenty years later, Galileo's troubles with the Inquisition reached their climax.

The finding of sunspots (and the reality of that finding was irrelevant) offended those mystics who found the Sun to be a representation of God, and some began to preach against him.

One of them was a Dominican friar who made use, very tellingly, of an amazingly apt quotation from the Bible. At the beginning of the Acts of the Apostles, the resurrected Jesus finally ascends to heaven and his Galilean apostles stare steadfastly upward at the point where he disappears until two angels recall them to their earthly duties with a reproof that begins with, "Ye men of Galilee, why stand ye gazing up into heaven?"

In Latin the first two words of the quotation are *Viri Galilaei*, and Galileo's family name was Galilei. In 1613, when the Dominican thundered out that phrase and used it as a biblical denunciation of Galileo's attempts to penetrate the mysteries of the heavens, many must have shuddered away from the angel-reproved astronomer. In 1615, Galileo's case was in the hands of the Inquisition and his long ordeal began.

Yet sunspots can be explained away. Their presence need not be accepted as a final disruption of Heaven's perfection. If the Sun is only the container of light, it might be imperfect and smudged. The thing contained, however, the heavenly light itself, the first creation of God on the first day, was another matter altogether. Who would dare deny *its* perfection?

That blasphemy came about in England in 1666, a place and time much safer for the purpose than the Italy of 1612. And the man who carried through the blasphemy was a quite pious twenty-four-year-old named Isaac Newton.

The young Newton was interested in the rainbow effect not for its own sake, but in connection with a more practical problem which concerned him but does not, at the moment, concern us.

Newton might have begun by arguing that if a rainbow is formed by the refraction of light by water drops, then it should also be formed in the laboratory, if refraction were carried through properly. Refraction takes place when light passes from air into glass at an oblique angle, but if the glass surface is bounded by two parallel planes (as ordinary window glass is, for instance), then, on emerging from the other surface, the same refraction takes place in reverse. The two refractions cancel and the ray of light passes through unrefracted.

One must, therefore, use a glass object with surfaces that

are not parallel and that refract the light entering the glass and the light leaving the glass in the same direction, so that the two effects add on instead of canceling.

For the purpose, Newton used a triangular prism of glass, which he knew, by Snell's Law, would refract light in the same direction on entering and on leaving, as he wanted it to do. He then darkened a room by covering the windows with shutters and made one little opening in one shutter to allow a single circular beam of light to enter and fall on the white wall opposite. A brilliant circle of white light appeared on the wall, of course.

Newton then placed the prism in the path of the light and the beam was refracted sharply. Its path was bent and the circle of white light was no longer where it had been but now struck the wall in a markedly different position.

What's more, it was no longer a circle but an oblong some five times longer than it was wide. Still more, colors had appeared, the same colors as in the rainbow and in the same order.

Was it possible that this rainbow was just a lucky freak resulting from the size of the hole or the position of the prism? He tried holes of different sizes and found that the artificial rainbow might get brighter or dimmer but the colors remained, and in the same order. They also remained if he had the light pass through the thicker or thinner part of the prism. He even tried the prism outside the window so that the sunlight went through it *before* it went through the hole in the shutter—and the rainbow still appeared.

So far, these experiments, though they had never been conducted with anything like such systematic care, did not introduce anything completely new. After all, rainbow effects had for centuries been observed and reported at oblique edges of glass which had been either broken or beveled, and that was essentially what Newton was now observing.

It had always been assumed before, though, that the effects were produced by the glass, and now Newton found himself wondering if that could possibly be so. The fact that changing the position of the glass or the thickness of the glass through which the light passed did not change the rainbow in any essential way made it seem the glass might not be involved, that it was the light itself that might be responsible.

It seemed to Newton that if he held the prism point down and then had the light that had passed through it pass through a second prism oriented in the opposite direction, with the point up, one of two things ought to happen:

1) If it was the glass producing the colors as light was refracted through it, more color would be produced by the glass of the second prism and the colored oblong of light would be still more elongated, and still more deeply colored.

2) If it was refraction alone that produced the colors and if the glass had nothing to do with it, then the second refraction, being opposite in direction, should cancel out the first so that the oblong would be a circle again, with all the colors gone.

Newton tried the experiment and the second alternative seemed to be it. The light, passing through two prisms that were identical except for being oppositely oriented, struck the wall where it would have struck if there had been no prisms at all, and struck it as a brilliant circle of pure white light. (If Newton had placed a piece of white cardboard between the prisms he would have seen that the oblong of colors still existed there.)

Newton decided, therefore, that the glass had nothing to do with the color, but served only as a vehicle of refraction. The colors were produced out of the sunlight itself.

Newton had, for the first time in man's history, clearly demonstrated the existence of color apart from matter. The colors he had produced with his prism were not colored this or colored that; they were not even colored air. They were *colored light*, as insubstantial and as immaterial as sunlight itself. Compared to the gross and palpable colored matter with which people had been familiar till then, the colors Newton had produced were a kind of ghost of color. It's not surprising, then, that the word he introduced for the band of colors was the Latin word for ghost—"spectrum."*

Newton went on to allow his beam of refracted light to fall on a board with a hole in it so that only the single color of a

*We still speak of "specters" and "spectral appearances," but the new meaning of the word, signifying a whole stretch of different colors, has taken over and is now a common metaphor. We can speak of "the spectrum of political attitudes," for instance.

small portion of the spectrum could pass through. This single-color portion of sunlight he passed through a second prism and found that although it was broadened somewhat, no new colors appeared. He also measured the degree to which each individual color was refracted by the second prism and found that red was always refracted less than orange, which was refracted less than yellow, and so on.

His final conclusion, then, was that sunlight (and white light generally) is not pure but is a mixture of colors, each of which is much more nearly pure than white light is. No one color by itself can appear white, but all of them together, properly mixed, will do so.

Newton further suggested that each different color has a different index of refraction in glass or in water. When light passes through a glass prism or through water droplets, the differences in index of refraction cause the different colored components of white light to bend, each by a different amount, and emerge from glass or water separated.

This was the final blow to the ancient/medieval view of the perfection of the heavens. The rainbow, that reminder of God's mercy, that bridge of the gods, was reduced to a giant spectrum high in the air, produced by countless tiny prisms (in the form of water droplets) all combining their effect.

To those who value the vision of the human mind organizing observations into natural law and then using natural law to grasp the workings of what had until then been mysterious, the rainbow has gained added significance and beauty through Newton's discovery, because, to a far greater extent than before, it can be *understood* and truly appreciated. To those of more limited fancy, who prefer mindless staring to understanding, and simple-minded fairy tales of gods crossing bridges to the dancing changes of direction of light in accordance with a system that can be written as an elegant mathematical expression, I suppose it is a loss.

Newton's announcement of his discoveries did not take the world by storm at once. It was so revolutionary, so opposed to what had been taken for granted for many centuries, that many hesitated.

For instance, there was the opposition of Robert Hooke, seven years Newton's senior, and with an important position at the Royal Society, which was the arbiter of science in those days. Hooke had been a sickly youngster. Smallpox had scarred his skin, but he had had to work his way through Oxford waiting on tables, and the scapegoatings and humiliations he had to endure at the hands of the young gentry who were infinitely his inferiors intellectually left deeper marks on him than the smallpox did.

The world was his enemy after that. He was one of the most brilliant scientific thinkers of his time and might easily have ranked a clear second after Newton himself if he had not put so much of his time into a delighted orgy of spiteful disputation.

In particular, he marked down Newton for his prey, out of sheer jealousy of the one man whose intellectual equal he could never be. Hooke used his position in the Royal Society to thwart Newton at every turn. He accused him of stealing his (Hooke's) ideas and nearly kept Newton's masterpiece, *Principia Mathematica*, in which the laws of motion and of universal gravitation are expounded, from being published, through such an accusation. When the book was published at last, it was not under Royal Society auspices, but at the private expense of Newton's friend Edmund Halley.

Newton, who was a moral coward, incapable of facing opposition openly although he was willing to use his friends for the purpose, and who was given to sniveling self-pity, was cowed and tormented by the raging, spiteful Hooke. At times Newton would vow he would engage in no more scientific research, and in the end he was driven into a mental breakdown.

It wasn't till Hooke's death that Newton was willing to publish his book *Opticks,* in which he finally organized all his optical findings. This book, published in 1704, was in English rather than in Latin as *Principia Mathematica* had been. Some have suggested that this was done deliberately in order to limit the extent to which it would be read outside England and, therefore, cut down on the controversies that would arise, since Newton, for various reasons, was not entirely a popular figure on the continent.

Opposition to the notion of white light as a mixture of colors did not disappear altogether even after the appearance of *Opticks*. As late as 1810 a German book entitled *Farbenlehre*

("Color-science") appeared and argued the case for white light being pure and unmixed. Its author was none other than the greatest of all German poets, Johann Wolfgang von Goethe, who, as a matter of fact, had done respectable scientific work.

Goethe was wrong, however, and his book dropped into the oblivion it deserved. It is only remembered now as the last dying wail against Newton's optical revolution.

Yet there is this peculiar point to be made. Newton's optical experiments, as I said earlier, were not carried through solely for the purpose of explaining the rainbow. Newton was far more interested in seeing whether there was any way of correcting a basic defect in the telescopes that, ever since Galileo's time a half-century before, had been used to study the heavens.

Till then, all the telescopes had used lenses that refracted light and that produced images that were fringed with color. Newton's experiments seemed to him to prove that color was inevitably produced by the spectrum-forming process of refraction and that no refracting telescope could possibly avoid these colored fringes.

Newton, therefore, went on to devise a telescope that made use of mirrors and reflection, thus introducing the reflecting telescope that today dominates the field of optical astronomy.

Yet Newton was wrong when he decided that refracting telescopes could never avoid those colored fringes. You see, in his marvelous optical experiments he had overlooked one small thing. But that is another story.

9

Belief

As we look into the past, we can watch with satisfaction as settled convictions are broken down and science is revolutionized in one way or another. After all, they are not our convictions that are being destroyed. We're part of the revolution.

In science fiction, our scientists of the future must break down our convictions, and that is hard. It is especially hard for me because I am conservative in my scientific views and I don't believe you can play fast and loose with the gravitational interaction. However, a story is a story, and I managed to write the one that follows.

"Did you ever dream you were flying?" asked Dr. Roger Toomey of his wife.

Jane Toomey looked up. "Certainly!"

Her quick fingers didn't stop their nimble manipulations of the yarn out of which an intricate and quite useless doily was being created. The television set made a muted murmur in the room and the posturings on its screen were, out of long custom, disregarded.

Roger said, "Everyone dreams of flying at some time or other. It's universal. I've done it many times. That's what worries me."

Jane said, "I don't know what you're getting at, dear. I hate to say so." She counted stitches in an undertone.

"When you think about it, it makes you wonder. It's not really flying that you dream of. You have no wings; at least I never had any. There's no effort involved. You're just floating. That's it. Floating."

"When I fly," said Jane, "I don't remember any of the details. Except once I landed on top of City Hall and hadn't any clothes on. Somehow, no one ever seems to pay any attention to you when you're dream-nude. Ever notice that? You're dying of embarrassment but people just pass by."

She pulled at the yarn and the ball tumbled out of the bag and half across the floor. She paid no attention.

Roger shook his head slowly. At the moment, his face was pale and absorbed in doubt. It seemed all angles with its high cheekbones, its long straight nose and the widow's-peak hairline that was growing more pronounced with the years. He was thirty-five.

He said, "Have you ever wondered what makes you dream you're floating?"

"No, I haven't."

Jane Toomey was blonde and small. Her prettiness was the fragile kind that does not impose itself upon you but rather creeps on you unaware. She had the bright blue eyes and pink cheeks of a porcelain doll. She was thirty.

Roger said, "Many dreams are only the mind's interpretation of a stimulus imperfectly understood. The stimuli are forced into a reasonable context in a split second."

Jane said, "What are you talking about, darling?"

Roger said, "Look, I once dreamed I was in a hotel, attending a physics convention. I was with old friends. Everything seemed quite normal. Suddenly there was a confusion of shouting and for no reason at all, I grew panicky. I ran to the door but it wouldn't open. One by one, my friends disappeared. They had no trouble leaving the room, but I couldn't see how they managed it. I shouted at them and they ignored me.

"It was borne in upon me that the hotel was on fire. I didn't smell smoke. I just knew there was a fire. I ran to the window and I could see a fire escape on the outside of the building. I

117

ran to each window in turn but none led to the fire escape. I was quite alone in the room now. I leaned out the window, calling desperately. No one heard me.

"Then the fire engines were coming, little red smears darting along the streets. I remember that clearly. The alarm bells clanged sharply to clear traffic. I could hear them, louder and louder till the sound was splitting my skull. I awoke and, of course, the alarm clock was ringing.

"Now I can't have dreamed a long dream designed to arrive at the moment of the alarm-clock ring in a way that builds the alarm neatly into the fabric of the dream. It's much more reasonable to suppose that the dream began at the moment the alarm began and crammed all its sensation of duration into one split second. It was just a hurry-up device of my brain to explain this sudden noise that penetrated the silence."

Jane was frowning now. She put down her crocheting. "Roger! you've been behaving queerly since you got back from the college. You didn't eat much, and now this ridiculous conversation. I've never heard you so morbid. What you need is a dose of bicarbonate."

"I need a little more than that," said Roger in a low voice. "Now what starts a floating dream?"

"If you don't mind, let's change the subject."

She rose and with firm fingers turned up the sound on the television set. A young gentleman with hollow cheeks and a soulful tenor suddenly raised his voice and assured her, dulcetly, of his never-ending love.

Roger turned it down again and stood with his back to the instrument.

"Levitation!" he said. "That's it. There is some way in which human beings can make themselves float. They have the capacity for it. It's just that they don't know how to use that capacity—except when they sleep. Then sometimes they lift up just a little bit, a tenth of an inch maybe. It wouldn't be enough for anyone to notice even if they were watching, but it would be enough to deliver the proper sensation for the start of a floating dream."

"Roger, you're delirious. I wish you'd stop. Honestly."

He drove on. "Sometimes we sink down slowly and the sensation is gone. Then again, sometimes the float-control ends suddenly and we drop. Jane, did you ever dream you were falling?"

"Yes, of c—"

"You're hanging on the side of a building or you're sitting at the edge of a seat and suddenly you're tumbling. There's the awful shock of falling and you snap awake, your breath gasping, your heart palpitating. You *did* fall. There's no other explanation."

Jane's expression, having passed slowly from bewilderment to concern, dissolved suddenly into sheepish amusement.

"Roger, you *devil*. And you fooled me! Oh, you rat!"

"What?"

"Oh, no. You can't play it out anymore. I know exactly what you're doing. You're making up a plot to a story and you're trying it out on me. I should know better than to listen to you."

Roger looked startled, even a little confused. He strode to her chair and looked down at her, "No, Jane."

"I don't see why not. You've been talking about writing fiction as long as I've known you. If you've got a plot, you might as well write it down. No use just frightening me with it." Her fingers flew as her spirits rose.

"Jane, this is no story."

"But what else—"

"When I woke up this morning, *I dropped to the mattress!*"

He stared at her without blinking. "I dreamed that I was flying," he said. "It was clear and distinct. I remember every minute of it. I was lying on my back when I woke up. I was feeling comfortable and quite happy. I just wondered a little why the ceiling looked so queer. I yawned and stretched and *touched* the ceiling. For a minute I just stared at my arm reaching upward and ending hard against the ceiling.

"Then I turned over. I didn't move a muscle, Jane. I just turned all in one piece because I wanted to. There I was, five feet above the bed. There you were on the bed, sleeping. I was frightened. I didn't know how to get down, but the minute I thought of getting down, I dropped. I dropped slowly. The whole process was under perfect control.

119

"I stayed in bed fifteen minutes before I dared move. Then I got up, washed, dressed and went to work."

Jane forced a laugh, "Darling, you had *better* write it up. But that's all right. You've just been working too hard."

"Please! Don't be banal."

"People work too hard, even though to say so is banal. After all, you were just dreaming fifteen minutes longer than you thought you were."

"It wasn't a dream."

"Of course it was. I can't even count the times I've dreamed I awoke and dressed and made breakfast, then really woke up and found it was all to do over again. I've even dreamed I was dreaming, if you see what I mean. It can be awfully confusing."

"Look, Jane. I've come to you with a problem because you're the only one I feel I can come to. Please take me seriously."

Jane's blue eyes opened wide. "Darling! I'm taking you as seriously as I can. You're the physics professor, not I. Gravitation is what you know about, not I. Would *you* take it seriously if I told you *I* had found myself floating?"

"No. *No!* That's the hell of it. I don't want to believe it, only I've got to. It was no dream, Jane. I tried to tell myself it was. You have no idea how I talked myself into that. By the time I got to class, I was sure it was a dream. You didn't notice anything queer about me at breakfast, did you?"

"Yes, I did, now that I think about it."

"Well, it wasn't very queer or you would have mentioned it. Anyway, I gave my nine-o'clock lecture perfectly. By eleven I had forgotten the whole incident. Then, just after lunch, I needed a book. I needed Page and—well, the book doesn't matter; I just needed it. It was on an upper shelf, but I could reach it. Jane—"

He stopped.

"Well, go on, Roger."

"Look, did you ever try to pick up something that's just a step away? You bend and automatically take a step toward it as you reach. It's completely involuntary. It's just your body's overall coordination."

"All right. What of it?"

"I reached for the book and automatically took a step upward. On air, Jane! On empty air!"

"I'm going to call Jim Sarle, Roger."

"I'm not sick, damn it."

"I think he ought to talk to you. He's a friend. It won't be a doctor's visit. He'll just talk to you."

"And what good will that do?" Roger's face turned red with sudden anger.

"We'll see. Now sit down, Roger. Please." She walked to the phone.

He cut her off, seizing her wrist. "You don't believe me."

"Oh, Roger."

"You don't."

"I believe you. Of course I believe you. I just want—"

"Yes. You just want Jim Sarle to talk to me. That's how much you believe me. I'm telling the truth but you want me to talk to a psychiatrist. Look, you don't have to take my word for anything. I can prove this. I can prove I can float."

"I *believe* you."

"Don't be a fool. I know when I'm being humored. Stand still! Now watch me."

He backed away to the middle of the room and without preliminary lifted off the floor. He *dangled,* with the toes of his shoes six empty inches from the carpet.

Jane's eyes and mouth were three round O's. She whispered, "Come down, Roger. Oh, dear heaven, come down."

He drifted down, his feet touching the floor without a sound. "You see?"

"Oh, my. Oh, my."

She stared at him, half-frightened, half-sick.

On the television set a chesty female sang mutedly that flying high with some guy in the sky was her idea of nothing at all.

Roger Toomey stared into the bedroom's darkness. He whispered, "Jane."

"What?"

"You're not sleeping?"

"No."

"I can't sleep either. I keep holding the headboard to make sure I'm . . . you know."

His hand moved restlessly and touched her face. She flinched, jerking away as though he carried an electric charge.

She said, "I'm sorry. I'm a little nervous."

"That's all right. I'm getting out of bed anyway."

"What are you going to do? You've got to sleep."

"Well, I can't, so there's no sense keeping you awake too."

"Maybe nothing will happen. It doesn't have to happen every night. It didn't happen before last night."

"How do I know? Maybe I just never went up so high. Maybe I just never woke up and caught myself. Anyway, now it's different."

He was sitting up in bed, his legs bent, his arms clasping his knees, his forehead resting on them. He pushed the sheet to one side and rubbed his cheek against the soft flannel of his pajamas.

He said, "It's bound to be different now. My mind's full of it. Once I'm asleep, once I'm not holding myself down consciously, why, up I'll go."

"I don't see why. It must be such an effort."

"That's the point. It isn't."

"But you're fighting gravity, aren't you?"

"I know, but there's still no effort. Look, Jane, if I only *could* understand it, I wouldn't mind so much."

He dangled his feet out of bed and stood up. "I don't want to talk about it."

His wife muttered, "I don't want to either." She started crying, fighting back the sobs and turning them into strangled moans, which sounded much worse.

Roger said, "I'm sorry, Jane. I'm getting you all wrought up."

"No, don't touch me. Just . . . just leave me alone."

He took a few uncertain steps away from the bed.

She said, "Where are you going?"

"To the studio couch. Will you help me?"

"How?"

"I want you to tie me down."

"Tie you down?"

"With a couple of ropes. Just loosely, so I can turn if I want to. Do you mind?"

Her bare feet were already seeking her mules on the floor at her side of the bed. "All right," she sighed.

Roger Toomey sat in the small cubbyhole that passed for his office and stared at the pile of examination papers before him. At the moment he didn't see how he was going to mark them.

He had given five lectures on electricity and magnetism since the first night he had floated. He had gotten through them somehow, though not swimmingly. The students asked ridiculous questions, so probably he wasn't making himself as clear as he once did.

Today he had saved himself a lecture by giving a surprise examination. He didn't bother making one up, just handed out copies of one given several years earlier.

Now he had the answer papers and would have to mark them. Why? Did it matter what they said? Or anyone? Was it so important to know the laws of physics? If it came to that, what were the laws? Were there any, really?

Or was it all just a mass of confusion out of which nothing orderly could ever be extracted? Was the Universe, for all its appearance, merely the original chaos, still waiting for the Spirit to move upon the face of its deep?

Insomnia wasn't helping him either. Even strapped in upon the couch, he slept only fitfully, and then always with dreams.

There was a knock at the door.

Roger cried angrily, "Who's there?"

A pause, and then the uncertain answer. "It's Miss Harroway, Dr. Toomey. I have the letters you dictated."

"Well, come in, come in. Don't just stand there."

The department secretary opened the door a minimum distance and squeezed her lean and unprepossessing body into his office. She had a sheaf of papers in her hand. To each was clipped a yellow carbon and a stamped, addressed envelope.

Roger was anxious to get rid of her. That was his mistake. He stretched forward to reach the letters as she approached and felt himself leave the chair.

He moved two feet forward, still in sitting position, before he could bring himself down hard, losing his balance and tumbling in the process. It was too late.

It was entirely too late. Miss Harroway dropped the letters in a fluttering handful. She screamed and turned, hitting the door with her shoulder, caroming out into the hall and dashing down the corridor in a clatter of high heels.

Roger rose, rubbing his aching hip. "Damn," he said forcefully.

But he couldn't help seeing her point. He pictured the sight as she must have seen it: a full-grown man lifting smoothly out of his chair and gliding toward her in a maintained squat.

He picked up the letters and closed his office door. It was quite late in the day; the corridors would be empty; she would probably be quite incoherent. Still—he waited anxiously for the crowd to gather.

Nothing happened. Perhaps she was lying somewhere in a dead faint. Roger felt it a point of honor to seek her out and do what he could do for her, but he told his conscience to go to the devil. Until he found out exactly what was wrong with him, exactly what this wild nightmare of his was all about, he must do nothing to reveal it.

Nothing, that is, more than he had done already.

He leafed through the letters, one to every major theoretical physicist in the country. Home talent was insufficient for this sort of thing.

He wondered if Miss Harroway grasped the contents of the letters. He hoped not. He had couched them deliberately in technical language; more so, perhaps, than was quite necessary. Partly that was to be discreet; partly to impress the addressees with the fact that he, Toomey, was a legitimate and capable scientist.

One by one, he put the letters in the appropriate envelopes. The best brains in the country, he thought. Could they help?

He didn't know.

The library was quiet. Roger Toomey closed the *Journal of Theoretical Physics*, placed it on end and stared at its backstrap somberly. The *Journal of Theoretical Physics*! What did any of the contributors to that learned bit of balderdash understand anyway? The thought tore at him. Until so recently they had been the greatest men in the world to him.

And still he was doing his best to live up to their code and philosophy. With Jane's increasingly reluctant help, he had made measurements. He had tried to weigh the phenomenon in the balance, extract its relationships, evaluate its quantities. He had tried, in short, to defeat it in the only way he knew how—by making of it just another expression of the eternal modes of behavior that all the Universe must follow.

(*Must* follow. The best minds said so.)

Only there was nothing to measure. There was absolutely no sensation of effort to his levitation. Indoors—he dare not test himself outdoors, of course—he could reach the ceiling as easily as he could rise an inch, except that it took more time. Given enough time, he felt he could continue rising indefinitely; go to the Moon, if necessary.

He could carry weights while levitating. The process became slower, but there was no increase in effort.

The day before he had come on Jane without warning, a stopwatch in one hand.

"How much do you weigh?" he asked.

"One hundred ten," she replied. She gazed at him uncertainly.

He seized her wrist with one arm. She tried to push him away but he paid no attention. Together they moved upward at a creeping pace. She clung to him, white and rigid with terror.

"Twenty-two minutes, thirteen seconds," he said when his head nudged the ceiling.

When they came down again, Jane tore away and hurried out of the room.

Some days before he had passed a drugstore scale, standing shabbily on a street corner. The street was empty, so he stepped on and put in his penny. Even though he suspected something of the sort, it was a shock to find himself weighing thirty pounds.

He began carrying handfuls of pennies and weighing himself under all conditions. He was heavier on days on which there was a brisk wind, as though he required weight to keep from blowing away.

Adjustment was automatic. Whatever it was that levitated

125

him maintained a balance between comfort and safety. But he could enforce conscious control upon his levitation just as he could upon his respiration. He could stand on a scale and force the pointer up to almost his full weight, and down, of course, to nothing.

He bought a scale two days before and tried to measure the rate at which he could change weight. That didn't help. The rate, whatever it was, was faster than the pointer could swing. All he did was collect data on moduli of compressibility and moments of inertia.

Well—what did it all amount to anyway?

He stood up and trudged out of the library, shoulders drooping. He touched tables and chairs as he walked to the side of the room and then kept his hand unobtrusively on the wall. He had to do that, he felt. Contact with matter kept him continually informed as to his status with respect to the ground. If his hand lost touch with a table or slid upward against the wall—that was it.

The corridor had the usual sprinkling of students. He ignored them. In these last days they had gradually learned to stop greeting him. Roger imagined that some had come to think of him as queer, and most were probably growing to dislike him.

He passed by the elevator. He never took it anymore; going down, particularly. When the elevator made its initial drop, he found it impossible not to lift into the air for just a moment. No matter how he lay in wait for the moment, he hopped and people would turn and look at him.

He reached for the railing at the head of the stairs and just before his hand touched it, one of his feet kicked the other. It was the most ungainly stumble that could be imagined. Three weeks earlier, Roger would have sprawled down the stairs.

This time his automatic system took over and, leaning forward, spread-eagled, fingers wide, legs half-buckled, he sailed down the flight gliderlike. He might have been on wires.

He was too dazed to right himelf, too paralyzed with horror to do anything. Within two feet of the window at the bottom of the flight, he came to an automatic halt and hovered.

There were two students on the flight he had come down, both now pressed against the wall, three more at the head of the stairs, two on the flight below, and one on the landing with him, so close they could almost touch one another.

It was very silent. They all looked at him.

Roger straightened himself, dropped to the ground and ran down the stairs, pushing one student roughly out of his way.

Conversation swirled up into exclamation behind him.

"Dr. Morton wants to see me?" Roger turned in his chair, holding one of its arms firmly.

The new department secretary nodded. "Yes, Dr. Toomey."

She left quickly. In the short time since Miss Harroway had resigned, she had learned that Dr. Toomey had something "wrong" with him. The students avoided him. In his lecture room today, the back seats had been full of whispering students. The front seats had been empty.

Roger looked into the small wall mirror near the door. He adjusted his jacket and brushed some lint off, but that operation did little to improve his appearance. His complexion had grown sallow. He had lost at least ten pounds since all this had started, though of course he had no way of really knowing his exact weight loss. He was generally unhealthy looking, as though his digestion perpetually disagreed with him and won every argument.

He had no apprehensions about this interview with the chairman of the department. He had reached a pronounced cynicism concerning the levitation incidents. Apparently witnesses didn't talk. Miss Harroway hadn't. There was no sign that the students on the staircase had.

With a last touch at his tie, he left his office.

Dr. Philip Morton's office was not too far down the hall, which was a gratifying fact to Roger. More and more, he was cultivating the habit of walking with systematic slowness. He picked up one foot and put it before him, watching. Then he picked up the other and put it before him, still watching. He moved along in a confirmed stoop, gazing at his feet.

Dr. Morton frowned as Roger walked in. He had little eyes, wore a poorly trimmed grizzled mustache and an untidy suit. He had a moderate reputation in the scientific world and a decided penchant for leaving teaching duties to the members of his staff.

He said, "Say, Toomey, I got the strangest letter from Linus Deering. Did you write to him on"—he consulted a paper on his desk—"the twenty-second of last month. Is this your signature?"

Roger looked and nodded. Anxiously he tried to read Deering's letter upside down. This was unexpected. Of the letters he had sent out the day of the Miss Harroway incident, only four had so far been answered.

Three of them had consisted of cold one-paragraph replies that read, more or less: "This is to acknowledge receipt of your letter of the 22nd. I do not believe I can help you in the matter you discuss." A fourth, from Ballantine of Northwestern Tech, had bumblingly suggested an institute for psychic research. Roger couldn't tell whether he was trying to be helpful or insulting.

Deering of Princeton made five. He had had hopes of Deering.

Dr. Morton cleared his throat loudly and adjusted a pair of glasses. "I want to read you what he says. Sit down, Toomey, sit down. He says: 'Dear Phil—'"

Dr. Morton looked up briefly with a slight, fatuous smile. "Linus and I met at Federation meetings last year. We had a few drinks together. Very nice fellow."

He adjusted his glasses again and returned to the letter: "'Dear Phil: Is there a Dr. Roger Toomey in your department? I received a very queer letter from him the other day. I didn't quite know what to make of it. At first I thought I'd let it go as another crank letter. Then I thought that since the letter carried your department heading, you ought to know of it. It's just possible someone may be using your staff as part of a confidence game. I'm enclosing Dr. Toomey's letter for your inspection. I hope to be visiting your part of the country—'"

"Well, the rest is personal." Dr. Morton folded the letter, took off his glasses, put them in a leather container and put that in his breast pocket. He twined his fingers together and leaned forward.

"Now," he said, "I don't have to read you your own letter. Was it a joke? A hoax?"

"Dr. Morton," said Roger, heavily, "I was serious. I don't

see anything wrong with my letter. I sent it to quite a few physicists. It speaks for itself. I've made observations on a case of . . . of levitation, and I wanted information about possible theoretical explanations for such a phenomenon."

"Levitation! Really!"

"It's a legitimate case, Dr. Morton."

"You've observed it yourself?"

"Of course."

"No hidden wires? No mirrors? Look here, Toomey, you're no expert on these frauds."

"This was a thoroughly scientific series of observations. There is no possibility of fraud."

"You might have consulted me, Toomey, before sending out these letters."

"Perhaps I should have, Dr. Morton, but, frankly, I thought you might be—unsympathetic."

"Well, thank you. I should hope so. And on department stationery. I'm really surprised, Toomey. Look here, Toomey, your life is your own. If you wish to believe in levitation, go ahead, but strictly on your own time. For the sake of the department and the college, it should be obvious that this sort of thing should not be injected into your scholastic affairs.

"In point of fact, you've lost some weight recently, haven't you, Toomey? Yes, you don't look well at all. I'd see a doctor if I were you. A nerve specialist, perhaps."

Roger said bitterly, "A psychiatrist might be better, you think?"

"Well, that's entirely your business. In any case, a little rest—"

The telephone had rung and the secretary had taken the call. She caught Dr. Morton's eye and he picked up his extension.

He said, "Hello . . . oh, Dr. Smithers, yes . . . um-m-m . . . yes. . . . Concerning whom? . . . Well, in point of fact, he's with me right now . . . yes . . . yes, immediately."

He cradled the phone and looked at Roger thoughtfully. "The dean wants to see both of us."

"What about, sir?"

"He didn't say." He got up and stepped to the door. "Are you coming, Toomey?"

129

"Yes, sir." Roger rose slowly to his feet, cramming the toe of one foot carefully under Dr. Morton's desk as he did so.

Dean Smithers was a lean man with a long, ascetic face. He had a mouthful of false teeth that fitted just badly enough to give his sibilants a peculiar half-whistle.

"Close the door, Miss Bryce," he said, "and I'll take no phone calls for a while. Sit down, gentlemen."

He stared at them portentously and added, "I think I had better get right to the point. I don't know exactly what Dr. Toomey is doing, but he must stop."

Dr. Morton turned upon Roger in amazement. "What have you been doing?"

Roger shrugged dispiritedly. "Nothing that I can help." He had underestimated student tongue-wagging after all.

"Oh, come, come." The dean registered impatience. "I'm sure I don't know how much of the story to discount, but it seems you must have been engaging in parlor tricks, silly parlor tricks quite unsuited to the spirit and dignity of this institution."

Dr. Morton said, "This is all beyond me."

The dean frowned. "It seems you haven't heard, then. It is amazing to me how the faculty can remain in complete ignorance of matters that fairly saturate the student body. I had never realized it before. I myself heard of it by accident; by a very fortunate accident, in fact, since I was able to intercept a newspaper reporter who arrived this morning looking for someone he called 'Dr. Toomey, the flying professor.'"

"What?" cried Dr. Morton.

Roger listened haggardly.

"That's what the reporter said. I quote him. It seems one of our students had called the paper. I ordered the newspaperman out and had the student sent to my office. According to him, Dr. Toomey flew—I use the word 'flew' because that's what the student insisted on calling it—down a flight of stairs and then back up again. He claimed there were a dozen witnesses."

"I went down the stairs only," muttered Roger.

Dean Smithers was tramping up and down along his carpet now. He had worked himself up into a feverish eloquence.

130

"Now mind you, Toomey, I have nothing against amateur theatricals. In my stay in office I have constantly fought against stuffiness and false dignity. I have encouraged friendliness between ranks in the faculty and have not even objected to reasonable fraternization with students. So I have no objection to your putting on a show for the students *in your own home*.

"Surely you see what could happen to the college once an irresponsible press is done with us. Shall we have a flying-professor craze succeed the flying-saucer craze? If the reporters get in touch with you, Dr. Toomey, I will expect you to deny all such reports categorically."

"I understand, Dean Smithers."

"I trust we shall escape this incident without lasting damage. I must ask you, with all the firmness at my command, never to repeat your . . . uh . . . performance. If you ever do, your resignation will be requested. Do you understand, Dr. Toomey?"

"Yes," said Roger.

"In that case, good day, gentlemen."

Dr. Morton steered Roger back into his office. This time he shooed his secretary and closed the door behind her carefully.

"Good heavens, Toomey," he whispered, "has this madness any connection with your letter on levitation?"

Roger's nerves were beginning to twang. "Isn't it obvious? I was referring to myself in those letters."

"You can fly? I mean, levitate?"

"Either word you choose."

"I never heard of such—damn it, Toomey, did Miss Harroway ever see you levitate?"

"Once. It was an accid—"

"Of course. It's obvious now. She was so hysterical it was hard to make out. She said you had jumped at her. It sounded as though she were accusing you of . . . of—" Dr. Morton looked embarrassed. "Well, I didn't believe that. She was a good secretary, you understand, but obviously not one designed to attract the attention of a young man. I was actually relieved when she left. I thought she would be carrying a small revolver next, or accusing *me*. You . . . you levitated, eh?"

131

"Yes."

"How do you do it?"

Roger shook his head. "That's my problem. I don't know."

Dr. Morton allowed himself a smile. "Surely you don't repeal the law of gravity?"

"You know, I think I do. There must be antigravity involved somehow."

Dr. Morton's indignation at having a joke taken seriously was marked. He said, "Look here, Toomey, this is nothing to laugh at."

"*Laugh* at. Great Scott, Dr. Morton, do I look as though I were laughing?"

"Well—you need a rest. No question about it. A little rest and this nonsense of yours will pass. I'm sure of it."

"It's not nonsense." Roger bowed his head a moment, then said in a quieter tone. "I tell you what, Dr. Morton, would you like to go into this with me? In some way this will open new horizons in physical science. I don't know how it works; I just can't conceive of any solution. The two of us together—"

Dr. Morton's look of horror penetrated by that time.

Roger said, "I know it all sounds queer. But I'll demonstrate for you. It's perfectly legitimate. I wish it weren't."

"Now, now." Dr. Morton sprang from his seat. "Don't exert yourself. You need a rest badly. I don't think you should wait till June. You go home right now. I'll see that your salary comes through and I'll look after your course. I used to give it myself once, you know."

"Dr. Morton. This is important."

"I know. I know." Dr. Morton clapped Roger on the shoulder. "Still, my boy, you look under the weather. Speaking frankly, you look like hell. You need a long rest."

"I *can* levitate." Roger's voice was climbing again. "You're just trying to get rid of me because you don't believe me. Do you think I'm lying? What would be my motive?"

"You're exciting yourself needlessly, my boy. You let me make a phone call. I'll have someone take you home."

"I tell you I *can* levitate," shouted Roger.

Dr. Morton turned red. "Look, Toomey, let's not discuss it. I don't care if you fly up in the air right this minute."

132

"You mean seeing isn't believing as far as you're concerned?"

"Levitation? Of course not." The department chairman was bellowing. "If I saw you fly, I'd see an optometrist or a psychiatrist. I'd sooner believe myself insane than that the laws of physics—"

He caught himself, harumphed loudly. "Well, as I said, let's not discuss it. I'll just make this phone call."

"No need, sir. No need," said Roger. "I'll go. I'll take my rest. Good-bye."

He walked out rapidly, moving more quickly than at any time in days. Dr. Morton, on his feet, hands flat on his desk, looked at his departing back with relief.

James Sarle, M.D., was in the living room when Roger arrived home. He was lighting his pipe as Roger stepped through the door, one large-knuckled hand enclosing the bowl. He shook out the match and his ruddy face crinkled into a smile.

"Hello, Roger. Resigning from the human race? Haven't heard from you in over a month."

His black eyebrows met above the bridge of his nose, giving him a rather forbidding appearance that somehow helped him establish the proper atmosphere with his patients.

Roger turned to Jane, who sat buried in an armchair. As usual lately, she had a look of wan exhaustion on her face.

Roger said to her, "Why did you bring him here?"

"Hold it! Hold it, man," said Sarle. "Nobody brought me. I met Jane downtown this morning and invited myself here. I'm bigger than she is. She couldn't keep me out."

"Met her by coincidence, I suppose? Do you make appointments for all your coincidences?"

Sarle laughed. "Let's put it this way. She told me a little about what's been going on."

Jane said wearily, "I'm sorry if you disapprove, Roger, but it was the first chance I had to talk to someone who would understand."

"What made you think he understands? Tell me, Jim, do you believe her story?"

Sarle said, "It's not an easy thing to believe. You'll admit that. But I'm trying."

"All right, suppose I flew. Suppose I levitated right now. What would you do?"

"Faint, maybe. Maybe I'd say, 'Holy Pete.' Maybe I'd burst out laughing. Why don't you try, and then we'll see?"

Roger stared at him. "You really want to see it?"

"Why shouldn't I?"

"The ones that have seen it screamed or ran or froze with horror. Can you take it, Jim?"

"I think so."

"Okay." Roger slipped two feet upward and executed a slow tenfold *entrechat*. He remained in the air, toes pointed downward, legs together, arms gracefully outstretched in bitter parody.

"Better than Nijinsky, eh, Jim?"

Sarle did none of the things he suggested he might do. Except for catching his pipe as it dropped, he did nothing at all.

Jane had closed her eyes. Tears squeezed quietly through the lids.

Sarle said, "Come down, Roger."

Roger did so. He took a seat and said, "I wrote to physicists, men of reputation. I explained the situation in an impersonal way. I said I thought it ought to be investigated. Most of them ignored me. One of them wrote to old man Morton to ask if I were crooked or crazy."

"Oh, Roger," whispered Jane.

"You think that's bad? The dean called me into his office today. I'm to stop my parlor tricks, he says. It seems I had stumbled down the stairs and automatically levitated myself to safety. Morton says he wouldn't believe I could fly if he saw me in action. Seeing isn't believing in his case, he says, and orders me to take a rest. I'm not going back."

"Roger," said Jane, her eyes opening wide. "Are you serious?"

"I can't go back. I'm sick of them. Scientists!"

"But what will you do?"

"I don't know." Roger buried his head in his hands. He said

in a muffled voice, "You tell me, Jim. You're the psychiatrist. Why won't they believe me?"

"Perhaps it's a matter of self-protection, Roger," said Sarle slowly. "People aren't happy with anything they can't understand. Even some centuries ago when many people *did* believe in the existence of extra-natural abilities, like flying on broomsticks, for instance, it was almost always assumed that these powers originated with the forces of evil.

"People still think so. They may not believe literally in the devil, but they do think that what is strange is evil. They'll fight against believing in levitation—or be scared to death if the fact is forced down their throats. That's true, so let's face it."

Roger shook his head. "You're talking about people, and I'm talking about scientists."

"Scientists are people."

"You know what I mean. I have here a phenomenon. It isn't witchcraft. I haven't dealt with the devil. Jim, there must be a natural explanation. We don't know all there is to know about gravitation. We know hardly anything, really. Don't you suppose it's just barely conceivable that there is some biological method of nullifying gravity? Perhaps I am a mutation of some sort. I have a . . . well, call it a muscle . . . which can abolish gravity. At least it can abolish the effect of gravity on myself. Well, let's investigate it. Why sit on our hands? If we have antigravity, imagine what it will mean to the human race."

"Hold it, Rog," said Sarle. "Think about the matter a while. Why are *you* so unhappy about it? According to Jane, you were almost mad with fear the first day it happened, *before* you had any way of knowing that science was going to ignore you and that your superiors would be unsympathetic."

"That's right," murmured Jane.

Sarle said, "Now why should that be? Here you had a great, new, wonderful power—a sudden freedom from the deadly pull of gravity."

Roger said, "Oh, don't be a fool. It was—horrible. I couldn't understand it. I still can't."

"Exactly, my boy. It was something you couldn't understand

135

and *therefore* something horrible. You're a physical scientist. You *know* what makes the Universe run. Or if you don't know, you know someone else knows. Even if no one understands a certain point, you know that some day someone will know. The key word is *know*. It's part of your life. Now you come face to face with a phenomenon which you consider to violate one of the basic laws of the Universe. Scientists say: Two masses will attract one another according to a fixed mathematical rule. It is an inalienable property of matter and space. There are no exceptions. And now you're an exception."

Roger said glumly, "And how."

"You see, Roger," Sarle went on, "for the first time in history, mankind really has what he considers unbreakable rules. I mean, unbreakable. In primitive cultures, a medicine man might use a spell to produce rain. If it didn't work, it didn't upset the validity of magic. It just meant that the shaman had neglected some part of his spell, or had broken a taboo, or offended a god. In modern theocratic cultures, the commandments of the Deity are unbreakable. Still, if a man were to break the commandments and yet prosper, it would be no sign that that particular religion was invalid. The ways of Providence are admittedly mysterious and some invisible punishment awaits.

"Today, however, we have rules that *really* can't be broken, and one of them is the existence of gravity. It works even though the man who invokes it has forgotten to mutter em-em-over-ahr-square."

Roger managed a twisted smile. "You're all wrong, Jim. The unbreakable rules have been broken over and over again. Radioactivity was impossible when it was discovered. Energy came out of nowhere, incredible quantities of it. It was as ridiculous as levitation."

"Radioactivity," said Sarle, "was an objective phenomenon that could be communicated and duplicated. Uranium would fog photographic film for anyone. A Crookes tube could be built by anyone and would deliver an electron stream in identical fashion for all. You—"

"I've tried communicating—"

"I know. But can you tell me, for instance, how *I* might levitate?"

"Of course not."

"That limits others to observation only without experimental duplication. It puts your levitation on the same plane with stellar evolution, something to theorize about but never experiment with."

"Yet scientists are willing to devote their lives to astrophysics."

"Scientists are people. They can't reach the stars, so they make the best of it. But they can reach you, and to be unable to touch your levitation would be infuriating."

"Jim, they haven't even tried. You talk as though I've been studied. Jim, they won't even consider the problem."

"They don't have to. Your levitation is part of a whole class of phenomena that won't be considered. Telepathy, clairvoyance, prescience and a thousand other extra-natural powers are practically never seriously investigated, even though reported with every appearance of reliability. Rhine's experiments on E.S.P. have annoyed far more scientists than they have intrigued. So you see, they don't have to study you to know they don't want to study you. They know that in advance."

"Is this funny to you, Jim? Scientists refuse to investigate facts; they turn their back on the truth. And you just sit there and grin and make droll statements."

"No, Roger, I know it's serious. And I have no glib explanations for mankind, really. I'm giving you my thoughts. It's what I think. But don't you see? What I'm doing, really, is to try to look at things as they are. It's what you must do. Forget your ideals, your theories, your notions as to what people *ought* to do. Consider what they *are* doing. Once a person is oriented to face facts rather than delusions, problems tend to disappear. At the very least they fall into their true perspective and become soluble."

Roger stirred restlessly. "Psychiatric gobbledygook! It's like putting your fingers on a man's temple and saying, 'Have faith and you will be cured!' If the poor chap isn't cured, it's because he didn't drum up enough faith. The witch doctor can't lose."

"Maybe you're right, but let's see. What *is* your problem?"

"No catechism, please. You know my problem so let's not horse around."

"You levitate. Is that it?"

"Let's say it is. It'll do as a first approximation."

"You're not being serious, Roger, but actually you're probably right. It's only a first approximation. After all, you're tackling that problem. Jane tells me you've been experimenting."

"Experimenting! Ye gods, Jim, I'm not experimenting. I'm drifting. I need high-powered brains and equipment. I need a research team, and I don't have it."

"Then what's your problem? Second approximation."

Roger said, "I see what you mean. My problem is to get a research team. But I've tried! Man, I've tried till I'm tired of trying."

"How have you tried?"

"I've sent out letters. I've asked— Oh, stop it, Jim. I haven't the heart to go through the patient-on-the-couch routine. You know what I've been doing."

"I know that you've said to people, 'I have a problem. Help me.' Have you tried anything else?"

"Look, Jim. I'm dealing with mature scientists."

"I know. So you reason that the straightforward request is sufficient. Again it's theory against fact. I've told you the difficulties involved in your request. When you thumb a ride on a highway, you're making a straightforward request, but most cars pass you by just the same. The point is that the straightforward request has failed. Now what's your problem? Third approximation!"

"To find another approach which won't fail? Is that what you want me to say?"

"It's what you have said, isn't it?"

"So I know it without your telling me."

"Do you? You're ready to quit school, quit your job, quit science. Where's your consistency, Rog? Do you abandon a problem when your first experiment fails? Do you give up when one theory is shown to be inadequate? The same philosophy of experimental science that holds for inanimate objects should hold for people as well."

"All right. What do you suggest I try? Bribery? Threats? Tears?"

James Sarle stood up. "Do you really want a suggestion?"

138

"Go ahead."

"Do as Dr. Morton said. Take a vacation and to hell with levitation. It's a problem for the future. Sleep in bed and float or don't float; what's the difference? Ignore levitation. Laugh at it, or even enjoy it. Do anything but worry about it, because it isn't your problem. That's the whole point. It's not your immediate problem. Spend your time considering how to make scientists study something they don't want to study. That is the immediate problem, and that is exactly what you've spent no thinking time on as yet."

Sarle walked to the hall closet and got his coat. Roger went with him. Minutes passed in silence.

Then Roger said without looking up, "Maybe you're right, Jim."

"Maybe I am. Try it and then tell me. Good-bye, Roger."

Roger Toomey opened his eyes and blinked at the morning brightness of the bedroom. He called out, "Hey, Jane, where are you?"

Jane's voice answered, "In the kitchen. Where do you think?"

"Come in here, will you?"

She came in. "The bacon won't fry itself, you know."

"Listen, did I float last night?"

"I don't know. I slept."

"You're a help." He got out of bed and slipped his feet into his mules. "Still, I don't think I did."

"Do you think you've forgotten how?" There was sudden hope in her voice.

"I haven't forgotten. See!" He slid into the dining room on a cushion of air. "I just have a feeling I haven't floated. I think it's three nights now."

"Well, that's good," said Jane. She was back at the stove. "It's just that a month's rest has done you good. If I had called Jim in the beginning—"

"Oh, please, don't go through that. A month's rest, my eye. It's just that last Sunday I made up my mind what to do. Since then I've relaxed. That's all there is to it."

"What are you going to do?"

139

"Every spring Northwestern Tech gives a series of seminars on physical topics. I'll attend."

"You mean, go way out to Seattle?"

"Of course."

"What will they be discussing?"

"What's the difference? I just want to see Linus Deering."

"But he's the one who called you crazy, isn't he?"

"He did." Roger scooped up a forkful of scrambled eggs. "But he's also the best man of the lot."

He reached for the salt and lifted a few inches out of his chair as he did so. He paid no attention.

He said, "I think maybe I can handle him."

The spring seminars at Northwestern Tech had become a nationally known institution since Linus Deering had joined the faculty. He was the perennial chairman and lent the proceedings their distinctive tone. He introduced the speakers, led the questioning periods, summed up at the close of each morning and afternoon session and was the soul of conviviality at the concluding dinner at the end of the week's work.

All this Roger Toomey knew by report. He could now observe the actual workings of the man. Professor Deering was rather under middle height, was dark of complexion, and had a luxuriant and quite distinctive mop of wavy brown hair. His wide, thin-lipped mouth when not engaged in active conversation looked perpetually on the point of a sly smile. He spoke quickly and fluently, without notes, and seemed always to deliver his comments from a level of superiority that his listeners automatically accepted.

At least so he had been on the first morning of the seminar. It was only during the afternoon session that the listeners began to notice a certain hesitation in his remarks. Even more, there was an uneasiness about him as he sat on the stage during the delivery of the scheduled papers. Occasionally he glanced furtively toward the rear of the auditorium.

Roger Toomey, seated in the very last row, observed all this tensely. His temporary glide toward normality that had begun when he first thought there might be a way out was beginning to recede.

On the Pullman to Seattle, he had not slept. He had had

140

visions of himself lifting upward in time to the wheel-clacking, of moving out quietly past the curtains and into the corridor, of being awakened into endless embarrassment by the hoarse shouting of a porter. So he had fastened the curtains with safety pins and had achieved nothing by that; no feeling of security; no sleep outside a few exhausting snatches.

He had napped in his seat during the day, while the mountains slipped past outside, and arrived in Seattle in the evening with a stiff neck, aching bones and a general sensation of despair.

He had made his decision to attend the seminar far too late to have been able to obtain a room to himself at the Institute's dormitories. Sharing a room was, of course, quite out of the question. He registered at a downtown hotel, locked the door, closed and locked all the windows, shoved his bed hard against the wall and the bureau against the open side of the bed, then slept.

He remembered no dreams, and when he awoke in the morning, he was still lying within the manufactured enclosure. He felt relieved.

When he arrived, in good time, at Physics Hall on the Institute's campus, he found, as he expected, a large room and a small gathering. The seminar sessions were held, traditionally, over the Easter vacation and students were not in attendance. Some fifty physicists sat in the auditorium designed to hold four hundred, clustering on either side of the central aisle up near the podium.

Roger took his seat in the last row, where he would not be seen by casual passersby looking through the high, small windows of the auditorium door, and where the others in the audience would have had to twist through nearly a hundred and eighty degrees to see him.

Except, of course, for the speaker on the platform—and for Professor Deering.

Roger did not hear much of the actual proceedings. He concentrated entirely on waiting for those moments when Deering was alone on the platform; when only Deering could see him.

As Deering grew obviously more disturbed, Roger grew

141

bolder. During the final summing up of the afternoon, he did his best.

Professor Deering stopped altogether in the middle of a poorly constructed and entirely meaningless sentence. His audience, which had been shifting in their seats for some time, stopped also and looked wonderingly at him.

Deering raised his hand and said gaspingly, "You! You there!"

Roger Toomey had been sitting with an air of complete relaxation—in the very center of the aisle. The only chair beneath him was composed of two and a half feet of empty air. His legs were stretched out before him on the armrest of an equally airy chair.

When Deering pointed, Roger slid rapidly sidewise. By the time fifty heads turned, he was sitting quietly in a very prosaic wooden seat.

Roger looked this way and that, then stared at Deering's pointing finger and rose.

"Are you speaking to me, Professor Deering?" he asked, with only the slightest tremble in his voice to indicate the savage battle he was fighting within himself to keep that voice cool and wondering.

"What are you doing?" demanded Deering, his morning's tension exploding.

Some of the audience were standing in order to see better. An unexpected commotion is as dearly loved by a gathering of research physicists as by a crowd at a baseball game.

"I'm not doing anything," said Roger. "I don't understand you."

"Get out! Leave this hall!"

Deering was beside himself with a mixture of emotions, or perhaps he would not have said that. At any rate, Roger sighed and took his opportunity prayerfully.

He said, loudly and distinctly, forcing himself to be heard over the gathering clamor, "I am Professor Roger Toomey of Carson College. I am a member of the American Physical Association. I have applied for permission to attend these sessions, have been accepted, and have paid my registration fee. I am sitting here as is my right and will continue to do so."

Deering could only say blindly, "Get out!"

"I will not," said Roger. He was actually trembling with a synthetic and self-imposed anger. "For what reason must I get out? What have I done?"

Deering put a shaking hand through his hair. He was quite unable to answer.

Roger followed up his advantage. "If you attempt to evict me from these sessions without just cause, I shall certainly sue the Institute."

Deering said hurriedly, "I call the first day's session of the Spring Seminars of Recent Advances in the Physical Sciences to a close. Our next session will be in this hall tomorrow at nine in—"

Roger left as he was speaking and hurried away.

There was a knock at Roger's hotel-room door that night. It startled him, froze him in his chair.

"Who is it?" he cried.

The answering voice was soft and hurried. "May I see you?"

It was Deering's voice. Roger's hotel as well as his room number were, of course, recorded with the seminar secretary. Roger had hoped, but scarcely expected, that the day's events would have so speedy a consequence.

He opened the door, said stiffly, "Good evening, Professor Deering."

Deering stepped in and looked about. He wore a very light topcoat that he made no gesture to remove. He held his hat in his hand and did not offer to put it down.

He said, "Professor Roger Toomey of Carson College. Right?" He said it with a certain emphasis, as though the name had significance.

"Yes. Sit down, Professor."

Deering remained standing. "Now what is it? What are you after?"

"I don't understand."

"I'm sure you do. You aren't arranging this ridiculous foolery for nothing. Are you trying to make me seem foolish, or is it that you expect to hoodwink me into some crooked scheme? I want you to know it won't work. And don't try to

143

use force now. I have friends who know exactly where I am at this moment. I'll advise you to tell the truth and then get out of town."

"Professor Deering! This is my room. If you are here to bully me, I'll ask you to leave. If you don't go, I'll have you put out."

"Do you intend to continue this . . . this persecution?"

"I have not been persecuting you. I don't know you, sir."

"Aren't you the Roger Toomey who wrote me a letter concerning a case of levitation he wanted me to investigate?"

Roger stared at the man. "What letter is this?"

"Do you deny it?"

"Of course I do. What are you talking about? Have you got the letter?"

Professor Deering's lips compressed. "Never mind that. Do you deny you were suspending yourself on wires at this afternoon's sessions?"

"On wires? I don't follow you at all."

"You were levitating!"

"Would you please leave, Professor Deering? I don't think you're well."

The physicist raised his voice. "Do you deny you were levitating?"

"I think you're mad. Do you mean to say I made magicians' arrangements in your auditorium? I was never in it before today and when I arrived, you were already present. Did you find wires or anything of the sort after I left?"

"I don't know how you did it and I don't care. *Do* you deny you were levitating?"

"Why, of course I do."

"I saw you. Why are you lying?"

"You saw me levitate? Professor Deering, will you tell me how that's possible? I suppose your knowledge of gravitational forces is enough to tell you that true levitation is a meaningless concept except in outer space. Are you playing some sort of joke on me?"

"Good heavens," said Deering in a shrill voice, "why won't you tell me the truth?"

"I am. Do you suppose that by stretching out my hand and

144

making a mystic pass . . . so . . . I can go sailing off into air?" And Roger did so, his head brushing the ceiling.

Deering's head jerked upward, "Ah! There . . . there—"

Roger returned to earth, smiling. "You *can't* be serious."

"You did it again. You just did it."

"Did what, sir?"

"You levitated. You just levitated. You can't deny it."

Roger's eyes grew serious. "I think you're sick, sir."

"I know what I saw."

"Perhaps you need a rest. Overwork—"

"It was *not* a hallucination."

"Would you care for a drink?" Roger walked to his suitcase while Deering followed his footsteps with bulging eyes. The toes of his shoes touched air two inches from the ground and went no lower.

Deering sank into the chair Roger had vacated.

"Yes, please," he said weakly.

Roger gave him the whiskey bottle, watched the other drink, then gag a bit. "How do you feel now?"

"Look here," said Deering, "have you discovered a way of neutralizing gravity?"

Roger stared. "Get hold of yourself, Professor. If I had antigravity, I wouldn't use it to play games on you. I'd be in Washington. I'd be a military secret. I'd be—well, I wouldn't be here! Surely all this is obvious to you?"

Deering jumped to his feet. "Do you intend sitting in on the remaining sessions?"

"Of course."

Deering nodded, jerked his hat down upon his head and hurried out.

For the next three days Professor Deering did not preside over the seminar sessions. No reason for his absence was given. Roger Toomey, caught between hope and apprehension, sat in the body of the audience and tried to remain inconspicuous. In this he was not entirely successful. Deering's public attack had made him notorious while his own strong defense had given him a kind of David-versus-Goliath popularity.

Roger returned to his hotel room Thursday night after an unsatisfactory dinner and remained standing in the doorway, one foot over the threshold. Professor Deering was gazing at him from within. And another man, a gray fedora shoved well back on his forehead, was seated on Roger's bed.

It was the stranger who spoke. "Come inside, Toomey."

Roger did so. "What's going on?"

The stranger opened his wallet and presented a cellophane window to Roger. He said, "I'm Cannon of the F.B.I."

Roger said, "You have influence with the government, I take it, Professor Deering."

"A little," said Deering.

Roger said, "Well, am I under arrest? What's my crime?"

"Take it easy," said Cannon. "We've been collecting some data on you, Toomey. Is this your signature?"

He held a letter out far enough for Roger to see but not to snatch. It was the letter Roger had written to Deering, which the latter had sent on to Morton.

"Yes," said Roger.

"How about this one?" The federal agent had a sheaf of letters.

Roger realized that he must have collected every one he had sent out, minus those that had been torn up. "They're all mine," he said wearily.

Deering snorted.

Cannon said, "Professor Deering tells us that you can float."

"Float? What the devil do you mean, float?"

"Float in the air," said Cannon stolidly.

"Do you believe anything as crazy as that?"

"I'm not here to believe or not to believe, Dr. Toomey," said Cannon. "I'm an agent of the government of the United States and I've got an assignment to carry out. I'd cooperate if I were you."

"How can I cooperate in something like this? If I came to you and told you that Professor Deering could float in air, you'd have me flat on a psychiatrist's couch in no time."

Cannon said, "Professor Deering has been examined by a psychiatrist at his own request. However, the government has been in the habit of listening very seriously to Professor Deering for a number of years now. Besides, I might as well tell you that we have independent evidence."

146

"Such as?"

"A group of students at your college have seen you float. Also, a woman who was once secretary to the head of your department. We have statements from all of them."

Roger said, "What kind of statements? Sensible ones that you would be willing to put into the record and show to my congressman?"

Professor Deering interrupted anxiously, "Dr. Toomey, what do you gain by denying the fact that you can levitate? Your own dean admits that you've done something of the sort. He has told me that he will inform you officially that your appointment will be terminated at the end of the academic year. He wouldn't do that for nothing."

"That doesn't matter," said Roger.

"But why won't you admit I saw you levitate?"

"Why should I?"

Cannon said, "I'd like to point out, Dr. Toomey, that if you have any device for counteracting gravity, it would be of great importance to your government."

"Really? I suppose you have investigated my background for possible disloyalty."

"The investigation," said the agent, "is proceeding."

"All right," said Roger, "let's take a hypothetical case. Suppose I admitted I could levitate. Suppose I didn't know how I did it. Suppose I had nothing to give the government but my body and an insoluble problem."

"How can you know it's insoluble?" asked Deering eagerly.

"I once asked you to study such a phenomenon," pointed out Roger mildly. "You refused."

"Forget that. Look," Deering spoke rapidly, urgently, "you don't have a position at the moment. I can offer you one in my department as Associate Professor of Physics. Your teaching duties will be nominal. Full-time research on levitation. What about it?"

"It sounds attractive," said Roger.

"I think it's safe to say that unlimited government funds will be available."

"What do I have to do? Just admit I can levitate?"

"I know you can. I saw you. I want you to do it now for Mr. Cannon."

Roger's legs moved upward and his body stretched out horizontally at the level of Cannon's head. He turned to one side and seemed to rest on his right elbow.

Cannon's hat fell backward onto the bed.

He yelled: "He floats!"

Deering was almost incoherent with excitement. "Do you see it, man?"

"I sure see something."

"Then report it. Put it right down in your report, do you hear me? Make a complete record of it. They won't say there's anything wrong with me. I didn't doubt for a minute that I had seen it."

But he couldn't have been so happy if that were entirely true.

"I don't even know what the climate is like in Seattle," wailed Jane, "and there are a million things I have to do."

"Need any help?" asked Jim Sarle from his comfortable position in the depths of the armchair.

"There's nothing you can do. Oh, dear." And she flew from the room, but unlike her husband, she did so figuratively only.

James Sarle came in.

"Jane, do we have the crates for the books yet?" called Roger. "Hello, Jim. When did you come in? And where's Jane?"

"I came in a minute ago and Jane's in the next room. I had to get past a policeman to get in. Man, they've got you surrounded."

"Um-m-m," said Roger absently. "I told them about you."

"I know you did. I've been sworn to secrecy. I told them it was a matter of professional confidence in any case. Why don't you let the movers do the packing? The government is paying, isn't it?"

"Movers wouldn't do it right," said Jane, suddenly hurrying in again and flouncing down on the sofa. "I'm going to have a cigarette."

"Break down, Roger," said Sarle, "and tell me what happened."

Roger smiled sheepishly. "As you said, Jim, I took my mind off the wrong problem and applied it to the right one. It

148

just seemed to me that I was forever being faced with two alternatives. I was either crooked or crazy. Deering said that flatly in his letter to Morton. The dean assumed I was crooked and Morton suspected that I was crazy.

"But supposing I could show them that I could really levitate. Well, Morton told me what would happen in that case. Either I would be crooked or the *witness* would be insane. Morton said that . . . he said that if he saw me fly, he'd prefer to believe himself insane than accept the evidence. Of course he was only being rhetorical. No man would believe in his own insanity while even the faintest alternative existed. I counted on that.

"So I changed my tactics. I went to Deering's seminar. I didn't *tell* him I could float; I showed him, *and then denied I had done it*. The alternative was clear. I was either lying or he . . . not I, mind you, but *he* . . . was mad. It was obvious that he would sooner believe in levitation than doubt his own sanity, once he was really put to the test. All his actions thereafter—his bullying, his trip to Washington, his offer of a job—were intended only to vindicate his own sanity, not to help me."

Sarle said, "In other words, you had made your levitation his problem and not your own."

Roger said, "Did you have anything like this in mind when we had our talk, Jim?"

Sarle shook his head. "I had vague notions, but a man must solve his own problems if they're to be solved effectively. Do you think they'll work out the principle of levitation now?"

"I don't know, Jim. I still can't communicate the subjective aspects of the phenomenon. But that doesn't matter. We'll be investigating them and that's what counts." He struck his balled right fist into the palm of his left hand. "As far as I'm concerned, the important point is that I made them help me."

"Is it?" asked Sarle softly. "I should say the important point is that you let them make *you* help *them*, which is a different thing altogether."

149

10

Euclid's Fifth

Mathematics has always seemed one step above the sciences. The sciences are, to a large extent, inductive—one observes, and from that one induces general rules. In mathematics one deduces consequences from first principles, a procedure that seems loftier and more certain, somehow.

But what if first principles are wrong? The shock of discovering that is even more shattering than finding out that an observation has been misinterpreted. I'm including two essays here that will serve to demonstrate this.

Some of my articles stir up more reader comment than others, and one of the most effective in this respect was one I once wrote in which I listed those who, in my opinion, were scientists of the first magnitude and concluded by working up a personal list of the ten greatest scientists of all time.

Naturally I received letters arguing for the omission of one or more of my ten best in favor of one or more others, and I still get them, even now, seven and a half years after the article was written.

Usually I reply by explaining that estimates as to the ten greatest scientists (always excepting the case of Isaac Newton, concerning whom there can be no reasonable disagreement) are largely a subjective matter and cannot really be argued out.

Recently I received a letter from a reader who argued that

Archimedes, one of my ten, ought to be replaced by Euclid, who was not one of my ten. I replied in my usual placating manner, but then went on to say that Euclid was "merely a systematizer" while Archimedes had made very important advances in physics and mathematics.

But later my conscience grew active. I still adhered to my own opinion of Archimedes taking pride of place over Euclid, but the phrase "merely a systematizer" bothered me. There is nothing necessarily "mere" about being a systematizer.*

For three centuries before Euclid (who flourished about 300 B.C.) Greek geometers had labored at proving one geometric theorem or another, and a great many had been worked out.

What Euclid did was to make a system out of it all. He began with certain definitions and assumptions and then used them to prove a few theorems. Using those definitions and assumptions plus the few theorems he had already proved, he proved a few additional theorems, and so on, and so on.

He was the first, as far as we know, to build an elaborate mathematical system based on the explicit attitude that it was useless to try to prove *everything*; that it was essential to make a beginning with some things that could not be proved but that could be accepted without proof because they satisfied intuition. Such intuitive assumptions, without proof, are called "axioms."

This was in itself a great intellectual advance, but Euclid did something more. He picked *good* axioms.

To see what this means, consider that you would want your list of axioms to be complete, that is, they should suffice to prove all the theorems that are useful in the particular field of knowledge being studied. On the other hand, they shouldn't be redundant. You don't want to be able to prove all those theorems even after you have omitted one or more of your axioms from the list; or to be able to prove one or more of your axioms by the use of the remaining axioms. Finally, your axioms must be consistent. That is, you do not want to use some axioms to prove that something is so and then use other axioms to prove the same thing to be *not* so.

For two thousand years Euclid's axiomatic system stood the

---

*Sometimes there is. In all my nonfiction writings I am "merely" a systematizer. —Just in case you think I'm *never* modest.

test. No one ever found it necessary to add another axiom, and no one was ever able to eliminate one or to change it substantially—which is a pretty good testimony to Euclid's judgment.

By the end of the nineteenth century, however, when notions of mathematical rigor had hardened, it was realized that there were many tacit assumptions in the Euclidean system; that is, assumptions that Euclid made without specifically saying that he had made them, and that all his readers also made, apparently without specifically saying so to themselves.

For instance, among his early theorems are several that demonstrate two triangles to the congruent (equal in both shape and size) by a course of proof that asks people to imagine that one triangle is moved in space so that it is superimposed on the other. That, however, presupposes that a geometrical figure doesn't change in shape and size when it moves. Of course it doesn't, you say. Well, you assume it doesn't and I assume it doesn't and Euclid assumed it doesn't—but Euclid never said he assumed it.

Again, Euclid assumed that a straight line could extend infinitely in both directions—but never said he was making that assumption.

Furthermore, he never considered that such important basic properties as the *order* of points in a line, and some of his basic definitions were inadequate—

But never mind. In the last century Euclidean geometry has been placed on a basis of the utmost rigor, and while that meant the system of axioms and definitions was altered, Euclid's geometry remained the same. It just meant that Euclid's axioms and definitions, *plus* his unexpressed assumptions, were adequate to the job.

Let's consider Euclid's axioms now. There were ten of them and he divided them into two groups of five. One group of five was called "common notions" because they were common to all sciences:

1) Things which are equal to the same thing are also equal to one another.

2) If equals are added to equals, the sums are equal.

3) If equals are subtracted from equals, the remainders are equal.

4) Things which coincide with one another are equal to one another.

5) The whole is greater than the part.

These "common notions" seem so common, indeed so obvious, so immediately acceptable by intuition, so incapable of contradiction, that they seem to represent absolute truth. They seem something a person could seize upon as soon as he had evolved the light of reason. Without ever sensing the Universe in any way, but living only in the luminous darkness of his own mind, he would see that things equal to the same thing are equal to one another and all the rest.

He might then, using Euclid's axioms, work out all the theorems of geometry and, therefore, the basic properties of the Universe from first principles, without having observed anything.

The Greeks were so fascinated with this notion that all mathematical knowledge comes from within that they lost one important urge that might have led to the development of experimental science. There were experimenters among the Greeks, notably Ctesibius and Hero, but their work was looked upon by the Greek scholars as a kind of artisanship rather than as science.

In one of Plato's dialogues, Socrates asks a slave certain questions about a geometric diagram and has him answer and prove a theorem in doing so. This was Socrates' method of showing that even an utterly uneducated man could draw truth from out of himself. Nevertheless, it took an extremely sophisticated man, Socrates, to ask the questions, and the slave was by no means uneducated, for merely by having been alive and perceptive for years, he had learned to make many assumptions by observation and example, without either himself or (apparently) Socrates being completely aware of it.

Still as late as 1800, influential philosophers such as Immanuel Kant held that Euclid's axioms represented absolute truth.

But do they? Would anyone question the statement that "the whole is greater than the part"? Since 10 can be broken up into $6 + 4$, are we not completely right in assuming that 10 is greater than either 6 or 4? If an astronaut can get into a space capsule, would we not be right in assuming that the volume of the capsule is greater than the volume of the astronaut? How could we doubt the general truth of the axiom?

Well, any list of consecutive numbers can be divided into odd numbers and even numbers, so that we might conclude that in any such list of consecutive numbers, the total of all numbers present must be greater than the total of even numbers. And yet if we consider an *infinite* list of consecutive numbers, it turns out that the total number of all the numbers is equal to the total number of all the even numbers. In what is called "transfinite mathematics" the particular axiom about the whole being greater than the part simply does not apply.

Again, suppose that two automobiles travel between points A and B by identical routes. The two routes coincide. Are they equal? Not necessarily. The first automobile traveled from A to B, while the second traveled from B to A. In other words, two lines might coincide and yet be unequal since the direction of one might be different from the direction of the other.

Is this just fancy talk? Can a line be said to have direction? Yes, indeed. A line with direction is a "vector," and in "vector mathematics" the rules aren't quite the same as in ordinary mathematics and things can coincide without being equal.

In short, then, axioms are *not* examples of absolute truth, and it is very likely that there is no such thing as absolute truth at all. The axioms of Euclid are axioms not because they appear as absolute truth out of some inner enlightenment, but only because they seem to be true in the context of the real world.

And that is why the geometric theorems derived from Euclid's axioms seem to correspond with what we call reality. They *started* with what we call reality.

It is possible to start with any set of axioms, provided they are not self-contradictory, and work up a system of theorems consistent with those axioms and with each other, even though they are *not* consistent with what we think of as the real world. This does not make the "arbitrary mathematics" less "true" than the one starting from Euclid's axioms, only less useful, perhaps. Indeed, an "arbitrary mathematics" may be *more* useful than ordinary "commonsense" mathematics in special regions such as those of transfinites or of vectors.

Even so, we must not confuse "useful" and "true." Even if an axiomatic system is so bizarre as to be useful in no conceivable practical sense, we can nevertheless say nothing about its "truth." If it is self-consistent, that is all we have a right to demand of any system of thought. "Truth" and "reality" are theological words, not scientific ones.

But back to Euclid's axioms. So far I have only listed the five "common notions." There were also five more axioms on the list that were specifically applicable to geometry, and these were later called "postulates." The first of these postulates was:

1) It is possible to draw a straight line from any point to any other point.

This seems eminently acceptable, but are you sure? Can you prove that you can draw a line from the Earth to the Sun? *If* you could somehow stand on the Sun safely and hold the Earth motionless in its orbit, and somehow stretch a string from the Earth to the Sun and pull it absolutely taut, that string would represent a straight line from Earth to Sun. You're sure that this is a reasonable "thought experiment" and I'm sure it is too, but we only *assume* that matters can be so. We can't ever demonstrate them or prove them mathematically.

And, incidentally, what is a straight line? I have just made the assumption that if a string is pulled absolutely taut, it has a shape we would recognize as what we call a straight line. But what is that shape? We simply can't do better than say, "A straight line is something very, very thin and very, very straight," or, to paraphrase Gertrude Stein, "A straight line is a straight line is a straight line—"

Euclid defines a straight line as "a line which lies evenly with the points on itself," but I would hate to have to try to describe what he means by that statement to a student beginning the study of geometry.

Another definition says that: A straight line is the shortest distance between two points.

But if a string is pulled absolutely taut, it cannot go from the point at one end to the point at the other in any shorter distance, so that to say that a straight line is the shortest distance between two points is the same as saying that it has the shape of an absolutely taut string, and we can still say, "And what shape is that?"

In modern geometry, straight lines are not defined at all. What is said, in essence, is this: Let us call something a line which has the following properties in connection with other undefined terms like "point," "plane," "between," "continuous," and so on. Then the properties are listed.

Be that as it may, here are the remaining postulates of Euclid:

2) A finite straight line can be extended continuously in a straight line.

3) A circle can be described with any point as center and any distance as radius.

4) All right angles are equal.

5) If a straight line falling on two straight lines makes the interior angles on the same side less than two right angles, the two straight lines, if produced indefinitely, meet on that side on which are the angles less than the two right angles.

I trust you notice something at once. Of all the ten axioms of Euclid, only one—the fifth postulate—is a long jawbreaker of a sentence, and only one—the fifth postulate—doesn't make instant sense.

Take any intelligent person who has studied arithmetic and who has heard of straight lines and circles, and give him the ten axioms one by one and let him think a moment and he will say, "Of course!" to each of the first nine. Then recite the fifth postulate and he will surely say, "What!"

And it will take a long time before he understands what's going on. In fact, I wouldn't undertake to explain it myself without a diagram like the one on the next page.

Consider two of the solid lines in the diagram: the one that runs from point C to point D through point M (call it line CD after the end points) and the one that runs through points G, L and H (line GH). A third line, which runs through points A, L, M and B (line AB), crosses both GH and CD, making angles with both.

If line CD is supposed to be perfectly horizontal and line AB is supposed to be perfectly vertical, then the four angles made in the crossing of the two lines (angles CMB, BMD, DML and LMC) are right angles and are all equal (by postulate 4). In particular, angles DML and LMC, which I have numbered in the diagram as 3 and 4, are equal, and are both right angles.

(I haven't bothered to define "perfectly horizontal" or "perfectly vertical" or "crosses" or to explain why the crossing of a perfectly horizontal line with a perfectly vertical line produces four right angles, but I am making no pretense of being completely rigorous. This sort of thing *can* be made rigorous but only at the expense of a lot more talk than I am prepared to give.)

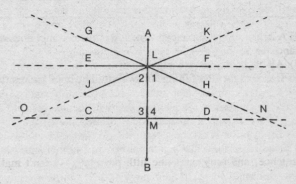

Now consider line GH. It is *not* perfectly horizontal. That means the angles it produces at its intersection (I haven't defined "intersection") with line AB are not right angles and are not all equal. It can be shown that angles ALH and GLB are equal and that angles HLB and GLA are equal but that either of the first pair is not equal to either of the second pair. In particular, angle GLB (labeled 2) is not equal to angle HLB (labeled 1).

Suppose we draw line EF, passing through L, and that line EF is (like line CD) perfectly horizontal. In that case it makes four equal right angles at its intersection with line AB. In particular, angles FLB and ELB are right angles. But angle HLB is contained within angle FLB (what does "is contained within" mean?) with room to spare. Since angle HLB is only part of FLB and the latter is a right angle, then angle HLB (angle 1) is less than a right angle, by the fifth "common notion."

In the same way, by comparing angle ELB, known to be a

157

right angle, with angle GLB (angle 2), we can show that angle 2 is greater than a right angle.

The "interior angles" of the diagram are those on the side of line GH that faces line CD, and those on the side of line CD that faces line GH. In other words, they are angles 1, 2, 3 and 4.

The fifth postulate talks about "the interior angles on the same side," that is, 1 and 4 on one side and 2 and 3 on the other. Since we know that 3 and 4 are right angles, that 1 is less than a right angle, and that 2 is more than a right angle, we can say that the interior angles on one side, 1 and 4, have a sum less than two right angles, while the interior angles on the other have a sum greater than two right angles.

The fifth postulate now states that if the lines GH and CD are extended, they will intersect on the side where the interior angles with a sum less than two right angles are located. And, indeed, if you look at the diagram you will see that if lines GH and CD are extended on both sides (dotted lines), they will intersect at point N on the side of interior angles 1 and 4. On the other side, they just move farther and farther apart and clearly will never intersect.

On the other hand, if you draw line JK through L, you would reverse the situation. Angle 2 would be less than a right angle and angle 1 would be greater than a right angle (where angle 2 is now angle JLB and angle 1 is now angle KLB). In that case interior angles 2 and 3 would have a sum less than two right angles and interior angles 1 and 4 would have a sum greater than two right angles. If lines JK and CD were extended (dotted lines), they would intersect at point O on the side of interior angles 2 and 3. On the other side they would merely diverge farther and farther.

Now that I've explained the fifth postulate at great length (and even then only at the cost of being very unrigorous), you might be willing to say, "Oh yes, of course. Certainly! It's obvious!"

Maybe, but if something is obvious, it shouldn't require hundreds of words of explanation. I didn't have to belabor any of the other nine axioms, did I?

Then again, having *explained* the fifth postulate, have I *proved* it? No, I have only interpreted the meaning of the words and then pointed to the diagram and said, "And indeed, if you look at the diagram, you will see—"

But that's only one diagram. And it deals with a perfectly vertical line crossing two lines of which one is perfectly horizontal. And what if none of the lines are either vertical or horizontal and none of the interior angles are right angles? The fifth postulate applies to *any* line crossing any two lines and I certainly haven't proved that.

I can draw a million diagrams of different types and show that in each specific case the postulate holds, but that is not enough. I must show that it holds in every conceivable case, and this can't be done by diagrams. A diagram can only make the proof clear; the proof itself must be derived by permissible logic from more basic premises already proved, or assumed. This I have not done.

Now let's consider the fifth postulate from the standpoint of moving lines. Suppose line GH is swiveled about L as a pivot in such a way that it comes closer and closer to coinciding with line EF. (Does a straight line remain a straight line while it swivels in this fashion? We can only *assume* it does.) As line GH swivels toward line EF, the point of intersection with line CD (point N) moves farther and farther to the right.

If you started with line JK and swiveled it so that it would eventually coincide with line EF, the intersection point O would move off farther and farther to the left. If you consider the diagram and make a few markings on it (if you have to), you will see this for yourself.

But consider line EF itself. When GH has finally swiveled so as to coincide with line EF, we might say that intersection point N has moved off an infinite distance to the right (whatever we mean by "infinite distance") and when line JK coincides with line EF, the intersection point O has moved off an infinite distance to the left. Therefore we can say that line EF and line CD intersect at *two* points, one an infinite distance to the right and one an infinite distance to the left.

Or let us look at it another way. Line EF, being perfectly horizontal, intersects line AB to make four equal right angles. In that case, angles 1, 2, 3 and 4 are *all* right angles and *all*

159

equal. Angles 1 and 4 have a sum equal to two right angles, and so do angles 2 and 3.

But the fifth postulate says the intersection comes on the side where the two interior angles have a sum *less* than two right angles. In the case of lines EF and CD crossed by line AB, neither set of interior angles has a sum less than two right angles and there can be an intersection on neither side.

We have now, by two sets of arguments, demonstrated first that lines EF and CD intersect at two points, each located an infinite distance away, and, second, that lines EF and CD do not intersect at all. Have we found a contradiction and thus shown that there is something wrong with Euclid's set of axioms?

To avoid a contradiction, we can say that having an intersection at an infinite distance is equivalent to saying there is no intersection. They are different ways of saying the same thing. To agree that "saying a" is equal to "saying b" in this case is consistent with all the rest of geometry, so we can get away with it.

Let us now say that two lines, such as EF and CD, which do not intersect with each other when extended any *finite* distance, however great, are "parallel."

Clearly there is only one line passing through L that can be parallel to line CD, and that is line EF. Any line through L that does not coincide with line EF is (however slightly) either of the type of line GH or of line JK, with an interior angle on one side or the other that is less than a right angle. This argument is sleight of hand, and not rigorous, but it allows us to see the point and say: Given a straight line and a point outside that line, it is possible to draw one and only one straight line through that point parallel to the given line.

This statement is entirely equivalent to Euclid's fifth postulate. If Euclid's fifth postulate is removed and this statement put in its place, the entire structure of Euclidean geometry remains standing without as much as a quiver.

The version of the postulate that refers to parallel lines *sounds* clearer and easier to understand than the way Euclid puts it because even the beginning student has some notion of what parallel lines look like, whereas he may not have the foggiest idea of what interior angles are. That is why it is in this "parallel" form that you usually see the postulate in elementary geometry books.

Actually, though, it isn't really simpler and clearer in this form, for as soon as you try to explain what you mean by "parallel," you're going to run into the matter of interior angles. Or, if you try to avoid that, you'll run into the problem of talking about lines of infinite length, of intersections at an infinite distance being equivalent to no intersection, and that's even worse.

But look, just because I didn't prove the fifth postulate doesn't mean it can't be proven. Perhaps by some line of argument, exceedingly lengthy, subtle and ingenious, it is possible to prove the fifth postulate by use of the other four postulates and the five common notions (or by use of some additional axiom not included in the list which, however, is much simpler and more "obvious" than the fifth postulate is).

Alas, no. For two thousand years mathematicians have now and then tried to prove the fifth postulate from the other axioms simply because that cursed fifth postulate was so long and so unobvious that it didn't seem possible that it could be an axiom. Well, they always failed and it seems certain they *must* fail. The fifth postulate is just not contained in the other axioms or in any list of axioms useful in geometry and simpler than itself.

It can be argued, in fact, that the fifth postulate is Euclid's greatest achievement. By some remarkable leap of insight, he realized that, given the nine brief and clearly "obvious" axioms, he could not prove the fifth postulate and he could not do without it either, and that, therefore, long and complicated though the fifth postulate was, *he had to include it among his assumptions*.

So for two thousand years the fifth postulate stood there: long, ungainly, puzzling. It was like a flaw in perfection, a standing reproach to a line of argument otherwise infinitely stately. It bothered the very devil out of mathematicians.

And then, in 1733, an Italian priest, Girolamo Saccheri, got the most brilliant notion concerning the fifth postulate that anyone had had since the time of Euclid, but wasn't brilliant enough himself to handle it—

Let's go into that in the following essay.

11

The Plane Truth

There are occasionally problems in immersing myself in these science essays I write. For instance, I watched a luncheon companion sprinkle salt on his dish after an unsatisfactory forkful, try another bite and say with satisfaction, "That's much better."

I stirred uneasily and said, "Actually, what you mean is, 'I like that much better.' In saying merely, 'That's much better,' you are making the unwarranted assumption that food can be objectively better or worse in taste and the further assumption that your own subjective sensation of taste is a sure guide to the objective situation."

I think I came within a quarter of an inch of getting that dish, salted to perfection as it was, right in the face; and would have well deserved it, too. The trouble, you see, was that I had just written the previous essay and was brimful on the subject of assumptions.

So let's get back to that. The subject under consideration is Euclid's "fifth postulate," which I will repeat here so you won't have to refer back to it:

If a straight line falling on two straight lines makes the interior angles on the same side less than two right angles, the two straight lines, if produced indefinitely, meet on that side on which are the angles less than the two right angles.

All Euclid's other axioms are extremely simple, but he apparently realized that this fifth postulate, complicated as it seemed, could not be proved from the other axioms, and must therefore be included as an axiom itself.

For two thousand years after Euclid other geometers kept trying to prove Euclid too hasty in having given up, and strove to find some ingenious method of proving the fifth postulate from the other axioms, so that it might therefore be removed from the list—if only because it was too long, too complicated, and too not immediately obvious to seem a good axiom.

One system of approaching the problem was to consider the following quadrilateral:

Two of the angles, DAB and ABC, are given as right angles in this quadrilateral, and side AD is equal in length to side BC. Given these facts, it is possible to prove that side DC is equal to side AB and that angles ADC and DCB are also right angles (so that the quadrilateral is actually a rectangle) *if* Euclid's fifth postulate is used.

If Euclid's fifth postulate is *not* used, then by using only the other axioms, all one can do is to prove that angles ADC and DCB are equal, but not that they are actually right angles.

The problem then arises as to whether it is possible to show that from the fact that angles ADC and DCB are equal, it is possible to show that they are also right angles. If one could do that, it would then follow from that fact that quadrilateral ABCD is a rectangle and that the fifth postulate is true. This would have been proven from the other axioms only and it would no longer be necessary to include Euclid's fifth among them.

Such an attempt was first made by the medieval Arabs, who carried on the traditions of Greek geometry while Western

Europe was sunk in darkness. The first to draw this quadrilateral and labor over its right angles was none other than Omar Khayyam (1050-1123).*

Omar pointed out that if angles ADC and DCB were equal, then there were three possibilities: 1) they were each a right angle, 2) they were each less than a right angle, that is "acute," or 3) they were each more than a right angle, or "obtuse."

He then went through a line of argument to show that the acute and obtuse cases were absurd, based on the assumption that two converging lines must intersect.

To be sure, it is perfectly commonsensical to suppose that two converging lines must intersect, but, unfortunately, common sense or not, that assumption is mathematically equivalent to Euclid's fifth postulate. Omar Khayyam ended, therefore, by "proving" the fifth postulate by assuming it to be true as one of the conditions of the proof. This is called either "arguing in a circle" or "begging the question," but whatever it is called, it is not allowed in mathematics.

Another Arabian mathematician, Nasir Eddin al-Tus (1201-74), made a similar attempt on the quadrilateral, using a different and more complicated assumption to outlaw the acute and obtuse cases. Alas, his assumption was also mathematically equivalent to Euclid's fifth.

Which brings us down to the Italian, Girolamo Saccheri (1667-1733), whom I referred to at the end of the previous essay and who was both a professor of mathematics at the University of Pisa and a Jesuit priest.

He knew of Nasir Eddin's work and he too tackled the quadrilateral. Saccheri, however, introduced something altogether new, something that in two thousand years no one had thought of doing in connection with Euclid's fifth.

Until then, people had omitted Euclid's fifth to see what would happen, or else had made assumptions that turned out to be equivalent to Euclid's fifth. What Saccheri did was to begin by assuming Euclid's fifth to be *false* and to substitute for it

---

*He wrote clever quatrains which Edward FitzGerald even more cleverly translated into English in 1859, making Omar forever famous as a hedonistic and agnostic poet, but the fact is that he ought to be remembered as a great mathematician and astronomer.

some other postulate that was contradictory to it. He planned then to try to build up a geometry based on Euclid's other axioms plus the "alternate fifth" until he came to a contradiction (proving that a particular theorem was both true *and* false, for instance).

When the contradiction was reached, the "alternate fifth" would have to be thrown out. If every possible "alternate fifth" is eliminated in this fashion, then Euclid's fifth must be true. This method of proving a theorem by showing all other possibilities to be absurd is a perfectly acceptable mathematical technique* and Saccheri was on the right road.

Working on this system, Saccheri therefore started by assuming that the angles ADC and DCB were both greater than a right angle. With this assumption, plus all the axioms of Euclid *other* than the fifth, he began working his way through what we might call "obtuse geometry." Quickly, he came across a contradiction. This meant that obtuse geometry could not be true and that angles ADC and DCB could not each be greater than a right angle.

This accomplishment was so important that the quadrilateral which Omar Khayyam had first used in connection with Euclid's fifth is now called the "Saccheri quadrilateral."

Greatly cheered by this, Saccheri then tackled "acute geometry," beginning with the assumption that angles ADC and DCB were each smaller than a right angle. He must have begun the task lightheartedly, sure that, as in the case of obtuse geometry, he would quickly find a contradiction in acute geometry. If that were so, Euclid's fifth would stand proven and his "right-angle geometry" would no longer require that uncomfortably long statement as an axiom.

As Saccheri went on from proposition to proposition in his acute geometry, his feeling of pleasure gave way to increasing anxiety, for he did not come across any contradiction. More and more he found himself faced with the possibility that one could build up a thoroughly self-consistent geometry based on at least one axiom that directly contradicted a Euclidean

---

*This is equivalent to Sherlock Holmes' famous dictum that when the impossible has been eliminated, whatever remains, however improbable, must be true.

axiom. The result would be a "non-Euclidean" geometry which might seem against common sense but which would be internally self-consistent and therefore mathematically valid.

For a moment Saccheri hovered on the very brink of mathematical immortality and—backed away.

He couldn't! To accept the notion of a non-Euclidean geometry took too much courage. So mistakenly had scholars come to confuse Euclidean geometry with absolute truth that any refutation of Euclid would have roused the deepest stirrings of anxiety in the hearts and minds of Europe's intellectuals. To doubt Euclid was to doubt absolute truth, and if there was no absolute truth in Euclid, might it not be quickly deduced that there was no absolute truth anywhere? And since the firmest claim to absolute truth came from religion, might not an attack on Euclid be interpreted as an attack on God?

Saccheri was clearly a mathematician of great potential, but he was also a Jesuit priest and a human being, so his courage failed him and he made the great denial.* When his gradual development of acute geometry went on to the point where he could take it no longer, he argued himself into imagining he had found an inconsistency where, in fact, he hadn't, and with great relief, he concluded that he had proved Euclid's fifth. In 1733 he published a book on his findings entitled (in English) *Euclid Cleared of Every Flaw* and, in that same year, died.

By his denial Saccheri had lost immortality and chosen oblivion. His book went virtually unnoticed until attention was called to it by a later Italian mathematician, Eugenio Beltrami (1835-1900), *after* Saccheri's failure had been made good by others. Now what we know of Saccheri is just this: that he had his finger on a major mathematical discovery a century before anybody else and had lacked the guts to keep his finger firmly on it.

Let us next move forward nearly a century to the German mathematician Karl F. Gauss (1777-1855). It can easily be argued that Gauss was the greatest mathematician who ever lived. Even as a young man he astonished Europe and the scientific world with his brilliance.

---

*I am not blaming him. Placed in his position, I would undoubtedly have done the same. It's just too bad, that's all.

He considered Euclid's fifth about 1815 and came to the same conclusion to which Euclid had come—that the fifth *had* to be made an axiom because it *couldn't* be proved from the other axioms. Gauss further came to the conclusion from which Saccheri had shrunk away—that there were other self-consistent geometries which were non-Euclidean, in that an alternate axiom replaced the fifth.

And then *he* lacked the guts to publish, too, and here I disclaim sympathy. The situation was different. Gauss had infinitely more reputation than Saccheri; Gauss was not a priest; Gauss lived in a land where, and at a time when, the hold of the Church was less to be feared. Gauss, genius or not, was just a coward.

Which brings us to the Russian mathematician Nikolai Ivanovich Lobachevski (1793-1856).* In 1826, Lobachevski also began to wonder if a geometry might not be non-Euclidean and yet consistent. With that in mind, he worked out the theorems of "acute geometry" as Saccheri had done a century earlier, but in 1829, Lobachevski did what neither Saccheri nor Gauss had done. He did *not* back away and he *did* publish. Unfortunately, what he published was an article in Russian called "On the Principles of Geometry" in a local periodical (he worked at the University of Kazan, deep in provincial Russia).

Who reads Russian? Lobachevski remained largely unknown. It wasn't until 1840 that he published his work in German and brought himself to the attention of the world of mathematics generally.

Meanwhile, though, a Hungarian mathematician, János Bolyai (1802-60), was doing much the same thing. Bolyai is one of the most romantic figures in the history of mathematics since he also specialized in such things as the violin and the dueling sword—in the true tradition of the Hungarian aristocrat. There is a story that he once fenced with thirteen swordsmen one after the other, vanquishing them all—and playing the violin between bouts.

---

*Nikolai Ivanovich Lobachevski is mentioned in one of Tom Lehrer's satiric songs, and to any Tom Lehrer fan (like myself), it seems strange to see the name mentioned in a serious connection, but Lehrer is a mathematician by trade and he made use of a real name.

In 1831, Bolyai's father published a book on mathematics. Young Bolyai had been pondering over Euclid's fifth for a number of years and now he persuaded his father to include a twenty-six-page appendix in which the principles of acute geometry were described. It was two years after Lobachevski had published but as yet no one had heard of the Russian, and nowadays, Lobachevski and Bolyai generally share the credit for having discovered non-Euclidean geometry.

Since the Bolyais published in German, Gauss was at once aware of the material. His commendation would have meant a great deal to the young Bolyai. Gauss still lacked the courage to put his approval into print, but he did praise Bolyai's work verbally. And then he couldn't resist—he told Bolyai he had had the same ideas years before but hadn't published, and showed him the work.

Gauss didn't have to do that. His reputation was unshakable; even without non-Euclidean geometry, he had done enough for a dozen mathematicians. Since he had lacked the courage to publish, he might have had the decency to let Bolyai take the credit. But he didn't. Genius or not, Gauss was a mean man in some ways.

Poor Bolyai was so embarrassed and humiliated by Gauss's disclosure that he never did any further work in mathematics.

And what about obtuse geometry? Saccheri had investigated that and found himself enmeshed in contradiction, so that it had been thrown out. Still, once the validity of non-Euclidean geometry had been established, was there no way of rehabilitating obtuse geometry too?

Yes, there was—but only at the cost of making a still more radical break with Euclid. Saccheri, in investigating obtuse geometry, had made use of an unspoken assumption that Euclid himself had also used—that a line could be infinite in length. This assumption introduced no contradiction in acute geometry or in right-angle geometry (Euclid's), but it did create trouble in obtuse geometry.

But then, drop that too. Suppose that, regardless of "common sense," you were to make the assumption that any line had to have some maximum finite length. In that case all the contradiction in obtuse geometry disappeared and there was a second valid variety of non-Euclidean geometry. This was first shown in 1854 by the German mathematician Georg F. Riemann (1826–66).

So now we have three kinds of geometry, which we can distinguish by using statements that are equivalent to the variety of fifth postulate used in each case:

A) Acute geometry (non-Euclidean): Through a point not on a given line, an infinite number of lines parallel to the given line may be drawn.

B) Right-angle geometry (Euclidean): Through a point not on a given line, one and only one line parallel to the given line may be drawn.

C) Obtuse geometry (non-Euclidean): Through a point not on a given line, no lines parallel to the given line may be drawn.

You can make the distinction in another and equivalent way:

A) Acute geometry (non-Euclidean): The angles of a triangle have a sum less than 180°.

B) Right-angle geometry (Euclidean): The angles of a triangle have a sum exactly equal to 180°.

C) Obtuse geometry (non-Euclidean): The angles of a triangle have a sum greater than 180°.

You may now ask: But which geometry is *true?*

If we define "true" as internally self-consistent, then all three geometries are equally true.

Of course they are inconsistent with each other, and perhaps only one corresponds with reality. We might therefore ask: Which geometry corresponds to the properties of the real Universe?

The answer is, again, that all do.

Let us, for instance, consider the problem of traveling from point A on Earth's surface to point B on Earth's surface, and suppose we want to go from A to B in such a way as to traverse the least distance.

In order to simplify the results, let us make two assumptions. First, let us assume that the Earth is a perfectly smooth sphere. This is almost true, as a matter of fact, and we can eliminate mountains and valleys, and even the equatorial bulge, without too much distortion.

Second, let us assume that we are confined in our travels to the surface of the sphere and cannot, for instance, burrow into its depth.

In order to determine the shortest distance from A to B on the surface of the Earth, we might stretch a thread from one point to the other and pull it taut. If we were to do this between two points on a plane, that is, on a surface like that of a flat blackboard extended infinitely in all directions, the result would be what we ordinarily call a "straight line."

On the surface of the sphere, the result, however, is a curve, and yet that curve is the analogue of a straight line, since that curve is the shortest distance between two points on the surface of a sphere. There is difficulty in forcing ourselves to accept a curve as analogous to a straight line because we've been thinking "straight" all our lives. Let us use a different word, then. Let us call the shortest distance between two points on any given surface a "geodesic."*

On a plane, a geodesic is a straight line; on a sphere, a geodesic is a curve, and, specifically, the arc of a "great circle." Such a great circle has a length equal to the circumference of the sphere and lies in a plane that passes through the center of the sphere. On the Earth, the equator is an example of a great circle and so are all the meridians. There are an infinite number of great circles that can be drawn on the surface of any sphere. If you choose any pair of points on a sphere and connect each pair by a thread which is pulled taut, you have in each case the arc of a different great circle.

You can see that on the surface of a sphere there is no such thing as a geodesic of infinite length. If it is extended, it simply meets itself as it goes around the sphere and becomes a closed curve. On the surface of the Earth, a geodesic can be no longer than 25,000 miles.

Furthermore, any two geodesics drawn on a sphere intersect if produced indefinitely, and do so at two points. On the surface of the Earth, for instance, any two meridians meet at the north pole and the south pole. This means that, on the surface of a sphere, through any point not on a given geodesic, no geodesic can be drawn parallel to the given geodesic. No

---

*"Geodesic" is from Greek words meaning "to divide the Earth," because any geodesic on the face of the Earth, if extended as far as possible, divides the surface of the Earth into two equal parts.

geodesic can be drawn through the point that won't sooner or later intersect the given geodesic.

Then, too, if you draw a triangle on the surface of a sphere, with each side the arc of a great circle, the angles will have a sum greater than 180°. If you own a globe, imagine a triangle with one of its vertices at the north pole, with a second at the equator and 10° west longitude, and the third at the equator and 100° west longitude. You will find that you will have an equilateral triangle with each one of its angles equal to 90°. The sum of the three angles is 270°.

This is precisely the geometry that Riemann worked out, if the geodesics are considered the analogues of straight lines. It is a geometry of finite lines, no parallels, and triangular angle-sums greater than 180°. What we have been calling "obtuse geometry" then might also be called "sphere geometry." And what we have been calling "right-angle geometry," or "Euclidean geometry," might also be called "plane geometry."

In 1865, Eugenio Beltrami drew attention to a shape called a "pseudosphere," which looks like two cornets joined wide mouth to wide mouth, and with each cornet extending infinitely out in either direction, ever narrowing but never quite closing. The geodesics drawn on the surface of a pseudosphere fulfill the requirements of acute geometry.

Geodesics on a pseudosphere are infinitely long, and it is possible for two particular geodesics to be extended indefinitely without intersecting and therefore to be parallel. In fact, it is possible to draw two geodesics on the surface of a pseudosphere that *do* intersect and yet have neither one intersecting a third geodesic lying outside the two.* In fact, since an infinite number of geodesics can be drawn in between the two intersecting geodesics, all intersecting in the same point, there are an infinite number of possible geodesics through a point, all of which are parallel to another geodesic not passing through the point.

*This sounds nonsensical because we are used to thinking in terms of planes, where the geodesics are straight lines and where two intersecting lines cannot possibly be both parallel to a third line. On a pseudosphere the geodesics curve, and curve in such a way as to make the two parallels possible.

In other words, "acute geometry" can be looked at as "pseudosphere geometry."

But now—granted that all three geometries are equally valid under circumstances suiting each—which is the best description of the universe as a whole?

This is not always easy to tell. If you draw a triangle with geodesics of a given length on a small sphere and then again on a large sphere, the sum of the angles of the triangle will be greater than 180° in either case, but the amount by which it is greater will be greater in the case of the small sphere.

If you imagine a sphere growing larger and larger, a triangle of a given size on its surface will have an angle-sum closer and closer to 180°, and eventually even the most refined possible measurement won't detect the difference. In short, a small section of a very large sphere is almost as flat as a plane and it becomes impossible to tell the difference.

This is true of the Earth, for instance. It is because the Earth is so large a sphere that small parts of it look flat that it took so long for mankind to satisfy himself that it was spherical.

Well, there is a similar problem in connection with the Universe generally.

Light travels from point to point in space: from the Sun to the Earth, or from one distant galaxy to another, over distances many times those possible on Earth's surface.

We assume that light in traveling across the parsecs travels in a straight line, but of course it really travels in a geodesic, which may or may not be a straight line. If the Universe obeys Euclidean geometry, the geodesic is a straight line. If the Universe obeys some non-Euclidean geometry, then the geodesics are curves of one sort or another.

It occurred to Gauss to form triangles with beams of light traveling through space from one mountaintop to another and measure the sum of the angles so obtained. To be sure, the sums turned out to be just about 180°, but were they *exactly* 180°? That was impossible to tell. If the Universe were a sphere millions of light-years in diameter and if the light beams followed the curvings of such a sphere, no conceivable direct measurement possible today could detect the tiny amount by which the angle sum exceeded 180°.

In 1916, however, Einstein worked out the General Theory

of Relativity and found that in order to explain the workings of gravitation, he had to assume a universe in which light (and everything else) traveled in non-Euclidean geodesics.

By Einstein's theory, the universe is non-Euclidean and is, in fact, an example of "obtuse geometry."

To put it briefly then, Euclidean geometry, far from being the absolute and eternal verity it was assumed to be for two thousand years, is only the highly restricted and abstract geometry of the plane, and one that is merely an approximation of the geometry of such important things as the universe and the Earth's surface.

It is not the plain truth so many have taken for granted it was—but only the plane truth.*

*Well, *I* think it's clever.

173

12

The Billiard Ball

Scientists (and even mathematicians) don't always get along like brethren. They are human beings and there is competitive envy, even hatred, between them on occasion. I don't know of any cases where this has gone to extremes greater than polemical denunciation in learned papers or attempts to steal credit, but one is free to imagine worse in one's fiction.

There follow two stories in which I manage to exacerbate scientific competition to the point of murder—and more.

James Priss—I suppose I ought to say Professor James Priss, though everyone is sure to know whom I mean even without the title—always spoke slowly.

I know. I interviewed him often enough. He had the greatest mind since Einstein, but it didn't work quickly. He admitted his slowness often. Maybe it was *because* he had so great a mind that it didn't work quickly.

He would say something in slow abstraction, then he would think, and then he would say something more. Even over trivial matters his giant mind would hover uncertainly, adding a touch here and then another there.

Would the Sun rise tomorrow, I can imagine him wondering. What do we mean by "rise"? Can we be certain that tomorrow will come? Is the term "Sun" completely unambiguous in this connection?

Add to this habit of speech a bland countenance, rather pale, with no expression except for a general look of uncertainty; gray hair, rather thin, neatly combed; business suits of an invariably conservative cut; and you have what Professor James Priss was—a retiring person, completely lacking in magnetism.

That's why nobody in the world, except myself, could possibly suspect him of being a murderer. And even I am not sure. After all, he *was* slow-thinking; he was *always* slow-thinking. Is it conceivable that at one crucial moment he managed to think quickly and act at once?

It doesn't matter. Even if he murdered, he got away with it. It is far too late now to try to reverse matters, and I wouldn't succeed in doing so even if I decided to let this be published.

Edward Bloom was Priss's classmate in college, and an associate, through circumstance, for a generation afterward. They were equal in age and in their propensity for the bachelor life, but opposites in everything else that mattered.

Bloom was a living flash of light; colorful, tall, broad, loud, brash and self-confident. He had a mind that resembled a meteor strike in the sudden and unexpected way it could seize the essential. He was no theoretician, as Priss was; Bloom had neither the patience for it nor the capacity to concentrate intense thought upon a single abstract point. He admitted that; he boasted of it.

What he did have was an uncanny way of seeing the application of a theory, of seeing the manner in which it could be put to use. In the cold marble block of abstract structure, he could see, without apparent difficulty, the intricate design of a marvelous device. The block would fall apart at his touch and leave the device.

It is a well-known story, and not too badly exaggerated, that nothing Bloom ever built had failed to work, or to be patentable, or to be profitable. By the time he was forty-five, he was one of the richest men on Earth.

And if Bloom the Technician was adapted to one particular matter more than anything else, it was to the way of thought of Priss the Theoretician. Bloom's greatest gadgets were built upon Priss's greatest thoughts, and as Bloom grew wealthy and famous, Priss gained phenomenal respect among his colleagues.

Naturally it was to be expected that when Priss advanced his Two-Field Theory, Bloom would set about at once to build the first practical antigravity device.

My job was to find human interest in the Two-Field Theory for the subscribers to *Tele-News Press*, and you get that by trying to deal with human beings and not with abstract ideas. Since my interviewee was Professor Priss, that wasn't easy.

Naturally I was going to ask about the possibilities of antigravity, which interested everyone, and not about the Two-Field Theory, which no one could understand.

"Antigravity?" Priss compressed his pale lips and considered. "I'm not entirely sure that it is possible, or ever will be. I haven't—uh—worked the matter out to my satisfaction. I don't entirely see whether the Two-Field equations would have a finite solution, which they would have to have, of course; if—" And then he went off into a brown study.

I prodded him. "Bloom says he thinks such a device can be built."

Priss nodded. "Well, yes, but I wonder. Ed Bloom has had an amazing knack at seeing the unobvious in the past. He has an unusual mind. It's certainly made him rich enough."

We were sitting in Priss's apartment. Ordinary middle-class. I couldn't help a quick glance this way and that. Priss was not wealthy.

I don't think he read my mind. He saw me look. And I think it was on *his* mind. He said, "Wealth isn't the usual reward for the pure scientist. Or even a particularly desirable one."

Maybe so at that, I thought. Priss certainly had his own kind of reward. He was the third person in history to win two Nobel prizes and the first to have both of them in the sciences and both of them unshared. You can't complain about that. And if he wasn't rich, neither was he poor.

But he didn't sound like a contented man. Maybe it wasn't Bloom's wealth alone that irked Priss; maybe it was Bloom's fame among the people of Earth generally; maybe it was the fact that Bloom was a celebrity wherever he went, whereas

176

Priss, outside scientific conventions and faculty clubs, was largely anonymous.

I can't say how much of all this was in my eyes or in the way I wrinkled the creases in my forehead, but Priss went on to say, "But we're friends, you know. We play billiards once or twice a week. I beat him regularly."

(I never published that statement. I checked it with Bloom, who made a long counterstatement that began: "He beats *me* at billiards. That jackass—" and grew increasingly personal thereafter. As a matter of fact, neither one was a novice at billiards. I watched them play once for a short while, after the statement and counterstatement, and both handled the cue with professional aplomb. What's more, both played for blood, and there was no friendship in the game that I could see.)

I said, "Would you care to predict whether Bloom will manage to build an antigravity device?"

"You mean would I commit myself to anything? Hmm. Well, let's consider, young man. Just what do we mean by antigravity? Our conception of gravity is built around Einstein's General Theory of Relativity, which is now a century and a half old but which, within its limits, remains firm. We can picture it—"

I listened politely. I'd heard Priss on the subject before, but if I was to get anything out of him—which wasn't certain—I'd have to let him work his way through in his own way.

"We can picture it," he said, "by imagining the Universe to be a flat, thin, superflexible sheet of untearable rubber. If we picture mass as being associated with weight, as it is on the surface of the Earth, then we would expect a mass, resting upon the rubber sheet, to make an indentation. The greater the mass, the deeper the indentation.

"In the actual Universe," he went on, "all sorts of masses exist, and so our rubber sheet must be pictured as riddled with indentations. Any object rolling along the sheet would dip into and out of the indentations it passed, veering and changing direction as it did so. It is this veer and change of direction that we interpret as demonstrating the existence of a force of gravity. If the moving object comes close enough to the center of the indentation and is moving slowly enough, it gets trapped and whirls round and round that indentation. In the absence of friction, it keeps up that whirl forever. In other words, what Isaac Newton interpreted as a force, Albert Einstein interpreted as geometrical distortion."

He paused at this point. He had been speaking fairly fluently—for him—since he was saying something he had said often before. But now he began to pick his way.

He said, "So in trying to produce antigravity, we are trying to alter the geometry of the Universe. If we carry on our metaphor, we are trying to straighten out the indented rubber sheet. We could imagine ourselves getting under the indenting mass and lifting it upward, supporting it so as to prevent it from making an indentation. If we make the rubber sheet flat in that way, then we create a Universe—or at least a portion of the Universe—in which gravity doesn't exist. A rolling body would pass the non-indenting mass without altering its direction of travel a bit, and we could interpret this as meaning that the mass was exerting no gravitational force. In order to accomplish this feat, however, we need a mass equivalent to the indenting mass. To produce antigravity on Earth in this way, we would have to make use of a mass equal to that of Earth and poise it above our heads, so to speak."

I interrupted him. "But your Two-Field Theory—"

"Exactly. General Relativity does not explain both the gravitational field and the electromagnetic fields in a single set of equations. Einstein spent half his life searching for that single set—for a Unified Field Theory—and failed. All who followed Einstein also failed. I, however, began with the assumption that there were two fields that could not be unified and followed the consequences, which I can explain, in part, in terms of the 'rubber sheet' metaphor."

Now we came to something I wasn't sure I had ever heard before. "How does that go?" I asked.

"Suppose that, instead of trying to lift the indenting mass, we try to stiffen the sheet itself, make it less indentable. It would contract, at least over a small area, and become flatter. Gravity would weaken and so would mass, for the two are essentially the same phenomenon in terms of the indented Universe. If we could make the rubber sheet completely flat, both gravity and mass would disappear altogether.

"Under the proper conditions, the electromagnetic field

could be made to counter the gravitational field and serve to stiffen the indented fabric of the Universe. The electromagnetic field is tremendously stronger than the gravitational field, so the former could be made to overcome the latter."

I said uncertainly, "But you say 'under the proper conditions.' Can those proper conditions you speak of be achieved, Professor?"

"That is what I don't know," said Priss thoughtfully and slowly. "If the Universe were really a rubber sheet, its stiffness would have to reach an infinite value before it could be expected to remain completely flat under an indenting mass. If that is also so in the real Universe, then an infinitely intense electromagnetic field would be required, and that would mean antigravity would be impossible."

"But Bloom says—"

"Yes, I imagine Bloom thinks a finite field will do, if it can be properly applied. Still, however ingenious he is," and Priss smiled narrowly, "we needn't take him to be infallible. His grasp on theory is quite faulty. He—he never earned his college degree, did you know that?"

I was about to say that I knew that. After all, everyone did. But there was a touch of eagerness in Priss's voice as he said it and I looked up in time to catch animation in his eye, as though he were delighted to spread that piece of news. So I nodded my head as if I were filing it for future reference.

"Then you would say, Professor Priss," I prodded again, "that Bloom is probably wrong and that antigravity is impossible?"

And finally Priss nodded and said, "The gravitational field can be weakened, of course, but if by antigravity we mean a true zero-gravity field—no gravity at all over a significant volume of space—then I suspect antigravity may turn out to be impossible, despite Bloom."

And I had, after a fashion, what I wanted.

I wasn't able to see Bloom for nearly three months after that, and when I did see him, he was in an angry mood.

He had grown angry at once, of course, when the news first broke concerning Priss's statement. He let it be known that Priss would be invited to the eventual display of the antigravity

179

device as soon as it was constructed, and would even be asked to participate in the demonstration. Some reporter—not I, unfortunately—caught him between appointments and asked him to elaborate on that and he said:

"I'll have the device eventually; soon, maybe. And you can be there, and so can anyone else the press would care to have there. And Professor James Priss can be there. He can represent Theoretical Science and after I have demonstrated antigravity, he can adjust his theory to explain it. I'm sure he will know how to make his adjustments in masterly fashion and show exactly why I couldn't possibly have failed. He might do it now and save time, but I suppose he won't."

It was all said very politely, but you could hear the snarl under the rapid flow of words.

Yet he continued his occasional game of billiards with Priss, and when the two met, they behaved with complete propriety. One could tell the progress Bloom was making by their respective attitudes to the press. Bloom grew curt and even snappish, while Priss developed an increasing good humor.

When my umpteenth request for an interview with Bloom was finally accepted, I wondered if perhaps that meant a break in Bloom's quest. I had a little daydream of him announcing final success to *me*.

It didn't work out that way. He met me in his office at Bloom Enterprises in upstate New York. It was a wonderful setting, well away from any populated area, elaborately landscaped, and covering as much ground as a rather large industrial establishment. Edison at his height, two centuries ago, had never been as phenomenally successful as Bloom.

But Bloom was not in a good humor. He came striding in ten minutes late and went snarling past his secretary's desk with the barest nod in my direction. He was wearing a lab coat, unbuttoned.

He threw himself into his chair and said, "I'm sorry if I've kept you waiting, but I didn't have as much time as I had hoped." Bloom was a born showman and knew better than to antagonize the press, but I had the feeling he was having a great deal of difficulty at that moment in adhering to this principle.

I made the obvious guess. "I am given to understand, sir, that your recent tests have been unsuccessful."

"Who told you that?"

"I would say it was general knowledge, Mr. Bloom."

"No, it isn't. Don't say that, young man. There is no general knowledge about what goes on in my laboratories and workshops. You're stating the professor's opinions, aren't you? Priss's, I mean."

"No, I'm—"

"Of course you are. Aren't you the one to whom he made that statement—that antigravity is impossible?"

"He didn't make the statement that flatly."

"He never says anything flatly, but it was flat enough for him and not as flat as I'll have his damned rubber-sheet Universe before I'm finished."

"Then does that mean you're making progress, Mr. Bloom?"

"You know I am," he said with a snap. "Or you should know. Weren't you at the demonstration last week?"

"Yes, I was."

I judged Bloom to be in trouble or he wouldn't be mentioning that demonstration. It worked but it was not a world beater. Between the two poles of a magnet a region of lessened gravity was produced.

It was done very cleverly. A Mössbauer-Effect Balance was used to probe the space between the poles. If you've never seen an M-E Balance in action, it consists primarily of a tight monochromatic beam of gamma rays shot down the low-gravity field. The gamma rays change wavelength slightly but measurably under the influence of the gravitational field and if anything happens to alter the intensity of the field, the wavelength change shifts correspondingly. It is an extremely delicate method for probing a gravitational field and it worked like a charm. There was no question but that Bloom had lowered gravity.

The trouble was that it had been done before by others. Bloom, to be sure, had made use of circuits that greatly increased the ease with which such an effect had been achieved—his system was typically ingenious and had been duly patented—and he maintained that it was by this method

181

that antigravity would become not merely a scientific curiosity, but a practical affair with industrial applications.

Perhaps. But it was an incomplete job and he didn't usually make a fuss over incompleteness. He wouldn't have done so this time if he weren't desperate to display *something*.

I said, "It's my impression that what you accomplished at that preliminary demonstration was $0.82\ g$, and better than that was achieved in Brazil last spring."

"That so? Well, calculate the energy input in Brazil and here, and then tell me the difference in gravity decrease per kilowatt-hour. You'll be surprised."

"But the point is, can you reach $0\ g$—zero gravity? That's what Professor Priss thinks may be impossible. Everyone agrees that merely lessening the intensity of the field is no great feat."

Bloom's fist clenched. I had the feeling that a key experiment had gone wrong that day and he was annoyed almost past endurance. Bloom hated to be balked by the Universe.

He said, "Theoreticians make me sick." He said it in a low, controlled voice, as though he were finally tired of not saying it and he was going to speak his mind and be damned. "Priss has won two Nobel prizes for sloshing around a few equations, but what has he done with it? Nothing! I *have* done something with it and I'm going to do more with it, whether Priss likes it or not.

"*I'm* the one people will remember. *I'm* the one who gets the credit. He can keep his damned title and his prizes and his kudos from the scholars. Listen, I'll tell you what gripes him. Plain old-fashioned jealousy. It kills him that I get what I get for doing. He wants it for *thinking*.

"I said to him once—we play billiards together, you know—"

It was at this point that I quoted Priss's statement about billiards and got Bloom's counterstatement. I never published either. That was just trivia.

"We play billiards," said Bloom, when he had cooled down, "and I've won my share of games. We keep things friendly enough. What the hell—college chums and all that—though how he got through, I'll never know. He made it in physics, of course, and in math, but he got a bare pass—out of pity, I think—in every humanities course he ever took."

"You did not get your degree, did you, Mr. Bloom?" That was sheer mischief on my part. I was enjoying his eruption.

"I quit to go into business, damn it. My academic average, over the three years I attended, was a strong B. Don't imagine anything else, you hear? Hell, by the time Priss got his PhD, I was working on my second million."

He went on, clearly irritated, "Anyway, we were playing billiards and I said to him, 'Jim, the average man will never understand why you get the Nobel Prize when I'm the one who gets the results. Why do you need two? Give me one!' He stood there, chalking up his cue, and then he said in his soft namby-pamby way, 'You have two billion, Ed. Give me one.' So you see, he wants the money."

I said, "I take it you don't mind his getting the honor?"

For a minute I thought he was going to order me out, but he didn't. He laughed instead, waved his hand in front of him as though he were erasing something from an invisible blackboard. He said, "Oh, well, forget it. All that is off the record. Listen, do you want a statement? Okay. Things didn't go right today and I blew my top a bit, but it will clear up. I think I know what's wrong. And if I don't, I'm going to know.

"Look, you can say that I say that we *don't* need infinite electromagnetic intensity; we *will* flatten out the rubber sheet; we *will* have zero gravity. And when we get it, I'll have the damndest demonstration you ever saw, exclusively for the press and for Priss, and you'll be invited. And you can say it won't be long. Okay?"

Okay!

I had time after that to see each man once or twice more. I even saw them together when I was present at one of their billiard games. As I said before, both of them were *good*.

But the call to the demonstration did not come as quickly as all that. It arrived six weeks less than a year after Bloom gave me his statement. And at that, perhaps it was unfair to expect quicker work.

I had a special, engraved invitation, with the assurance of a cocktail hour first. Bloom never did things by halves, and he was planning to have a pleased and satisfied group of reporters on hand. There was an arrangement for trimensional TV too. Bloom felt completely confident, obviously; confident enough to be willing to trust the demonstration in every living room on the planet.

I called up Professor Priss, to make sure he was invited too. He was.

"Do you plan to attend, sir?"

There was a pause and the professor's face on the screen was a study in uncertain reluctance. "A demonstration of this sort is most unsuitable where a serious scientific matter is in question. I do not like to encourage such things."

I was afraid he would beg off, and the dramatics of the situation would be greatly lessened if he were not there. But then, perhaps , he decided he dared not play the chicken before the world. With obvious distaste he said, "Of course Ed Bloom is not really a scientist and he must have his day in the sun. I'll be there."

"Do you think Mr. Bloom can produce zero gravity, sir?"

"Uh . . . Mr. Bloom sent me a copy of the design of his device and . . . and I'm not certain. Perhaps he can do it, if . . . uh . . . he says he can do it. Of course"—he paused again for quite a long time—"I think I would like to see it."

So would I, and so would many others.

The staging was impeccable. A whole floor of the main building at Bloom Enterprises—the one on the hilltop—was cleared. There were the promised cocktails and a splendid array of hors d'oeuvres, soft music and lighting, and a carefully dressed and thoroughly jovial Edward Bloom playing the perfect host, while a number of polite and unobtrusive menials fetched and carried. All was geniality and amazing confidence.

James Priss was late and I caught Bloom watching the corners of the crowd and beginning to grow a little grim about the edges. Then Priss arrived, dragging a volume of colorlessness in with him, a drabness that was unaffected by the noise and the absolute splendor (no other word would describe it— or else it was the two martinis glowing inside me) that filled the room.

184

Bloom saw him and his face was illuminated at once. He bounced across the floor, seized the smaller man's hand and dragged him to the bar.

"Jim! Glad to see you! What'll you have? Hell, man, I'd have called it off if you hadn't showed. Can't have this thing without the star, you know." He wrung Priss's hand. "It's your theory, you know. We poor mortals can't do a thing without you few, you damned *few* few, pointing the way."

He was being ebullient, handing out the flattery, because he could afford to do so now. He was fattening Priss for the kill.

Priss tried to refuse a drink, with some sort of mutter, but a glass was pressed into his hand and Bloom raised his voice to a bull roar.

"Gentlemen! A moment's quiet, please. To Professor Priss, the greatest mind since Einstein, two-time Nobel Laureate, father of the Two-Field Theory and inspirer of the demonstration we are about to see—even if he didn't think it would work and had the guts to say so publicly."

There was a distinct titter of laughter that quickly faded out and Priss looked grim as his face could manage.

"But now that Professor Priss is here," said Bloom, "and we've had our toast, let's get on with it. Follow me, gentlemen!"

The demonstration was in a much more elaborate place than had housed the earlier one. This time it was on the top floor of the building. Different magnets were involved—smaller ones, by heaven—but as nearly as I could tell, the same M-E Balance was in place.

One thing was new, however, and it staggered everybody, drawing much more attention than anything else in the room. It was a billiard table, resting under one pole of the magnet. Beneath it was the companion pole. A round hole, about a foot across, was stamped out of the very center of the table, and it was obvious that the zero-gravity field, if it was to be produced, would be produced through that hole in the center of the billiard table.

It was as though the whole demonstration had been designed, surrealist fashion, to point up the victory of Bloom over Priss. This was to be another version of their everlasting billiards competition and Bloom was going to win.

I don't know if the other newsmen took matters in that fashion, but I think Priss did. I turned to look at him and saw that he was still holding the drink that had been forced into his hand. He rarely drank, I knew, but now he lifted the glass to his lips and emptied it in two swallows. He stared at that billiard ball and I needed no gift of E.S.P. to realize that he took it as a deliberate snap of fingers under his nose.

Bloom led us to the twenty seats that surrounded three sides of the table, leaving the fourth free as a working area. Priss was carefully escorted to the seat commanding the most convenient view. Priss glanced quickly at the trimensional cameras, which were now working. I wondered if he were thinking of leaving but deciding that he couldn't in the full glare of the eyes of the world.

Essentially the demonstration was simple; it was the production that counted. There were dials in plain view that measured the energy expenditure. There were others that transferred the M-E Balance readings into a position and a size that were visible to all. Everything was arranged for easy trimensional viewing.

Bloom explained each step in a genial way, with one or two pauses in which he turned to Priss for a confirmation that had to come. He didn't do it often enough to make it obvious, but just enough to turn Priss upon the spit of his own torment. From where I sat I could look across the table and see Priss on the other side.

He had the look of a man in Hell.

As we all know, Bloom succeeded. The M-E Balance showed the gravitational intensity to be sinking steadily as the electromagnetic field was intensified. There were cheers when it dropped below the $0.52\ g$ mark. A red line indicated that on the dial.

"The $0.52\ g$ mark, as you know," said Bloom confidently, "represents the previous record low in gravitational intensity. We are now lower than that at a cost in electricity that is less than ten percent what it cost at the time that mark was set. And we will go lower still."

Bloom—I think deliberately, for the sake of the suspense—

slowed the drop toward the end, letting the trimensional cameras switch back and forth between the gap in the billiard table and the dial on which the M-E Balance reading was lowering.

Bloom said suddenly, "Gentlemen, you will find dark goggles in the pouch on the side of each chair. Please put them on now. The zero-gravity field will soon be established and it will radiate a light rich in ultraviolet."

He put goggles on himself, and there was a momentary rustle as others went on too.

I think no one breathed during the last minute, when the dial reading dropped to zero and held fast. And just as that happened, a cylinder of light sprang into existence from pole to pole through the hole in the billiard table.

There was a ghost of twenty sighs at that. Someone called out, "Mr. Bloom, what is the reason for the light?"

"It's characteristic of the zero-gravity field," said Bloom smoothly, which was no answer, of course.

Reporters were standing up now, crowding about the edge of the table. Bloom waved them back. "Please, gentlemen, stand clear!"

Only Priss remained sitting. He seemed lost in thought, and I have been certain ever since that it was the goggles that obscured the possible significance of everything that followed. I didn't see his eyes. I couldn't. And that meant neither I nor anyone else could ever begin to make a guess as to what was going on behind those eyes. Well, maybe we couldn't have made such a guess, even if the goggles hadn't been there, but who can say?

Bloom was raising his voice again. "Please! The demonstration is not yet over. So far we've only repeated what I have done before. I have now produced a zero-gravity field and I have shown it can be done practically. But I want to demonstrate something of what such a field can do. What we are going to see next will be something that has never been seen, not even by myself. I have not experimented in this direction, much as I would have liked to, because I have felt that Professor Priss deserved the honor of—"

Priss looked up sharply. "What—what—"

"Professor Priss," said Bloom, smiling broadly, "I would

187

like you to perform the first experiment involving the interaction of a solid object with a zero-gravity field. Notice that the field has been formed in the center of a billiard table. The world knows your phenomenal skill in billiards, Professor, a talent second only to your amazing aptitude in theoretical physics. Won't you send a billiard ball into the zero-gravity volume?"

Eagerly he was handing a ball and cue to the professor. Priss, his eyes hidden by the goggles, stared at them and only very slowly, very uncertainly, reached out to take them.

I wonder what his eyes were showing. I wonder, too, how much of the decision to have Priss play billiards at the demonstration was due to Bloom's anger at Priss's remark about their periodic game, the remark I had quoted. Had I been, in my way, responsible for what followed?

"Come, stand up, Professor," said Bloom, "and let me have your seat. The show is yours from now on. Go ahead!"

Bloom seated himself and still talked—in a voice that grew more organlike with each moment. "Once Professor Priss sends the ball into the volume of zero gravity, it will no longer be affected by Earth's gravitational field. It will remain truly motionless while the Earth rotates about its axis and travels about the Sun. In this latitude, and at this time of day, I have calculated that the Earth, in its motions, will sink downward. We will move with it and the ball will stand still. To us it will seem to rise up and away from the Earth's surface. Watch."

Priss seemed to stand in front of the table in frozen paralysis. Was it surprise? Astonishment? I don't know. I'll never know. Did he make a move to interrupt Bloom's little speech, or was he just suffering from an agonized reluctance to play the ignominious part into which he was being forced by his adversary?

Priss turned to the billiard table, looking first at it, then back at Bloom. Every reporter was on his feet, crowding as closely as possible in order to get a good view. Only Bloom himself remained seated, smiling and isolated. He, of course, was not watching the table, or the ball, or the zero-gravity field. As nearly as I could tell through the goggles, he was watching Priss.

Priss turned to the table and placed his ball. He was going to

188

be the agent that was to bring final and dramatic triumph to Bloom and make himself—the man who said it couldn't be done—the goat to be mocked forever.

Perhaps he felt there was no way out. Or perhaps—

With a sure stroke of his cue, he set the ball into motion. It was not going quickly, and every eye followed it. It struck the side of the table and caromed. It was going even slower now as though Priss himself were increasing the suspense and making Bloom's triumph the more dramatic.

I had a perfect view, for I was standing on the side of the table opposite from that where Priss was. I could see the ball moving toward the glitter of the zero-gravity field, and beyond it I could see those portions of the seated Bloom which were not hidden by that glitter.

The ball approached the zero-gravity volume, seemed to hang on the edge for a moment, and then was gone, with a streak of light, the sound of a thunderclap, and the sudden smell of burning cloth.

We yelled. We all yelled.

I've seen the scene on television since—along with the rest of the world. I can see myself in the film during that fifteen-second period of wild confusion, but I don't really recognize my face.

Fifteen seconds!

And then we discovered Bloom. He was still sitting in the chair, his arms still folded, but there was a hole the size of a billiard ball through forearm, chest, and back. The better part of his heart, as it later turned out under autopsy, had been neatly punched out.

They turned off the device. They called in the police. They dragged off Priss, who was in a state of utter collapse. I wasn't much better off, to tell the truth, and if any reporter then on the scene ever tried to say he remained a cool observer of that scene, then he's a cool liar.

It was some months before I got to see Priss again. He had lost some weight but seemed well otherwise. Indeed, there was color in his cheeks and an air of decision about him. He was better dressed than I had ever seen him to be.

He said, "I know what happened *now*. If I had had time to

think, I would have known then. But I am a slow thinker, and poor Ed Bloom was so intent on running a great show and doing it so well that he carried me along with him. Naturally I've been trying to make up for some of the damage I unwittingly caused."

"You can't bring Bloom back to life," I said soberly.

"No, I can't," he said just as soberly. "But there's Bloom Enterprises to think of too. What happened at the demonstration, in full view of the world, was the worst possible advertisement for zero gravity, and it's important that the story be made clear. That is why I have asked to see *you*."

"Yes?"

"If I had been a quicker thinker, I would have known Ed was speaking the purest nonsense when he said that the billiard ball would slowly rise in the zero-gravity field. It *couldn't* be so! If Bloom hadn't despised theory so, if he hadn't been so intent on being proud of his own ignorance of theory, he'd have known it himself.

"The Earth's motion, after all, isn't the only motion involved, young man. The Sun itself moves in a vast orbit about the center of the Milky Way Galaxy. And the galaxy moves too, in some not very clearly defined way. If the billiard ball were subjected to zero gravity, you might think of it as being unaffected by any of these motions and therefore as suddenly falling into a state of absolute rest—when there is no such thing as absolute rest."

Priss shook his head slowly. "The trouble with Ed, I think, was that he was thinking of the kind of zero gravity one gets in a spaceship in free fall, when people float in mid-air. He expected the ball to float in mid-air. However, in a spaceship, zero gravity is not the result of an absence of gravitation, but merely the result of two objects, a ship and a man within the ship, falling at the same rate, responding to gravity in precisely the same way, so that each is motionless with respect to the other.

"In the zero-gravity field produced by Ed, there was a flattening of the rubber-sheet Universe, which means an actual loss of mass. Everything in that field, including molecules of air caught within it and the billiard ball I pushed into it, was completely massless as long as it remained within it. A completely massless object can move in only one way."

He paused, inviting the question. I asked, "What motion would that be?"

"Motion at the speed of light. Any massless object, such as a neutrino or a photon, must travel at the speed of light as long as it exists. In fact, light moves at that speed only because it is made up of photons. As soon as the billiard ball entered the zero-gravity field and lost its mass, it too assumed the speed of light at once and left."

I shook my head. "But didn't it regain its mass as soon as it left the zero-gravity volume?"

"It certainly did, and at once it began to be affected by the gravitational field and to slow up in response to the friction of the air and the top of the billiard table. But imagine how much friction it would take to slow up an object the mass of a billiard ball going at the speed of light. It went through the hundred-mile thickness of our atmosphere in a thousandth of a second and I doubt that it was slowed more than a few miles a second in doing so, a few miles out of 186,282 of them. On the way, it scorched the top of the billiard table, broke cleanly through the edge, went through poor Ed and the window too, punching out neat circles because it had passed through before the neighboring portions of something even as brittle as glass had a chance to split and splinter.

"It is extremely fortunate we were on the top floor of a building set in a countrified area. If we were in the city, it might have passed through a number of buildings and killed a number of people. By now that billiard ball is off in space, far beyond the edge of the solar system, and it will continue to travel so forever, at nearly the speed of light, until it happens to strike an object large enough to stop it. And then it will gouge out a sizable crater."

I played with the notion and was not sure I liked it. "How is that possible? The billiard ball entered the zero-gravity volume almost at a standstill. I saw it. And you say it left with an incredible quantity of kinetic energy. Where did the energy come from?"

Priss shrugged. "It came from nowhere! The law of conservation of energy only holds under the conditions in which general relativity is valid; that is, in an indented rubber-sheet Universe. Wherever the indentation is flattened out, general relativity no longer holds, and energy can be created and destroyed freely. That accounts for the radiation along the cylindrical surface of the zero-gravity volume. That radiation, you remember, Bloom did not explain and, I fear, could not explain. If he had only experimented further first; if he had only not been so foolishly anxious to put on his show——"

"What accounts for the radiation, sir?"

"The molecules of air inside the volume. Each assumes the speed of light and comes smashing outward. They're only molecules, not billiard balls, so they're stopped, but the kinetic energy of their motion is converted into energetic radiation. It's continuous because new molecules are always drifting in, attaining the speed of light and smashing out."

"Then energy is being created continuously?"

"Exactly. And that is what we must make clear to the public. Antigravity is not primarily a device to lift spaceships or to revolutionize mechanical movement. Rather it is the source of an endless supply of free energy, since part of the energy produced can be diverted to maintain the field that keeps that portion of the Universe flat. What Ed Bloom invented, without knowing it, was not just antigravity, but the first successful perpetual-motion machine of the first class—one that manufactures energy out of nothing."

I said slowly, "Any one of us could have been killed by that billiard ball, is that right. Professor? It might have come out in any direction."

Priss said, "Well, massless photons emerge from any light source at the speed of light in any direction; that's why a candle casts light in all directions. The massless air molecules come out of the zero-gravity volume in all directions, which is why the entire cylinder radiates. But the billiard ball was only one object. It could have come out in any direction, but it had to come out in some one direction, chosen at random, and the chosen direction happened to be the one that caught Ed."

That was it. Everyone knows the consequences. Mankind had free energy and so we have the world we have now. Professor Priss was placed in charge of its development by the board of Bloom Enterprises, and in time he was as rich and famous as ever Edward Bloom had been. And Priss still has two Nobel prizes in addition.

Only. . . .

I keep thinking. Photons smash out from a light source in all directions because they are created at the moment and there is no reason for them to move in one direction more than in another. Air molecules come out of a zero-gravity field in all directions because they enter it in all directions.

But what about a single billiard ball, entering a zero-gravity field from one particular direction? Does it come out in the same direction or in any direction?

I've inquired delicately, but theoretical physicists don't seem to be sure, and I can find no record that Bloom Enterprises, which is the only organization working with zero-gravity fields, has ever experimented in the matter. Someone at the organization once told me that the uncertainty principle guarantees the random emersion of an object entering in any direction. But then why don't they try the experiment?

Could it be, then . . .

Could it be that for once Priss's mind had been working quickly? Could it be that, under the pressure of what Bloom was trying to do to him, Priss had suddenly seen everything? He had been studying the radiation surrounding the zero-gravity volume. He might have realized its cause and been certain of the speed-of-light motion of anything entering the volume.

Why, then, had he said nothing?

One thing is certain. *Nothing* Priss would do at the billiard table could be accidental. He was an expert, and the billiard ball did exactly what he wanted it to. I was standing right there. I saw him look at Bloom and then at the table as though he were judging angles.

I watched him hit that ball. I watched it bounce off the side of the table and move into the zero-gravity volume, heading in one particular direction.

For when Priss sent that ball toward the zero-gravity volume—and the tri-di films bear me out—it was *already* aimed directly at Bloom's heart!

Accident? Coincidence?

. . . Murder?

13

The Winds of Change

Jonas Dinsmore walked into the President's Room of the Faculty Club in a manner completely characteristic of himself, as though conscious of being in a place in which he belonged but in which he was not accepted. The belonging showed in the sureness of his stride and the casual noise of his feet as he walked. The nonacceptance lay in his quick look from side to side as he entered, a quick summing-up of the enemies present.

He was an associate professor of physics and he was not liked.

There were two others in the room, and Dinsmore might well have considered them enemies without being thought paranoid for doing so.

One was Horatio Adams, the aging chairman of the department who, without ever having done any single thing that was remarkable, had yet accumulated a vast respect for the numerous unremarkable but perfectly correct things he had done. The other was Carl Muller, whose work on Grand Unified Field Theory had put him in line for the Nobel Prize (he thought probably) and the presidency of the university (he thought certainly).

It was hard to say which prospect Dinsmore found more distasteful. It was quite fair to say he detested Muller.

Dinsmore seated himself at one corner of the couch, which

was old, slippery and chilly. The two comfortable armchairs were taken by the others. Dinsmore smiled.

He frequently smiled, though his face never seemed either friendly or pleased as a result. Though there was nothing in the smile that was not the normal drawing back of the corners of the mouth, it invariably had a chilling effect on those at whom he aimed the gesture. His round face, his sparse but carefully combed hair, his full lips would all have taken on joviality with such a smile, or should have—but didn't.

Adams stirred with what seemed to be a momentary spasm of irritation crossing his long, New Englandish face. Muller, his hair nearly black and his eyes an incongruous blue, seemed impassive.

Dinsmore said, "I intrude, gentlemen, I know. Yet I have no choice. I have been asked by the Board of Trustees to be present. It may seem to you to be a cruel action, perhaps. I am sure you expect, Muller, that at any moment a communication will be received from the trustees to the effect that you have been named for the presidency. It would seem proper that the renowned Professor Adams, your mentor and patron, should know of it. But why, Muller, should they reserve a similar privilege for me, your humble and ever failing rival?

"I suspect, in fact, that your first act as president, Muller, would be to inform me that it would be in all ways better if I would seek another position elsewhere since my appointment will not be renewed past this academic year. It might be convenient to have me on the spot in order that there be no delay. It would be unkind, but efficient.

"You look troubled, both of you. I may be unjust. My instant dismissal may not be in your mind; you may have been willing to wait till tomorrow. Can it be that it is the trustees who would rather be quick and who would rather have me on the spot? It doesn't matter. Either way, it would seem that you are in and I am out. And perhaps that seems just. The respected head of a great department approaching the evening of his career, with his brilliant protégé, whose grasp of concept and whose handling of mathematics is unparalleled, are ready for the laurels; while I, without respect or honor—

"Since this is so, it is kind of you to let me talk without interrupting. I have a feeling that the message we wait for may

195

not arrive for some minutes, for an hour, perhaps. A presentiment. The trustees themselves would not be averse to building suspense. This is their moment in the sun, their fleeting time of glory. And since the time must be passed, I am willing to speak.

"Some, before execution, are granted a last meal, some a last cigarette; I, a last few words. You needn't listen, I suppose, or even bother to look interested.

"—Thank you. The look of resignation, Professor Adams, I will accept as agreement. Professor Muller's slight smile, let us say of contempt, will also do.

"You will not blame me, I know, for wishing the situation were changed. In what way? A good question. I would not wish to change my character and personality. It may be unsatisfactory, but it is mine. Nor would I change the polite efficiency of Adams or the brilliance of Muller, for what would such a change do but make them no longer Adams and Muller? I would have them be they, and yet—have the results different. If one could go back in time, what small change then might produce a large and desirable change now?

"That's what's needed. Time travel!

"Ah, *that* grinds a reaction out of you, Muller. That was the clear beginning of a snort. Time travel! Ridiculous! Impossible!

"Not only impossible in the sense that the state of the art is inadequate for the purpose, but in the greater sense that it will be forever inadequate. Time travel, in the sense of going backward to change reality, is not only technologically impossible now, but it is theoretically impossible altogether.

"Odd you should think so, Muller, because your theories, those very analyses which have brought the four forces, even gravitation, measurably close to inclusion under the umbrella of a single set of relationships, make time travel no longer theoretically impossible.

"No, don't rise to protest. Keep your seat, Muller, and relax. For you it is impossible, I'm sure. For most people it would be. Perhaps for almost everyone. But there might be exceptions and it just might be that I'm one of them. Why myself? Who knows? I don't claim to be brighter than either of you, but what has that to do with it?

196

"Let us argue by analogy. Consider— Tens of thousands of years ago, human beings, little by little, either as a mass endeavor or through the agency of a few brilliant individuals, learned to communicate. Speech was invented and delicate modulations of sounds were invested with abstract meaning.

"For thousands of years every normal human being has been able to communicate, but how many have been able to tell a story superlatively well? Shakespeare, Tolstoy, Dickens, Hugo—a handful compared to all the human beings who have lived—can use those modulated sounds to wrench at heartstrings and reach for sublimity. Yet they use the same sounds that all of us use.

"I am prepared to admit that Muller's IQ, for instance, is higher than that of Shakespeare or Tolstoy. Muller's knowledge of language must be as good as that of any writer alive; his understanding of meaning as great. Yet Muller could not put words together and achieve the effect that Shakespeare could. Muller himself wouldn't deny it for a moment, I'm sure. What then is it that Shakespeare and Tolstoy can do that Muller or Adams or I cannot; what wisdom do they have that we cannot penetrate? You don't know and I don't know. What is worse, *they* didn't know. Shakespeare could in no manner have instructed you—or anyone—how to write as he did. He didn't know how—he merely could.

"Next consider the consciousness of time. As far as we can guess, only human beings of all life forms can grasp the significance of time. All other species live in the present only; might have vague memories; might have dim and limited forethought—but surely only human beings truly understand the past, present and future and can speculate on its meaning and significance, can wonder about the flow of time, of how it carries us along with it, and of how that flow might be altered.

"When did this happen? How did it come about? Who was the first human being, or hominid, that suddenly grasped the manner in which the river of time carried him from the dim past into the dim future, and wondered if it might be dammed or diverted?

"The flow is not invariant. Time races for us at times; hours vanish in what seem like minutes—and lag unconscionably at other times. In dream states, in trances, in drug experiences, time alters its properties.

"You seem about to comment, Adams. Don't bother. You are going to say that those alterations are purely psychological. I know it, but what else is there but the psychological?

"Is there *physical* time? If so, what *is* physical time? Surely it is whatever we choose to make it. *We* design the instruments. *We* interpret the measurements. *We* create the theories and then interpret those. And from absolute, we have changed time and made it the creature of the speed of light and decided that simultaneity is indefinable.

"From your theory, Muller, we know that time is altogether subjective. In theory, someone understanding the nature of the flow of time can, given enough talent, move with or against the flow independently, or stand still in it. It is analogous to the manner in which, given the symbols of communication, someone, given enough talent, can write *King Lear*. Given enough talent.

"What if I had enough talent? What if I could be the Shakespeare of the time flow? Come, let us amuse ourselves. At any moment the message from the Board of Trustees will arrive and I will have to stop. Until it does, however, allow me to push along with my chatter. It serves its turn. Come, I doubt that you are aware that fifteen minutes have passed since I began talking.

"Think, then— If I could make use of Muller's theory and find within myself the odd ability to take advantage of it as Homer did of words, what would I do with my gift? I might wander back through time perhaps, wraithlike, observing from without all the pattern of time and events in order to reach in at one place or another and make a change.

"Oh, yes, I would be outside the time-stream as I travel. Your theory, Muller, properly interpreted, does not insist that in moving backward in time, or forward, one must move through the thick of the flow, stumbling across events and knocking them down in passage. That would indeed be theoretically impossible. To remain *outside* is where the possibility comes in and to slip in and out at will is where the talent comes in.

"Suppose, then, I did this; that I slipped in and made a

change. That one change would breed another—which would breed another— Time would be set in a new path which would take on a life of its own, curving and foaming until, in a very little time—

"No, that is an inadequate expression. 'Time would, in a very little time—' It is as though we are imagining some abstract and absolute timelike reference against which our time may be measured; as though our own background of time were flowing against another, deeper background. I confess it's beyond me, but pretend you understand.

"Any change in the events of time would, after a—while—alter everything unrecognizably.

"But I wouldn't want *that*. I told you at the start, I do not wish to cease to be me. Even if in my place I would create someone who was more intelligent, more sensible, more successful, it would still not be *me*.

"Nor would I want to change you, Muller, or you, Adams. I've said that already too. I would not want to triumph over a Muller who is less ingenious and spectacularly bright, or over an Adams who has been less politic and deft at putting together an imposing structure of respect. I would want to triumph over you as you are, and not over lesser beings.

"Well, yes, it is triumph I wish.

"—Oh, come. You stir as though I had said something unworthy. Is a sense of triumph so alien to you? Are you so dead to humanity that you seek no honor, no victory, no fame, no rewards? Am I to suppose that the respected Professor Adams does not wish to possess his long list of publications, his revered string of honorary degrees, his numerous medals and plaques, his post as head of one of the most prestige-filled departments of physics in the world?

"And would you be satisfied to have all that, Adams, if no one were to know of it; if its existence were to be wiped out of all records and histories; if it were to remain a secret between you and the Almighty? A silly question. I certainly won't demand an answer when we all know what it would be.

"And I needn't go through the same rigmarole of inquiry concerning Muller's potential Nobel Prize and what seems like a certain university presidency—and of this university too.

"What is it you both want in all of this, considering that you want not only the things themselves but the public knowledge of your ownership of these things? Surely you want triumph! You want triumph over your competitors as an abstract class, triumph over your fellow human beings. You want to do something others cannot do and to have all those others know that you have done something they cannot do, so that they must then look up at you in helpless awareness of that knowledge and in envy and enforced admiration.

"Shall I be more noble than you? Why? Let me have the privilege of wanting what you want, of hungering for the triumph you have hungered for. Why should I not want the long respect, the great prize, the high position that waits on you two? And to do so in your place? To snatch it from you at the moment of its attainment? It is no more disgraceful for me to glory in such things than for you to do so.

"Ah, but you deserve it and I do not. There is precisely the point. What if I could so arrange the flow and content of time as to have me deserve it and you not?

"Imagine! I would still be I; the two of you, the two of you. You would be no less worthy and I no more worthy—that being the condition I have set myself, that none of us change—and yet I deserve and you do not. I want to beat you, in other words, as you are and not as inferior substitutes.

"In a way, that is a tribute to you, isn't it? I see from your expression you think it is. I imagine you both feel a kind of contemptuous pride. It is something after all to be the standard by which victory is measured. You enjoy earning the merits I lust for—especially if that lust must go unsatisfied.

"I don't blame you for feeling so. In your place, I would feel the same.

"But must the lust go unsatisfied? Think it out—

"Suppose I were to go back in time, say twenty-five years. A nice figure, an even quarter-century. You, Adams, would be forty. You would have just arrived here, a full professor, from your stint at Case Institute. You would have done your work in diamagnetics, though your unreported effort to do something with bismuth hypochromite had been a rather laughable failure.

"Heavens, Adams, don't look so surprised. Do you think I don't know your professional life to the last detail—

"And as for you, Muller, you were twenty-six, and just in the process of turning out a doctor's thesis on general relativity, which was fascinating at the time but is much less satisfying in retrospect than it was at the time. Had it been correctly interpreted, it would have anticipated most of Hawking's later conclusions, as you now know. You did not correctly interpret it at the time and you have successfully managed to hide that fact.

"I'm afraid, Muller, you are not good at interpretation. You did not interpret your own doctor's thesis to its best advantage and you have not properly interpreted your great Field Theory. Perhaps, Muller, it isn't a disgrace, either. The lack of interpretation is a common event. We can't all have the interpretative knack, and the talent to shake loose consequences may not occur in the same mind that possesses the talent for brilliance of concept. I have the former without the latter so why should you not have the latter without the former?

"If you could only create your marvelous thoughts, Muller, and leave it to me to see the equally marvelous conclusions. What a team we would make, you and I, Muller—but you wouldn't have me. I don't complain about that, for I wouldn't have you.

"In any case, these are trifles. I could in no way damage you, Adams, with the pinprick of your silly handling of the bismuth salts. After all, you did, with some difficulty, catch your mistake before you embalmed it in the pages of a learned journal—if you could have gotten past the referees. And I could not cloud the sunshine that plays on you, Muller, by making a point of your failure to deduce what might be deduced from your concepts. It might even be looked upon as a measure of your brilliance; that so much crowded into your thoughts that even *you* were not bright enough to wring them dry of consequence.

"But if that would not do, what would? How could matters be changed properly? Fortunately, I could study the situation for a length of—something—that my consciousness would interpret as years, and yet there would be no physical time passage and therefore no aging. My thought processes would continue, but my physical metabolism would not.

"You smile again. No, I don't know how that could be. Surely our thought processes are part of our metabolic changes. I can only suppose that outside the time-stream, thought processes are not thought processes in the physical sense, but are something else that is equivalent.

"And if I study a moment in time, and search for a change that will accomplish what I want it to accomplish, how could I do that? Could I make a change, move forward in time, study the consequences, and if I didn't like it, move back, unchange the change and try another? If I did it fifty times, a thousand times, could I ever find the right change? The number of changes, each with numberless consequences, each with further numberless consequences, is beyond computation or comprehension. How could I find the change I was seeking?

"Yet I could. I could learn how, and I can't tell you how I learned or what I did after I learned. Would it be so difficult? Think of the things we *do* learn.

"We stand, we walk, we run, we hop—and we do it all even though we are tipped on end. We are in an utter state of instability. We remain standing only because the large muscles of our legs and torso are forever lightly contracting and pulling this way and that, like a circus performer balancing a stick on the end of his nose.

"Physically, it's hard. That is why standing still takes it out of us and makes us glad to sit down after a while. That is why standing at attention for an unfairly long period of time will lead to collapse. Yet, except when we take it to extremes, we do it so well, we're not even aware we do it. We can stand and walk and run and hop and start and stop all day long and never fall or even become seriously unsteady. Well, then, describe how you do it so that someone who has never tried can do it. You can't.

"Another example. We can talk. We can stretch and contract the muscles of our tongue and lips and cheeks and palate in a rapid and unrhythmic set of changes that produce just the modulation of sound that we want. It was hard enough to learn when we were infants, but once we learned, we could produce dozens of words a minute without any conscious effort. Well, how do we do it? What changes do we produce to say, 'How do we do it?' Describe those changes to someone

202

who has never spoken so that he can make that sound! It can't be done.

"But we can make the sound. And without effort too.

"Given enough time—I don't even know how to describe the passage of what I mean. It was not time; call it 'duration.' Given enough duration *without* the passage of time, I learned how to adjust reality as desired. It was like a child babbling but gradually learning to pick and choose among the babbles to construct words. I learned to choose.

"It was risky, of course. In the process of learning, I might have done something irreversible; or at least something which, for reversal, would have required subtle changes that were beyond me. I did not. Perhaps it was more good fortune than anything else.

"And I came to enjoy it. It was like the painting of a picture, the construction of a piece of sculpture. It was much more than that; it was the carving of a new reality. —A new reality unchanged from our own in key ways. I remained exactly what I am; Adams remained the eternal Adams; Muller, the quintessential Muller. The university remained the university; science, science.

"Well, then, did nothing change? —But I'm losing your attention. You no longer believe me and, if I am any judge, feel scornful with what I am saying. I seem to have slipped in my enthusiasm and I have begun acting as though time-travel were real and that I have really done what I would like to do. Forgive me. Consider it imagination—fantasy—I say what I *might* have done *if* time-travel were real and *if* I truly had the talent for it.

"In that case—in my imagination—did nothing change? There would have to be *some* change, one that would leave Adams exactly Adams and yet unfit to be head of the department; Muller to be precisely Muller and yet without any likelihood of becoming university president and without much chance of being voted the Nobel Prize.

"And I would have to be myself, unlovable and plodding, and unable to create—and yet possessing the qualities that would make *me* university president.

"It could be nothing scientific; it would have to be

something outside science; something disgraceful and sordid that would disqualify you fine gentlemen—

"Come, now. I don't deserve those looks of mingled disdain and smug self-satisfaction. You are sure, I take it, that you can do nothing disgraceful and sordid? How can you be sure? There's not one of us who, if conditions were right, would not slip into—shall we call it sin? Who among us would be without sin, given the proper temptation? Who among us *is* without sin?

"Think, think— Are you sure your souls are pure? Have you done nothing wrong, ever? Have you never at least nearly fallen into the pit? And if you have, was it not a narrow escape, brought about more through some fortunate circumstance than inner virtue? And if someone had closely studied all your actions and noted the strokes of fortune that kept you safe and deflected just one of them, might you not then have done wrong?

"Of course, if you had lived openly foul and sordid lives so that people turned from you in disdain and disgust, you would not have reached your present states of reverence. You would have fallen long since and I would not have to step over your disgraced bodies for you would not be here to serve me as stepping stones.

"You see how complex it all is?

"But then, it is all the more exciting, you see. If I were to go back in time and find that the solution was not complex, that in one stroke I could achieve my aim, I might manage to gain pleasure out of it but there would be a lack of intellectual excitement.

"If we were to play chess and I were to win by a fool's mate in three moves, it would be a victory that was worse than defeat. I would have played an unworthy opponent and I would be disgraced for having done so.

"No. The victory that is worthwhile is the one snatched slowly and with pain from the reluctant grip of the adversary; a victory that seems unattainable; a victory that is as wearying, as torturing, as hopelessly bone-breaking as the worst and most tedious defeat but that has, as its difference, the fact that while you are panting and gasping in total exhaustion, it is the flag you hold in your hand, the trophy.

"The duration I spent playing with that most intractable of all materials, reality, was filled with the difficulty I had set myself. I insisted stubbornly not only on having my aim, but on my having that aim my way; on rejecting everything that was not *exactly* as I wanted it to be. A near miss I considered a miss; an almost hit I eliminated as not a hit. In my target, I had a bull's-eye and nothing else.

"And even after I won, it would have to be a victory so subtle that you would not know I had won until I had carefully explained it to you. To the final moment you would not know your life had been turned wrong end up. That is what—

"But wait, I have left out something. I have been so caught up in the intensity of my intention of leaving us and the university and science all the same that I have not explained that other things might indeed change. There would bound to be changes in social, political and economic forces, and in international relationships. Who would care about such things after all? Certainly not we three.

"That is the marvel of science and the scientist, is it not? What is it to us whom we elect in our dear United States, or what votes were taken in the United Nations, or whether the stock market went up or down, or whether the unending pavane of the nations followed this pattern or that? As long as science is there and the laws of nature hold fast and the game we play continues, the background against which we play it is just a meaningless shifting of light and shadow.

"Perhaps you don't feel this openly, Muller. I know well you have, in your time, felt yourself part of society and have placed yourself on record with views on this and that. To a lesser extent so did you, Adams. Both of you have had exalted views concerning humanity and the earth and various abstractions. How much of that, however, was a matter of greasing your conscience because inside—deep inside—you don't really care as long as you can sit brooding over your scientific thoughts?

"That's one big difference between us. I don't care what happens to humanity as long as I am left to my physics. I am open about it; everyone knows me as cynical and callous. You two *secretly* don't care. To the cynicism and callousness that characterize me, you add hypocrisy, which plasters over your sins to the unthinking but makes them worse when found out.

"Oh, don't shake your heads. In my searching out your lives, I discovered as much about you as you yourselves know; more, since I see your peccadilloes clearly, and you two hide them even from yourselves. It is the most amusing thing about hypocrisy that once it is adhered to sternly enough, it numbers the hypocrite himself among its victims. He is his own chief victim, in fact, for it is quite usual that when the hypocrite is exposed to all the world, he still seems, quite honestly, a plaster saint to himself.

"But I tell you this not in order to vilify you. I tell it to you in order to explain that if I found it necessary to change the world in order to keep ourselves all the same, yet place me on top instead of you, you wouldn't really mind. Not about the world, that is.

"You wouldn't mind if the Republicans were up and the Democrats were down, or vice versa; if feminism was in flower and professional sports were under a cloud; if this fashion or that in clothing, furniture, music or comedy was in or out. What would any of that matter to you?

"Nothing.

"In fact, less than nothing, for if the world were changed, it would be a new reality; *the* reality as far as people in the world were concerned; the *only* reality, the reality of the history books, the reality that was *real* over the last twenty-five years.

"If you believed me, if you thought I were spinning more than a fantasy, you would still be helpless. Could you go to someone in authority and say: 'This is not the way things are supposed to be. It has been altered by a villain'? What would that prove but that you were insane? Who could believe that reality is not reality, when it is the fabric and tapestry that have been woven all these twenty-five years in incredibly intricate fashion, and when everyone remembers and lives it as woven?

"But you yourselves do *not* believe me. You dare not believe that I am not merely speculating about having gone back into the past, about having studied you both, about having labored to bring about a new reality in which we are unchanged but, alas, the world is changed. I have *done* it; I have done it *all*. And I alone remember both realities because I was outside time when the change was made, and *I* made it.

"And still you don't believe me. You dare not believe me, for you yourselves would feel you were insane if you did. Could I have altered this familiar world of 1982? Impossible.

"If I did, what could the world have been like before I tampered with it? I'll tell you—it was chaotic! It was full of license! People were laws to themselves! In a way I'm glad I changed it. Now we have a government and the land is governed. Our rulers have views and the views are enforced. Good!

"But, gentlemen, in that world that was, that old reality that no one can know or conceive, you two gentlemen were laws to yourselves and fought for license and anarchy. It was no crime in the old reality. It was admirable to many.

"In the new reality, I left you unchanged. You remained fighters for license and anarchy, and that *is* a crime in the present reality, the only reality you know. I made sure you could cover it up. No one knew about your crimes, and you were able to rise to your present heights. But I know where the evidence was and how it might be uncovered, and at the proper time—I uncovered it.

"Now I think that for the first time I catch expressions on your faces that don't ring the changes of weary tolerance, of contempt, of amusement, of annoyance. Do I catch a whiff of fear? Do you remember what I am talking about?

"Think! Think! Who were members of the League of Constitutional Freedoms? Who helped circulate the *Free Thought Manifesto*? It was very brave and honorable of you to do this, some people thought. You were much applauded by the underground. —Come, come, you know whom I mean by the underground. You're not active in it any longer. Your position is too exposed and you have too much to lose. You have position and power, and there is more on the way. Why risk it for something that people don't want?

"You wear your pendants, and you're numbered among the godly. But my pendant is larger and I am more godly, for I have not committed your crimes. What is more, gentlemen, I get the credit of having informed against you.

"A shameful act? A scandalous act? My informing? Not at

all. I shall be rewarded. I have been horrified at the hypocrisy of my colleagues, disgusted and nauseated at their subversive past, concerned for what they might be plotting now against the best and noblest and most godly society ever established on Earth. As a result, I brought all this to the attention of the decent men who help conduct the policies of that society in true sobriety of thought and humility of spirit.

"They will wrestle with your evils to save your souls and to make you true children of the Spirit. There will be some damage to your bodies in the process, I imagine, but what of that? It would be a trivial cost compared to the vast and eternal good they will bring you. And I shall be rewarded for making it all possible.

"I think you are really frightened now, gentlemen, for the message we have all been waiting for is now coming, and you see now why I have been asked to remain here with you. The presidency is mine, and my interpretation of the Muller theory, combined with the disgrace of Muller, will make it the Dinsmore theory in the textbooks and may bring me the Nobel Prize. As for you—"

There was the sound of footsteps in cadence outside the door; a ringing cry of "Halt!"

The door was flung open. In stepped a man whose sober gray garb, wide white collar, tall buckled hat and large bronze cross proclaimed him a captain in the dreaded Legion of Decency.

He said nasally, "Horatio Adams, I arrest you in the name of God and the Congregation of the crime of devilry and witchcraft. Carl Muller, I arrest you in the name of God and the Congregation for the crime of devilry and witchcraft."

His hand beckoned briefly and quickly. Two legionnaires from the ranks came up to the two physicists, who sat in stupefied horror in their chairs, yanked them to their feet, placed cuffs on their wrists, and with an initial gesture of humility to the sacred symbol, tore the small crosses that were pendant from their lapels.

The captain turned to Dinsmore. "Yours in sanctity, sir. I have been asked to deliver this communication from the Board of Trustees."

"Yours in sanctity, Captain," said Dinsmore gravely,

fingering his own pendant cross. "I rejoice to receive the words of those godly men."

He knew what the communication contained.

As the new president of the university, he might, if he chose, lighten the punishment of the two men. His triumph would be enough even so.

—But only if it were safe.

—And in the grip of the Moral Majority, he must remember, no one was ever *truly* safe.

14

The Figure of the Fastest

Sometimes making a careful measurement can be of supreme importance; more important than the scientists initially trying to make the measurement can realize. No one at the start, for instance, had the faintest idea how fundamental a quantity the speed of light is. And sometimes the measurement, when it is made successfully (or reasonably so), is obtained in an unexpected way from an unexpected source, as in the case described in the next essay.

As you can all imagine, I frequently receive outlines of odd theories invented by some of my readers. Most of them deal with vast concepts like the basic laws underlying all of space and time. Most of them are unreadable (or over my head, if you prefer). Many of them are produced by earnest teenagers, some by retired engineers. These theorists appear to think I possess some special ability to weigh deep and subtle concepts, combined with the imagination not to be deterred by the wildly creative.

It is all, of course, useless. I am no judge of great, new theories. All I can do is send back the material (which sometimes extends to many pages and forces me to incur substantial expense in postage) and try to explain, humbly, that I cannot help them.

Once in a while, though—once in all too long a while—I get

a letter that I find amusing. One such came years ago. It was in fourteen vituperative, increasingly incoherent, pages of prose which boiled down to a diatribe against Albert Einstein, one that came under two headings:

1) Albert Einstein had gained world renown (my correspondent said) through the advancement of a great and subtle theory of relativity which he had stolen from some poor hardworking scientist. Einstein's victim thereupon died in obscurity and neglect without ever receiving the appreciation he deserved for this monumental discovery.

2) Albert Einstein had gained world renown (my correspondent also said) by inventing a completely false and ridiculous theory of relativity, which had been foisted on the world by a conspiracy of physicists.

My correspondent argued *both* these alternately with equal vehemence and clearly never saw that they were incompatible. Naturally, I didn't answer.

But what is there that causes some people to react so violently against the theory of relativity? Most of the people who object (usually much more rationally than my unfortunate correspondent, of course) know very little about the theory. About the only thing they know (and all that almost any non-physicist knows) is that according to the theory, nothing can go faster than light, and that offends them.

I won't go into the question of why scientists believed that nothing possessing mass can go faster than light. I would, however, like to talk about the actual speed limit, the speed of light, what it actually is and how that was determined.

Olaus Roemer, the Danish astronomer, was the first to advance a reasonable figure for the speed of light through a study of the eclipses of Jupiter's satellites by Jupiter.

In 1676 he estimated that it took light 22 minutes to cross the extreme width of Earth's orbit about the Sun. At that time the total width of Earth's orbit was thought to be in the neighborhood of 174,000,000 miles, so Roemer's results implied a speed of light of 132,000 miles per second.

That is not bad. The figure is roughly 30 percent low but it is in the right ball park, and for a first effort it is quite respectable. Roemer at least determined, correctly, the first

211

figure of the value. The speed of light is indeed between 100,000 and 200,000 miles per second.

The next measurement of the speed of light came about, quite accidentally, a half-century later.

The English astronomer James Bradley was trying to detect the parallax (that is, tiny shifts in position) of the nearer stars relative to the farther ones. This shift would result from the change in the position of the Earth as it moved around the Sun.

Ideally, every star in the heaven should move in an ellipse in the course of one year, the size and shape of that ellipse depending on the distance of the star from the Sun and its position with respect to the plane of Earth's orbit.

The farther the star, the smaller the ellipse, and for all but the nearest stars, the ellipse would be too small to measure. Those farther stars could, therefore, be considered motionless, and the displacement of the nearer stars relative to them would be the parallax Bradley was looking for.

Bradley *did* detect displacements of stars, but they were not what would be expected if Earth's motion around the Sun were responsible. The displacements could not be caused by parallax but had to be caused by something else. In 1728 he was on a pleasure sail on the Thames River and noted that the pennant on top of the mast changed direction according to the relative motion of ship and wind and *not* according to the direction of the wind alone.

That set him to thinking. Suppose you are standing still in a rainstorm with all the raindrops falling vertically downward because there is no wind. If you have an umbrella, you hold it directly over your head and remain dry. If you are walking, however, you will walk into some raindrops that have just cleared the umbrella if you continue to hold the umbrella directly over your head. You must angle the umbrella a little in the direction you are walking if you want to remain dry.

The faster you walk or the slower the raindrops fall, the farther you must tilt your umbrella to avoid walking into the raindrops. The exact angle through which you must tilt your umbrella depends on the ratio of the two velocities, that of the raindrops and that of yourself.

The situation is similar in astronomy. Light is falling on the Earth from some star in some direction and at some velocity.

Meanwhile the Earth is moving around the Sun at another velocity. The telescope, like the umbrella, cannot be aimed directly at the star to gather the light but must be tilted a little in the direction the Earth is moving. (This is called "the aberration of light.") Because light is traveling very much faster than the Earth is moving in its orbit, the velocity ratio is high and the telescope must be tilted only very slightly indeed.

The tilt can be measured, and from that, the ratio of the speed of light to the speed of the Earth in its orbit can be calculated. Since the Earth's orbital speed was known with fair accuracy, the speed of light could be calculated. Bradley calculated that the speed was such that light would cross the full width of the Earth's orbit in 16 minutes, 26 seconds.

If the width of the Earth's orbit were 174,000,000 miles, this meant that light must travel at a rate of about 176,000 miles per second. This second try at the determination of the speed was considerably higher than Roemer's and considerably closer to the figure we now accept. It was still nearly 5 percent low, however.

The methods of Roemer and Bradley both involved astronomical observations and had the disadvantage of depending for their accuracy on knowledge concerning the distance of the Earth from the Sun. This knowledge was still not very precise even through the nineteenth century. (If the width of the orbit had been known as accurately in Bradley's time as it is now, his figure for the speed of light would have been within 1.6 percent of what we now consider it to be.)

Was it possible, then, to devise some method for measuring the speed of light directly by Earthbound experiments? In that case, the shakiness of astronomical statistics would be irrelevant. But how? Measuring a velocity that seems to be not too far below 200,000 miles per second presents a delicate problem.

In 1849 a French physicist, Armand Hippolyte Louis Fizeau, devised a way to turn the trick. He placed a light source on a hilltop and a mirror on another hilltop 5 miles away. Light flashed from the source to the mirror and back, a total distance of 10 miles, and it was Fizeau's intention to measure the time lapse. Since that time lapse was sure to be less than 1/10,000 of a second, Fizeau couldn't very well use a wristwatch, and he didn't.

What he did do was to place a toothed disc in front of the light source. If he held the disc motionless, the light would shoot out between two adjacent teeth, reach the mirror, and be reflected back between the teeth.

Suppose the disc were set to rotating. Light would travel so quickly that it would be at the mirror and back before the space between the teeth would have a chance to move out of the way. But now speed up the rate of rotation of the disc. At some speed the light ray would flash to the mirror and back only to find that the disc had turned sufficiently to move a tooth in the way. The reflected light ray could no longer be observed.

Make the disc move still more rapidly. The light ray would then flash outward between two teeth and be reflected back at a time when the tooth had moved past and the *next* gap was in the path of the light ray. You could see its reflection again.

If you knew how rapidly the disc rotated, you would know the fraction of a second it would take for a tooth to move in the way of the reflected ray and how long for that tooth to move out of the way of the reflected ray. You would then know how much time it took light to cover 10 miles and, therefore, how far it would go in a second.

The value Fizeau settled on turned out to be about 196,000 miles per second. This was no better than Bradley's value and was still 5 percent off, but it was now too high rather than too low.

Helping Fizeau in his experiments was another French physicist, Jean Bernard Léon Foucault. Foucault eventually went on to attempt to measure the speed of light on his own, according to a slightly different type of experiment.

In Foucault's scheme, the light still flashed from a source to a mirror and then back. Foucault arranged it, however, so that on its return, the light ray fell on a second mirror, which reflected the ray onto a screen.

Suppose, now, you set the second mirror to revolving. When the light returns, it hits the second mirror after it has changed its angle just slightly, and the light ray is then reflected on the screen in a slightly different place than it would be if the second mirror had been motionless.

Foucault set up the experiment in such a way that he was able to measure this displacement of the light ray. From this displacement and knowing how fast the second mirror was revolving, Foucault could calculate the speed of light.

Foucault's best measurement, made in 1862, was about 185,000 miles per second. This was the most nearly accurate measurement yet made. It was only 0.7 percent low, and Foucault was the first to get the second figure correct. The speed of light was indeed somewhere between 180,000 and 190,000 per second.

Foucault's measurement was so delicate that he didn't even have to use particularly great distances. He didn't use adjacent hilltops but carried out the whole thing in a laboratory with a light ray that traveled a total distance of about 66 feet.

The use of such a short distance led to something else. If light is expected to travel 10 miles, it is very difficult to have it travel through anything but air or some other gas. A liquid or solid may be transparent in short lengths, but 10 miles of any liquid or solid is simply opaque. Over a distance of 66 feet, however, it is possible to make a beam of light shine through water or through any of a variety of other media.

Foucault passed light through water and found that by his method its velocity was considerably slower, only three-fourths of its velocity in air. It turned out, in fact, that the speed of light depended on the index of refraction of the medium it traveled through. The higher the index of refraction, the lower the speed of light.

But air itself has an index of refraction too, though a very small one. Therefore, the speed of light, as measured by Fizeau and Foucault, had to be a trifle too low no matter how perfect the measurement. In order to get the maximum speed of light, one would have to measure it in a vacuum.

As it happens, the astronomical methods of Roemer and Bradley involved the passage of light through the vacuum of interplanetary and interstellar space. The light in each case also passed through the full height of the atmosphere but that length was insignificant compared to the millions of miles of vacuum the light had crossed. However, the astronomical methods of the eighteenth and nineteenth centuries had sources of error that utterly swamped the tiny advantage inherent in substituting vacuum for air.

The next important figure in the determination of the speed of light was the German-American physicist Albert Abraham Michelson. He began working on the problem in 1878 by using Foucault's scheme but improving the accuracy considerably. Whereas Foucault had to work with a displacement of the spot of light of only a little over 1/40 of an inch, Michelson managed to produce a displacement of some 5 inches.

In 1879 he reported the speed of light to be 186,355 miles per second. This value is only 0.04 percent too high and was by far the most accurate yet obtained. Michelson was the first to get the third figure right, for the speed of light was indeed betwen 186,000 and 187,000 miles per second.

Michelson kept working, using every possible way of increasing the precision of the measurement, especially since, by 1905, Einstein's theory of relativity made the speed of light seem a fundamental constant of the Universe.

In 1923 Michelson picked two mountaintops in California, two that were not 5 miles apart as Fizeau's had been, but 22 miles apart. He surveyed the distance between them till he had that down to the nearest inch! He used a special eight-sided revolving mirror and by 1927 announced that the speed of light was about 186,295 miles per second. This was only 0.007 percent too high, and now he had the first four figures correct. The speed of light was indeed between 186,200 and 186,300 miles per second.

Michelson still wasn't satisfied. He wanted the speed of light *in a vacuum*. It was that speed and nothing else that was a fundamental constant of the Universe.

Michelson therefore used a long tube of accurately known length and evacuated it. Within it he set up a system that sent light back and forth in that tube till he made it pass through 10 miles of vacuum. Over and over he made his measurements, and it wasn't till 1933 that the final figure was announced (two years after he had died).

The final figure was 186,271 miles per second, and that was

a small further approach to the truth, for it was only 0.006 percent too low.

In the four decades since Michelson's final determinaton, physicists have developed a variety of new techniques and instruments which might be applied to the determination of the speed of light.

For instance, it became possible to produce light of a single wavelength by means of a laser beam and to measure that wavelength to a high degree of precision. It was also possible to determine the frequency of the wavelength (the number of oscillations per second) with equally high precision.

If you multiply the length of one wavelength by the number of wavelengths per second, the product is the distance covered by light in one second—in other words, the speed of light.

This was done with greater and greater precision, and in October 1972 by far the most accurate measurement ever made was announced by a research team headed by Kenneth M. Evenson, working with a chain of laser beams at the National Bureau of Standards laboratories in Boulder, Colorado.

The speed they announced was 186,282.3959 miles per second.

The accuracy of the measurement is within a yard in either direction so, since there are 1,760 yards in a mile, we can say that the speed of light is somewhere between 327,857,015 and 327,857,017 yards per second.

Of course I have been giving all the measurements in common units of miles, yards and so on. Despite all my scientific training, I still can't visualize measurements in the metric system. It's the fault of the stupid education all American children get—but that's another story.

Still, if I don't think in the metric system instinctively, I can at least handle it mathematically and I intend to use it more and more in these essays. The proper way to give the speed of light is not in miles per second or in yards per second, but in kilometers per second and in meters per second. Using the proper language, the speed of light is now set at 299,792.4562 kilometers per second. If we multiply it by 1,000 (the beauty of the metric system is that so many multiplications and divisions are so simple), it is equal to 299,792,456.2 meters per second, give or take a meter.

There are few measurements we can make that are as accurate as the present value of the speed of light. One of them is the length of the year which is, in fact, known with even greater precision.

Since the number of seconds in a year is 31,556,925.9747, we can calculate the length of a light-year (the distance light will travel in one year) as 5,878,499,776,000 miles, or 9,460,563,614,000 kilometers. (There's no use trying to figure out that final 000. Even now the speed of light is not accurately enough known to give the light-year to closer than a thousand miles or so.)

All these figures are, of course, un-round and are troublesome to memorize exactly. This is too bad since the speed of light is so fundamental a quantity, but it is to be expected. The various units—miles, kilometers, and seconds—were all determined for reasons that had nothing to do with the speed of light and therefore it is in the highest degree unlikely that that speed would come out even. That we even come near a round figure is merely a highly fortunate coincidence.

In miles per second, the common value given for the speed of light in, let us say, a newspaper story, is 186,000 miles per second, which is only 0.15 percent low. This is good enough but there are three figures that must be memorized—186.

In kilometers per second we have a much better situation, since if we say the speed of light is 300,000 kilometers per second, we are only 0.07 percent low. The approximation is twice as close as in the miles-per-second case, and only one figure need be remembered, the 3. (Of course you must also remember the order of magnitude—that the speed is in the hundreds of thousands of kilometers per second and not in the tens of thousands or in the millions.)

The beauty of the metric system again displays itself. The fact that the speed of light is about 300,000 kilometers per second means that it is about 300,000,000 meters per second and about 30,000,000,000 centimeters per second, all three figures being at the same approximation to the truth.

If we use exponential figures, we can say that the speed of light is 3×10^5 kilometers per second, or 3×10^8 meters per second, or 3×10^{10} centimeters per second. You need only memorize one of these since the others are easily calculated from the one, provided you understand the metric system. The exponential figure 10^{10} is particularly easy to remember, so if you associate that with "centimeters per second" and then don't forget to multipy it by 3, you've got it made.

The fact that the speed of light is so close to a pretty round number in the metric system is, of course, a coincidence. Let's locate that coincidence.

One of the most convenient measures of distance that people use is the distance from the nose to the tip of the fingers of an arm stretched horizontally away from the body. You can imagine someone selling a length of textile or rope or anything flexible by stretching out successive lengths in this manner. Consequently, almost every culture has some common unit of about this length. In the Anglo-American culture it is the "yard."

When the French Revolutionary committee was preparing a new system of measurements in the 1790s, they needed a fundamental unit of length to begin with and it was natural to choose one that would approximate the good old nose-to-fingertip length. To make it non-anthropocentric, however, they wanted to tie it to some natural measurement.

In the previous decades, as it happened, Frenchmen had taken the lead in two expeditions designed to make exact measurements of the curvature of the Earth in order to see if it were flattened at the poles, as Isaac Newton had predicted. That placed the exact size and shape of the Earth very much in the consciousness of French intellectuals.

The Earth proved to be slightly flattened, so the circumference of the Earth passing through both poles was somewhat less than the circumference around the equator. It seemed very up-to-date to recognize this by tying the fundamental unit of length to one of these particularly. The polar circumference was chosen because one of these could be made to go through Paris, whereas the equatorial circumference (the one and only) certainly did not go through that City of Light.

By the measurements of the time, the polar circumference was roughly equal to 44,000,000 yards, and that quadrant of

219

the circumference from the equator to the North Pole, passing through Paris, was about 11,000,000 yards long. It was decided to make the length of the quadrant just 10,000,000 times the fundamental unit and to define the new units as 1/10,000,000 of that quadrant and give it the name of "meter."

This definiton of the meter was romantic but foolish, for it implied that the polar circumference was known with great precision, which of course it was not. As better measurements of the Earth's vital statistics were made, it turned out that the quadrant was very slightly longer than had been thought. The length of the meter could not be adjusted to suit—too many measurements had already been made with it; and the quadrant is now know to be *not* 10,000,000 meters long as it ought to be by French logic, but 10,002,288.3 meters long.

Of course the meter is no longer tied to the Earth. It was eventualy defined as the distance between two marks on a platinum-iridium rod kept with great care in a vault at constant temperature and, finally, as so many wavelengths of a particular ray of light (the orange-red light emitted by the noble gas isotope krypton-86, to be exact).

Now for the coincidences.

1) It so happens that the speed of light is very close to 648,000 times as great as the speed at which the Earth's surface at the equator moves as our planet rotates on its axis. This is just a coincidence, for the Earth could be rotating at any velocity and was in the past rotating considerably faster and will in the future be rotating considerably slower.

2) A single rotation of the Earth is defined as a day and our short units of time are based on exact divisions of the day. Thanks to the Babylonians and their predecessors, we use the factors 24 and 60 in dividing the day into smaller units, and by coincidence, 24 and 60 are also factors of 648,000. As a result of coincidences 1 and 2, anything moving at the speed of light will make a complete circle at Earth's equator almost exactly 450 times per minute, or almost exactly 7.5 times per second—which are simple numbers.

3) Since, by a third coincidence, the French commissioners decided to tie the meter to the circumference of the Earth and make it an even fraction of that circumference, the result is an inevitable near-round number for the speed of light in the

metric system. There are 40,000,000 meters (roughly) to Earth's circumference and if you multiply this by 7.5, you come out with 300,000,000 meters per second.

Can we do better? Can we just have an exponential figure without having to multiply it? Can we express the speed as a certain number of units of length per unit of time with a number that consists of a 1 followed by a number of zeros and come fairly close to the truth?

If we multiply 3 by 36 we come out with a product of 108. If we remember that there are 3,600 seconds in the hour, it follows that the speed of light is 1,079,252,842 kilometers per hour. This is just about eight percent over the figure of 1,000,000,000 kilometers per hour. If we were to say that the speed of light is 10^9 kilometers per hour, we'd be only 8 percent low of the facts and that's not too bad, I suppose.

As for the light-year, we can say it is 6,000,000,000,000 (six trillion) miles and be only 2 percent high. To express that exponentially, however, we must say 6×10^{12} miles, and that multiplication by 6 is a nuisance. In the metric system we can say that a light-year is ten trillion kilometers, or 10^{13} kilometers, and be only 6 percent high. The lesser accuracy might be more than counterbalanced by the elegance of the simple figure 10^{13}.

However, honesty compels me to say that the despised common measurements happen to offer a closer way of approaching the light-year in a purely exponential way. If we say the light-year is equal to 10^{16} yards, we are only 3.5 percent high.

15

The Dead Past

The scientist isn't always a hero. Think of the scientists who developed the nuclear bomb and those who are working on weapons development today. It's hard to fit them out with white hats.

But what is "good" and what is "bad"? The nuclear bomb is "bad," but we were in a death struggle with that malignant villain, Adolf Hitler, back in 1942. What if he had gotten the bomb first?

Then, too, even something which is clearly "good" may have unexpectedly "bad" side effects, and vice versa. I tackle that problem in the following story, in which (as though that weren't enough) I also consider the increasing difficulty of scientific communicaton as the content of science grows steadily greater and the specialization of scientists steadily more extreme.

Arnold Potterley, PhD, was a Professor of Ancient History. That in itself was not dangerous. What changed the world beyond all dreams was the fact that he *looked* like a Professor of Ancient History.

Thaddeus Araman, Department Head of the Division of Chronoscopy, might have taken proper action if Dr. Potterley had been owner of a large, square chin, flashing eyes, aquiline nose and broad shoulders.

As it was, Thaddeus Araman found himself staring over his desk at a mild-mannered individual whose faded blue eyes looked at him wistfully from either side of a low-bridged button nose; whose small, neatly dressed figure seemed stamped "milk-and-water" from thinning brown hair to the neatly brushed shoes that complete a conservative middle-class costume.

Araman said pleasantly, "And now what can I do for you, Dr. Potterley?"

Dr. Potterley said in a soft voice that went well with the rest of him. "Mr. Araman, I came to you because you're top man in chronoscopy."

Araman smiled. "Not exactly. Above me is the World Commissioner of Research and above him is the Secretary-General of the United Nations. And above both of them, of course, are the sovereign peoples of Earth."

Dr. Potterley shook his head. "They're not interested in chronoscopy. I've come to you, sir, because for two years I have been trying to obtain permission to do some time-viewing—chronoscopy, that is—in connection with my researches on ancient Carthage. I can't obtain such permission. My research grants are all proper. There is no irregularity in any of my intellectual endeavors and yet—"

"I'm sure there is no question of irregularity," said Araman soothingly. He flipped the thin reproduction sheets in the folder to which Potterley's name had been attached. They had been produced by Multivac, whose vast analogical mind kept all the department records. When this was over, the sheets could be destroyed, then reproduced on demand in a matter of minutes.

And while Araman turned the pages, Dr. Potterley's voice continued in a soft monotone.

The historian was saying, "I must explain that my problem is quite an important one. Carthage was ancient commercialism brought to its zenith. Pre-Roman Carthage was the nearest ancient analogue to pre-atomic America, at least insofar as its attachment to trade, commerce and business in general was concerned. They were the most daring seamen and explorers before the Vikings; much better at it than the overrated Greeks.

"To know Carthage would be very rewarding, yet the only knowledge we have of it is derived from the writings of its bitter enemies, the Greeks and Romans. Carthage itself never wrote in its own defense or, if it did, the books did not survive. As a result, the Carthaginians have been one of the favorite sets of villains of history and perhaps unjustly so. Time-viewing may set the record straight."

He said much more.

Araman said, still turning the reproduction sheets before him, "You must realize, Dr. Potterley, that chronoscopy, or time-viewing, if you prefer, is a difficult process."

Dr. Potterley, who had been interrupted, frowned and said, "I am asking for only certain selected views at times and places I would indicate."

Araman sighed. "Even a few views, even one. . . . It is an unbelievably delicate art. There is the question of focus, getting the proper scene in view and holding it. There is the synchronization of sound, which calls for completely independent circuits."

"Surely my problem is important enough to justify considerable effort."

"Yes, sir. Undoubtedly," said Araman at once. To deny the importance of someone's research problem would be unforgivably bad manners. "But you must understand how long-drawn-out even the simplest view is. And there is a long waiting line for the chronoscope and an even longer waiting line for the use of Multivac, which guides us in our use of the controls."

Potterley stirred unhappily. "But can nothing be done? For two years—"

"A matter of priority, sir. I'm sorry. . . . Cigarette?"

The historian started back at the suggestion, eyes suddenly widening as he stared at the pack thrust out toward him. Araman looked surprised, withdrew the pack, made a motion as though to take a cigarette for himself and thought better of it.

Potterley drew a sigh of unfeigned relief as the pack was put out of sight. He said, "Is there any way of reviewing matters, putting me as far forward as possible? I don't know how to explain—"

Araman smiled. Some had offered money under similar circumstances, which, of course, had gotten them nowhere either. He said, "The decisions on priority are computer-processed. I could in no way alter those decisions arbitrarily."

Potterley rose stiffly to his feet. He stood five and a half feet tall. "Then, good day, sir."

"Good day, Dr. Potterley. And my sincerest regrets."

He offered his hand and Potterley touched it briefly.

The historian left, and a touch of the buzzer brought Araman's secretary into the room. He handed her the folder.

"These," he said, "may be disposed of."

Alone again, he smiled bitterly. Another item in his quarter-century's service to the human race. Service through negation.

At least this fellow had been easy to dispose of. Sometimes academic pressure had to be applied, and even withdrawal of grants.

Five minutes later he had forgotten Dr. Potterley. Nor, thinking back on it later, could he remember feeling any premonition of danger.

During the first year of his frustration, Arnold Potterley had experienced only that—frustration. During the second year, though, his frustration gave birth to an idea that first frightened and then fascinated him. Two things stopped him from trying to translate the idea into action, and neither barrier was the undoubted fact that his notion was a grossly unethical one.

The first was merely the continuing hope that the government would finally give its permission and make it unnecessary for him to do anything more. That hope had perished finally in the interview with Araman just completed.

The second barrier had been not a hope at all but a dreary realization of his own incapacity. He was not a physicist and he knew no physicists from whom he might obtain help. The Department of Physics at the university consisted of men well stocked with grants and well immersed in specialty. At best, they would not listen to him. At worst, they would report him for intellectual anarchy and even his basic Carthaginian grant might easily be withdrawn.

That he could not risk. And yet chronoscopy was the only way to carry on his work. Without it, he would be no worse off if his grant were lost.

The first hint that the second barrier might be overcome had come a week earlier than his interview with Araman, and it had gone unrecognized at the time. It had been at one of the faculty teas. Potterley attended these sessions unfailingly because he conceived attendance to be a duty, and he took his duties seriously. Once there, however, he conceived it to be no responsibility of his to make light conversation or new friends. He sipped abstemiously at a drink or two, exchanged a polite word with the dean or such department heads as happened to be present, bestowed a narrow smile on others and finally left early.

Ordinarily he would have paid no attention, at that most recent tea, to a young man standing quietly, even diffidently, in one corner. He would never have dreamed of speaking to him. Yet a tangle of circumstance persuaded him this once to behave in a way contrary to his nature.

That morning at breakfast, Mrs. Potterley had announced somberly that once again she had dreamed of Laurel; but this time a Laurel grown up, yet retaining the three-year-old face that stamped her as their child. Potterley had let her talk. There had been a time when he fought her too frequent preoccupation with the past and death. Laurel would not come back to them, either through dreams or through talk. Yet if it appeased Caroline Potterley—let her dream and talk.

But when Potterley went to school that morning, he found himself for once affected by Caroline's inanities. Laurel grown up! She had died nearly twenty years ago; their only child, then and ever. In all that time, when he thought of her, it was as a three-year-old.

Now he thought: But if she were alive now, she wouldn't be three; she'd be nearly twenty-three.

Helplessly he found himself trying to think of Laurel as growing progressively older, as finally becoming twenty-three. He did not quite succeed.

Yet he tried. Laurel using makeup. Laurel going out with boys. Laurel—getting married!

So it was that when he saw the young man hovering at the outskirts of the coldly circulating group of faculty men, it occurred to him quixotically that, for all he knew, a youngster just such as this might have married Laurel. That youngster himself, perhaps. . . .

226

Laurel might have met him here at the university, or some evening when he might be invited to dinner at the Potterleys'. They might grow interested in one another. Laurel would surely have been pretty and this youngster looked well. He was dark in coloring, with a lean, intent face and an easy carriage.

The tenuous daydream snapped, yet Potterley found himself staring foolishly at the young man, not as a strange face but as a possible son-in-law in the might-have-been. He found himself threading his way toward the man. It was almost a form of autohypnotism.

He put out his hand. "I am Arnold Potterley of the History Department. You're new here, I think?"

The youngster looked faintly astonished and fumbled with his drink, shifting it to his left hand in order to shake with his right. "Jonas Foster is my name, sir. I'm a new instructor in physics. I'm just starting this semester."

Potterley nodded. "I wish you a happy stay here and great success."

That was the end of it then. Potterley had come uneasily to his senses, found himself embarrassed and moved off. He stared back over his shoulder once, but the illusion of relationship had gone. Reality was quite real once more and he was angry with himself for having fallen prey to his wife's foolish talk about Laurel.

But a week later, even while Araman was talking, the thought of that young man had come back to him. An instructor in physics. A new instructor. Had he been deaf at the time? Was there a short circuit between ear and brain? Or was it an automatic self-censorship because of the impending interview with the Head of Chronoscopy?

But the interview failed, and it was the thought of the young man with whom he had exchanged two sentences that prevented Potterley from elaborating his pleas for consideration. He was almost anxious to get away.

And in the autogiro express back to the university, he could almost wish he were superstitious. He could then console himself with the thought that the casual meaningless meeting had really been directed by a knowing and purposeful Fate.

* .* *

227

Jonas Foster was not new to academic life. The long and rickety struggle for the doctorate would make anyone a veteran. Additional work as a postdoctorate teaching fellow acted as a booster shot.

But now he was Instructor Jonas Foster. Professorial dignity lay ahead. And he now found himself in a new sort of relationship toward other professors.

For one thing, they would be voting on future promotions. For another, he was in no position to tell so early in the game which particular member of the faculty might or might not have the ear of the dean, or even of the university president. He did not fancy himself as a campus politician and was sure he would make a poor one, yet there was no point in kicking his own rear into blisters just to prove that to himself.

So Foster listened to this mild-mannered historian, who in some vague way seemed nevertheless to radiate tension, and did not shut him up abruptly and toss him out. Certainly that was his first impulse.

He remembered Potterly well enough. Potterley had approached him at that tea (which had been a grisly affair). The fellow had spoken two sentences to him stiffly, somehow glassy-eyed, and then come to himself with a visible start and hurried off.

It had amused Foster at the time, but now. . . .

Potterley might have been deliberately trying to make his acquaintance, or, rather, to impress his own personality on Foster as that of a queer sort of duck, eccentric but harmless. He might now be probing Foster's views, searching for unsettling opinions. Surely they ought to have done so before granting him his appointment. Still. . . .

Potterley might be serious, might honestly not realize what he was doing. Or he might realize quite well what he was doing; he might be nothing more or less than a dangerous rascal.

Foster mumbled, "Well, now—" to gain time and fished out a package of cigarettes, intending to offer one to Potterley and to light it and one for himself very slowly.

But Potterley said at once, "Please, Dr. Foster. No cigarettes."

Foster looked startled. "I'm sorry, sir."

"No. The regrets are mine. I cannot stand the odor. An idiosyncrasy. I'm sorry."

He was positively pale. Foster put away the cigarettes.

Foster, feeling the absence of the cigarette, took the easy way out. "I'm flattered that you ask my advice and all that, Dr. Potterley, but I'm not a neutrinics man. I can't very well do anything professional in that direction. Even stating an opinion would be out of line, and, frankly, I'd prefer that you didn't go into any particulars."

The historian's prim face set hard. "What do you mean, you're not a neutrinics man? You're not anything yet. You haven't received any grant, have you?"

"This is only my first semester."

"I know that. I imagine you haven't even applied for any grant yet."

Foster half-smiled. In three months at the university he had not succeeded in putting his initial requests for research grants into good enough shape to pass on to a professional science writer, let alone to the Research Commission.

(His department head, fortunately, took it quite well. "Take your time now, Foster," he said, "and get your thoughts well organized. Make sure you know your path and where it will lead, for once you receive a grant, your specialization will be formally recognized and, for better or for worse, it will be yours for the rest of your career." The advice was trite enough, but triteness has often the merit of truth, and Foster recognized that.)

Foster said, "By education and inclination, Dr. Potterley, I'm a hyperoptics man with a gravitics minor. It's how I described myself in applying for this position. It may not be my official specialization yet, but it's going to be. It can't be anything else. As for neutrinics, I never even studied the subject."

"Why not?" demanded Potterley at once.

Foster stared. It was the kind of rude curiosity about another man's professional status that was always irritating. He said, with the edge of his own politeness just a trifle blunted, "A course in neutrinics wasn't given at my university."

"Good Lord, where did you go?"

"M.I.T.," said Foster quietly.

"And they don't teach neutrinics?"

"No, they don't." Foster felt himself flush and was moved to a defense. "It's a highly specialized subject with no great value. Chronoscopy, perhaps, has some value, but it is the only practical application and that's a dead end."

The historian stared at him earnestly. "Tell me this. Do you know where I can find a neutrinics man?"

"No, I don't," said Foster bluntly.

"Well, then, do you know a school which teaches neutrinics?"

"No, I don't."

Potterley smiled tightly and without humor.

Foster resented that smile, found he detected insult in it and grew sufficiently annoyed to say, "I would like to point out, sir, that you're stepping out of line."

"What?"

"I'm saying that, as a historian, your interest in any sort of physics, your *professional* interest, is—" He paused, unable to bring himself quite to say the word.

"Unethical?"

"That's the word, Dr. Potterley."

"My researches have driven me to it," said Potterley in an intense whisper.

"The Research Commission is the place to go. If they permit—"

"I have gone to them and have received no satisfaction."

"Then obviously you must abandon this." Foster knew he was sounding stuffily virtuous, but he wasn't going to let this man lure him into an expression of intellectual anarchy. It was too early in his career to take stupid risks.

Apparently, though, the remark had its effect on Potterley. Without any warning, the man exploded into a rapid-fire verbal storm of irresponsibility.

Scholars, he said, could be free only if they could freely follow their own free-swinging curiosity. Research, he said, forced into a predesigned pattern by the powers that held the purse strings became slavish and had to stagnate. No man, he said, had the right to dictate the intellectual interests of another.

Foster listened to all of it with disbelief. None of it was

strange to him. He had heard college boys talk so in order to shock their professors, and he had once or twice amused himself in that fashion too. Anyone who studied the history of science knew that many men had once thought so.

Yet it seemed strange to Foster, almost against nature, that a modern man of science could advance such nonsense. No one would advocate running a factory by allowing each individual worker to do whatever pleased him at the moment, or of running a ship according to the casual and conflicting notions of each individual crewman. It would be taken for granted that some sort of centralized supervisory agency must exist in each case. Why should direction and order benefit a factory and a ship but not scientific research?

People might say that the human mind was somehow qualitatively different from a ship or factory, but the history of intellectual endeavor proved the opposite.

When science was young and the intricacies of all or most of the known was within the grasp of an individual mind, there was no need for direction, perhaps. Blind wandering over the uncharted tracts of ignorance could lead to wonderful finds by accident.

But as knowledge grew, more and more data had to be absorbed before worthwhile journeys into ignorance could be organized. Men had to specialize. The researcher needed the resources of a library he himself could not gather, then of instruments he himself could not afford. More and more, the individual researcher gave way to the research team and the research institution.

The funds necessary for research grew greater as tools grew more numerous. What college was so small today as not to require at least one nuclear microreactor and at least one three-stage computer?

Centuries before, private individuals could no longer subsidize research. By 1940 only the government, large industries and large universities or research institutions could properly subsidize basic research.

By 1960 even the largest universities depended entirely upon government grants, while research institutions could not exist without tax concessions and public subscriptions. By 2000 the industrial combines had become a branch of the

231

world government, and thereafter the financing of research, and therefore its direction, naturally became centralized under a department of the government.

It all worked itself out naturally and well. Every branch of science was fitted neatly to the needs of the public, and the various branches of science were coordinated decently. The material advance of the last half-century was argument enough for the fact that science was not falling into stagnation.

Foster tried to say a very little of this and was waved aside impatiently by Potterley, who said, "You are parroting official propaganda. You're sitting in the middle of an example that's squarely against the official view. Can you believe that?"

"Frankly, no."

"Well, why do you say time-viewing is a dead end? Why is neutrinics unimportant? You say it is. You say it categorically. Yet you've never studied it. You claim complete ignorance of the subject. It's not even given in your school—"

"Isn't the mere fact that it isn't given proof enough?"

"Oh, I see. It's not given because it's unimportant. And it's unimportant because it's not given. Are you satisfied with that reasoning?"

Foster felt a growing confusion. "It's all in the books."

"That's all? The books say neutrinics is unimportant. Your professors tell you so because they read it in the books. The books say so because professors write them. Who says it from personal experience and knowledge? Who does research in it? Do you know of anyone?"

Foster said, "I don't see that we're getting anywhere, Dr. Potterley. I have work to do—"

"One minute. I just want you to try this on. See how it sounds to you. I say the government is actively suppressing basic research in neutrinics and chronoscopy. They're suppressing application of chronoscopy."

"Oh, no."

"Why not? They could do it. There's your centrally directed research. If they refuse grants for research in any portion of science, that portion dies. They've killed neutrinics. They can do it and have done it."

"But why?"

"I don't know why. I want to find out. I'd do it myself if I knew enough. I came to you because you're a young fellow with a brand-new education. Have your intellectual arteries hardened already? Is there no curiosity in you? Don't you want to *know?* Don't you want *answers?"*

The historian was peering intently into Foster's face. Their noses were only inches apart, and Foster was so lost that he did not think to draw back.

He should, by rights, have ordered Potterley out. If necessary, he should have thrown Potterley out.

It was not respect for age and position that stopped him. It was certainly not that Potterley's arguments had convinced him. Rather, it was a small point of college pride.

Why didn't M.I.T. give a course in neutrinics? For that matter, now that he came to think of it, he doubted that there was a single book on neutrinics in the library. He could never recall having seen one.

He stopped to think about that.

And that was ruin.

Caroline Potterley had once been an attractive woman. There were occasions, such as dinners or university functions, when, by considerable effort, remnants of the attraction could be salvaged.

On ordinary occasions, she sagged. It was the word she applied to herself in moments of self-abhorrence. She had grown plumper with the years, but the flaccidity about her was not a matter of fat entirely. It was as though her muscles had given up and grown limp so that she shuffled when she walked while her eyes grew baggy and her cheeks jowly. Even her graying hair seemed tired rather than merely stringy. Its straightness seemed to be the result of a supine surrender to gravity, nothing else.

Caroline Potterley looked at herself in the mirror and admitted this was one of her bad days. She knew the reason too.

It had been the dream of Laurel. The strange one, with Laurel grown up. She had been wretched ever since.

Still, she was sorry she had mentioned it to Arnold. He didn't say anything; he never did anymore; but it was bad for him. He was particularly withdrawn for days afterward. It might have been that he was getting ready for that important conference with the big government official (he kept saying he expected no success), but it might also have been her dream.

It was better in the old days when he would cry sharply at her, "Let the dead past *go*, Caroline! Talk won't bring her back, and dreams won't either."

It had been bad for both of them. Horribly bad. She had been away from home and had lived in guilt ever since. If she had stayed at home, if she had not gone on an unnecessary shopping expedition, there would have been two of them available. One would have succeeded in saving Laurel.

Poor Arnold had not managed. Heaven knew he tried. He had nearly died himself. He had come out of the burning house, staggering in agony, blistered, choking, half-blinded, with the dead Laurel in his arms.

The nightmare of that lived on, never lifting entirely.

Arnold slowly grew a shell about himself afterward. He cultivated a low-voiced mildness through which nothing broke, no lightning struck. He grew puritanical and even abandoned his minor vices, his cigarettes, his penchant for an occasional profane exclamation. He obtained his grant for the preparation of a new history of Carthage and subordinated everything to that.

She tried to help him. She hunted up his references, typed his notes and microfilmed them. Then that ended suddenly.

She ran from the desk suddenly one evening, reaching the bathroom in bare time and retching abominably. Her husband followed her in confusion and concern.

"Caroline, what's wrong?"

It took a drop of brandy to bring her around. She said, "Is it true? What they did?"

"Who did?"

"The Carthaginians."

He stared at her and she got it out by indirection. She couldn't say it right out.

The Carthaginians, it seemed, worshiped Moloch, in the form of a hollow, brazen idol with a furnace in its belly. At times of national crisis, the priests and the people gathered, and infants, after the proper ceremonies and invocations, were dextrously hurled, alive, into the flames.

They were given sweetmeats just before the crucial moment in order that the efficacy of the sacrifice not be ruined by displeasing cries of panic. The drums rolled just after the moment, to drown out the few seconds of infant shrieking. The parents were present, presumably gratified, for the sacrifice was pleasing to the gods. . . .

Arnold Potterley frowned darkly. Vicious lies, he told her, on the part of Carthage's enemies. He should have warned her. After all, such propagandistic lies were not uncommon. According to the Greeks, the ancient Hebrews worshiped an ass's head in their Holy of Holies. According to the Romans, the primitive Christians were haters of all men who sacrificed pagan children in the catacombs.

"Then they didn't do it?" asked Caroline.

"I'm sure they didn't. The primitive Phoenicians may have. Human sacrifice is commonplace in primitive cultures. But Carthage in her great days was not a primitive culture. Human sacrifice often gives way to symbolic actions such as circumcision. The Greeks and Romans might have mistaken some Carthaginian symbolism for the original full rite, either out of ignorance or out of malice."

"Are you sure?"

"I can't be sure yet, Caroline, but when I've got enough evidence, I'll apply for permission to use chronoscopy, which will settle the matter once and for all."

"Chronoscopy?"

"Time-viewing. We can focus on ancient Carthage at some time of crisis, the landing of Scipio Africanus in 202 B.C., for instance, and see with our own eyes exactly what happens. And you'll see, I'll be right."

He patted her and smiled encouragingly, but she dreamed of Laurel every night for two weeks thereafter and she never helped him with his Carthage project again. Nor did he ever ask her to.

But now she was bracing herself for his coming. He had called her after arriving back in town, told her he had seen the government man and that it had gone as expected. That meant failure, and yet the little telltale sign of depression had been absent from his voice and his features had appeared quite

235

composed in the teleview. He had another errand to take care of, he said, before coming home.

It meant he would be late, but that didn't matter. Neither one of them was particular about eating hours or cared when packages were taken out of the freezer or even which packages or when the self-warming mechanism was activated.

When he did arrive, he surprised her. There was nothing untoward about him in any obvious way. He kissed her dutifully and smiled, took off his hat and asked if all had been well while he was gone. It was almost perfectly normal. Almost.

She had learned to detect small things, though, and his pace in all this was a trifle hurried. Enough to show her accustomed eye that he was under tension.

She said, "Has something happened?"

He said, "We're going to have a dinner guest night after next, Caroline. You don't mind?"

"Well, no. Is it anyone I know?"

"No. A young instructor. A newcomer. I've spoken to him." He suddenly whirled toward her and seized her arms at the elbow, held them a moment, then dropped them in confusion as though disconcerted at having shown emotion.

He said, "I almost didn't get through to him. Imagine that. Terrible, *terrible*, the way we have all bent to the yoke, the affection we have for the harness about us."

Mrs. Potterley wasn't sure she understood, but for a year she had been watching him grow quietly more rebellious, little by little more daring in his criticism of the government. She said, "You haven't spoken foolishly to him, have you?"

"What do you mean, foolishly? He'll be doing some neutrinics for me."

"Neutrinics" was trisyllabic nonsense to Mrs. Potterley, but she knew it had nothing to do with history. She said faintly, "Arnold, I don't like you to do that. You'll lose your position. It's—"

"It's intellectual anarchy, my dear," he said. "That's the phrase you want. Very well. I am an anarchist. If the government will not allow me to push my researches, I will push them on my own. And when I show the way, others will

236

follow. . . . And if they don't, it makes no difference. It's Carthage that counts and human knowledge, not you and I."

"But you don't know this young man. What if he is an agent for the Commissioner of Research?"

"Not likely, and I'll take that chance." He made a fist of his right hand and rubbed it gently against the palm of his left. "He's on my side now. I'm sure of it. He can't help but be. I can recognize intellectual curiosity when I see it in a man's eyes and face and attitude, and it's a fatal disease for a tame scientist. Even today it takes time to beat it out of a man, and the young ones are vulnerable. . . . Oh, why stop at anything? Why not build our own chronoscope and tell the government to go to—"

He stopped abruptly, shook his head and turned away.

"I hope everything will be all right," said Mrs. Potterley, feeling helplessly certain that everything would not be, and frightened, in advance, for her husband's professional status and the security of their old age.

It was she alone, of them all, who had a violent presentiment of trouble. Quite the wrong trouble, of course.

Jonas Foster was nearly half an hour late in arriving at the Potterleys' off-campus house. Up to that very evening he had not quite decided he would go. Then, at the last moment, he found he could not bring himself to commit the social enormity of breaking a dinner appointment an hour before the appointed time. That, and the nagging of curiosity.

The dinner itself passed interminably. Foster ate without appetite. Mrs. Potterley sat in distant absentmindedness, emerging out of it only once to ask if he were married and to make a deprecating sound at the news that he was not. Dr. Potterley himself asked neutrally after his professional history and nodded his head primly.

It was as staid, stodgy—boring, actually—as anything could be.

Foster thought: He seems so harmless.

Foster had spent the last two days reading up on Dr. Potterley. Very casually, of course, almost sneakily. He wasn't particularly anxious to be seen in the social-science library. To be sure, history was one of those borderline affairs, and historical works were frequently read for amusement or edification by the general public.

Still, a physicist wasn't quite the "general public." Let Foster take to reading histories and he would be considered queer, sure as relativity, and after a while the head of the department would wonder if his new instructor were really "the man for the job."

So he had been cautious. He sat in the more secluded alcoves and kept his head bent when he slipped in and out at odd hours.

Dr. Potterley, it turned out, had written three books and some dozen articles on the ancient Mediterranean worlds, and the later articles (all in *Historical Reviews*) had all dealt with pre-Roman Carthage from a sympathetic viewpoint.

That, at least, checked with Potterley's story and had soothed Foster's suspicions somewhat. . . . And yet Foster felt that it would have been much wiser, much safer, to have scotched the matter at the beginning.

A scientist shouldn't be too curious, he thought in bitter dissatisfaction with himself. It's a dangerous trait.

After dinner he was ushered into Potterley's study and he was brought up sharply at the threshold. The walls were simply lined with books.

Not merely films. There were films, of course, but these were far outnumbered by the books—print on paper. He wouldn't have thought so many books would exist in usable condition.

That bothered Foster. Why should anyone want to keep so many books at home? Surely all were available in the university library, or, at the very worst, at the Library of Congress, if one wished to take the minor trouble of checking out a microfilm.

There was an element of secrecy involved in a home library. It breathed of intellectual anarchy. That last thought, oddly, calmed Foster. He would rather Potterley be an authentic anarchist than a play-acting *agent provocateur*.

And now the hours began to pass quickly and astonishingly.

"You see," Potterley said in a clear, unflurried voice, "it was a matter of finding, if possible, anyone who had ever used chronoscopy in his work. Naturally I couldn't ask baldly, since that would be unauthorized research."

"Yes," said Foster dryly. He was a little surprised that such a small consideration would stop the man.

"I used indirect methods—"

He had. Foster was amazed at the volume of correspondence dealing with small, disputed points of ancient Mediterranean culture which somehow managed to elicit the casual remark over and over again: "Of course, having never made use of chronoscopy—" or, "Pending approval of my request for chronoscopic data, which appears unlikely at the moment—"

"Now these aren't blind questionings," said Potterley. "There's a monthly booklet put out by the Institute for Chronoscopy in which items concerning the past as determined by time-viewing are printed. Just one or two items.

"What impressed me first was the triviality of most of the items, their insipidity. Why should such researches get priority over my work? So I wrote to people who would be most likely to do research in the directions described in the booklet. Uniformly, as I have shown you, they did *not* make use of the chronoscope. Now let's go over it point by point."

At last Foster, his head swimming with Potterley's meticulously gathered details, asked, "But why?"

"I don't know why," said Potterley, "but I have a theory. The original invention of the chronoscope was by Sterbinski— you see, I know that much—and it was well publicized. Then the government took over the instrument and decided to suppress further research in the matter or any use of the machine. But then people might be curious as to why it wasn't being used. Curiosity is such a vice, Dr. Foster."

Yes, agreed the physicist to himself.

"Imagine the effectiveness, then," Potterley went on, "of pretending that the chronoscope was being used. It would then be not a mystery, but a commonplace. It would no longer be a fitting object for legitimate curiosity or an attractive one for illicit curiosity."

"You were curious," pointed out Foster.

Potterley looked a trifle restless. "It was different in my case," he said angrily. "I have something that *must* be done,

239

and I wouldn't submit to the ridiculous way in which they kept putting me off."

A bit paranoid too, thought Foster gloomily.

Yet he had ended up with something, paranoid or not. Foster could no longer deny that something peculiar was going on in the matter of neutrinics.

But what was Potterley after? That still bothered Foster. If Potterley didn't intend this as a test of Foster's ethics, what *did* he want?

Foster put it to himself logically. If an intellectual anarchist with a touch of paranoia wanted to use a chronoscope and was convinced that the powers-that-be were deliberately standing in his way, what would he do?

Supposing it were I, he thought. What would I do?

He said slowly, "Maybe the chronoscope doesn't exist at all?"

Potterley started. There was almost a crack in his general calmness. For an instant Foster found himself catching a glimpse of something not at all calm.

But the historian kept his balance and said, "Oh, no, there *must* be a chronoscope."

"Why? Have you seen it? Have I? Maybe that's the explanation of everything. Maybe they're not deliberately holding out on a chronoscope they've got. Maybe they haven't got it in the first place."

"But Sterbinski lived. He built a chronoscope. That much is a fact."

"The book says so," said Foster coldly.

"Now listen." Potterley actually reached over and snatched at Foster's jacket sleeve. "I need the chronoscope. I must have it. Don't tell me it doesn't exist. What we're going to do is find out enough about neutrinics to be able to—"

Potterley drew himself up short.

Foster drew his sleeve away. He needed no ending to that sentence. He supplied it himself. He said, "Build one of our own?"

Potterley looked sour, as though he would rather not have said it point-blank. Nevertheless, he said, "Why not?"

"Because that's out of the question," said Foster. "If what I've read is correct, then it took Sterbinski twenty years to

240

build his machine and several millions in composite grants. Do you think you and I can duplicate that illegally? Suppose we had the time, which we haven't, and suppose I could learn enough out of books, which I doubt, where would we get the money and equipment? The chronoscope is supposed to fill a five-story building, for heaven's sake."

"Then you won't help me?"

"Well, I'll tell you what. I have one way in which I may be able to find out something—"

"What is that?" asked Potterley at once.

"Never mind. That's not important. But I may be able to find out enough to tell you whether the government is deliberately suppressing research by chronoscope. I may confirm the evidence you already have or I may be able to prove that your evidence is misleading. I don't know what good it will do you in either case, but it's as far as I can go. It's my limit."

Potterley watched the young man go finally. He was angry with himself. Why had he allowed himself to grow so careless as to permit the fellow to guess that he was thinking in terms of a chronoscope of his own? That was premature.

But then why did the young fool have to suppose that a chronoscope might not exist at all?

It *had* to exist. It *had* to. What was the use of saying it didn't?

And why couldn't a second one be built? Science had advanced in the fifty years since Sterbinski. All that was needed was knowledge.

Let the youngster gather knowledge. Let him think a small gathering would be his limit. Having taken the path to anarchy, there would be no limit. If the boy were not driven onward by something in himself, the first steps would be error enough to force the rest. Potterley was quite certain he would not hesitate to use blackmail.

Potterley waved a last good-bye and looked up. It was beginning to rain.

Certainly! Blackmail if necessary, but he would not be stopped.

* * *

Foster steered his car across the bleak outskirts of town and scarcely noticed the rain.

He *was* a fool, he told himself, but he couldn't leave things as they were. He had to know. He damned his streak of undisciplined curiosity, but he had to know.

But he would go no further than Uncle Ralph. He swore mightily to himself that it would stop there. In that way there would be no evidence against him, no real evidence. Uncle Ralph would be discreet.

In a way he was secretly ashamed of Uncle Ralph. He hadn't mentioned him to Potterley partly out of caution and partly because he did not wish to witness the lifted eyebrow, the inevitable half-smile. Professional science writers, however useful, were a little outside the pale, fit only for patronizing contempt. The fact that, as a class, they made more money than did research scientists only made matters worse, of course.

Still, there were times when a science writer in the family could be a convenience. Not being really educated, they did not have to specialize. Consequently, a good science writer knew practically everything. . . . And Uncle Ralph was one of the best.

Ralph Nimmo had no college degree and was rather proud of it. "A degree," he once said to Jonas Foster, when both were considerably younger, "is a first step down a ruinous highway. You don't want to waste it so you go on to graduate work and doctoral research. You end up a thorough-going ignoramus on everything in the world except for one subdivisional sliver of nothing.

"On the other hand, if you guard your mind carefully and keep it blank of any clutter of information till maturity is reached, filling it only with intelligence and training it only in clear thinking, you then have a powerful instrument at your disposal and you can become a science writer."

Nimmo received his first assignment at the age of twenty-five, after he had completed his apprenticeship and been out in the field for less than three months. It came in the shape of a clotted manuscript whose language would impart no glimmering of understanding to any reader, however qualified, without

242

careful study and some inspired guesswork. Nimmo took it apart and put it together again (after five long and exasperating interviews with the authors, who were biophysicists), making the language taut and meaningful and smoothing the style to a pleasant gloss.

"Why not?" he would say tolerantly to his nephew, who countered his strictures on degrees by berating him with his readiness to hang on the fringes of science. "The fringe is important. Your scientists can't write. Why should they be expected to? They aren't expected to be grand masters at chess or virtuosos at the violin, so why expect them to know how to put words together? Why not leave that for specialists too?

"Good Lord, Jonas, read your literature of a hundred years ago. Discount the fact that the science is out of date and that some of the expressions are out of date. Just try to read it and make sense out of it. It's just jaw-cracking, amateurish. Pages are published uselessly; whole articles which are either noncomprehensible or both."

"But you don't get recognition, Uncle Ralph," protested young Foster, who was getting ready to start his college career and was rather starry-eyed about it. "You could be a terrific researcher."

"I get recognition," said Nimmo. "Don't think for a minute I don't. Sure, a biochemist or a strato-meteorologist won't give me the time of day, but they pay me well enough. Just find out what happens when some first-class chemist finds the Commission has cut his year's allowance for science writing. He'll fight harder for enough funds to afford me, or someone like me, than to get a recording ionograph."

He grinned broadly and Foster grinned back. Actually, he was proud of his paunchy, round-faced, stub-fingered uncle, whose vanity made him brush his fringe of hair futilely over the desert on his pate and made him dress like an unmade haystack because such negligence was his trademark. Ashamed, but proud too.

And now Foster entered his uncle's cluttered apartment in no mood at all for grinning. He was nine years older now and so was Uncle Ralph. For nine more years, papers in every branch of science had come to him for polishing and a little of each had crept into his capacious mind.

Nimmo was eating seedless grapes, popping them into his mouth one at a time. He tossed a bunch to Foster, who caught them by a hair, then bent to retrieve individual grapes that had torn loose and fallen to the floor.

"Let them be. Don't bother," said Nimmo carelessly. "Someone comes in here to clean once a week. What's up? Having trouble with your grant application write-up?"

"I haven't really got into that yet."

"You haven't? Get a move on, boy. Are you waiting for me to offer to do the final arrangement?"

"I couldn't afford you, Uncle."

"Aw, come on. It's all in the family. Grant me all popular-publication rights and no cash need change hands."

Foster nodded. "If you're serious, it's a deal."

"It's a deal."

It was a gamble, of course, but Foster knew enough of Nimmo's science writing to realize it could pay off. Some dramatic discovery of public interest on primitive man or on a new surgical technique, or on any branch of spationautics could mean a very cash-attracting article in any of the mass media of communication.

It was Nimmo, for instance, who had written up, for scientific consumption, the series of papers by Bryce and co-workers that elucidated the fine structure of two cancer viruses, for which job he asked the picayune payment of fifteen hundred dollars, provided popular-publication rights were included. He then wrote up, exclusively, the same work in semidramatic form for use in trimensional video for a twenty-thousand-dollar advance plus rental royalties that were still coming in after five years.

Foster said bluntly, "What do you know about neutrinics, Uncle?"

"Neutrinics?" Nimmo's small eyes looked surprised. "Are you working in that? I thought it was pseudo-gravitic optics."

"It is p.g.o. I just happen to be asking about neutrinics."

"That's a devil of a thing to be doing. You're stepping out of line. You know that, don't you?"

"I don't expect you to call the Commission because I'm a little curious about things."

"Maybe I should before you get into trouble. Curiosity is an occupational danger with scientists. I've watched it work. One of them will be moving quietly along on a problem, then curiosity leads him up a strange creek. Next thing you know, he's done so little on his proper problem, he can't justify for a project renewal. I've seen more—''

"All I want to know," said Foster patiently, "is what's been passing through your hands lately on neutrinics."

Nimmo leaned back, chewing at a grape thoughtfully. "Nothing. Nothing ever. I don't recall ever getting a paper on neutrinics."

"What!" Foster was openly astonished. "Then who does get the work?"

"Now that you ask," said Nimmo, "I don't know. Don't recall anyone talking about it at the annual conventions. I don't think much work is being done there."

"Why not?"

"Hey, there, don't bark. I'm not doing anything. My guess would be—"

Foster was exasperated. "Don't you know?"

"Hmp. I'll tell you what I know about neutrinics. It concerns the applications of neutrino movements and the forces involved—''

"Sure. Sure. Just as electronics deals with the applications of electron movements and the forces involved, and pseudogravitics deals with the applications of artificial gravitational fields. I didn't come to you for that. Is that all you know?"

"And," said Nimmo with equanimity, "neutrinics is the basis of time-viewing and that *is* all I know."

Foster slouched back in his chair and massaged one lean cheek with great intensity. He felt angrily dissatisfied. Without formulating it explicitly in his own mind, he had felt sure, somehow, that Nimmo would come up with some late reports, bring up interesting facets of modern neutrinics, send him back to Potterley able to say that the elderly historian was wrong, that his data was misleading, his deductions mistaken.

Then he could have returned to his proper work.

But now. . . .

He told himself angrily: So they're not doing much work in the field. Does that make it deliberate suppression? What if neutrinics is a sterile discipline? Maybe it is. I don't know. Potterley doesn't. Why waste the intellectual resources of humanity on nothing? Or the work might be secret for some legitimate reason. It might be. . . .

The trouble was, he had to know. He couldn't leave things as they were now. *He couldn't!*

He said, "Is there a text on neutrinics, Uncle Ralph? I mean a clear and simple one. An elementary one."

Nimmo thought, his plump cheeks puffing out with a series of sighs. "You ask the damnedest questions. The only one I ever heard of was Sterbinski and somebody. I've never seen it, but I viewed something about it once. . . . Sterbinski and LaMarr, that's it."

"Is that the Sterbinski who invented the chronoscope?"

"I think so. Proves the book ought to be good."

"Is there a recent edition? Sterbinski died thirty years ago."

Nimmo shrugged and said nothing.

"Can you find out?"

They sat in silence for a moment while Nimmo shifted his bulk to the creaking tune of the chair he sat on. Then the science writer said, "Are you going to tell me what this is all about?"

"I can't. Will you help me anyway, Uncle Ralph? Will you get me a copy of the text?"

"Well, you've taught me all I know on pseudo-gravitics. I should be grateful. Tell you what—I'll help you on one condition."

"Which is?"

The old man was suddenly very grave. "That you be careful, Jonas. You're obviously way out of line, whatever you're doing. Don't blow up your career just because you're curious about something you haven't been assigned to and which is none of your business. Understand?"

Foster nodded, but he hardly heard. He was thinking furiously.

A full week later Ralph Nimmo eased his rotund figure into Jonas Foster's on-campus two-room combination and said in a hoarse whisper, "I've got something."

"What?" Foster was immediately eager.

"A copy of Sterbinski and LaMarr." He produced it, or rather a corner of it, from his ample topcoat.

Foster almost automatically eyed door and windows to make sure they were closed and shaded respectively, then held out his hand.

The film case was flaking with age, and when he cracked it, the film was faded and growing brittle. He said sharply, "Is this all?"

"Gratitude, my boy, gratitude!" Nimmo sat down with a grunt and reached into a pocket for an apple.

"Oh, I'm grateful, but it's so old."

"And lucky to get it at that. I tried to get a film run from the Congressional Library. No go. The book was restricted."

"Then how did you get this?"

"Stole it." He was biting crunchingly around the core. "New York Public."

"What?"

"Simple enough. I had access to the stacks, naturally. So I stepped over a chained railing when no one was around, dug this up, and walked out with it. They're very trusting out there. Meanwhile, they won't miss it for years. . . . Only you'd better not let anyone see it on you, Nephew."

Foster stared at the film as though it were literally hot.

Nimmo discarded the core and reached for a second apple. "Funny thing, now. There's nothing more recent in the whole field of neutrinics. Not a monograph, not a paper, not a progress note. Nothing since the chronoscope."

"Uh-huh," said Foster absently.

Foster worked evenings in the Potterley home. He could not trust his own on-campus rooms for the purpose. The evening work grew more real to him than his own grant applications. Sometimes he worried about it, but then that stopped too.

His work consisted, at first, simply in viewing and reviewing the text film. Later it consisted in thinking (sometimes while a section of the book ran itself off through the pocket projector, disregarded).

Sometimes Potterley would come down to watch, to sit with prim, eager eyes, as though he expected thought processes to solidify and become visible in all their convolutions. He interfered in only two ways. He did not allow Foster to smoke and sometimes he talked.

It wasn't conversation talk, never that. Rather it was a low-voiced monologue with which, it seemed, he scarcely expected to command attention. It was much more as though he were relieving a pressure within himself.

Carthage! Always Carthage!

Carthage, the New York of the ancient Mediterranean. Carthage, commercial empire and queen of the seas. Carthage, all that Syracuse and Alexandria pretended to be. Carthage, maligned by her enemies and inarticulate in her own defense.

She had been defeated once by Rome and then driven out of Sicily and Sardinia, but came back to more than recoup her losses by new dominions in Spain, and raised up Hannibal to give the Romans sixteen years of terror.

In the end she lost a second time, reconciled herself to fate and built again with broken tools a limping life in shrunken territory, succeeding so well that jealous Rome deliberately forced a third war. And then Carthage, with nothing but bare hands and tenacity, built weapons and forced Rome into a two-year war that ended only with complete destruction of the city, the inhabitants throwing themselves into their flaming houses rather than surrender.

"Could people fight so for a city and a way of life as bad as the ancient writers painted it? Hannibal was a better general than any Roman and his soldiers were absolutely faithful to him. Even his bitterest enemies praised him. There was a Carthaginian. It is fashionable to say that he was an atypical Carthaginian, better than the others, a diamond placed in garbage. But then why was he so faithful to Carthage, even to his death after years of exile? They talk of Moloch—"

Foster didn't always listen but sometimes he couldn't help himself and he shuddered and turned sick at the bloody tale of child sacrifice.

But Potterley went on earnestly, "Just the same, it isn't true. It's a twenty-five-hundred-year-old canard started by the Greeks and Romans. They had their own slaves, their crucifixions and torture, their gladiatorial contests. They weren't holy. The Moloch story is what later ages would have called war propaganda, the big lie. I can prove it was a lie. I can prove it and, by heaven, I will—I will—"

He would mumble that promise over and over again in his earnestness.

Mrs. Potterley visited him also, but less frequently, usually on Tuesdays and Thursdays when Dr. Potterley himself had an evening course to take care of and was not present.

She would sit quietly, scarcely talking, face slack and doughy, eyes blank, her whole attitude distant and withdrawn.

The first time, Foster tried, uneasily, to suggest that she leave.

She said tonelessly, "Do I disturb you?"

"No, of course not," lied Foster restlessly. "It's just that—that—" He couldn't complete the sentence.

She nodded, as though accepting an invitation to stay. Then she opened a cloth bag she had brought with her and took out a quire of vitron sheets which she proceeded to weave together by rapid, delicate movements of a pair of slender, tetra-faceted depolarizers whose battery-fed wires made her look as though she were holding a large spider.

One evening she said softly, "My daughter, Laurel, is your age."

Foster started, as much at the sudden, unexpected sound of speech as at the words. He said, "I didn't know you had a daughter, Mrs. Potterley."

"She died. Years ago."

The vitron grew under the deft manipulations into the uneven shape of some garment Foster could not yet identify. There was nothing left for him to do but mutter inanely, "I'm sorry."

Mrs. Potterley sighed. "I dream about her often." She raised her blue, distant eyes to him.

Foster winced and looked away.

Another evening she asked, pulling at one of the vitron sheets to loosen its gentle clinging to her dress, "What is time-viewing anyway?"

That remark broke into a particularly involved chain of thought, and Foster said snappishly, "Dr. Potterley can explain."

"He's tried to. Oh, my, yes. But I think he's a little impatient with me. He calls it chronoscopy most of the time. Do you actually see things in the past, like the trimensionals? Or does it just make little dot patterns like the computer you use?"

Foster stared at his hand computer with distaste. It worked well enough, but every operation had to be manually controlled and the answers were obtained in code. Now if he could use the school computer . . . well, why dream? He felt conspicuous enough as it was, carrying a hand computer under his arm every evening as he left his office.

He said, "I've never seen the chronoscope myself, but I'm under the impression that you actually see pictures and hear sound."

"You can hear people talk, too?"

"I think so." Then, half in desperation, "Look here, Mrs. Potterley, this must be awfully dull for you. I realize you don't like to leave a guest all to himself, but really, Mrs. Potterley, you mustn't feel compelled—"

"I don't feel compelled," she said. "I'm sitting here waiting."

"Waiting? For what?"

She said composedly, "I listened to you that first evening. The time you first spoke to Arnold. I listened at the door."

He said, "You did?"

"I know I shouldn't have, but I was awfully worried about Arnold. I had a notion he was going to do something he oughtn't and I wanted to hear what. And then when I heard—" She paused, bending close over the vitron and peering at it.

"Heard what, Mrs. Potterley?"

"That you wouldn't build a chronoscope."

"Well, of course not."

"I thought maybe you might change your mind."

Foster glared at her. "Do you mean you're coming down here hoping I'll build a chronoscope, waiting for me to build one?"

"I hope you do, Dr. Foster. Oh, I hope you do."

It was as though, all at once, a fuzzy veil had fallen off her face, leaving all her features clear and sharp, putting color into

250

her cheeks, life into her eyes, the vibrations of something approaching excitement into her voice.

"Wouldn't it be wonderful," she whispered, "to have one? People of the past could live again. Pharaohs and kings and— just people. I hope you build one, Dr. Foster. I really— hope—"

She choked, it seemed, on the intensity of her own words and let the vitron sheets slip off her lap. She rose and ran up the basement stairs while Foster's eyes followed her awkwardly fleeing body with astonishment and distress.

It cut deeper into Foster's nights and left him sleepless and painfully stiff with thought. It was almost a mental indigestion.

His grant requests went limping in, finally, to Ralph Nimmo. He scarcely had any hope for them. He thought numbly: They won't be approved.

If they weren't, of course, it would create a scandal in the department and probably mean his appointment at the university would not be renewed, come the end of the academic year.

He scarcely worried. It was the neutrino, the neutrino, only the neutrino. Its trail curved and veered sharply and led him breathlessly along unchartered pathways that even Sterbinski and LeMarr did not follow.

He called Nimmo. "Uncle Ralph, I need a few things. I'm calling from off the campus."

Nimmo's face in the video plate was jovial but his voice was sharp. He said, "What you need is a course in communication. I'm having a hell of a time pulling your application into one intelligible piece. If that's what you're calling about—"

Foster shook his head impatiently. "That's *not* what I'm calling about. I need these." He scribbled quickly on a piece of paper and held it up before the receiver.

Nimmo yiped. "Hey, how many tricks do you think I can wangle?"

"You can get them, Uncle. You know you can."

Nimmo reread the list of items with silent motions of his plump lips and looked grave.

"What happens when you put those things together?" he asked.

251

Foster shook his head. "You'll have exclusive popular-publication rights to whatever turns up, the way it's always been. But please don't ask any questions now."

"I can't do miracles, you know."

"Do this one. You've got to. You're a science writer, not a research man. You don't have to account for anything. You've got friends and connections. They can look the other way, can't they, to get a break from you next publication time?"

"Your faith, Nephew, is touching. I'll try."

Nimmo succeeded. The material and equipment were brought over late one evening in a private touring car. Nimmo and Foster lugged it in with the grunting of men unused to manual labor.

Potterley stood at the entrance of the basement after Nimmo had left. He asked softly, "What's this for?"

Foster brushed the hair off his forehead and gently massaged a sprained wrist. He said, "I want to conduct a few simple experiments."

"Really?" The historian's eyes glittered with excitement.

Foster felt exploited. He felt as though he were being led along a dangerous highway by the pull of pinching fingers on his nose; as though he could see the ruin clearly that lay in wait at the end of the path, yet walked eagerly and determinedly. Worst of all, he felt the compelling grip on his nose to be his own.

It was Potterley who began it, Potterley who stood there now, gloating; but the compulsion was his own.

Foster said sourly, "I'll be wanting privacy now, Potterley. I can't have you and your wife running down here and annoying me."

He thought: If that offends him, let him kick me out. Let him put an end to this.

In his heart, though, he did not think being evicted would stop anything.

But it did not come to that. Potterley was showing no signs of offense. His mild gaze was unchanged. He said, "Of course, Dr. Foster, of course. All the privacy you wish."

Foster watched him go. He was left still marching along the highway, perversely glad of it and hating himself for being glad.

252

He took to sleeping over on a cot in Potterley's basement and spending his weekends there entirely.

During that period, preliminary word came through that his grants (as doctored by Nimmo) had been approved. The department head brought the word and congratulated him.

Foster stared back distantly and mumbled, "Good. I'm glad," with so little conviction that the other frowned and turned away without another word.

Foster gave the matter no further thought. It was a minor point, worth no notice. He was planning something that really counted, a climactic test for that evening.

One evening, a second and third and then, haggard and half beside himself with excitement, he called in Potterley.

Potterley came down the stairs and looked about at the homemade gadgetry. He said in his soft voice, "The electric bills are quite high. I don't mind the expense, but the City may ask questions. Can anything be done?"

It was a warm evening but Potterley wore a tight collar and a semi-jacket. Foster, who was in his undershirt, lifted bleary eyes and said shakily, "It won't be for much longer, Dr. Potterley. I've called you down to tell you something. A chronoscope can be built. A small one, of course, but it can be built."

Potterley seized the railing. His body sagged. He managed a whisper. "Can it be built here?"

"Here in the basement," said Foster wearily.

"Good Lord. You said—"

"I know what I said," cried Foster impatiently. "I said it couldn't be done. I didn't know anything then. Even Sterbinski didn't know anything."

Potterley shook his head. "Are you sure? You're not mistaken, Dr. Foster? I couldn't endure it if—"

Foster said, "I'm not mistaken. Damn it, sir, if just theory had been enough, we could have had a time-viewer over a hundred years ago, when the neutrino was first postulated. The trouble was, the original investigators considered it only a mysterious particle without mass or charge that could not be detected. It was just something to even up the bookkeeping and save the law of conservation of mass and energy."

He wasn't sure Potterley knew what he was talking about. He didn't care. He needed a breather. He had to get some of this out of his clotting thoughts. . . . And he needed background for what he would have to tell Potterley next.

He went on. "It was Sterbinski who first discovered that the neutrino broke through the space-time cross-sectional barrier, that it traveled through time as well as through space. It was Sterbinski who first devised a method for stopping neutrinos. He invented a neutrino recorder and learned how to interpret the pattern of the neutrino stream. Naturally the stream had been affected and deflected by all the matter it had passed through in its passage through time, and the deflections could be analyzed and converted into the images of the matter that had done the deflecting. Time-viewing was possible. Even air vibrations could be detected in this way and converted into sound."

Potterley was definitely not listening. He said, "Yes. Yes. But when can you build a chronoscope?"

Foster said urgently, "Let me finish. Everything depends on the method used to detect and analyze the neutrino stream. Sterbinski's method was difficult and roundabout. It required mountains of energy. But I've studied pseudo-gravitics, Dr. Potterley, the science of artificial gravitational fields. I've specialized in the behavior of light in such fields. It's a new science. Sterbinski knew nothing of it. If he had, he would have seen—anyone would have—a much better and more efficient method of detecting neutrinos using a pseudo-gravitic field. If I had known more neutrinics to begin with, I would have seen it at once."

Potterley brightened a bit. "I knew it," he said. "Even if they stop research in neutrinics, there is no way the government can be sure that discoveries in other segments of science won't reflect knowledge on neutrinics. So much for the value of centralized direction of science. I thought this long ago, Dr. Foster, before you ever came to work here."

"I congratulate you on that," said Foster, "but there's one thing—"

"Oh, never mind all this. Answer me. Please. When can you build a chronoscope?"

"I'm trying to tell you something, Dr. Potterley. A

254

chronoscope won't do you any good." (This is it, Foster thought.)

Slowly Potterley descended the stairs. He stood facing Foster. "What do you mean? Why won't it help me?"

"You won't see Carthage. It's what I've got to tell you. It's what I've been leading up to. You can never see Carthage."

Potterley shook his head slightly. "Oh, no, you're wrong. If you have the chronoscope, just focus it properly—"

"No, Dr. Potterley. It's not a question of focus. There are random factors affecting the neutrino stream, as they affect all subatomic particles. What we call the uncertainty principle. When the stream is recorded and interpreted, the random factor comes out as fuzziness, or 'noise,' as the communications boys speak of it. The farther back in time you penetrate, the more pronounced the fuzziness, the greater the noise. After a while the noise drowns out the picture. Do you understand?"

"More power," said Potterley in a dead kind of voice.

"That won't help. When the noise blurs out detail, magnifying detail magnifies the noise too. You can't see anything in a sun-burned film by enlarging it, can you? Get this through your head now. The physical nature of the Universe sets limits. The random thermal motions of air molecules set limits to how weak a sound can be detected by any instrument. The length of a light wave or of an electron wave sets limits to the size of objects that can be seen by any instrument. It works that way in chronoscopy too. You can only time-view so far."

"How far? How far?"

Foster took a deep breath. "A century and a quarter. That's the most."

"But the monthly bulletin the Commission puts out deals with ancient history almost entirely." The historian laughed shakily. "You must be wrong. The government has data as far back as 3000 B.C."

"When did you switch to believing them?" demanded Foster scornfully. "You began this business by proving they were lying, that no historian had made use of the chronoscope. Don't you see why now? No historian, except one interested in contemporary history, could. No chronoscope can possibly see back in time farther than 1920 under any conditions."

255

"You're wrong. You don't know everything," said Potterley.

"The truth won't bend itself to your convenience either. Face it. The government's part in this is to perpetrate a hoax."

"Why?"

"I don't know why."

Potterley's snubby nose was twitching. His eyes were bulging. He pleaded, "It's only theory, Dr. Foster. Build a chronoscope. Build one and try."

Foster caught Potterley's shoulders in a sudden, fierce grip. "Do you think I haven't? Do you think I would tell you this before I had checked it every way I knew? I *have* built one. It's all around you. Look!"

He ran to the switches at the power leads. He flicked them on, one by one. He turned a resistor, adjusted other knobs, put out the cellar lights. "Wait. Let it warm up."

There was a small glow near the center of one wall. Potterley was gibbering incoherently but Foster only cried again, "Look!"

The light sharpened and brightened, broke up into a light-and-dark pattern. Men and women! Fuzzy. Features blurred. Arms and legs mere streaks. An old-fashioned ground car, unclear but recognizable as one of the kind that had once used gasoline-powered internal-combustion engines, sped by.

Foster said, "Mid-twentieth century, somewhere. I can't hook up an audio yet so this is soundless. Eventually we can add sound. Anyway, mid-twentieth is almost as far back as you can go. Believe me, that's the best focusing that can be done."

Potterley said, "Build a larger machine, a stronger one. Improve your circuits."

"You can't lick the uncertainty principle, man, any more than you can live on the sun. There are physical limits to what can be done."

"You're lying. I won't believe you. I—"

A new voice sounded, raised shrilly to make itself heard.

"Arnold! Dr. Foster!"

The young physicist turned at once. Dr. Potterley froze for a long moment, then said without turning, "What is it, Caroline? Leave us."

"No!" Mrs. Potterley descended the stairs. "I heard. I

couldn't help hearing. Do you have a time-viewer here, Dr. Foster? Here in the basement?"

"Yes, I do, Mrs. Potterley. A kind of time-viewer. Not a good one. I can't get sound yet and the picture is darned blurry, but it works."

Mrs. Potterley clasped her hands and held them tightly against her breast. "How wonderful. How wonderful."

"It's not at all wonderful," snapped Potterley. "The young fool can't reach farther back than—"

"Now, look," began Foster in exasperation.

"Please!" cried Mrs. Potterley. "Listen to me. Arnold, don't you see that as long as we can use it for twenty years back, we can see Laurel once again? What do we care about Carthage and ancient times? It's Laurel we can see. She'll be alive for us again. Leave the machine here, Dr. Foster. Show us how to work it."

Foster stared at her, then at her husband. Dr. Potterley's face had gone white. Though his voice stayed low and even, its calmness was somehow gone. He said, "You're a fool!"

Caroline said weakly, "Arnold!"

"You're a fool, I say. What will you see? The past. The dead past. Will Laurel do one thing she did not do? Will you see one thing you haven't seen? Will you live three years over and over again, watching a baby who'll never grow up no matter how long you watch?"

His voice came near to cracking, but held. He stepped closer to her, seized her shoulder and shook her roughly. "Do you know what will happen to you if you do that? They'll come to take you away because you'll go mad. Yes, mad. Do you want mental treatment? Do you want to be shut up, to undergo the psychic probe?"

Mrs. Potterley tore away. There was no trace of softness or vagueness about her. She had twisted into a virago. "I want to see my child, Arnold. She's in that machine and I want her."

"She's *not* in the machine. An image is. Can't you understand? An image! Something that's not real!"

"I want my child. Do you hear me?" She flew at him, screaming, fists beating. *"I want my child."*

The historian retreated at the fury of the assault, crying out.

Foster moved to step between them, when Mrs. Potterley dropped, sobbing wildly, to the floor.

Potterley turned, eyes desperately seeking. With a sudden heave, he snatched at a Lando-rod, tearing it from its support and whirling away before Foster, numbed by all that was taking place, could move to stop him.

"Stand back!" gasped Potterley, "or I'll kill you. I swear it."

He swung with force, and Foster jumped back.

Potterley turned with fury on every part of the structure in the cellar, and Foster, after the first crash of glass, watched dazedly.

Potterley spent his rage and then he was standing quietly amid shards and splinters, with a broken Lando-rod in his hand. He said to Foster in a whisper, "Now get out of here! Never come back! If any of this cost you anything, send me a bill and I'll pay for it. I'll pay double."

Foster shrugged, picked up his shirt and moved up the basement stairs. He could hear Mrs. Potterley sobbing loudly, and as he turned at the head of the stairs for a last look, he saw Dr. Potterley bending over her, his face convulsed with sorrow.

Two days later, with the school day drawing to a close and Foster looking wearily about to see if there were any data on his newly approved projects that he wished to take home, Dr. Potterley appeared once more. He was standing at the open door of Foster's office.

The historian was neatly dressed as ever. He lifted his hand in a gesture that was too vague to be a greeting, too abortive to be a plea. Foster stared stonily.

Potterley said, "I waited till five, till you were . . . may I come in?"

Foster nodded.

Potterley said, "I suppose I ought to apologize for my behavior. I was dreadfully disappointed, not quite master of myself. Still, it was inexcusable."

"I accept your apology," said Foster. "Is that all?"

"My wife called you, I think."

"Yes, she has."

"She has been quite hysterical. She told me she had but I couldn't be quite sure—"

"She has called me."

"Could you tell me—would you be so kind as to tell me what she wanted?"

"She wanted a chronoscope. She said she had some money of her own. She was willing to pay."

"Did you—make any commitments?"

"I said I wasn't in the manufacturing business."

"Good," breathed Potterley, his chest expanding with a sign of relief. "Please don't take any calls from her. She's not—quite—"

"Look, Dr. Potterley," said Foster, "I'm not getting into any domestic quarrels, but you'd better be prepared for something. Chronoscopes can be built by anybody. Given a few simple parts that can be bought through some etherics sales center, they can be built in the home workshop. The video part, anyway."

"But no one else will think of it besides you, will they? No one has."

"I don't intend to keep it secret."

"But you can't publish. It's illegal research."

"That doesn't matter anymore, Dr. Potterley. If I lose my grants, I lose them. If the university is displeased, I'll resign. It just doesn't matter."

"But you can't do that!"

"Till now," said Foster, "you didn't mind my risking loss of grants and position. Why do you turn so tender about it now? Now let me explain something to you. When you first came to me, I believed in organized and directed research; the situation as it existed, in other words. I considered you an intellectual anarchist, Dr. Potterley, and dangerous. But for one reason or another, I've been an anarchist myself for months now and I have achieved great things.

"Those things have been achieved not because I am a brilliant scientist. Not at all. It was just that scientific research had been directed from above and holes were left that could be filled in by anyone who looked in the right direction. And anyone might have if the government hadn't actively tried to prevent it.

259

"Now understand me. I still believe directed research can be useful. I'm not in favor of a retreat to total anarchy. But there must be a middle ground. Directed research can retain flexibility. A scientist must be allowed to follow his curiosity, at least in his spare time."

Potterley sat down. He said ingratiatingly, "Let's discuss this, Foster. I appreciate your idealism. You're young. You want the moon. But you can't destroy yourself through fancy notions of what research must consist of. I got you into this. I am responsible and I blame myself bitterly. I was acting emotionally. My interest in Carthage blinded me and I was a damned fool."

Foster broke in. "You mean you've changed completely in two days? Carthage is nothing? Government suppression of research is nothing?"

"Even a damned fool like myself can learn, Foster. My wife taught me something. I understand the reason for government suppression of neutrinics now. I didn't two days ago. And, understanding, I approve. You saw the way my wife reacted to the news of a chronoscope in the basement. I had envisioned a chronoscope used for research purposes. All *she* could see was the personal pleasure of returning neurotically to a personal past, a dead past. The pure researcher, Foster, is in the minority. People like my wife would outweigh us.

"For the government to encourage chronoscopy would have meant that everyone's past would be visible. The government officers would be subjected to blackmail and improper pressure, since who on Earth has a past that is absolutely clean? Organized government might become impossible."

Foster licked his lips. "Maybe the government has some justification in its own eyes. Still, there's an important principle involved here. Who knows what other scientific advances are being stymied because scientists are being stifled into walking a narrow path? If the chronoscope becomes the terror of a few politicians, it's a price that must be paid. The public must realize that science must be free and there is no more dramatic way of doing it than to publish my discovery, one way or another, legally or illegally."

Potterley's brow was damp with perspiration, but his voice remained even. "Oh, not just a few politicians, Dr. Foster.

Don't think that. It would be my terror too. My wife would spend her time living with our dead daughter. She would retreat farther from reality. She would go mad living the same scenes over and over. And not just my terror. There would be others like her. Children searching for their dead parents or their own youth. We'll have a whole world living in the past. Midsummer madness."

Foster said, "Moral judgments can't stand in the way. There isn't one advance at any time in history that mankind hasn't had the ingenuity to pervert. Mankind must also have the ingenuity to prevent. As for the chronoscope, your delvers into the dead past will get tired soon enough. They'll catch their loved parents in some of the things their loved parents did and they'll lose their enthusiasm for it all. But all this is trivial. With me, it's a matter of important principle."

Potterley said, "Hang your principle. Can't you understand men and women as well as principle? Don't you understand that my wife will live through the fire that killed our baby? She won't be able to help herself. I know her. She'll follow through each step, trying to prevent it. She'll live it over and over again, hoping each time that it won't happen. How many times do you want to kill Laurel?" A huskiness had crept into his voice.

A thought crossed Foster's mind. "What are you really afraid she'll find out, Dr. Potterley? What happened the night of the fire?"

The historian's hands went up quickly to cover his face and they shook with his dry sobs. Foster turned and stared uncomfortably out the window.

Potterley said after a while, "It's a long time since I've had to think of it. Caroline was away. I was baby-sitting. I went into the baby's bedroom midevening to see if she had kicked off the bedclothes. I had my cigarette with me . . . I smoked in those days. I must have stubbed it out before putting it in the ashtray on the chest of drawers. I was always careful. The baby was all right. I returned to the living room and fell asleep before the video. I awoke, choking, surrounded by fire. I don't know how it started."

"But you think it may have been the cigarette, is that it?"

said Foster. "A cigarette which, for once, you forgot to stub out?"

"I don't know. I tried to save her, but she was dead in my arms when I got out."

"You never told your wife about the cigarette, I suppose."

Potterley shook his head. "But I've lived with it."

"Only now, with a chronoscope, she'll find out. Maybe it wasn't the cigarette. Maybe you did stub it out. Isn't that possible?"

The scant tears had dried on Potterley's face. The redness had subsided. He said, "I can't take the chance . . . but it's not just myself, Foster. The past has its terrors for most people. Don't loose those terrors on the human race."

Foster paced the floor. Somehow this explained the reason for Potterley's rabid, irrational desire to boost the Carthaginians, deify them, most of all disprove the story of their fiery sacrifices to Moloch. By freeing them of the guilt of infanticide by fire, he symbolically freed himself of the same guilt.

So the same fire that had driven him on to causing the construction of a chronoscope was now driving him on to the destruction.

Foster looked sadly at the older man. "I see your position, Dr. Potterley, but this goes above personal feelings. I've got to smash this throttling hold on the throat of science."

Potterley said savagely, "You mean you want the fame and wealth that goes with such a discovery."

"I don't know about the wealth, but that too, I suppose. I'm no more than human."

"You won't 'suppress your knowledge?"

"Not under any circumstances."

"Well, then—" And the historian got to his feet and stood for a moment, glaring.

Foster had an odd moment of terror. The man was older than he, smaller, feebler, and he didn't look armed. Still. . . .

Foster said, "If you're thinking of killing me or anything insane like that, I've got the information in a safe-deposit vault where the proper people will find it in case of my disappearance or death."

Potterley said, "Don't be a fool," and stalked out.

262

Foster closed the door, locked it and sat down to think. He felt silly. He had no information in a safe-deposit vault, of course. Such a melodramatic action would not have occurred to him ordinarily. But now it had.

Feeling even sillier, he spent an hour writing out the equations and the application of pseudo-gravitic optics to neutrinic recording, and some diagrams for the engineering details of construction. He sealed it in an envelope and scrawled Ralph Nimmo's name over the outside.

He spent a rather restless night and the next morning, on the way to school, dropped the envelope off at the bank, with appropriate instructions to an official, who made him sign a paper permitting the box to be opened after his death.

He called Nimmo to tell him of the existence of the envelope, refusing querulously to say anything about its contents.

He had never felt so ridiculously self-conscious as at that moment.

That night and the next, Foster spent in only fitful sleep, finding himself face to face with the highly practical problem of the publication of data unethically obtained.

The *Proceedings of the Society of Pseudo-Gravitics*, which was the journal with which he was best acquainted, would certainly not touch any paper that did not include the magic footnote: "The work described in this paper was made possible by Grant No. so-and-so from the Commission of Research of the United Nations."

Nor, doubly so, would the *Journal of Physics*.

There were always the minor journals that might overlook the nature of the article for the sake of the sensation, but that would require a little financial negotiation on which he hesitated to embark. It might, on the whole, be better to pay the cost of publishing a small pamphlet for general distribution among the scholars. In that case, he would even be able to dispense with the services of a science writer, sacrificing polish for speed. He would have to find a reliable printer. Uncle Ralph might know one.

He walked down the corridor to his office and wondered anxiously if perhaps he ought to waste no further time, give himself no further chance to lapse into indecision and take the risk of calling Ralph from his office phone. He was so absorbed in his own heavy thoughts that he did not notice that his room was occupied until he turned from the clothes closet and approached his desk.

Dr. Potterley was there and a man whom Foster did not recognize.

Foster stared at them. "What's this?"

Potterley said, "I'm sorry, but I had to stop you."

Foster continued staring. "What are you talking about?"

The stranger said, "Let me introduce myself." He had large teeth, a little uneven, and they showed prominently when he smiled. "I am Thaddeus Araman, Department Head of the Division of Chronoscopy. I am here to see you concerning information brought to me by Professor Arnold Potterley and confirmed by our own sources—"

Potterley said breathlessly, "I took all the blame, Dr. Foster. I explained that it was I who persuaded you against your will into unethical practices. I have offered to accept full responsibility and punishment. I don't wish you harmed in any way. It's just that chronoscopy must not be permitted!"

Araman nodded. "He has taken the blame as he says, Dr. Foster, but this thing is out of his hands now."

Foster said, "So? What are you going to do? Blackball me from all consideration for research grants?"

"This is in my power," said Araman.

"Order the university to discharge me?"

"That, too, is in my power."

"All right, go ahead. Consider it done. I'll leave my office now, with you. I can send for my books later. If you insist, I'll leave my books. Is that all?"

"Not quite," said Araman. "You must engage to do no further research in chronoscopy, to publish none of your findings in chronoscopy and, of course, to build no chronoscope. You will remain under surveillance indefinitely to make sure you keep that promise."

"Supposing I refuse to promise? What can you do? Doing research out of my field may be unethical, but it isn't a criminal offense."

"In the case of chronoscopy, my young friend," said

Araman patiently, "it is a criminal offense. If necessary, you will be put in jail and kept there."

"Why?" shouted Foster. "What's magic about chronoscopy?"

Araman said, "That's the way it is. We cannot allow further developments in the field. My own job is, primarily, to make sure of that, and I intend to do my job. Unfortunately, I had no knowledge, nor did anyone in the department, that the optics of pseudo-gravity fields had such immediate application to chronoscopy. Score one for general ignorance, but henceforward research will be steered properly in that respect too."

Foster said, "That won't help. Something else may apply that neither you nor I dream of. All science hangs together. It's one piece. If you want to stop one part, you've got to stop it all."

"No doubt that is true," said Araman, "in theory. On the practical side, however, we have managed quite well to hold chronoscopy down to the original Sterbinski level for fifty years. Having caught you in time, Dr. Foster, we hope to continue doing so indefinitely. And we wouldn't have come this close to disaster, either, if I had accepted Dr. Potterley at something more than face value."

He turned toward the historian and lifted his eyebrows in a kind of humorous self-deprecation. "I'm afraid, sir, that I dismissed you as a history professor and no more on the occasion of our first interview. Had I done my job properly and checked on you, this would not have happened."

Foster said abruptly, "Is anyone allowed to use the government chronoscope?"

"No one outside our division under any pretext. I say that since it is obvious to me that you have already guessed as much. I warn you, though, that any repetition of that fact will be criminal, not an ethical, offense."

"And your chronoscope doesn't go back more than a hundred twenty-five years or so, does it?"

"It doesn't."

"Then your bulletin with its stories of time-viewing ancient times is a hoax?"

Araman said coolly, "With the knowledge you now have, it

is obvious you know that for a certainty. However, I confirm your remark. The monthly bulletin is a hoax."

"In that case," said Foster, "I will not promise to suppress my knowledge of chronoscopy. If you wish to arrest me, go ahead. My defense at the trial will be enough to destroy the vicious card house of directed research and bring it tumbling down. Directing research is one thing; suppressing it and depriving mankind of its benefits is quite another."

Araman said, "Oh, let's get something straight, Dr. Foster. If you do not cooperate, you will go to jail directly. You will *not* see a lawyer, you will *not* be charged, you will *not* have a trial. You will simply stay in jail."

"Oh, no," said Foster, "you're bluffing. This is not the twentieth century, you know."

There was a stir outside the office, the clatter of feet, a high-pitched shout that Foster was sure he recognized. The door crashed open, the lock splintering, and three intertwined figures stumbled in.

As they did so, one of the men raised a blaster and brought its butt down hard on the skull of another.

There was a whoosh of expiring air, and the one whose head was struck went limp.

"Uncle Ralph!" cried Foster.

Araman frowned. "Put him down in that chair," he ordered, "and get some water."

Ralph Nimmo, rubbing his head with a gingerly sort of disgust, said, "There was no need to get rough, Araman."

Araman said, "The guard should have been rougher sooner and kept you out of here, Nimmo. You'd have been better off."

"You know each other?" asked Foster.

"I've had dealings with the man," said Nimmo, still rubbing. "If he's here in your office, Nephew, you're in trouble."

"And you too," said Araman angrily. "I know Dr. Foster consulted you on neutrinics literature."

Nimmo corrugated his forehead, then straightened it with a wince as though the action had brought pain. "So?" he said. "What else do you know about me?"

"We will know everything about you soon enough. Meanwhile, that one item is enough to implicate you. What are you doing here?"

"My dear Dr. Araman," said Nimmo, some of his jauntiness restored, "yesterday, my jackass of a nephew called me. He had placed some mysterious information—"

"Don't tell him! Don't say anything!" cried Foster.

Araman glanced at him coldly. "We know all about it, Dr. Foster. The safe-deposit box has been opened and its contents removed."

"But how can you know—" Foster's voice died away in a kind of furious frustration.

"Anyway," said Nimmo, "I decided the net must be closing around him and after I took care of a few items, I came down to tell him to get off this thing he's doing. It's not worth his career."

"Does that mean you know what he's doing?" asked Araman.

"He never told me," said Nimmo, "but I'm a science writer with a hell of a lot of experience. I know which side of an atom is electronified. The boy, Foster, specializes in pseudo-gravitic optics and coached me on the stuff himself. He got me to get him a textbook on neutrinics and I kind of skip-viewed it myself before handing it over. I can put two and two together. He asked me to get him certain pieces of physical equipment, and that was evidence too. Stop me if I'm wrong, but my nephew has built a semiportable, low-power chronoscope. Yes, or—yes?"

"Yes." Araman reached thoughtfully for a cigarette and paid no more attention to Dr. Potterley (watching silently, as though all were a dream), who shied away, gasping, from the white cylinder. "Another mistake for me. I ought to resign. I should have put tabs on you too, Nimmo, instead of concentrating too hard on Potterley and Foster. I didn't have much time of course and you've ended up safely here, but that doesn't excuse me. You're under arrest, Nimmo."

"What for?" demanded the science writer.

"Unauthorized research."

"I wasn't doing any. I can't, not being a registered scientist. And even if I did, it's not a criminal offense."

267

Foster said savagely, "No use, Uncle Ralph. This bureaucrat is making his own laws."

"Like what?" demanded Nimmo.

"Like life imprisonment without trial."

"Nuts," said Nimmo. "This isn't the twentieth cen—"

"I tried that," said Foster. "It doesn't bother him."

"Well, nuts," shouted Nimmo. "Look here, Araman. My nephew and I have relatives who haven't lost touch with us, you know. The professor has some also, I imagine. You can't just make us disappear. There'll be questions and a scandal. This *isn't* the twentieth century. So if you're trying to scare us, it isn't working."

The cigarette snapped between Araman's fingers and he tossed it away violently. He said, "Damn it, I don't know *what* to do. It's never been like this before. . . . Look! You three fools know nothing of what you're trying to do. You understand nothing. Will you listen to me?"

"Oh, we'll listen," said Nimmo grimly.

(Foster sat silently, eyes angry, lips compressed. Potterley's hands writhed like two intertwined snakes.)

Araman said, "The past to you is the dead past. If any of you have discussed the matter, it's dollars to nickels you've used that phrase. The dead past. If you knew how many times I've heard those three words, you'd choke on them too.

"When people think of the past, they think of it as dead, far away and gone, long ago. We encourage them to think so. When we report time-viewing, we always talk of views centuries in the past, even though you gentlemen know seeing more than a century or so is impossible. People accept it. The past means Greece, Rome, Carthage, Egypt, the Stone Age. The deader, the better.

"Now you three know a century or a little more is the limit, so what does the past mean to you? Your youth. Your first girl. Your dead mother. Twenty years ago. Thirty years ago. Fifty years ago. The deader, the better. . . . But when does the past really begin?"

He paused in anger. The others stared at him and Nimmo stirred uneasily.

"Well," said Araman, "when did it begin? A year ago? Five minutes ago? One second ago? Isn't it obvious that the past begins an instant ago? The dead past is just another name for the living present. What if you focus the chronoscope in the past of one-hundredth of a second ago? Aren't you watching the present? Does it begin to sink in?"

Nimmo said, "Damnation."

"Damnation," mimicked Araman. "After Potterley came to me with his story last night, how do you suppose I checked up on both of you? I did it with the chronoscope, spotting key moments to the very instant of the present."

"And that's how you knew about the safe-deposit box?" said Foster.

"And every other important fact. Now what do you suppose would happen if we let news of a home chronoscope get out? People might start out by watching their youth, their parents, and so on, but it wouldn't be long before they'd catch on to the possibilities. The housewife will forget her poor, dead mother and take to watching her neighbor at home and her husband at the office. The businessman will watch his competitor; the employer his employee.

"There will be no such thing as privacy. The party line, the prying eye behind the curtain will be nothing compared to it. The video stars will be closely watched at all times by everyone. Every man his own Peeping Tom, and there'll be no getting away from the watcher. Even darkness will be no escape because chronoscopy can be adjusted to the infrared, and human figures can be seen by their own body heat. The figures will be fuzzy, of course, and the surroundings will be dark, but that will make the titillation of it all the greater, perhaps. . . . Hmp, the men in charge of the machine now experiment sometimes in spite of the regulations against it."

Nimmo seemed sick. "You can always forbid private manufacture—"

Araman turned on him fiercely. "You can, but do you expect it to do any good? Can you legislate successfully against drinking, smoking, adultery or gossiping over the back fence? And this mixture of nosiness and prurience will have a worse grip on humanity than any of those. Good Lord, in a thousand years of trying we haven't even been able to wipe out the heroin traffic and you talk about legislating against a device for watching anyone you please at any time you please that can be built in a home workshop."

Foster said suddenly, "I won't publish."

Potterley burst out, half in sobs, "None of us will talk. I regret—"

Nimmo broke in. "You said you didn't tab me on the chronoscope, Araman."

"No time," said Araman wearily. "Things don't move any faster on the chronoscope than in real life. You can't speed it up like the film in a book viewer. We spent a full twenty-four hours trying to catch the important moments during the last six months of Potterley and Foster. There was no time for anything else and it was enough."

"It wasn't," said Nimmo.

"What are you talking about?" There was a sudden infinite alarm on Araman's face.

"I told you my nephew, Jonas, had called me to say he had put important information in a safe-deposit box. He acted as though he were in trouble. He's my nephew. I had to try to get him off the spot. It took a while, then I came here to tell him what I had done. I told you when I got here, just after your man conked me, that I had taken care of a few items."

"What? For heaven's sake—"

"Just this: I sent the details of the portable chronoscope off to half a dozen of my regular publicity outlets."

Not a word. Not a sound. Not a breath. They were all past any demonstration.

"Don't stare like that," cried Nimmo. "Don't you see my point? I had popular-publication rights. Jonas will admit that. I knew he couldn't publish scientifically in any legal way. I was sure he was planning to publish illegally and was preparing the safe-deposit box for that reason. I thought if I put through the details prematurely, all the responsibility would be mine. His career would be saved. And if I were deprived of my science-writing license as a result, my exclusive possession of the chronometric data would set me up for life. Jonas would be angry, I expected that, but I could explain the motive and we would split fifty-fifty. . . . Don't stare at me like that. How did I know—"

"Nobody knew anything," said Araman bitterly, "but you

all just took it for granted that the government was stupidly bureaucratic, vicious, tyrannical, given to suppressing research for the hell of it. It never occurred to any of you that we were trying to protect mankind as best we could."

"Don't sit there talking," wailed Potterley. "Get the names of the people who were told—"

"Too late," said Nimmo, shrugging. "They've had better than a day. There's been time for the word to spread. My outlets will have called any number of physicists to check my data before going on with it and they'll call one another to pass on the news. Once scientists put neutrinics and pseudo-gravitics together, home chronoscopy becomes obvious. Before the week is out, five hundred people will know how to build a small chronoscope and how will you catch them all?" His plump cheeks sagged. "I suppose there's no way of putting the mushroom cloud back into that nice, shiny uranium sphere."

Araman stood up. "We'll try, Potterley, but I agree with Nimmo. It's too late. What kind of world we'll have from now on, I don't know, I can't tell, but the world we know has been destroyed completely. Until now, every custom, every habit, every tiniest way of life has always taken a certain amount of privacy for granted, but that's all gone now."

He saluted each of the three with elaborate formality.

"You have created a new world among the three of you. I congratulate you. Happy goldfish bowl to you, to me, to everyone, and may each of you fry in hell forever. Arrest rescinded."

16

The Fateful Lightning

We expect an astonishing scientific discovery to have a chance of revolutionizing some applicable aspect of science. It is even more exciting, though, when a discovery revolutionizes human society in general and alters the way in which human beings (even "ordinary" human beings) look upon the Universe. There is a case in which (in my opinion) exactly this happened, and the man who made the discovery is not even thought of as a scientist by Americans. He was one, of course, and a good one, but he was so many other things as well that the scientist in him was drowned out.

In the last five years or so, I have turned to writing history. I don't mean the history of science (I've been doing that for a long time); I mean "straight" history. As of now, I have published seven history books, with more to come.

This is valuable to me in a number of ways. It keeps my fingers nimbly stroking the typewriter keys and it keeps my mind exercised in new and refreshing directions. And, both least and most important, it inveigles me into new games.

No one who reads these essays can help knowing that I love to play with numbers— Well, I discovered I love to play with turning points too. There's the excitement of tracing down an event and saying: "At this point, at this exact point, man's history forked and man moved irrevocably into this path rather than the other."

To be sure, I'm somewhat of a fatalist and believe that "man's history" is the product of rather massive forces that will not be denied; that if a certain turning is prevented at this point, it will come about at another point eventually. Yet even so, it remains interesting to find the point where the turning *was* made.

Of course the most fun of all is to find a brand-new turning point; one which has never (to one's knowledge) been pointed out. My own chance at finding a new turning point is made somewhat better than it might be, in my opinion, by my advantage of being equally at home in history and in science.

By and large, historians tend to be weak in science and they find their turning points in political and military events for the most part. Such watershed years of history as 1453, 1492, 1517, 1607, 1789, 1815 and 1917 have nothing directly to do with science. Scientists, on the other hand, tend to think of science in terms rather divorced from society and such turning-point years as 1543, 1687, 1774, 1803, 1859, 1895, 1900 and 1905 tend to have no immediate and direct connection with society.*

To me, however, a turning point of the first magnitude, one that is *equally* important both to science and to society, took place in 1752, and no one, to my knowledge, has ever made an issue of it. So, Gentle Reader, *I* will—

As far as our records go back, and presumably much farther, men have turned to experts for protection against the vagaries of nature.

That protection they surely needed, for men have been subjected to seasons of bad hunting when they were hunters and to seasons of sparse rainfall when they were farmers. They have fallen prey to mysterious toothaches and intestinal gripings; they have sickened and died; they have perished in storms and wars; they have fallen prey to mischance and accident.

*You're welcome to join the fun of turning-pointing by trying to figure out what happened in these years, without looking them up, but you don't have to. The details are not relevant to the remainder of the essay.

All the Universe seemed to conspire against poor, shivering man, and yet it was, in a way, his transcendent triumph that he felt there must be some way in which the tables could be turned. If only he had the right formula, the right mystic sign, the right lucky object, the right way of threatening or pleading—why, then, game would be plentiful, rain would be adequate, mischance would not befall, and life would be beautiful.

If he didn't believe that, then he lived in a Universe that was unrelievedly capricious and hostile, and few men, from the Neanderthal who buried his dead with the proper ceremony, to Albert Einstein who refused to believe that God would play dice with the Universe, were willing to live in such a world.

Much of human energies in prehistory, then, and in most of historical times too, went into the working out of the proper ritual for control of the Universe and into the effort of establishing rigid adherence to that ritual. The tribal elder, the patriarch, the shaman, the medicine man, the wizard, the magician, the seer, the priest, those who were wise because they were old, or wise because they had entry into secret teachings, or wise simply because they had the capacity to foam at the mouth and go into a trance, were in charge of the rituals, and it was to them that men turned for protection.

In fact, much of this remains. Verbal formulas, uttered by specialists, are relied on to bring good luck to a fishing fleet, members of which would be uneasy about leaving port without it. If we think this is but a vagary of uneducated fishermen, I might point out that the Congress of the United States would feel most uneasy about beginning its deliberations without a chaplain mimicking biblical English in an attempt to rain down good judgment upon them from on high—a device that seems very rarely to have done the Congress much good.

It is not long since it was common to sprinkle fields with holy water to keep off the locusts, to ring church bells to comets, to use united supplications according to agreed-upon wording to bring on needed rain. In short, we have not really abandoned the attempt to control the Universe by magic.

The point is that well into the eighteenth century there was no other way to find security. Either the Universe was controlled by magic (whether through spells or through prayer) or it couldn't be controlled at all.

It might *seem* as though there *was* an alternative. What about science? By the mid-eighteenth century, the "scientific revolution" was two centuries old and had already reached its climax with Isaac Newton, three-quarters of a century before. Western Europe, and France in particular, was in the very glory of the "Age of Reason."

And yet science was not an alternative.

In fact, science in the mid-eighteenth century still meant nothing to men generally. There was a tiny handful of scholars and dilettantes who were interested in the new science as an intellectual game suitable for gentlemen of high IQ, but that was all. Science was a thoroughly abstract matter that did not (and indeed, according to many scientists in a tradition that dated back to the ancient Greeks, *should* not) involve practical matters.

Copernicus might argue that the Earth went around the Sun, rather than vice versa; Galileo might get into serious trouble over the matter; Newton might work out the tremendous mechanical structure that explained the motions of the heavenly bodies—yet how did any of that affect the farmer, the fisherman or the artisan?

To be sure, there were technological advances prior to the mid-eighteenth century that did affect the ordinary man, sometimes even very deeply; but those advances seemed to have nothing to do with science. Inventions such as the catapult, the mariner's compass, the horseshoe, gunpowder and printing were all revolutionary, but they were the product of ingenious thinking that had nothing to do with the rarefied cerebrations of the scientist (who, in the eighteenth century, was called a natural philosopher, for the term "scientist" had not yet been invented).

In short, as late as the mid-eighteenth century, the general population not only did not consider science as an alternative to superstition, it never dreamed that science could have any application at all to ordinary life.

It was in 1752, exactly, that that began to change; and it was in connection with lightning that the change began.

* * *

Of all the fatal manifestations of nature, the most personal one, the one which is most clearly an overwhelming attack of a divine being against an individual man, is the lightning bolt.

War, disease and famine are all wholesale forms of destruction. Even if to the true believers these misfortunes are all the punishment of sin, they are at least punishment on a mass scale. Not you alone, but all your friends and neighbors suffer the ravages of a conquering army, the agony of the Black Death, the famishes that follows drought-killed grainfields. Your sin is drowned and therefore diminished in the mighty sin of the village, the region, the nation.

The man who is struck by lightning, however, is a personal sinner, for his neighbors are spared and are not even singed. The victim is selected, singled out. He is even more a visible mark of a god's displeasure than the man who dies of a sudden apoplectic stroke. In the latter case the cause is invisible and may be anything, but in the former there can be no doubt. The divine displeasure is blazoned forth and there is thus a kind of superlative disgrace to the lightning stroke that goes beyond death and lends an added dimension of shame and horror to the thought of being its victim.

Naturally, lightning is closely connected with the divine in our best-known myths. To the Greeks, it was Zeus who hurled the lightning, and to the Norse, the lightning was Thor's hammer. If you care to turn to the 18th Psalm (verse 14 in particular), you will find that the biblical God also hurls lightning. Or as Julia Ward Howe says in her "Battle Hymn of the Republic"—"He hath loosed the fateful lightning of His terrible, swift sword."

And yet, if the lightning stroke were obviously the wrathful weapon of a supernatural being, there were some difficult-to-explain consequences.

As it happens, high objects are more frequently struck by lightning than low objects are. As it also happens, the highest man-made object in the small European town of early modern times was the steeple of the village church. It followed, embarrassingly enough, that the most frequent target of the lightning bolt, then, was the church itself.

I have read that over a thirty-three-year period in eighteenth-century Germany, no less than four hundred church towers were damaged by lightning. What's more, since church bells were often rung during thunderstorms in an attempt to avert the wrath of the Lord, the bell ringers were in unusual danger and in that same thirty-three-year period, 120 of them were killed.

Yet none of this seemed to shake the preconceived notion that connected lightning with sin and punishment. Until science took a hand.

In the mid-eighteenth century, scientists were fascinated by the Leyden jar. Without going into detail, this was a device which enabled one to build up a sizable electric charge; one which, on discharge, could sometimes knock a man down. The charge on a Leyden jar could be built up to the point where it might discharge across a small air gap, and when that happened, there was a brief spark and a distinct crackling sound.

It must have occurred to a number of scholars that the discharge of a Leyden jar seemed to involve a tiny lightning bolt with an accompanying pygmyish roll of thunder. Or, in reverse, it must have occurred to a number of them that in a thunderstorm, earth and sky played the role of a gigantic Leyden jar and that the massive lightning stroke and the rolling thunder were but the spark and crackle on a huge scale.

But thinking it and demonstrating it were two different things. The man who demonstrated it was our own Benjamin Franklin—the "Renaissance Man" of the American colonies.

In June 1752, Franklin prepared a kite, and to its wooden framework he tied a pointed metal rod. He attached a length of twine to the rod and connected the other end to the cord which held the kite. At the lower end of the cord he attached an electrical conductor in the shape of an iron key.

The idea was that if an electric charge built up in the clouds, it would be conducted down the pointed rod and the rain-wet cord to the iron key. Franklin was no fool; he recognized that it might also be conducted down to himself. He therefore tied a nonconducting silk thread to the kite cord and held that silk thread rather than the kite cord itself. What's more, he remained under a shed so that he and the silk thread would stay dry. He was thus effectively insulated from the lightning.

The strong wind kept the kite aloft and the storm clouds gathered. Eventually the kite vanished into one of the clouds and Franklin noted that the fibers of the kite cord were standing apart. He was certain that an electric charge was present.

With great courage (and this was the riskiest part of the experiment), Franklin brought his knuckle near the key. A spark leaped across the gap from key to knuckle. Franklin heard the crackle and felt the tingle. It was the same spark, crackle and tingle he had experienced a hundred times with Leyden jars. Franklin then took the next step. He had brought with him an uncharged Leyden jar. He brought it to the key and charged it with electricity from the heavens. When he had done so, he found that electricity behaved exactly as did ordinary earthly electricity produced by ordinary earthly means.

Franklin had demonstrated that lightning was an electrical discharge, different from that of the Leyden jar only in being immensely larger.

This meant that the rules that applied to the Leyden jar discharge would also apply to the lightning discharge.

Franklin had noted, for instance, that an electrical discharge took place more readily and quietly through a fine point than through a blunt projection. If a needle were attached to a Leyden jar, the charge leaked quietly through the needle point so readily that the jar could never be made to spark and crackle.

Well, then— If a sharp metal rod were placed at the top of some structure and if that were properly grounded, any electric charge accumulating on the structure during a thunderstorm would be quietly discharged and the chances of its building up to the catastrophic loosing of a lightning bolt were greatly diminished.

Franklin advanced the notion of this "lightning rod" in the 1753 edition of *Poor Richard's Almanac*. The notion was so simple, the principle so clear, the investment in time and material so minute, the nature of the possible relief so great that lightning rods began to rise over buildings in Philadelphia by the hundreds almost at once, then in New York and Boston, and soon even in Europe.

And it worked! Where the lightning rods rose, the lightning

stroke ceased. For the first time in the history of mankind, one of the scourges of the Universe had been beaten, not by magic and spells and prayer, not by an attempt to subvert the laws of nature—but by science, by an understanding of the laws of nature and by intelligent cooperation with them.

What's more, the lightning rod was a device that was important to every man. It was not a scholar's toy; it was a lifesaver for every mechanic's house and for every farmer's barn. It was not a distant theory; it was a down-to-earth fact. Most of all, it was the product not of an ingenious tinkerer, but of a logical working out of scientific observations. It was clearly a product of science.

Naturally the forces of superstition did not give in without a struggle. For one thing, they made the instant point that since the lightning bolt was God's vengeance, it was the height of impiety to try to ward it off.

This, however, was easy to counter. If the lightning were God's artillery and if it could be countered by a piece of iron, then God's powers were puny indeed and no minister dared imply that they were. Furthermore, the rain was also sent by God and if it was improper to use lightning rods, it was also improper to use umbrellas or, indeed, to use overcoats to ward off God's wintry winds.

The great Lisbon earthquake of 1755 was a temporary source of exultation for the ministers in the churches of Boston. There were not wanting those who pointed out that in his just wrath against the citizens of Boston, God had, with a mighty hand, destroyed the city of Lisbon. This merely succeeded, however, in giving the parishioners a poor notion of the accuracy of the divine aim.

The chief resistance, however, was negative. There was an embarrassed reluctance about putting up lightning rods on churches. It seemed to betray a lack of confidence in God, or worse still, a fullness of confidence in science that would seem to countenance atheism.

But the results of refusing to put up lightning rods proved insupportable. The church steeples remained the highest objects in town and they continued to be hit. It became all too noticeable to all men that the town church, unprotected by lightning rods, was hit while the town brothel, if protected by lightning rods, was not.

One by one, and most reluctantly, the lightning rods went up even over the churches. It became quite noticeable then that a particular church whose steeple had been damaged over and over would stop having any of this kind of trouble once the lightning rod went up.

According to one story I've read, the crowning incident took place in the Italian city of Brescia. The church of San Nazaro in that city was unprotected by lightning rods but so confident was the population in its sanctity that they stored a hundred tons of gunpowder in its vaults, considering those vaults to be the safest possible place for it.

But then, in 1767, the church was struck by lightning and the gunpowder went up in a gigantic explosion that destroyed one-sixth of the city and killed three thousand people.

That was too much. The lightning rod had won and superstition surrendered. Every lightning rod on a church was evidence of the victory and of the surrender and no one could be so blind as not to see that evidence. It was plain to anyone who would devote any thought to the problem that the proper road to God was not through the self-will of man-made magical formulas, but through the humble exploration of the laws governing the Universe.

Although the victory over lightning was a minor one in a way, for the number killed by lightning in the course of a year is minute compared to the number killed by famine, war or disease, it was crucial. From that moment on, the forces of superstition* could fight only rearguard actions and never won a major battle.

Here's one example. In the 1840s the first really effective anesthetics were introduced and the possibility arose that pain might be abolished as a necessary accompaniment of surgery and that hospitals might cease to be the most exquisitely organized torture chambers in the history of man. In particular, anesthesia might be used to ease the pains of childbirth.

---

*I am saying superstition, *not* religion. The ethical and moral side of religion is not involved in the fight against the lightning rod or against any other scientific finding. Only traditional superstitious beliefs are in the fight and it may well be argued that these are even more harmful to real religion than they are to science and rationality.

In 1847 a Scottish physician, James Young Simpson, began to use anesthesia for women in labor, and at once the holy men mounted their rostrums and began their denunciations.

From pulpit after pulpit there thundered forth a reminder of the curse visited upon Eve by God after she had eaten of the fruit of the tree of the knowledge of good and evil. Male ministers, personally safe from the pain and deadly danger of childbearing, intoned: "Unto the woman he said, I will greatly multiply thy sorrow and thy conception; in sorrow thou shalt bring forth children. . . ." (Genesis 3:16)

The usual story is that those apostles of mothers' anguish, these men who worshiped a God whom they viewed as willing to see hundreds of millions of agonized childbirths in each generation, when the means were at hand to ease the pain, were defeated by Simpson himself through a counterquotation from the Bible.

The first "childbirth" recorded in the Bible was that of Eve herself, for she was born of Adam's rib. And how did that childbirth come about? It is written in Genesis 2:21, "And the Lord God caused a deep sleep to fall upon Adam, and he slept: and he took one of his ribs, and closed up the flesh instead thereof."

In short, said Simpson, God had used anesthesia.

Actually, I am not impressed with the counterquotation. Eve was formed while Adam was still in the Garden and before he had eaten of the fruit and, therefore, before sin had entered the world. It was only after the fruit had been eaten that sin and pain entered the world. Simpson's argument was, therefore, worthless.

It was just as well it was, too, for to defeat superstition by superstition is useless. What really defeated the forces of mythology in this case was a revolt by women. They insisted on anesthesia and refused to go along with a curse that applied to them but not to the divines who revered it. Queen Victoria herself accepted anesthesia at her next accouchement and that settled *that*.

Then came 1859 and Charles Robert Darwin's *Origin of Species*. This time the forces of superstition rallied for the greatest battle of all and the preponderance of power seemed on their side. The field of battle was ideally suited to superstition and now, surely, science would be defeated.

The target under attack was the theory of evolution by natural selection, a theory that struck at the very heart and core of human vanity.

It was not a verifiable statement to the effect that a piece of metal would protect man against lightning or that a bit of vapor would protect him against pain that was being considered this time. It was, rather, a thoroughly abstract statement that was dependent upon subtle and hard-to-understand evidence that made it seem that man was an animal much like other animals and had arisen from ancestors that were apelike in nature.

Men might fight on the side of science and against superstition in order to be protected from lightning and from pain for they had much to gain in doing so. Surely they would not do so merely in order to be told they were apes, when the opposition told them they were made "in the image of God."

The prominent Conservative Member of Parliament, Benjamin Disraeli (later to be prime minister), expressed the matter so succinctly in 1864 as to add a phrase to the English language. He said, "Is man an ape or an angel? Now I am on the side of the angels."

Who would not be?

For once, it seemed, science would have to lose, for the public simply was not on its side.

Yet there were not wanting men to face down the angry multitude, and one of them was Thomas Henry Huxley, a largely self-educated English biologist. He had been against evolution to start with but after reading *Origin of Species*, he cried out, "Now why didn't *I* think of that?" and took to the lecture platform as "Darwin's Bulldog."

In 1860, at a meeting of the British Association for the Advancement of Science, at Oxford, the Bishop of Oxford undertook to "smash Darwin" in public debate. He was Samuel Wilberforce, an accomplished orator, with so unctuous a voice that he was universally known as "Soapy Sam."

Wilberforce rose to speak and for half an hour he held an overflow crowd of seven hundred in delighted thrall, while Huxley somberly waited his turn. And as the Bishop approached the end of his speech, he turned toward Huxley and, muting his organ tones to sugar-sweet mockery, begged leave to ask his honorable opponent whether it was through his grandmother or his grandfather that he claimed descent from an ape.

At that, Huxley muttered, "The Lord has delivered him into my hands." He rose, faced the audience, and gravely and patiently waited for the laughter to die down.

He then said: "If then, the question is put to me, would I rather have a miserable ape for a grandfather or a man highly endowed by nature and possessing great means and influence, and yet who employs those faculties and that influence for the mere purpose of introducing ridicule into a grave scientific discussion—I unhesitatingly affirm my preference for the ape."

Few debates have ever resulted in so devastating a biter-bit smash, and the last offensive against science by superstition was condemned to defeat from that moment.

Huxley had made it clear that it was science now that spoke with the thunders of Sinai, and it was the older orthodoxy that, in the fashion of Wilberforce's unfortunate remark, was capering about the golden calf of man-made myth.

The fight did not end, to be sure. Disraeli was still to make his own unctuous remark, and pulpits were to thunder for decades. I am still, even in this very year in which we now live, frequently made a target by sincere members of the Jehovah's Witnesses' sect, who send me publication after publication designed to disprove the theory of evolution.

But the real battle is over. There may be skulking skirmishes in the backwoods and it may even be incumbent upon the astronauts of Apollo 8 to stumble their way haltingly through the first few verses of Genesis 1 as they circle the Moon (in an absolute masterpiece of incongruity), but no man of *stature* from outside science arises to denounce science.

When some aspect of science threatens mankind with danger, as in the case of the atom bomb, or bacteriological warfare, or environmental pollution; or when it merely wastes effort and resources as (a few maintain) in the case of the space program, the warnings and criticisms are mounted from within science.

Science is the secular religion of today and scientists are, in a very literal sense, the new priesthood. And it all began when Ben Franklin flew his kite in a thunderstorm in the crucial year of 1752.

17

Breeds There a Man?

The danger with setting fictional scientists to work in the too-near future is that events may outdate the story. This doesn't necessarily ruin a story, of course. Novels by Jules Verne and H. G. Wells are still popular even though the nineteenth-century aura is unmistakable. Nevertheless, if the author is still alive at the time of outdating and if said author is proud of the accuracy of his science, he may become a little embarrassed about it. Certainly I become embarrassed.

The story that follows is accurate in that we are now indeed concerned with a defense against nuclear weapons, but the nature of the proposed defense in reality is totally different from the one I dreamed up in my story.

But never mind! Nuclear defense isn't the point of the story, anyhow!

Police Sergeant Mankiewicz was on the telephone and he wasn't enjoying it. His conversation was sounding like a one-sided view of a firecracker.

He was saying, "That's right! He came in here and said, 'Put me in jail, because I want to kill myself.'

". . . I can't help that. Those were his exact words. It sounds crazy to me too.

". . . Look, mister, the guy answers the description. You asked me for information and I'm giving it to you.

". . . He has exactly that scar on his right cheek and he said his name was John Smith. He didn't say it was doctor anything-at-all.

". . . Well, sure it's a phony. Nobody is named John Smith. Not in a police station, anyway.

". . . He's in jail now.

". . . Yes. I mean it.

". . . Resisting an officer; assault and battery; malicious mischief. That's three counts.

". . . I don't care who he is.

". . . All right. I'll hold on."

He looked up at Officer Brown and put his hand over the mouthpiece of the phone. It was a ham of a hand that nearly swallowed up the phone altogether. His blunt-featured face was ruddy and steaming under a thatch of pale yellow hair.

He said, "Trouble! Nothing but trouble at a precinct station. I'd rather be pounding the beat any day."

"Who's on the phone?" asked Brown. He had just come in and didn't really care. He thought Mankiewicz would look better on a suburban beat too.

"Oak Ridge. Long distance. A guy called Grant. Head of the somethingological division, and now he's getting somebody else at seventy-five cents a min . . . hello!"

Mankiewicz got a new grip on the phone and held himself down.

"Look," he said, "let me go through this from the beginning. I want you to get it straight and then if you don't like it, you can send someone down here. The guy doesn't want a lawyer. He claims he just wants to stay in jail and, brother, that's all right with me.

"Well, will you listen? He came in yesterday, walked right up to me, and said, 'Officer, I want you to put me in jail because I want to kill myself.' So I said, 'Mister, I'm sorry you want to kill yourself. Don't do it, because if you do, you'll regret it the rest of your life.'

". . . I *am* serious. I'm just telling you what I said. I'm not saying it was a funny joke, but I've got my own troubles here, if you know what I mean. Do you think all I've got to do here is to listen to cranks who walk in and—

". . . Give me a chance, will you? I said, 'I can't put you

285

in jail for wanting to kill yourself. That's no crime.' And he said, 'But I don't want to die.' So I said, 'Look, bud, get out of here.' I mean if a guy wants to commit suicide, all right, and if he doesn't want to, all right, but I don't want him weeping on my shoulder.

". . . I'm *getting* on with it. So he said to me, 'If I commit a crime, will you put me in jail?' I said, 'If you're caught and if someone files a charge and you can't put up bail, we will. Now beat it.' So he picked up the inkwell on my desk and before I could stop him, he turned it upside down on the open police blotter.

". . . That's right! Why do you think we have 'malicious mischief' tabbed on him? The ink ran down all over my pants.

". . . Yes, assault and battery too! I came hopping down to shake a little sense into him, and he kicked me in the shins and handed me one in the eye.

". . . I'm not making this up. You want to come down here and look at my face?

". . . He'll be up in court one of these days. About Thursday maybe.

". . . Ninety days is the least he'll get, unless the psychos say otherwise. I think he belongs in the loony bin myself.

". . . Officially he's John Smith. That's the only name he'll give.

". . . No, sir, he doesn't get released without the proper legal steps.

". . . Okay, you do that if you want to, bud! I just do my job here."

He banged the phone into its cradle, glowered at it, then picked it up again and began dialing. He said, "Gianetti?" got the proper answer and began talking: "What's the AEC? I've been talking to some Joe on the phone and he says—

". . . No, I'm not kidding, lunkhead. If I were kidding, I'd put up a sign. What's the alphabet soup?"

He listened, said "Thanks" in a small voice and hung up again.

He had lost some of his color. "That second guy was the head of the Atomic Energy Commission," he said to Brown. "They must have switched me from Oak Ridge to Washington."

Brown lounged to his feet. "Maybe the FBI is after this John Smith guy. Maybe he's one of these here scientists." He felt moved to philosophy. "They ought to keep atomic secrets away from those guys. Things were okay as long as General Groves was the only fella who knew about the atom bomb. Once they cut in these here scientists on it, though—"

"Ah, shut up," snarled Mankiewicz.

Dr. Oswald Grant kept his eyes fixed on the white line that marked the highway and handled the car as though it were an enemy of his. He always did. He was tall and knobby, with a withdrawn expression stamped on his face. His knees crowded the wheel, and his knuckles whitened whenever he made a turn.

Inspector Darrity sat beside him with his legs crossed so that the sole of his left shoe came up hard against the door. It would leave a sandy mark when he took it away. He tossed a nut-brown penknife from hand to hand. Earlier he had unsheathed its wicked, gleaming blade and scraped casually at his nails as they drove, but a sudden swerve had nearly cost him a finger and he desisted.

He said, "What do you know about this Ralson?"

Dr. Grant took his eyes from the road momentarily, then returned them. He said uneasily, "I've known him since he took his doctorate at Princeton. He's a very brilliant man."

"Yes? Brilliant, huh? Why is it that all you scientific men describe one another as 'brilliant'? Aren't there any mediocre ones?"

"Many. I'm one of them. But Ralson isn't. You ask anyone. Ask Oppenheimer. Ask Bush. He was the youngest observer at Alamogordo."

"Okay. He was brilliant. What about his private life?"
Grant waited. "I wouldn't know."

"You know him since Princeton. How many years is that?"
They had been scouring north along the highway from Washington for two hours with scarcely a word between them. Now Grant felt the atmosphere change and the grip of the law on his coat collar.

"He got out in '43."

"You've known him eight years then."

"That's right."

"And you don't know about his private life?"

"A man's life is his own, Inspector. He wasn't very sociable. A great many of the men are like that. They work under pressure and when they're off the job, they're not interested in continuing the lab acquaintanceships."

"Did he belong to any organizations that you know of?"

"No."

The inspector said, "Did he ever say anything to you that might indicate he was disloyal?"

Grant shouted, "No!" and there was silence for a while.

Then Darrity said, "How important is Ralson in atomic research?"

Grant hunched over the wheel and said, "As important as any one man can be. I grant you that no one is indispensable, but Ralson has always seemed to be rather unique. He has the engineering mentality."

"What does that mean?"

"He isn't much of a mathematician himself, but he can work out the gadgets that put someone else's math into life. There's no one like him when it comes to that. Time and again, Inspector, we've had a problem to lick and no time to lick it in. There were nothing but blank minds all around until he put some thought into it and said, 'Why don't you try so-and-so?' Then he'd go away. He wouldn't even be interested enough to see if it worked. But it always did. Always! Maybe we would have got it ourselves eventually, but it might have taken months of additional time. I don't know how he does it. It's no use asking him either. He just looks at you and says, 'It was obvious,' and walks away. Of course, once he's shown us how to do it, it *is* obvious."

The inspector let him have his say out. When no more came, he said, "Would you say he was queer mentally? Erratic, you know."

"When a person is a genius, you wouldn't expect him to be normal, would you?"

"Maybe not. But just how abnormal was this particular genius?"

"He never talked, particularly. Sometimes he wouldn't work."

"Stayed at home and went fishing instead?"

"No. He came to the labs all right, but he would just sit at his desk. Sometimes that would go on for weeks. Wouldn't answer you, or even look at you, when you spoke to him."

"Did he ever actually leave work altogether?"

"Before now, you mean? Never!"

"Did he ever claim he wanted to commit suicide? Ever say he wouldn't feel safe except in jail?"

"No."

"You're sure this John Smith is Ralson?"

"I'm almost positive. He had a chemical burn on his right cheek that can't be mistaken."

"Okay. That's that, then. I'll speak to him and see what he sounds like."

The silence fell for good this time. Dr. Grant followed the snaking line as Inspector Darrity tossed the penknife in low arcs from hand to hand.

The warden listened to the call box and looked up at his visitors. "We can have him brought up here, Inspector, regardless."

"No," Dr. Grant shook his head. "Let's go to him."

Darrity said, "Is that normal for Ralson, Dr. Grant? Would you expect him to attack a guard trying to take him out of his prison cell?"

Grant said, "I can't say."

The warden spread a calloused palm. His thick nose twitched a little. "We haven't tried to do anything about him so far because of the telegram from Washington, but, frankly, he doesn't belong here. I'll be glad to have him taken off my hands."

"We'll see him in his cell," said Darrity.

They went down the hard, bar-lined corridor. Empty, incurious eyes watched their passing.

Dr. Grant felt his flesh crawl. "Has he been kept *here* all the time?"

Darrity did not answer.

The guard, pacing before them, stopped. "This is the cell."

Darrity said, "Is that Dr. Ralson?"

Dr. Grant looked silently at the figure upon the cot. The man had been lying down when they first reached the cell, but now he had risen to one elbow and seemed to be trying to shrink into the wall. His hair was sandy and thin, his figure slight, his eyes blank and china-blue. On his right cheek there was a raised pink patch that tailed off like a tadpole.

Dr. Grant said, "That's Ralson."

The guard opened the door and stepped inside, but Inspector Darrity sent him out again with a gesture. Ralson watched them mutely. He had drawn both feet up to the cot and was pushing backward. His Adam's apple bobbled as he swallowed.

Darrity said quietly, "Dr. Elwood Ralson?"

"What do you want?" The voice was a surprising baritone.

"Would you come with us, please? We have some questions we would like to ask you."

"No! Leave me alone!"

"Dr. Ralson," said Grant, "I've been sent here to ask you to come back to work."

Ralson looked at the scientist and there was a momentary glint of something other than fear in his eyes. He said, "Hello, Grant." He got off his cot. "Listen, I've been trying to have them put me into a padded cell. Can't you make them do that for me? You know me, Grant. I wouldn't ask for something I didn't feel was necessary. Help me. I can't stand the hard walls. It makes me want to . . . bash—" He brought the flat of his palm thudding down against the hard, dull-gray concrete behind his cot.

Darrity looked thoughtful. He brought out his penknife and unbent the gleaming blade. Carefully he scraped at his thumbnail and said, "Would you like to see a doctor?"

But Ralson didn't answer that. He followed the gleam of metal and his lips parted and grew wet. His breath became ragged and harsh.

He said, "Put that away!"

Darrity paused. "Put what away?"

"The knife. Don't hold it in front of me. I can't stand looking at it."

Darrity said, "Why not?" He held it out. "Anything wrong with it? It's a good knife."

Ralson lunged. Darrity stepped back and his left hand came

290

down on the other's wrist. He lifted the knife high in the air. "What's the matter, Ralson? What are you after?"

Grant cried a protest but Darrity waved him away.

Darrity said, "What do you want, Ralson?"

Ralson tried to reach upward and bent under the other's appalling grip. He gasped, "Give me the knife.".

"Why, Ralson? What do you want to do with it?"

"Please. I've got to—" He was pleading. "I've got to stop living."

"You want to die?"

"No. But I must."

Darrity shoved. Ralson flailed backward and tumbled into his cot so that it squeaked noisily. Slowly Darrity bent the blade of his penknife into its sheath and put it away. Ralson covered his face. His shoulders were shaking but otherwise he did not move.

There was the sound of shouting from the corridor as the other prisoners reacted to the noise issuing from Ralson's cell. The guard came hurrying down, yelling "Quiet!" as he went.

Darrity looked up. "It's all right, guard."

He was wiping his hands upon a large handkerchief. "I think we'll get a doctor for him."

Dr. Gottfried Blaustein was small and dark and spoke with a trace of an Austrian accent. He needed only a small goatee to be the layman's caricature of a psychiatrist. But he was clean-shaven and very carefully dressed. He watched Grant carefully, assessing him, blocking in certain observations and deductions. He did this automatically now with everyone he met.

He said, "You give me a sort of picture. You describe a man of great talent, perhaps even genius. You tell me he has always been uncomfortable with people, that he has never fitted in with his laboratory environment, even though it was there that he met the greatest of success. Is there another environment to which he has fitted himself?"

"I don't understand."

"It is not given to all of us to be so fortunate as to find a congenial type of company at the place or in the field where we find it necessary to make a living. Often one compensates by

291

playing an instrument, or going hiking, or joining some club. In other words, one creates a new type of society when not working, in which one can feel more at home. It need not have the slightest connection with what his ordinary occupation is. It is an escape, and not necessarily an unhealthy one." He smiled and added, "Myself, I collect stamps. I am an active member of the American Society of Philatelists."

Grant shook his head. "I don't know what he did outside working hours. I doubt that he did anything like what you've mentioned."

"Um-m-m. Well, that would be sad. Relaxation and enjoyment are wherever you find them; but you must find them somewhere, no?"

"Have you spoken to Dr. Ralson yet?"

"About his problem? No."

"Aren't you going to?"

"Oh, yes. But he has been here only a week. One must give him a chance to recover. He was in a highly excited state when he first came here. It was almost a delirium. Let him rest and become accustomed to the new environment. I will question him then."

"Will you be able to get him back to work?"

Blaustein smiled. "How should I know? I don't even know what his sickness is."

"Couldn't you at least get rid of the worst of it, this suicidal obsession of his, and take care of the rest of the cure while he's at work?"

"Perhaps. I couldn't even venture an opinion so far without several interviews."

"How long do you suppose it will take?"

"In these matters, Dr. Grant, nobody can say."

Grant brought his hands together in a sharp slap. "Do what seems best then. But this is more important than you know."

"Perhaps you may be able to help me, Dr. Grant."

"How?"

"Can you get me certain information which may be classified as top secret."

"What kind of information?"

"I would like to know the suicide rate, since 1945, among nuclear scientists. Also, how many have left their jobs to go into other types of scientific work, or to leave science altogether."

"Is this in connection with Ralson?"

"Don't you think it might be an occupational disease, this terrible unhappiness of his?"

"Well—a good many have left their jobs, naturally."

"Why naturally, Dr. Grant?"

"You must know how it is, Dr. Blaustein. The atmosphere in modern atomic research is one of great pressure and red tape. You work with the government; you work with military men. You can't talk about your work; you have to be careful what you say. Naturally, if you get a chance at a job in a university, where you can fix your own hours, do your own work, write papers that don't have to be submitted to the AEC, attend conventions that aren't held behind locked doors, you take it."

"And abandon your field of specialty forever?"

"There are always nonmilitary applications. Of course there was one man who did leave for another reason. He told me once he couldn't sleep nights. He said he'd hear one hundred thousand screams coming from Hiroshima when he put the lights out. The last I heard of him he was a clerk in a haberdashery."

"And do you ever hear a few screams yourself?"

Grant nodded. "It isn't a nice feeling to know that even a little of the responsibility of atomic destruction might be your own."

"How did Ralson feel?"

"He never spoke of anything like that."

"In other words, if he felt it, he never even had the safety-valve effect of letting off steam to the rest of you."

"I guess he hadn't."

"Yet nuclear research must be done, no?"

"I'll say."

"What would you do, Dr. Grant, if you felt you *had* to do something that you *couldn't* do?"

Grant shrugged. "I don't know."

"Some people kill themselves."

"You mean that's what has Ralson down?"

"I don't know. I do not know. I will speak to Dr. Ralson this

293

evening. I can promise nothing of course, but I will let you know whatever I can."

Grant rose. "Thanks, Doctor. I'll try to get the information you want."

Elwood Ralson's appearance had improved in the week he had been at Dr. Blaustein's sanitarium. His face had filled out and some of the restlessness had gone out of him. He was tieless and beltless. His shoes were without laces.

Blaustein said, "How do you feel, Dr. Ralson?"

"Rested."

"You have been treated well?"

"No complaints, Doctor."

Blaustein's hand fumbled for the letter opener with which it was his habit to play during moments of abstraction, but his fingers met nothing. It had been put away, of course, with anything else possessing a sharp edge. There was nothing on his desk now but papers.

He said, "Sit down, Dr. Ralson. How do your symptoms progress?"

"You mean, do I have what you would call a suicidal impulse? Yes. It gets worse or better depending on my thoughts, I think. But it's always with me. There is nothing you can do to help."

"Perhaps you are right. There are often things I cannot help. But I would like to know as much as I can about you. You are an important man—"

Ralson snorted.

"You do not consider that to be so?" asked Blaustein.

"No, I don't. There are no important men, any more than there are important individual bacteria."

"I don't understand."

"I don't expect you to."

"And yet it seems to me that behind your statement there must have been much thought. It would certainly be of the greatest interest to have you tell me some of this thought."

For the first time, Ralson smiled. It was not a pleasant smile. His nostrils were white. He said, "It is amusing to watch you, Doctor. You go about your business so conscientiously. You must listen to me, mustn't you, with just that air of

294

phony interest and unctuous sympathy? I can tell you the most ridiculous things and still be sure of an audience, can't I?"

"Don't you think my interest can be real, even granted that it is professional too?"

"No, I don't."

"Why not?"

"I'm not interested in discussing it."

"Would you rather return to your room?"

"If you don't mind. No!" His voice had suddenly suffused with fury as he stood up, then almost immediately sat down again, "Why shouldn't I use you? I don't like to talk to people. They're stupid. They don't see things. They stare at the obvious for hours and it means nothing to them. If I spoke to them, they wouldn't understand; they'd lose patience; they'd laugh. Whereas you must listen. It's your job. You can't interrupt to tell me I'm mad, even though you may think so."

"I'd be glad to listen to whatever you would like to tell me."

Ralson drew a deep breath. "I've known something for a year now, that very few people know. Maybe it's something no *live* person knows. Do you know that human cultural advances come in spurts? Over a space of two generations in a city containing thirty thousand free men, enough literary and artistic genius of the first rank arose to supply a nation of millions for a century under ordinary circumstances. I'm referring to the Athens of Pericles.

"There are other examples. There is the Florence of the Medicis, the England of Elizabeth, the Spain of the Cordovan Emirs. There was the spasm of social reformers among the Israelites of the eighth and seventh centuries before Christ. Do you know what I mean?"

Blaustein nodded. "I see that history is a subject that interests you."

"Why not? I suppose there's nothing that says I must restrict myself to nuclear cross-sections and wave mechanics."

"Nothing at all. Please proceed."

"At first I thought I could learn more of the true inwardness of historical cycles by consulting a specialist. I had some conferences with a professional historian. A waste of time!"

"What was his name, this professional historian?"

"Does it matter?"

"Perhaps not, if you would rather consider it confidential. What did he tell you?"

"He said I was wrong, that history only appeared to go in spasms. He said that after closer studies, the great civilizations of Egypt and Sumeria did not arise suddenly or out of nothing, but upon the basis of a long-developing subcivilization that was already sophisticated in its arts. He said that Periclean Athens was built upon a pre-Periclean Athens of lower accomplishments, without which the age of Pericles could not have been.

"I asked him why was there not a post-Periclean Athens of higher accomplishments still, and he told me that Athens was ruined by a plague and by the long war with Sparta. I asked about other cultural spurts and each time it was a war that ended them, or, in some cases, even accompanied them. He was like all the rest. The truth was there; he had only to bend and pick it up, but he didn't."

Ralson stared at the floor and said in a tired voice, "They come to me in the laboratory sometimes, Doctor. They say, 'How the devil are we going to get rid of the such-and-such effect that is ruining all our measurements, Ralson?' They show me the instruments and the wiring diagrams and I say, 'It's staring at you. Why don't you do so-and-so? A child could tell you that.' Then I walk away because I can't endure the slow puzzling of their stupid faces. Later they come to me again and say, 'It worked, Ralson. How did you figure it out?' I can't explain to them, Doctor; it would be like explaining that water is wet. And I couldn't explain to the historian. And I can't explain to you. It's a waste of time."

"Would you like to go back to your room?"

"Yes."

Blaustein sat and wondered for many minutes after Ralson had been escorted out of his office. His fingers found their way automatically into the upper right drawer of his desk and lifted out the letter opener. He twiddled it in his fingers.

Finally he lifted the telephone and dialed the unlisted number he had been given.

He said, "This is Blaustein. There is a professional historian who was consulted by Dr. Ralson some time in the past, probably a bit over a year ago. I don't know his name. I don't even know if he was connected with a university. If you could find him, I would like to see him."

Thaddeus Milton, PhD, blinked thoughtfully at Blaustein and brushed his hand through his iron-gray hair. He said, "They came to me and I said that I had indeed met this man. However, I have had very little connection with him. None, in fact, beyond a few conversations of a professional nature."

"How did he come to you?"

"He wrote me a letter; why me, rather than someone else, I do not know. A series of articles written by myself had appeared in one of the semilearned journals of semipopular appeal about that time. I may have attracted his attention."

"I see. With what general topic were the articles concerned?"

"They were a consideration of the validity of the cyclic approach to history. That is, whether one can really say that a particular civilization must follow the laws of growth and decline in any matter analogous to those involving individuals."

"I have read Toynbee, Dr. Milton."

"Well then, you know what I mean."

Blaustein said, "And when Dr. Ralson consulted you, was it with reference to this cyclic approach to history?"

"U-m-m-m. In a way, I suppose. Of course the man is not an historian and some of his notions about cultural trends are rather dramatic and . . . what shall I say . . . tabloidish. Pardon me, Doctor, if I ask a question which may be improper. Is Dr. Ralson one of your patients?"

"Dr. Ralson is not well and is in my care. This and all else we say here is confidential, of course."

"Quite. I understand that. However, your answer explains something to me. Some of his ideas almost verged on the irrational. He was always worried, it seemed to me, about the connection between what he called 'cultural spurts' and calamities of one sort or another. Now such connections have been noted frequently. The time of a nation's greatest vitality may come at a time of great national insecurity. The Netherlands is a good case in point. Its great artists, statesmen and

297

explorers belong to the early seventeenth century, at the time when she was locked in a death struggle with the greatest European power of the time, Spain. When at the point of destruction at home, she was building an empire in the Far East and had secured footholds on the northern coast of South America, the southern tip of Africa and the Hudson Valley of North America. Her fleets fought England to a standstill. And then, once her political safety was assured, she declined.

"Well, as I say, that is not unusual. Groups, like individuals, will rise to strange heights in answer to a challenge and vegetate in the absence of a challenge. Where Dr. Ralson left the paths of sanity, however, was in insisting that such a view amounted to confusing cause and effect. He declared that it was not times of war and danger that stimulated 'cultural spurts,' but rather vice versa. He claimed that each time a group of men showed too much vitality and ability, a war became necessary to destroy the possibility of their further development."

"I see," said Blaustein.

"I rather laughed at him, I am afraid. It may be that that was why he did not keep the last appointment we made. Just toward the end of the last conference he asked me, in the most intense fashion imaginable, whether I did not think it queer that such an improbable species as man was dominant on Earth, when all he had in his favor was intelligence. There I laughed aloud. Perhaps I should not have, poor fellow."

"It was a natural reaction," said Blaustein, "but I must take no more of your time. You have been most helpful."

They shook hands and Thaddeus Milton took his leave.

"Well," said Darrity, "there are your figures on the recent suicides among scientific personnel. Get any deductions out of it?"

"I should be asking you that," said Blaustein gently. "The FBI must have investigated thoroughly."

"You can bet the national debt on that. They *are* suicides. There's no mistake about it. There have been people checking on it in another department. The rate is about four times above normal, taking age, social status, economic class into consideration."

"What about British scientists?"

"Just about the same."

"And the Soviet Union?"

"Who can tell?" The investigator leaned forward. "Doc, you don't think the Soviets have some sort of ray that can make people want to commit suicide, do you? It's sort of suspicious that men in atomic research are the only ones affected."

"Is it? Perhaps not. Nuclear physicists may have peculiar strains imposed upon them. It is difficult to tell without thorough study."

"You mean complexes might be coming through?" asked Darrity warily.

Blaustein made a face. "Psychiatry is becoming too popular. Everybody talks of complexes and neuroses and psychoses and compulsions and what-not. One man's guilt complex is another man's good night's sleep. If I could talk to one of the men who committed suicide, maybe I could know something."

"You're talking to Ralson."

"Yes, I'm talking to Ralson."

"Has *he* got a guilt complex?"

"Not particularly. He has a background out of which it would not surprise me if he obtained a morbid concern with death. When he was twelve, he saw his mother die under the wheels of an automobile. His father died slowly of cancer. Yet the effect of that on his present troubles is not clear."

Darrity picked up his hat. "Well, I wish you would get a move on, Doc. There's something big on, bigger than the H-bomb. I don't know how anything *can* be bigger than that, but it is."

Ralson insisted on standing. "I had a bad night last night, Doctor."

"I hope," said Blaustein, "these conferences are not disturbing you."

"Well, maybe they are. It has me thinking on the subject again. It also makes things bad, when I do that. How do you imagine it feels being part of a bacterial culture, Doctor."

299

"I had never thought of that. To a bacterium, it probably feels quite normal."

Ralson did not hear. He said slowly, "A culture in which intelligence is being studied. We study all sorts of things as far as their genetic relationships are concerned. We take fruit flies and cross red eyes with white eyes to see what happens. We don't care anything about red eyes and white eyes, but we try to gather from them certain basic genetic principles. You see what I mean?"

"Certainly."

"Even in humans we can follow various physical characteristics. There is the Hapsburg lip, and the hemophilia that started with Queen Victoria and cropped up in her descendants among the Spanish and Russian royal families. We can even follow feeble-mindedness in the Jukes and Kallikaks. You learn about it in high-school biology. But you can't breed human beings the way you do fruit flies. Humans live too long. It would take centuries to draw conclusions. It's a pity we don't have a special race of men that reproduce at weekly intervals, eh?"

He waited for an answer, but Blaustein only smiled.

Ralson said, "Only that's exactly what we would be for another group of beings whose life span might be thousands of years. To them, we would reproduce rapidly enough. We would be short-lived creatures and they could study the genetics of such things as musical aptitude, scientific intelligence and so on. Not that those things would interest them as such, any more than the white eyes of the fruit fly interest us as white eyes."

"This is a very interesting notion," said Blaustein.

"It is not simply a notion. It is true. To me, it is obvious, and I don't care how it seems to you. Look around you. Look at the planet, Earth. What kind of ridiculous animal are we to be lords of the world after the dinosaurs had failed? Sure, we're intelligent, but what's intelligence? We think it is important because we have it. If the Tyrannosaurus could have picked out the one quality that he thought would ensure species domination, it would be size and strength. And he would make a better case for it. He lasted longer than we're likely to.

300

"Intelligence in itself isn't much as far as survival values are concerned. The elephant makes out very poorly indeed when compared to the sparrow even though he is much more intelligent. The dog does well under man's protection, but not as well as the housefly, against whom every human hand is raised. Or take the primates as a group. The small ones cower before their enemies; the large ones have always been remarkably unsuccessful in doing more than barely holding their own. The baboons do their best and that is because of their canines, not their brains."

A light film of perspiration covered Ralson's forehead. "And one can see that man has been tailored, made to careful specifications for those things that study us. Generally the primate is short-lived. Naturally the larger ones live longer, which is a fairly general rule in animal life. Yet the human being has a life span twice as long as any of the other great apes; considerably longer even than the gorilla that outweighs him. We mature later. It's as though we've been carefully bred to live a little longer so that our life cycle might be more of a convenient length."

He jumped to his feet, shaking his fists above his head. "A thousand years is a day—"

Blaustein punched a button hastily.

For a moment Ralson struggled against the white-coated orderly who entered, and then he allowed himself to be led away.

Blaustein looked after him, shook his head and picked up the telephone.

He got Darrity. "Inspector, you may as well know that this may take a long time."

He listened and shook his head again. "I know. I don't minimize the urgency."

The voice in the receiver was tinny and harsh. "Doctor, you *are* minimizing it. I'll send Dr. Grant to you. He'll explain the situation."

Dr. Grant asked how Ralson was, then asked somewhat wistfully if he could see him. Blaustein shook his head gently.

Grant said, "I've been directed to explain the current situation in atomic research to you."

"So that I will understand, no?"

"I hope so. It's a measure of desperation. I'll have to remind you—"

"Not to breathe a word of it. Yes, I know. This insecurity on the part of you people is a very bad symptom. You must know these things cannot be hidden."

"You live with secrecy. It's contagious."

"Exactly. What is the current secret?"

"There is . . . or at least there might be, a defense against the atomic bomb."

"And that is a secret? It would be better it should be shouted to all the people of the world instantly."

"For heaven's sake, no. Listen to me, Dr. Blaustein. It's only on paper so far. It's at the E-equals-mc-square stage, almost. It may not be practical. It would be bad to raise hopes we would have to disappoint. On the other hand, if it were known that we *almost* had a defense, there *might* be a desire to start and win a war before the defense were completely developed."

"That I earnestly hope would not happen. But, nevertheless, I distract you. What is the nature of this defense, or have you told me as much as you dare?"

"No, I can go as far as I like, as far as it is necessary to convince you we have to have Ralson—and fast!"

"Well, then tell me, and I too will know the secret. I'll feel like a member of the cabinet."

"You'll know more than most. Look, Dr. Blaustein, let me explain it in lay language. So far, military advances have been made fairly equally in both offensive and defensive weapons. Once before there seemed to be a definite and permanent tipping of all warfare in the direction of the offense, and that was with the invention of gunpowder. But the defense caught up. The medieval man-in-armor-on-horse became the modern man-in-tank-on-treads, and the stone castle became the concrete pillbox. The same thing, you see, except that everything has been boosted several orders of magnitude."

"Very good. You make it clear. But with the atomic bomb comes more orders of magnitude, no? You must go past concrete and steel for protection."

"Right. Only we can't just make thicker and thicker walls. We've run out of materials that are strong enough. So we must abandon materials altogether. If the atom attacks, we must let the atom defend. We will use energy itself, a force field."

"And what," asked Dr. Blaustein gently, "is a force field?"

"I wish I could tell you. Right now it's an equation on paper. Energy can be so channeled as to create a wall of matterless inertia theoretically. In practice, we don't know how to do it."

"It would be a wall you could not go through, is that it? Even for atoms?"

"Even for atom bombs. The only limit of its strength would be the amount of energy we could pour into it. It could theoretically be made to be impermeable to radiation. It would bounce off the gamma rays. What we're dreaming of is a screen that would be in permanent place about cities, at minimum strength, using practically no energy. It could then be triggered to maximum intensity in a fraction of a millisecond at the impingement of shortwave radiation, say the amount radiating from a mass of plutonium large enough to be an atomic warhead. All this is theoretically possible."

"And why must you have Ralson?"

"Because he is the only one who can reduce it to practice, if it can be made practical at all, quickly enough. Every minute counts these days. You know what the international situation is like. Atomic defense *must* arrive before atomic war."

"You are so sure of Ralson?"

"I am as sure of him as I can be of anything. The man is amazing, Dr. Blaustein. He is always right. Nobody in the field knows how he does it."

"A sort of intuition, no?" The psychiatrist looked disturbed. "A kind of reasoning that goes beyond ordinary human capacities. Is that it?"

"I make no pretense of knowing what it is."

"Let me speak to him once more, then. I will let you know."

"Good." Grant rose to leave; then, as if in afterthought, he said, "I might say, Doctor, that if you don't do something, the Commission plans to take Dr. Ralson out of your hands."

"And try another psychiatrist? If they wish to do that, of course I will not stand in their way. It is my opinion, however,

303

that no reputable practitioner will pretend there is a rapid cure."

"We may not intend further mental treatment. He may simply be returned to work."

"That, Dr. Grant, I will fight. You will get nothing out of him. It will be his death."

"We get nothing out of him anyway."

"This way there is at least a chance, no?"

"I hope so. And by the way, please don't mention the fact that I said anything about taking Ralson away."

"I will not, and I thank you for the warning. Good-bye, Dr. Grant."

"I made a fool of myself last time, didn't I, Doctor?" said Ralson. He was frowning.

"You mean you don't believe what you said then?"

"I *do!*" Ralson's slight form trembled with the intensity of his affirmation.

He rushed to the window, and Blaustein swiveled in his chair to keep him in view. There were bars in the window. He couldn't jump. The glass was unbreakable.

Twilight was ending, and the stars were beginning to come out. Ralson stared at them in fascination; then he turned to Blaustein and flung a finger outward. "Every single one of them is an incubator. They maintain temperatures at the desired point. Different experiments; different temperatures. And the planets that circle them are just huge cultures, containing different nutrient mixtures and different life forms. The experimenters are economical too—whatever and whoever they are. They've cultured many types of life forms in this particular test tube. Dinosaurs in a moist, tropical age and ourselves among the glaciers. They turn the sun up and down and we try to work out the physics of it. Physics!" He drew his lips back in a snarl.

"Surely," said Dr. Blaustein, "it is not possible that the sun can be turned up and down at will."

"Why not? It's just like a heating element in an oven. You think bacteria know what it is that works the heat that reaches them? Who knows? Maybe they evolve theories too. Maybe they have their cosmogonies about cosmic catastrophes, in

304

which clashing light bulbs create strings of Petri dishes. Maybe they think there must be some beneficent creator that supplies them with food and warmth and says to them, 'Be fruitful and multiply!'

"We breed like them, not knowing why. We obey the so-called laws of nature, which are only our interpretation of the not-understood forces imposed upon us.

"And now they've got the biggest experiment of any yet on their hands. It's been going on for two hundred years. They decided to develop a strain for mechanical aptitude in England in the seventeen hundreds, I imagine. We call it the Industrial Revolution. It began with steam, went on to electricity, then atoms. It was an interesting experiment, but they took their chances on letting it spread. Which is why they'll have to be very drastic indeed in ending it."

Blaustein said, "And how would they plan to end it? Do you have an idea about that?"

"You ask *me* how they plan to end it? You can look about the world today and still ask what is likely to bring our technological age to an end? All the Earth fears an atomic war and would do anything to avoid it; yet all the Earth fears that an atomic war is inevitable."

"In other words, the experimenters will arrange an atomic war, whether we want it or not, to kill off the technological era we are in and to start fresh. That is it, no?"

"Yes. It's logical. When we sterilize an instrument, do the germs know where the killing heat comes from? Or what has brought it about? There is some way the experimenters can raise the heat of our emotions, some way they can handle us that passes our understanding."

"Tell me," said Blaustein, "is that why you want to die? Because you think the destruction of civilization is coming and can't be stopped?"

Ralson said, "I *don't* want to die. It's just that I must." His eyes were tortured. "Doctor, if you had a culture of germs that were highly dangerous and that you had to keep under absolute control, might you not have an agar medium impregnated with, say, penicillin, in a circle at a certain distance from the center of inoculation? Any germs spreading out too far from that center would die. You would have nothing against the particular germs who were killed; you might not even know that any germs had spread that far in the first place. It would be purely automatic.

"Doctor, there is a penicillin ring about our intellects. When we stray too far, when we penetrate the true meaning of our own existence, we have reached into the penicillin and we must die. It works slowly—but it's hard to stay alive."

He smiled briefly and sadly. Then he said, "May I go back to my room now, Doctor?"

Dr. Blaustein went to Ralson's room about noon the next day. It was a small room, and featureless. The walls were gray with padding. Two small windows were high up and could not be reached. The mattress lay directly on the padded floor. There was nothing of metal in the room, nothing that could be utilized in tearing life from body. Even Ralson's nails were clipped short.

Ralson sat up. "Hello!"

"Hello, Dr. Ralson. May I speak to you?"

"Here? There isn't any seat I can offer you."

"It is all right. I'll stand. I have a sitting job and it is good for my sitting-down place that I should stand sometimes. Dr. Ralson, I have thought all night of what you told me yesterday and in the days before."

"And now you are going to apply treatment to rid me of what you think are delusions."

"No. It is just that I wish to ask questions and perhaps to point out some consequences of your theories which . . . you will forgive me? . . . you may not have thought of."

"Oh?"

"You see, Dr. Ralson, since you have explained your theories, I too know what you know. Yet I have no feeling about suicide."

"Belief is more than something intellectual, Doctor. You'd have to believe this with all your insides, which you don't."

"Do you not think perhaps it is rather a phenomenon of adaptation?"

"How do you mean?"

"You are not really a biologist, Dr. Ralson. And although you are very brilliant indeed in physics, you do not think of

306

everything with respect to these bacterial cultures you use as analogies. You know that it is possible to breed bacterial strains that are resistant to penicillin or to almost any bacterial poison."

"Well?"

"The experimenters who breed us have been working with humanity for many generations, no? And this particular strain which they have been culturing for two centuries shows no signs of dying out spontaneously. Rather, it is a vigorous strain and a very infective one. Older high-culture strains were confined to single cities or to small areas and lasted only a generation or two. This one is spreading throughout the world. It is a *very* infective strain. Do you not think it may have developed penicillin immunity? In other words, the methods the experimenters used to wipe out other cultures may not work too well anymore, no?"

Ralson shook his head. "It's working on me."

"You are perhaps nonresistant. Or you have stumbled into a very high concentration of penicillin indeed. Consider all the people who have been trying to outlaw atomic warfare and to establish some form of world government and lasting peace. The effort has risen in recent years, without too awful results."

"It isn't stopping the atomic war that's coming."

"No, but maybe only a little more effort is all that is required. The peace advocates do not kill themselves. More and more humans are immune to the experimenters. Do you know what they are doing in the laboratory?"

"I don't want to know."

"You *must* know. They are trying to invent a force field that will stop the atom bomb. Dr. Ralson, if I am culturing a virulent and pathological bacterium, then even with all precautions, it may sometimes happen that I will start a plague. We may be bacteria to them, but we are dangerous to them, also, or they wouldn't wipe us out so carefully after each experiment.

"They are not quick, no? To them a thousand years is as a day, no? By the time they realize we are out of the culture, past the penicillin, it will be too late for them to stop us. They have brought us to the atom, and if we can only prevent ourselves from using it upon one another, we may turn out to be too much even for the experimenters."

307

Ralson rose to his feet. Small though he was, he was an inch and a half taller than Blaustein. "They are really working on a force field?"

"They are trying to. But they need you."

"No, I can't."

"They must have you in order that you might see what is so obvious to you. It is not obvious to them. Remember, it is your help or else—defeat of man by the experimenters."

Ralson took a few rapid steps away, staring into the blank, padded wall. He muttered, "But there must be that defeat. If they build a force field, it will mean death for all of them before it can be completed."

"Some or all of them may be immune, no? And in any case, it will be death for them anyhow. They are trying."

Ralson said, "I'll try to help them."

"Do you still want to kill yourself?"

"Yes."

"But you'll try not to, no?"

"I'll *try* not to, Doctor." His lip quivered. "I'll have to be watched."

Blaustein climbed the stairs and presented his pass to the guard in the lobby. He had already been inspected at the outer gate, but he, his pass, and its signature were now scrutinized once again. After a moment, the guard retired to his little cubby and made a phone call. The answer satisfied him. Blaustein took a seat and in half a minute was up again, shaking hands with Dr. Grant.

"The President of the United States would have trouble getting in here, no?" said Blaustein.

The lanky physicist smiled. "You're right, if he came without warning."

They took an elevator, which traveled twelve floors. The office to which Grant led the way had windows in three directions. It was soundproofed and air-conditioned. Its walnut furniture was in a state of high polish.

Blaustein said, "My goodness. It is like the office of the chairman of a board of directors. Science is becoming big business."

Grant looked embarrassed. "Yes, I know, but government

308

money flows easily and it is difficult to persuade a congress-man that your work is important unless he can see, smell and touch the surface shine."

Blaustein sat down and felt the upholstered seat give way slowly. He said, "Dr. Elwood Ralson has agreed to return to work."

"Wonderful. I was hoping you would say that. I was hoping that that was why you wanted to see me." As though inspired by the news, Grant offered the psychiatrist a cigar, which was refused.

"However," said Blaustein, "he remains a very sick man. He will have to be treated carefully and with insight."

"Of course. Naturally."

"It's not quite as simple as you may think. I want to tell you something of Ralson's problems so that you will really understand how delicate the situation is."

He went on talking and Grant listened, first in concern and then in astonishment. "But then the man is out of his head, Dr. Blaustein. He'll be of no use to us. He's crazy."

Blaustein shrugged. "It depends on how you define 'crazy.' It's a bad word; don't use it. He has delusions, certainly. Whether they will affect his peculiar talents one cannot know."

"But surely no sane man could possibly—"

"Please. Please. Let us not launch into long discussions on psychiatric definitions of sanity and so on. The man has delusions, and ordinarily I would dismiss them from all consideration. It is just that I have been given to understand that the man's particular ability lies in his manner of proceeding to the solution of a problem by what seems to be outside ordinary reason. That is so, no?"

"Yes. That *must* be admitted."

"How can you and I judge then as to the worth of his conclusions? Let me ask you, do *you* have suicidal impulses lately?"

"No, of course not."

"And other scientists here?"

"I don't think so."

"I would suggest, however, that while research on the force field proceeds, the scientists concerned be watched here and at home. It might even be a good enough idea that they should

309

not go home. Offices like these could be arranged to be a small dormitory—"

"Sleep at work? You would never get them to agree."

"Oh, yes. If you do not tell them the real reason but say it is for security purposes, they will agree. 'Security purposes' is a wonderful phrase these days, no? Ralson must be watched more than anyone."

"Of course."

"But all this is minor. It is something to be done to satisfy my conscience in case Ralson's theories are correct. Actually, I don't believe them. They *are* delusions, but once that is granted, it is necessary to ask what the causes of those delusions are. What is it in Ralson's mind, in his background, in his life, that makes it so necessary for him to have these particular delusions? One cannot answer that simply. It may well take years of constant psychoanalysis to discover the answer. And until the answer is discovered, he will not be cured.

"But, meanwhile, we can perhaps make intelligent guesses. He has had an unhappy childhood, which in one way or another has brought him face to face with death in very unpleasant fashion. In addition, he has never been able to form associations with other children, or, as he grew older, with other men. He was always impatient with their slower forms of reasoning. Whatever difference there is between his mind and that of others, it has built a wall between him and society as strong as the force field you are trying to design. For similar reasons, he has been unable to enjoy a normal sex life. He has never married; he has had no sweethearts.

"It is easy to see that he could easily compensate to himself for this failure to be accepted by his social milieu by taking refuge in the thought that other human beings are inferior to himself. Which is, of course, true as far as mentality is concerned. There are, of course, many, many facets to the human personality and in not all of them is he superior. No one is. Others, then, who are more prone to see merely what is inferior, just as he himself is, would not accept his affected preeminence of position. They would think him queer, even laughable, which would make it even more important to Ralson to prove how miserable and inferior the human species was. How could he better do that than to show that mankind was simply a form of bacteria to other superior creatures who experiment upon them? And then his impulses to suicide would be a wild desire to break away completely from being a man at all, to stop this identification with the miserable species he has created in his mind. You see?"

Grant nodded. "Poor guy."

"Yes, it is a pity. Had he been properly taken care of in childhood— Well, it is best for Dr. Ralson that he have no contact with any of the other men here. He is too sick to be trusted with them. You yourself must arrange to be the only man who will see him or speak to him. Dr. Ralson has agreed to that. He apparently thinks you are not so stupid as some of the others."

Grant smiled faintly. "That is agreeable to me."

"You will, of course, be careful. I would not discuss anything with him but his work. If he should volunteer information about his theories, which I doubt, confine yourself to something noncommittal and leave. And at all times, keep away anything that is sharp and pointed. Do not let him reach a window. Try to have his hands kept in view. You understand. I leave my patient in your care, Dr. Grant."

"I will do my best, Dr. Blaustein."

For two months Ralson lived in a corner of Grant's office, and Grant lived with him. Gridwork had been built up before the windows; wooden furniture was removed and upholstered sofas brought in. Ralson did his thinking on the couch and his calculating on a desk pad atop a hassock.

The "Do Not Enter" sign was a permanent fixture outside the office. Meals were left outside. The adjoining men's room was marked off for private use and the door between it and the office removed. Grant switched to an electric razor. He made certain that Ralson took sleeping pills each night and waited till the other slept before sleeping himself.

And always reports were brought to Ralson. He read them while Grant watched and tried to seem not to watch.

Then Ralson would let them drop and stare at the ceiling, with one hand shading his eyes.

"Anything?" asked Grant.

311

Ralson shook his head from side to side.

Grant said, "Look, I'll clear the building during the swing shift. It's important that you see some of the experimental jigs we've been setting up."

They did so, wandering through the lighted, empty buildings like drifting ghosts, hand in hand. Always hand in hand. Grant's grip was tight. But after each trip, Ralson would still shake his head from side to side.

Half a dozen times he would begin writing; each time there would be a few scrawls and then he would kick the hassock over on its side.

Until, finally, he began writing once again and covered half a page rapidly. Automatically Grant approached. Ralson looked up, covering the sheet of paper with a trembling hand.

He said, "Call Blaustein."

"What?"

"I said, call Blaustein. Get him here. Now!"

Grant moved to the telephone.

Ralson was writing rapidly now, stopping only to brush wildly at his forehead with the back of a hand. It came away wet.

He looked up and his voice was cracked, "Is he coming?"

Grant looked worried. "He isn't at his office."

"Get him at his home. Get him wherever he is. *Use* that telephone. Don't play with it."

Grant used it; and Ralson pulled another sheet toward him.

Five minutes later Grant said, "He's coming. What's wrong? You're looking sick."

Ralson could only speak thickly. "No time—can't talk—"

He was writing, scribbling, scrawling, shakily diagramming. It was as though he were driving his hands, fighting it.

"Dictate!" urged Grant. "I'll write."

Ralson shook him off. His words were unintelligible. He held his right wrist with this other hand, shoving it as though it were a piece of wood, and then collapsed over the papers.

Grant edged them out from under and laid Ralson down on the couch. He hovered over him restlessly until Blaustein arrived.

Blaustein took one look. "What happened?"

Grant said, "I think he's alive," but by that time Blaustein

312

had verified that for himself, and Grant told him what had happened.

Blaustein used a hypodermic and they waited. Ralson's eyes were blank when they opened. He moaned.

Blaustein leaned close. "Ralson."

Ralson's hands reached out blindly and clutched at the psychiatrist. "Doc. Take me back."

"I will. Now. It is that you have the force field worked out, no?"

"It's on the papers. Grant, it's on the papers."

Grant had them and was leafing through them dubiously. Ralson said weakly, "It's not *all* there. It's all I can write. You'll *have* to make it out of that. Take me back, Doc!"

"Wait," said Grant. He whispered urgently to Blaustein, "Can't you leave him here till we test this thing? I can't make out what most of this is. The writing is illegible. Ask him what makes him think this will work."

"Ask *him*?" said Blaustein gently. "Isn't he the one who always knows?"

"Ask me anyway," said Ralson, overhearing from where he lay on the couch. His eyes were suddenly wide and blazing.

They turned to him.

He said, "*They* don't want a force field. *They!* The experimenters! As long as I had no true grasp, things remained as they were. But I hadn't followed up that thought—*that* thought which is there in the papers—I hadn't followed it up for thirty seconds before I felt . . . I felt—Doctor—"

Blaustein said, "What is it?"

Ralson was whispering again. "I'm deeper in the penicillin. I could feel myself plunging in and in, the farther I went with that. I've never been in . . . so deep. That's how I knew I was right. Take me away."

Blaustein straightened. "I'll have to take him away, Grant. There's no alternative. If you can make out what he's written, that's it. If you can't make it out, I can't help you. That man can do no more work in his field without dying, do you understand?"

"But," said Grant, "he's dying of something imaginary."

"All right. Say that he is. But he will be really dead just the same, no?"

313

Ralson was unconscious again and heard nothing of this. Grant looked at him somberly, then said, "Well, take him away, then."

Ten of the top men at the Institute watched glumly as slide after slide filled the illuminated screen. Grant faced them, expression hard and frowning.

He said, "I think the idea is simple enough. You're mathematicians and you're engineers. The scrawl may seem illegible, but it was done with meaning behind it. That meaning must somehow remain in the writing, distorted though it is. The first page is clear enough. It should be a good lead. Each one of you will look at every page over and over again. You're going to put down every possible version of each page as it seems it might be. You will work independently. I want no consultations."

One of them said, "How do you know it means *anything*, Grant?"

"Because those are Ralson's notes."

"*Ralson!* I thought he was—"

"You thought he was sick," said Grant. He had to shout over the rising hum of conversation. "I know. He is. That's the writing of a man who was nearly dead. It's all we'll ever get from Ralson anymore. Somewhere in that scrawl is the answer to the force-field problem. If we can't find it, we may have to spend ten years looking for it elsewhere."

They bent to their work. The night passed. Two nights passed. Three nights—

Grant looked at the results. He shook his head. "I'll take your word for it that it is all self-consistent. I can't say I understand it."

Lowe, who in the absence of Ralson would readily have been rated the best nuclear engineer in the Institute, shrugged. "It's not exactly clear to me. If it works, he hasn't explained why."

"He had no time to explain. Can you build a generator as he describes it?"

"I could try."

"Would you look at all the other versions of the pages?"

"The others are definitely not self-consistent."

"Would you double-check?"

"Sure."

"And you could start construction anyway?"

"I'll get the shop started. But I tell you frankly that I'm pessimistic."

"I know. So am I."

The thing grew. Hal Ross, Senior Mechanic, was put in charge of the actual construction, and he stopped sleeping. At any hour of the day or night he could be found at it, scratching his bald head.

He asked questions only once. "What is it, Dr. Lowe? Never saw anything like it? What's it supposed to do?"

Lowe said, "You know where you are, Ross. You know we don't ask questions here. Don't ask again."

Ross did not ask again. He was known to dislike the structure that was being built. He called it ugly and unnatural. But he stayed at it.

Blaustein called one day.

Grant said, "How's Ralson?"

"Not good. He wants to attend the testing of the Field Projector he designed."

Grant hesitated. "I suppose he should. It's his after all."

"I would have to come with him."

Grant looked unhappier. "It might be dangerous, you know. Even in a pilot test, we'd be playing with tremendous energies."

Blaustein said, "No more dangerous for us than for you."

"Very well. The list of observers will have to be cleared through the Commission and the FBI, but I'll put you in."

Blaustein looked about him. The Field Projector squatted in the very center of the huge testing laboratory, but all else had been cleared. There was no visible connection with the plutonium pile which served as energy source, but from what the psychiatrist heard in scraps about him—he knew better than to ask Ralson—the connection was from beneath.

At first the observers had circled the machine, talking in incomprehensibles, but they were drifting away now. The gallery was filling up. There were at least three men in generals' uniforms on the other side, and a real coterie of lower scale military. Blaustein chose an unoccupied portion of the railing; for Ralson's sake, most of all.

He said, "Do you still think you would like to stay?"

It was warm enough within the laboratory, but Ralson was in his coat, with his collar turned up. It made little difference, Blaustein felt. He doubted that any of Ralson's former acquaintances would now recognize him.

Ralson said, "I'll stay."

Blaustein was pleased. He wanted to see the test. He turned again at a new voice.

"Hello, Dr. Blaustein."

For a minute Blaustein did not place him; then he said, "Ah, Inspector Darrity. What are you doing here?"

"Just what you would suppose." He indicated the watchers. "There isn't any way you can weed them out so that you can be sure there won't be any mistakes. I once stood as near to Klaus Fuchs as I am standing to you." He tossed his pocketknife into the air and retrieved it with a dexterous motion.

"Ah, yes. Where shall one find perfect security? What man can trust even his own unconscious? And you will now stand near to me, no?"

"Might as well." Darrity smiled. "You were very anxious to get in here, weren't you?"

"Not for myself, Inspector. And would you put away the knife, please."

Darrity turned in surprise in the direction of Blaustein's gentle head gesture. He put his knife away and looked at Blaustein's companion for the second time. He whistled softly.

He said, "Hello, Dr. Ralson."

Ralson croaked, "Hello."

Blaustein was not surprised at Darrity's reaction. Ralson had lost twenty pounds since returning to the sanitarium. His face was yellow and wrinkled, the face of a man who had suddenly become sixty.

Blaustein said, "Will the test be starting soon?"

Darrity said, "It looks as if they're starting now."

He turned and leaned on the rail. Blaustein took Ralson's

elbow and began leading him away, but Darrity said softly, "Stay here, Doc. I don't want you wandering about."

Blaustein looked across the laboratory. Men were standing about with the uncomfortable air of having turned half to stone. He could recognize Grant, tall and gaunt, moving his hand slowly to light a cigarette, then changing his mind and putting lighter and cigarette in his pocket. The young men at the control panels waited tensely.

Then there was a low humming and the faint smell of ozone filled the air.

Ralson said harshly, "Look!"

Blaustein and Darrity looked along the pointing finger. The Projector seemed to flicker. It was as though there were heated air rising between it and them.

An iron ball came swinging down pendulum fashion and passed through the flickering area.

"It slowed up, no?" said Blaustein excitedly.

Ralson nodded. "They're measuring the height of rise on the other side to calculate the loss of momentum. Fools! I *said* it would work." He was speaking with obvious difficulty.

Blaustein said, "Just watch, Dr. Ralson. I would not allow myself to grow needlessly excited."

The pendulum was stopped in its swinging, drawn up. The flickering about the Projector became a little more intense and the iron sphere arced down once again.

Over and over again, and each time the sphere's motion was slowed with more of a jerk. It made a clearly audible sound as it struck the flicker. And eventually it *bounced*. First soggily, as though it hit putty, and then ringingly, as though it hit steel, so that the noise filled the place.

They drew back the pendulum bob and used it no longer. The Projector could hardly be seen behind the haze that surrounded it.

Grant gave an order and the odor of ozone was suddenly sharp and pungent. There was a cry from the assembled observers, each one exclaiming to his neighbor. A dozen fingers were pointing.

Blaustein leaned over the railing, as excited as the rest. Where the Projector had been, there was now only a huge semiglobular mirror. It was perfectly and beautifully clear. He

317

could see himself in it, a small man standing on a balcony that curved up on each side. He could see the fluorescent lights reflected in spots of glowing illumination. It was wonderfully sharp.

He was shouting, "Look, Ralson. It is reflecting energy. It is reflecting light waves like a mirror. Ralson—"

He turned, "Ralson! Inspector, where is Ralson?"

"What?" Darrity whirled. "I haven't seen him."

He looked about wildly. "Well, he won't get away. No way of getting out of here now. You take the other side." And then he clapped hand to thigh, fumbled for a moment in his pocket, and said, "My knife is gone."

Blaustein found him. He was inside the small office belonging to Hal Ross. It led off the balcony, but under the circumstances, of course, it had been deserted. Ross himself was not even an observer. A senior mechanic need not observe. But his office would do very well for the final end of the long fight against suicide.

Blaustein stood in the doorway for a sick moment, then turned. He caught Darrity's eye as the latter emerged from a similar office a hundred feet down the balcony. He beckoned, and Darrity came at a run—

Dr. Grant was trembling with excitement. He had taken two puffs at each of two cigarettes and trodden each underfoot thereafter. He was fumbling with the third now.

He was saying, "This is better than any of us could possibly have hoped. We'll have the gun-fire test tomorrow. I'm sure of the result now, but we've planned it; we'll go through with it. We'll skip the small arms and start with bazooka levels. Or maybe not. It might be necessary to construct a special testing structure to take care of the ricocheting problem."

He discarded his third cigarette.

A general said, "We'd have to try a literal atom-bombing, of course."

"Naturally. Arrangements have already been made to build a mock city at Eniwetok. We could build a generator on the spot and drop the bomb. There'd be animals inside."

"And you really think the Field in full power would hold the bomb?"

"It's not just that, General. There'd be no noticeable Field when the bomb is dropped. The radiation of the plutonium would have to energize the Field before explosion. As we did here in the last step. That's the essence of it all."

"You know," said a Princeton professor, "I see disadvantages too. When the Field is on full, anything it protects is in total darkness as far as the sun is concerned. Besides that, it strikes me that the enemy can adopt the practice of dropping harmless radioactive missiles to set off the Field at frequent intervals. It would have nuisance value and be a considerable drain on our pile as well."

"Nuisances," said Grant, "can be survived. These difficulties will be met eventually, I'm sure, now that the main problem has been solved."

The British observer had worked his way toward Grant and was shaking hands. He said, "I feel better about London already. I cannot help but wish your government would allow me to see the complete plans. What I have seen strikes me as completely ingenious. It seems obvious now, of course, but how did anyone ever come to think of it?"

Grant smiled. "That question has been asked before with reference to Dr. Ralson's devices—"

He turned at the touch of a hand upon his shoulder. "Dr. Blaustein! I have nearly forgotten. Here, I want to talk to you."

He dragged the small psychiatrist to one side and hissed in his ear, "Listen, can you persuade Ralson to be introduced to these people. This is his triumph."

Blaustein said, "Ralson is dead."

"*What!*"

"Can you leave these people for a time?"

"Yes . . . yes—gentlemen, you will excuse me for a few minutes?"

He hurried off with Blaustein.

The federal men had already taken over. Unobtrusively they barred the doorway to Ross's office. Outside there was the milling crowd discussing the answer to Alamogordo that they had just witnessed. Inside, unknown to them, was the death of the answerer. The G-men barrier divided to allow Grant and Blaustein to enter. It closed behind them again.

319

For a moment Grant raised the sheet. He said, "He looks peaceful."

"I would say—happy," said Blaustein.

Darrity said colorlessly, "The suicide weapon was my own knife. It was my negligence; it will be reported as such."

"No, no," said Blaustein, "that would be useless. He was my patient and I am responsible. In any case, he would not have lived another week. Since he invented the Projector, he was a dying man."

Grant said, "How much of this has been placed in the federal files? Can't we forget all about his madness?"

"I'm afraid not, Dr. Grant," said Darrity.

"I have told him the whole story," said Blaustein sadly.

Grant looked from one to the other. "I'll speak to the director. I'll go to the President, if necessary. I don't see that there need be any mention of suicide or of madness. He'll get full publicity as inventor of the Field Projector. It's the least we can do for him." His teeth were gritting.

Blaustein said, "He left a note."

"A note?"

Darrity handed him a sheet of paper and said, "Suicides almost always do. This is one reason the doctor told me about what really killed Ralson."

The note was addressed to Blaustein and it went:

"The Projector works; I knew it would. The bargain is done. You've got it and you don't need me anymore. So I'll go. You needn't worry about the human race, Doc. You were right. They've bred us too long; they've taken too many chances. We're out of the culture now and they won't be able to stop us. I know. That's all I can say. I know."

He had signed his name quickly and then underneath there was one scrawled line, and it said:

"Provided enough men are penicillin-resistant."

Grant made a motion to crumple the paper, but Darrity held out a quick hand.

"For the record, Doctor," he said.

Grant gave it to him and said, "Poor Ralson! He died believing all that trash."

Blaustein nodded. "So he did. Ralson will be given a great funeral, I suppose, and the fact of his invention will be publicized without the madness and the suicide. But the government men will remain interested in his mad theories. They may not be so mad, no, Mr. Darrity?"

"That's ridiculous, Doctor," said Grant. "There isn't a scientist on the job who has shown the least uneasiness about it at all."

"Tell him, Mr. Darrity," said Blaustein.

Darrity said, "There has been another suicide. No, not one of the scientists. No one with a degree. It happened this morning, and we investigated because we thought it might have some connection with today's test. There didn't seem any, and we were going to keep it quiet till the test was over. Only now there seems to be a connection.

"The man who died was just a guy with a wife and three kids. No reason to die. No history of mental illness. He threw himself under a car. We have witnesses, and it's certain he did it on purpose. He didn't die right away and they got a doctor to him. He was horribly mangled, but his last few words were, 'I feel much better now,' and he died."

"But who was he?" cried Grant.

"Hal Ross. The guy who actually built the Projector. The guy whose office this is."

Blaustein walked to the window. The evening sky was darkening into starriness.

He said, "The man knew nothing about Ralson's views. He had never spoken to Ralson, Mr. Darrity tells me. Scientists are probably resistant as a whole. They must be or they are quickly driven out of the profession. Ralson was an exception, a penicillin-sensitive who insisted on remaining. You see what happened to him. But what about the others, those who have remained in walks of life where there is no constant weeding out of the sensitive ones? How much of humanity *is* penicillin-resistant?"

"You *believe* Ralson?" asked Grant in horror.

"I don't really know."

Blaustein looked at the stars.

Incubators?

18

The Man Who Massed the Earth

Sometimes, instead of the shock of a sudden discovery or the "Eureka!" of a flash of inspiration, it is the very careful measurement of a tiny phenomenon in the laboratory that instantly gives you the answer to some related phenomenon that just happens to be huge.

Just a few days ago I was at a dinner party and a nice lady, whom I did not know, cornered me and, for some reason unknown to myself, began telling me in superfluous detail of the manifold achievements of her son.

Now as it happens I have a very low attention span when the topic of conversation is something other than myself* and so I tried, rather desperately, to break the flow by asking some question or other.

The first that occurred to me was: "And is this admirable young man your only son?"

To which the lady replied most earnestly, "Oh, *no!* I also have a daughter."

It had all been worth it, after all. The lady could not

---

*I am told this, with varying degrees of mordacity (so look it up in the dictionary) by my nearest and dearest, but I maintain that this is not an evil peculiar to myself but is a common, and even necessary, attribute of writers generally.

understand why I had broken into delighted laughter and even after I explained she had trouble seeing the humor of her reply.

Naturally, the juice of the situation was not just that the lady didn't hear me (that might have happened to anyone), but that it seemed to me to reflect, perfectly, the manner in which outmoded traditions of thought interfere with an understanding of the Universe as it is.

In pre-industrial society, for instance, male infants were much more valuable than female infants. Baby boys would grow into men and therefore presented, in potential, desperately needed help at the farm or in the army. Baby girls merely grew into women who had to be married off at great expense. Consequently, there was a great tendency to ignore daughters and to equate "child" with "son."

The attitude still lingers, I think, even now, and even though the owner of such an attitude may be unaware of it and would deny its existence heatedly if accused of harboring it. I think that when the nice lady heard the phrase "your only son" she honestly recognized no difference between that and "your only child" and answered accordingly.

What has all this to do with this chapter? Well, scientists have similar problems and to this day they cannot free themselves utterly and entirely from outmoded ways of thought.

For instance, we all think we know what we mean when we speak of the "weight" of something, and we all think we know what we mean when we say we are "weighing" something or that one thing is "heavier" or "lighter" than another thing.

Except that I'm not at all sure we really do. Even physicists who are perfectly aware of what weight really is and can define and explain it adequately tend to slip into inaccurate ways of thought if not careful.

Let me explain.

The inevitable response to a gravitational field is an acceleration. Imagine, for instance, a material object suddenly appearing in space with no acceleration (relative to some large nearby astronomical body) at the moment of its appearance. Either it is motionless relative to that body or it is moving at a constant velocity.

If there were no gravitational field at the point in space where the body appeared, the body would continue to remain at rest or to move at constant velocity. If, however, there *is* a gravitational field at that point, as there must be from that large nearby astronomical body, the object beings to accelerate. It moves faster and faster, or slower and slower, or it curves out of its original line of motion, or it undergoes some combination of these effects.

Since in any Universe that contains matter at all, a gravitational field (however weak) must exist at all points, accelerated motion is the norm for those objects in space which are subjected to gravitational fields only, and non-accelerated motion is an unrealizable ideal.

To be sure, if two objects are both accelerating precisely the same way relative to a third body, the two objects seem at rest with respect to each other. That is why you so often seem to yourself to be at rest. You *are* at rest with respect to the Earth, but that is because both you and the Earth are accelerating in response to the Sun's gravitational field in precisely the same way.

But then what about you and the *Earth's* gravitational field? You may be at rest with respect to the Earth, but suppose a hole suddenly gaped below you. Instantly, in response to Earth's gravitational field, you would begin to accelerate downward.

The only reason you don't do so ordinarily is that there is matter solidly packed in the direction in which you would otherwise move and the electromagnetic forces set up by the atoms composing that matter hold those atoms together and easily block you from responding to the gravitational field.

In a sense, though, any material object prevented from responding to a gravitational field with an acceleration "tries" to do so just the same.* It pushes in the direction it would "like" to move in. It is this "attempt" to accelerate in response to gravitation that makes itself evident as a force and it is this force which we can measure and call weight.

---

*In this paragraph I am deliberately putting in quotes all the words that appear to give inanimate objects human desires and motivations. This is the "pathetic fallacy" and it should be avoided, except that it's such a convenient way of explaining things that sometimes I simply cannot resist being pathetic.

Suppose we use a coiled spring to measure force, for instance. If we pull at such a spring, the spring lengthens. If we pull twice as hard, it will lengthen twice as much. Within the limits of the spring's elasticity, the amount of lengthening will be proportional to the intensity of the force.

If, now, you fix one end of the spring to a beam in the ceiling and suspend a material object on the other end of the spring, the spring lengthens, just as though a force had been applied. A force *has* been applied. The material object "tries" to accelerate downward and the force produced as a result of this "attempt" lengthens the spring.

We can calibrate the spring by noting the amount of lengthening produced by bodies whose weights we have arbitrarily defined in terms of some standard weight somewhere. Once that is done, we can read off the weight of any object, having a pointer (attached to the lengthening spring) mark off a number on a scale.

All right so far, but our notion of weight is derived, at its most primitive, from the feeling we have when an object rests on our hand or on some other part of our body and we must exert a muscular effort to keep it motionless with respect to Earth's gravitational field. Since we take Earth's gravitational field for granted and never experience any significant change in it, we attribute the sensation of weight entirely to the object.

An object is heavy, we think, because it is just naturally heavy and that's it, and we are so used to the thought that we don't allow ourselves to be disturbed by obvious evidence to the contrary. The weight of an object immersed in a liquid is decreased because the upward force of buoyancy must be subtracted from the downward force imposed by the gravitational field. If the buoyant force is great enough, the object will float, and the denser the liquid, the greater the buoyant force. Thus wood will float on water and iron will float on mercury.

We can actually feel an iron sphere to be lighter under water than in open air, yet we dismiss that. We don't think of weight as a force that can be countered by other forces. We insist on thinking of it as an intrinsic property of matter and when, under certain conditions, weight falls to zero, we are astonished, and we view the weightless cavortings of astronauts as something almost against nature. (They are "beyond the reach of gravity," to quote the illiterate mouthings of too many newscasters.)

It is true that weight depends in part on a certain property innate in the object, but it also depends on the intensity of the gravitational field to which that object is responding. If we were standing on the surface of the Moon and were holding an object in our hand, that object would be "attempting" to respond to a gravitational field that was only one-sixth as intense as that on the surface of the Earth. It would therefore weigh only one-sixth as much.

What is the innate property of matter on which weight partly depends? That is "mass," a term and concept Newton introduced.

The force produced by a body "attempting" to respond to a gravitational field is proportional to its mass as well as to the intensity of the gravitational field. If the gravitational field remains constant in intensity at all times (as is true, to all intents and purposes, of the Earth's gravitational field if we remain on or near its surface), we can ignore that field. We can then say that the force produced by a body "attempting" to respond to Earth's gravitational field under ordinary circumstances is simply proportional to its mass.

(Actually, Earth's gravitational field varies from point to point, depending on the exact distance from the point to the Earth's center and on the exact distribution of matter in the neighborhood of the point. These variations are far too tiny to detect through changes in the muscular effort required to counter the effect of weight, but they can be detected by delicate instruments.)

Since weight, under ordinary circumstances, is proportional to mass and vice versa, it is almost unbearably tempting to treat the two as identical. When the notion of mass was first established, it was given units ("pounds," for instance) which had earlier been used for weight. To this day we speak of a mass of two kilograms and a weight of two kilograms and this is wrong. Units such as kilograms should be applied to mass only and weight should be given the units of force, but go talk to a brick wall.

The units have been so arranged that on the Earth's surface,

326

a mass of six kilograms also has a weight of six kilograms, but on the Moon's surface that same body will have a mass of six kilograms and a weight of only one kilogram.

A satellite orbiting the Earth is in free fall with respect to the Earth and is already responding in full to Earth's gravitational field. There is nothing further for it to "attempt" to do. Therefore a mass of six pounds on the satellite has a weight of zero pounds and the same is true of all objects, however massive. Objects on an orbiting satellite are therefore weightless. (To be sure, objects on an orbiting satellite ought to "attempt" to respond to the gravitational fields of the satellite itself and of other objects on it, but these fields are so negligibly small, they can be ignored.)

Does it matter that the close match of weight and mass to which we are accustomed on the surface of the Earth fails elsewhere? Sure it does. An object's inertia, that is the force required to accelerate it, depends entirely on its mass. A large metal beam is just as difficult to maneuver (to get moving when it is at rest, or to stop it when it is moving) on the Moon as on Earth, even though its weight is much less on the Moon. The difficulty of maneuver is the same on a space station even though weight is essentially zero.

Astronauts will have to be careful and if they don't forget Earth-born notions, they may die. If you are caught between two rapidly moving beams, you will be killed even though they are weightless. You will not be able to stop them with a flick of your finger even though they weigh less than a feather.

How can we measure mass? One way is to use the kind of balance consisting of two pans pivoting around a central fulcrum. Suppose an object of unknown weight is placed in the left pan. The left pan sinks and the right rises.

Suppose, next, a series of metal slivers, weighing exactly one gram each, are added to the right pan. As long as all the slivers, put together, weigh less than the unknown object, the right pan remains raised. When the sum of the slivers weighs more than the unknown, the right pan sinks and the left pan rises. When the two pans balance at the same level, the two weights are equal and you can say that the unknown weighs (let us say) seventy-two grams.

But now two weights at once are being subjected to the

action of the gravitational field and the effect of that field cancels out. If the field is intensified or weakened, it is intensified or weakened on both pans simultaneously and the fact that the two pans are balanced is not affected. The two pans would remain in balance on the Moon, for instance. Such a balance is, therefore, to all intents and purposes measuring the one other property on which weight develops—mass.

Scientists prefer to measure mass rather than weight and so they train themselves to say "more massive" and "less massive" instead of "heavier" and "lighter" (though only with an effort and with frequent slips).

And yet they haven't freed themselves utterly from pre-Newtonian thinking even now, three centuries after Newton.

Picture this situation. A chemist carefully measures the mass of an object by using a delicate chemical balance and brings two pans into equilibrium as we have described. What has he done? He has "measured the mass" of an object. Is there any shorter way of saying that correctly? No, there isn't. The English language doesn't offer anything. He can't say he has "massed" the object, or "massified" it or "massicated" it.

The only thing he can say is that he has "weighed" the object, and he *does* say it. I say it too.

But to weigh an object is to determine its weight, not its mass. The unreformed English language forces us to be pre-Newtonian.

Again, these little slivers of metal that weigh a gram each (or any other convenient quantity or variety of quantities) should be called "standard masses" if we are to indicate they are used in measuring mass. They are not. They are called "weights."

Again, chemists must frequently deal with the relative average masses of the atoms making up the different elements. These relative average masses are universally called "atomic weights." They are *not* weights, they are masses.

In short, no matter how well any scientist knows (in his head) the difference between mass and weight, he will never really know it (in his heart) as long as he uses a language in which hangover traditions are retained. Like the lady who saw no difference between "only son" and "only child."

328

Now let's move on. Jupiter is 318 times as massive as the Earth; the Sun is 330,000 times as massive as Earth; the Moon is 1/81 times as massive as Earth, and so on.

But what is the mass of the Earth itself in kilograms (or any other unit of mass that we can equate with familiar everyday objects)?

To determine that we must make use of Newton's equation, which is:

$$F = GmM/d^2 \qquad \text{(Equation 1)}$$

If this equation is applied to a falling rock, for instance, F is the gravitational force to which the rock is responding by accelerating downward, G is the universal gravitational constant, m is the mass of the rock, M is the mass of the Earth, and d is the distance of the center of the rock from the center of the Earth.

Unfortunately, of the five quantities, the men of the eighteenth century could only determine three. The mass of the rock (m) could easily be determined, and the distance of the rock from the center of the earth (d) was known as far back as the time of the ancient Greeks. The gravitational force (F) could be determined by measuring the acceleration with which the rock was responding to the gravitational field, and that had been done by Galileo.

Only the values of G, the gravitational constant, and M, the mass of the Earth, remained unknown. If only the value of G were known, the mass of the Earth could be calculated at once. Conversely, if M were known, the universal gravitational constant could be quickly determined.

What to do?

The mass of the Earth could be determined directly if it could be manipulated; if it could be placed on a balance pan against standard weights or something like that. However, the Earth cannot be manipulated, at least by men in a laboratory, so forget that.

Then what about determining G? This is the universal gravitational constant and it is the same for *any* gravitational field. That means we don't have to use the Earth's gravitational field to determine it. We might use the gravitational field of some smaller object which we can freely manipulate.

Suppose, for instance, we suspend an object from a spring and lengthen the spring thanks to the effect of Earth's gravitational field. Next we take a large boulder and place it under the suspended object. The gravitational field of the boulder is now added to the Earth's gravitational field and the spring is extended a little farther as a result.

From the amount of the additional lengthening of the spring, we could determine the intensity of the gravitational field of the boulder.

Now let us use the following variation of Newton's equation:

$$f = Gmm'/d^2 \qquad \text{(Equation 2)}$$

where f is the gravitational field intensity of the boulder (measured by the additional extension of the spring), G is the gravitational constant, m the mass of the object suspended from the spring, m' the mass of the boulder, and d the distance between the center of the boulder and the center of the suspended object.

Every one of these quantities can be determined except G, so we rearrange Equation 2 thus:

$$G = fd^2/mm' \qquad \text{(Equation 3)}$$

and at once have the value of G. Once we know that value, we can substitute it in Equation 1, which we can then solve for M (the mass of the Earth), as follows:

$$M = Fd^2/Gm \qquad \text{(Equation 4)}$$

But there is a catch. Gravitational fields are so incredibly weak in relation to mass that it takes a hugely massive object to have a gravitational field intense enough to measure easily. The boulder held under the suspended object would simply not produce a measurable farther extension of the spring, that's all.

There is no way of making the gravitational field more intense, so if the problem of the mass of the Earth was to be solved at all, some exceedingly delicate device would have to be used. What was needed was something that would measure the vanishingly small force produced by the vanishingly small gravitational field produced by an object small enough to be handled in the laboratory.

The necessary refinement in measurement came about with the invention of the "torsion balance" by the French physicist Charles Augustin Coulomb in 1777 and (independently) by the English geologist John Michell as well.

Instead of having a force extend a spring or pull a pan about a fulcrum, it was used to twist a string or wire.

If the spring or wire was very fine, only a tiny force would be required to twist it quite a bit. To detect the twist, one need attach to the vertical wire a long horizontal rod balanced at the center. Even a tiny twist would produce a large movement at the end of the rods. If a thin wire is used and a long rod, a torsion balance could be made enormously delicate, delicate enough even to detect the tiny gravitational field of an ordinary object.

In 1798 the English chemist Henry Cavendish put the principle of the torsion balance to use in determining the value of G.

Suppose you take a rod six feet long and place on each end a two-inch-in-diameter lead ball. Suppose you next suspend the rod from its center by a fine wire.

If a very small force is applied to the one lead ball on one side and an equally small force to the other lead ball on the other side, the horizontal rod will rotate and the wire to which it is attached will twist. The twisting wire "attempts" to untwist. The more it is twisted, the stronger the force to untwist becomes. Eventually the force to untwist balances the force, causing it to twist, and the rod remains in a new equilibrium position. From the extent to which the rod's position has shifted, the amount of force upon the lead balls can be determined.

(Naturally, you must enclose the whole thing in a box and place it in a sealed, constant-temperature room so that no air currents—produced either by temperature differences or mechanical motions—confuse the situation.)

Where the rod takes up only a slightly different position, it means that even a tiny twist of the fine wire produces enough counterforce to balance the applied force. What a tiny force it must then be that was applied—and that was exactly what Cavendish had in mind.

He suspended a lead ball eight inches in diameter on one side of one of the small lead balls at the end of the horizontal rod. He suspended another such ball on the opposite side of the other small lead ball.

The gravitational field of the large lead balls would now serve to twist the rod and force it into a new position (*see Figure 1*).

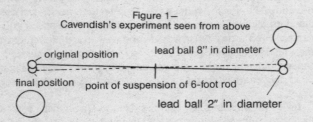

Figure 1—
Cavendish's experiment seen from above

original position

lead ball 8" in diameter

final position   point of suspension of 6-foot rod

lead ball 2" in diameter

Cavendish repeated the experiment over and over again, and from the shift in the position of the rod and, therefore, from the twist of the wire, he determined the value of f in Equation 3. Since he knew the values of m, m' and d, he could calculate the value of G at once.

Cavendish's value was off by less than one percent from the value now accepted, which is 0.0000000000667 meters^3/kilogram-second^2. (Don't ask about the significance of that unit; it is necessary to make the equations balance).

Once we have the value for G in the units given, we can solve Equation 4, and if we use the proper units, out will pop the mass of the Earth in kilograms. This turns out to be 5,983,000,000,000,000,000,000,000, or 5.983 × 10^{24}, kilograms. (If you want it, roughly, in words, say, "About six septillion kilograms.")

Once we have the Earth's mass in kilograms, we can determine the mass of other objects too, provided only their mass relative to that of the Earth is known.

The Moon, which has a mass 1/81 that of the Earth, has a mass of 7.4 × 10^{22} kilograms. Jupiter, with a mass 318 times that of the Earth, has a mass of 1.9 × 10^{27} kilograms. The

Sun, with a mass 330,000 times that of the Earth, has a mass of 2×10^{30} kilograms.

Thus, Cavendish not only measured the mass of the Earth, but he measured (at least potentially) the mass of every other object in the Universe just by noticing the small shift in position of a pair of lead balls when a pair of larger balls was placed nearby.

How's that for the power of a simple equation?

But—and here is the point of the whole essay—when someone wishes to mention this astonishing achievement of Cavendish's, what does he say? He says: "Cavendish weighed the Earth."

Even physicists and astronomers speak of Cavendish as the man who "weighed the Earth."

He did no such thing! He determined the *mass* of the Earth. He *massed* the Earth. It may be that English has no such verb, but that's the fault of the language, not of me. To me, Cavendish is the man who massed the earth, and English can like it or lump it.

Which leaves one question: What *is* the weight of the Earth?

The answer is simple. The Earth is in free fall, and like any object in free fall, it is responding in full to the gravitational fields to which it is subject. It is not "attempting" to make any further response and therefore it is weightless.

The weight of the Earth, then, is zero.

19

Nightfall

Could a book such as this be complete without a consideration of nonhuman scientists? In this story, the scientists are not very nonhuman, for just as one can translate a foreign language into English in order to make the story understandable, so one can translate nonhumanity into familiar terms if one wishes. I did this.

On the other hand, the problem under consideration is certainly un-Earthly.

> "If the stars should appear one night in a thousand years, how would men believe and adore, and preserve for many generations the remembrance of the city of God?"
>
> EMERSON

Aton 77, director of Saro University, thrust out a belligerent lower lip and glared at the young newspaperman in a hot fury.

Theremon 762 took that fury in his stride. In his earlier days, when his now widely syndicated column was only a mad idea in a cub reporter's mind, he had specialized in "impossible" interviews. It had cost him bruises, black eyes and broken bones; but it had given him an ample supply of coolness and self-confidence.

334

So he lowered the outthrust hand that had been so pointedly ignored and calmly waited for the aged director to get over the worst. Astronomers were queer ducks anyway, and if Aton's actions of the last two months meant anything, this same Aton was the queer-duckiest of the lot.

Aton 77 found his voice, and though it trembled with restrained emotion, the careful, somewhat pedantic phraseology, for which the famous astronomer was noted, did not abandon him.

"Sir," he said, "you display an infernal gall in coming to me with that impudent proposition of yours."

The husky telephotographer of the Observatory, Beenay 25, thrust a tongue's tip across dry lips and interposed nervously, "Now, sir, after all—"

The director turned to him and lifted a white eyebrow. "Do not interfere, Beenay. I will credit you with good intentions in bringing this man here; but I will tolerate no insubordination now."

Theremon decided it was time to take a part. "Director Aton, if you'll let me finish what I started saying, I think—"

"I don't believe, young man," retorted Aton, "that anything you could say now would count much as compared with your daily columns of these last two months. You have led a vast newspaper campaign against the efforts of myself and my colleagues to organize the world against the menace which it is now too late to avert. You have done your best with your highly personal attacks to make the staff of this Observatory objects of ridicule."

The director lifted a copy of the Saro City *Chronicle* from the table and shook it at Theremon furiously. "Even a person of your well-known impudence should have hesitated before coming to me with a request that he be allowed to cover today's events for his paper. Of all newsmen, you!"

Aton dashed the newspaper to the floor, strode to the window and clasped his arms behind his back.

"You may leave," he snapped over his shoulder. He stared moodily out at the skyline where Gamma, the brightest of the planet's six suns, was setting. It had already faded and yellowed into the horizon mists, and Aton knew he would never see it again as a sane man.

335

He whirled. "No, wait, come here!" He gestured peremptorily. "I'll give you your story."

The newsman had made no motion to leave, and now he approached the old man slowly. Aton gestured outward. "Of the six suns, only Beta is left in the sky. Do you see it?"

The question was rather unnecessary. Beta was almost at zenith, its ruddy light flooding the landscape to an unusual orange as the brilliant rays of setting Gamma died. Beta was at aphelion. It was small; smaller than Theremon had ever seen it before, and for the moment it was undisputed ruler of Lagash's sky.

Lagash's own sun, Alpha, the one about which it revolved, was at the antipodes, as were the two distant companion pairs. The red dwarf Beta—Alpha's immediate companion—was alone, grimly alone.

Aton's upturned face flushed redly in the sunlight. "In just under four hours," he said, "civilization, as we know it, comes to an end. It will do so because, as you see, Beta is the only sun in the sky." He smiled grimly. "Print that! There'll be no one to read it."

"But if it turns out that four hours pass—and another four—and nothing happens?" asked Theremon softly.

"Don't let that worry you. Enough will happen."

"Granted! And *still*—if nothing happens?"

For a second time Beenay 25 spoke. "Sir, I think you ought to listen to him."

Theremon said, "Put it to a vote, Director Aton."

There was a stir among the remaining five members of the Observatory staff, who till now had maintained an attitude of wary neutrality.

"That," stated Aton flatly, "is not necessary." He drew out his pocket watch. "Since your good friend, Beenay, insists so urgently, I will give you five minutes. Talk away."

"Good! Now, just what difference would it make if you allowed me to take down an eyewitness account of what's to come? If your prediction comes true, my presence won't hurt; for in that case my column would never be written. On the other hand, if nothing comes of it, you will just have to expect ridicule or worse. It would be wise to leave that ridicule to friendly hands."

Aton snorted. "Do you mean yours when you speak of friendly hands?"

"Certainly!" Theremon sat down and crossed his legs. "My columns may have been a little rough, but I gave you people the benefit of the doubt every time. After all, this is not the century to preach 'The end of the world is at hand' to Lagash. You have to understand that people don't believe the *Book of Revelations* anymore, and it annoys them to have scientists turn about-face and tell us the Cultists are right after all—"

"No such thing, young man," interrupted Aton. "While a great deal of our data has been supplied us by the Cult, our results contain none of the Cult's mysticism. Facts are facts, and the Cult's so-called mythology *has* certain facts behind it. We've exposed them and ripped away their mystery. I assure you that the Cult hates us now worse than you do."

"I don't hate you. I'm just trying to tell you that the public is in an ugly humor. They're angry."

Aton twisted his mouth in derision. "Let them be angry."

"Yes, but what about tomorrow?"

"There'll be no tomorrow!"

"But if there is. Say that there is—just to see what happens. That anger might take shape into something serious. After all, you know, business has taken a nosedive these last two months. Investors don't really believe the world is coming to an end, but just the same, they're being cagey with their money until it's all over. Johnny Public doesn't believe you either, but the new spring furniture might just as well wait a few months—just to make sure.

"You see the point. Just as soon as this is all over, the business interests will be after your hide. They'll say that if crackpots—begging your pardon—can upset the country's prosperity any time they want, simply by making some cockeyed prediction, it's up to the planet to prevent them. The sparks will fly, sir."

The director regarded the columnist sternly. "And just what were you proposing to do to help the situation?"

"Well"—Theremon grinned—"I was proposing to take charge of the publicity. I can handle things so that only the ridiculous side will show. It would be hard to stand, I admit, because I'd have to make you all out to be a bunch of gibbering idiots, but if I can get people laughing at you, they might forget to be angry. In return for that, all my publisher asks is an exclusive story."

Beenay nodded and burst out, "Sir, the rest of us think he's right. These last two months we've considered everything but the million-to-one chance that there is an error somewhere in our theory or in our calculations. We ought to take care of that too."

There was a murmur of agreement from the men grouped about the table, and Aton's expression became that of one who found his mouth full of something bitter and couldn't get rid of it.

"You may stay if you wish, then. You will kindly refrain, however, from hampering us in our duties in any way. You will also remember that I am in charge of all activities here, and in spite of your opinions as expressed in your columns, I will expect full cooperation and full respect—"

His hands were behind his back, and his wrinkled face thrust forward determinedly as he spoke. He might have continued indefinitely but for the intrusion of a new voice.

"Hello, hello, hello!" It came in a high tenor, and the plump cheeks of the newcomer expanded in a pleased smile. "What's this morguelike atmosphere about here? No one's losing his nerve, I hope."

Aton started in consternation and said peevishly, "Now what the devil are you doing here, Sheerin? I thought you were going to stay behind in the Hideout."

Sheerin laughed and dropped his tubby figure into a chair. "Hideout be blowed! The place bored me. I wanted to be here, where things are getting hot. Don't you suppose I have my share of curiosity? I want to see these Stars the Cultists are forever speaking about." He rubbed his hands and added in a soberer tone, "It's freezing outside. The wind's enough to hang icicles on your nose. Beta doesn't seem to give any heat at all, at the distance it is."

The white-haired director ground his teeth in sudden exasperation. "Why do you go out of your way to do crazy things, Sheerin? What kind of good are you around here?"

"What kind of good am I around there?" Sheerin spread his palms in comical resignation. "A psychologist isn't worth his

338

salt in the Hideout. They need men of action and strong, healthy women that can breed children. Me? I'm a hundred pounds too heavy for a man of action, and I wouldn't be a success at breeding children. So why bother them with an extra mouth to feed? I feel better over here."

Theremon spoke briskly. "Just what is the Hideout, sir?"

Sheerin seemed to see the columnist for the first time. He frowned and blew his ample cheeks out. "And just who in Lagash are you, redhead?"

Aton compressed his lips and then muttered sullenly, "That's Theremon 762, the newspaper fellow. I suppose you've heard of him."

The columnist offered his hand. "And, of course, you're Sheerin 501 of Saro University. I've heard of you." Then he repeated, "What is this Hideout, sir?"

"Well," said Sheerin, "we have managed to convince a few people of the validity of our prophecy of—er—doom, to be spectacular about it, and those few have taken proper measures. They consist mainly of the immediate members of the families of the Observatory staff, certain of the faculty of Saro University, and a few outsiders. Altogether they number about three hundred, but three-quarters are women and children."

"I see! They're supposed to hide where the Darkness and the—er—Stars can't get at them, and then hold out when the rest of the world goes poof."

"If they can. It won't be easy. With all of mankind insane, with the great cities going up in flames—environment will not be conducive to survival. But they have food, water, shelter and weapons—"

"They've got more," said Aton. "They've got all our records, except for what we will collect today. Those records will mean everything to the next cycle, and *that's* what must survive. The rest can go hang."

Theremon uttered a long, low whistle and sat brooding for several minutes. The men about the table had brought out a multi-chessboard and started a six-member game. Moves were made rapidly and in silence. All eyes bent in furious concentration on the board. Theremon watched them intently and then rose and approached Aton, who sat apart in whispered conversation with Sheerin.

"Listen," he said, "let's go somewhere where we won't bother the rest of the fellows. I want to ask some questions."

The aged astronomer frowned sourly at him, but Sheerin chirped up, "Certainly. It will do me good to talk. It always does. Aton was telling me about your ideas concerning world reaction to a failure of the prediction—and I agree with you. I read your column pretty regularly, by the way, and as a general thing, I like your views."

"Please, Sheerin," growled Aton.

"Eh? Oh, all right. We'll go into the next room. It has softer chairs anyway."

There were softer chairs in the next room. There were also thick red curtains on the windows and a maroon carpet on the floor. With the bricky light of Beta pouring in, the general effect was one of dried blood.

Theremon shuddered. "Say, I'd give ten credits for a decent dose of white light for just a second. I wish Gamma or Delta were in the sky."

"What are your questions?" asked Aton. "Please remember that our time is limited. In a little over an hour and a quarter we're going upstairs, and after that there will be no time for talk."

"Well, here it is." Theremon leaned back and folded his hands on his chest. "You people seem so all-fired serious about this that I'm beginning to believe you. Would you mind explaining what it's all about?"

Aton exploded, "Do you mean to sit there and tell me that you've been bombarding us with ridicule without even finding out what we've been trying to say?"

The columnist grinned sheepishly. "It's not that bad, sir. I've got the general idea. You say there is going to be a worldwide Darkness in a few hours and that all mankind will go violently insane. What I want now is the science behind it."

"No, you don't. No, you don't," broke in Sheerin. "If you ask Aton for that—supposing him to be in the mood to answer at all—he'll trot out pages of figures and volumes of graphs. You won't make head or tail of it. Now if you were to ask me, I could give you the layman's standpoint."

340

"All right; I ask you."

"Then first I'd like a drink." He rubbed his hands and looked at Aton.

"Water?" grunted Aton.

"Don't be silly!"

"Don't you be silly. No alcohol today. It would be too easy to get my men drunk. I can't afford to tempt them."

The psychologist grumbled wordlessly. He turned to Theremon, impaled him with his sharp eyes, and began.

"You realize, of course, that the history of civilization on Lagash displays a cyclic character—but I mean *cyclic!*"

"I know," replied Theremon cautiously, "that that is the current archaeological theory. Has it been accepted as a fact?"

"Just about. In this last century it's been generally agreed upon. This cyclic character is—or rather, was—one of the great mysteries. We've located series of civilizations, nine of them definitely, and indications of others as well, all of which have reached heights comparable to our own, and all of which, without exception, were destroyed by fire at the very height of their culture.

"And no one could tell why. All centers of culture were thoroughly gutted by fire, with nothing left behind to give a hint as to the cause."

Theremon was following closely. "Wasn't there a Stone Age too?"

"Probably, but as yet practically nothing is known of it, except that men of that age were little more than rather intelligent apes. We can forget about that."

"I see. Go on."

"There have been explanations of these recurrent catastrophes, all of a more or less fantastic nature. Some say that there are periodic rains of fire; some that Lagash passes through a sun every so often; some even wilder things. But there is one theory, quite different from all of these, that has been handed down over a period of centuries."

"I know. You mean this myth of the 'Stars' that the Cultists have in their *Book of Revelations*."

"Exactly," rejoined Sheerin with satisfaction. "The Cultists said that every two thousand and fifty years Lagash entered a huge cave, so that all the suns disappeared and there came

341

total darkness all over the world! And then, they say, things called Stars appeared, which robbed men of their souls and left them unreasoning brutes, so that they destroyed the civilization they themselves had built up. Of course they mix all this up with a lot of religio-mystic notions, but that's the central idea."

There was a short pause in which Sheerin drew a long breath. "And now we come to the theory of Universal Gravitation." He pronounced the phrase so that the capital letters sounded—and at that point Aton turned from the window, snorted loudly and stalked out of the room.

The two stared after him and Theremon said, "What's wrong?"

"Nothing in particular," replied Sheerin. "Two of the men were due several hours ago and haven't shown up yet. He's terrifically shorthanded, of course, because all but the really essential men have gone to the Hideout."

"You don't think the two deserted, do you?"

"Who? Faro and Yimot? Of course not. Still, if they're not back within the hour, things would be a little sticky." He got to his feet suddenly and his eyes twinkled. "Anyway, as long as Aton is gone—"

Tiptoeing to the nearest window, he squatted, and from the low window box beneath withdrew a bottle of red liquid that gurgled suggestively when he shook it.

"I *thought* Aton didn't know about this," he remarked as he trotted back to the table. "Here! We've only got one glass so, as the guest, you can have it. I'll keep the bottle." And he filled the tiny cup with judicious care.

Theremon rose to protest, but Sheerin eyed him sternly. "Respect your elders, young man."

The newsman seated himself with a look of anguish on his face. "Go ahead then, you old villain."

The psychologist's Adam's apple wobbled as the bottle upended, and then, with a satisfied grunt and a smack of the lips, he began again. "But what do you know about gravitation?"

"Nothing, except that it is a very recent development, not too well established, and that the math is so hard that only twelve men in Lagash are supposed to understand it."

342

"Tcha! Nonsense! Baloney! I can give you all the essential math in a sentence. The Law of Universal Gravitation states that there exists a cohesive force among all bodies of the Universe, such that the amount of this force between any two given bodies is proportional to the product of their masses divided by the square of the distance between them."

"Is that all?"

"That's enough! It took four hundred years to develop it."

"Why that long? It sounded simple enough, the way you said it."

"Because great laws are not divined by flashes of inspiration, whatever you may think. It usually takes the combined work of a world full of scientists over a period of centuries. After Genovi 41 discovered that Lagash rotated about the sun Alpha rather than vice versa—and that was four hundred years ago—astronomers have been working. The complex motions of the six suns were recorded and analyzed and unwoven. Theory after theory was advanced and checked and counter-checked and modified and abandoned and revived and converted to something else. It was a devil of a job."

Theremon nodded thoughtfully and held out his glass for more liquor. Sheerin grudgingly allowed a few ruby drops to leave the bottle.

"It was twenty years ago," he continued after remoistening his own throat, "that it was finally demonstrated that the Law of Universal Gravitation accounted exactly for the orbital motions of the six suns. It was a great triumph."

Sheerin stood up and walked to the window, still clutching his bottle. "And now we're getting to the point. In the last decade, the motions of Lagash about Alpha were computed according to gravity, and *it did not account for the orbit observed;* not even when all perturbations due to the other suns were included. Either the law was invalid, or there was another, as yet unknown, factor involved."

Theremon joined Sheerin at the window and gazed out past the wooded slopes to where the spires of Saro City gleamed bloodily on the horizon. The newsman felt the tension of uncertainty grow within him as he cast a short glance at Beta. It glowered redly at zenith, dwarfed and evil.

"Go ahead, sir," he said softly.

343

Sheerin replied, "Astronomers stumbled about for years, each proposed theory more untenable than the one before—until Aton had the inspiration of calling in the Cult. The head of the Cult, Sor 5, had access to certain data that simplified the problem considerably. Aton set to work on a new track.

"What if there were another nonluminous planetary body such as Lagash? If there were, you know, it would shine only by reflected light, and if it were composed of bluish rock, as Lagash itself largely is, then, in the redness of the sky, the eternal blaze of the suns would make it invisible—drown it out completely."

Theremon whistled. "What a screwy idea!"

"You think *that's* screwy? Listen to this: Suppose this body rotated about Lagash at such a distance and in such an orbit and had such a mass that its attraction would exactly account for the deviations of Lagash's orbit from theory—do you know what would happen?"

The columnist shook his head.

"Well, sometimes this body would get in the way of a sun." And Sheerin emptied what remained in the bottle at a draft.

"And it does, I suppose," said Theremon flatly.

"Yes! But only one sun lies in its plane of revolution." He jerked a thumb at the shrunken sun above. "Beta! And it has been shown that the eclipse will occur only when the arrangement of the suns is such that Beta is alone in its hemisphere and at maximum distance, at which time the moon is invariably at minimum distance. The eclipse that results, with the moon seven times the apparent diameter of Beta, covers all of Lagash and lasts well over half a day, so that no spot on the planet escapes the effects. *That eclipse comes once every two thousand and forty-nine years.*"

Theremon's face was drawn into an expressionless mask. "And that's my story?"

The psychologist nodded. "That's all of it. First the eclipse—which will start in three-quarters of an hour—then universal Darkness and, maybe, these mysterious Stars—then madness, and end of the cycle."

He brooded. "We had two months' leeway—we at the Observatory—and that wasn't enough time to persuade Lagash of the danger. Two centuries might not have been enough. But

344

our records are at the Hideout, and today we photograph the eclipse. The next cycle will *start off* with the truth, and when the *next* eclipse comes, mankind will at last be ready for it. Come to think of it, that's part of your story too."

A thin wind ruffled the curtains at the window as Theremon opened it and leaned out. It played coldly with his hair as he stared at the crimson sunlight on his hand. Then he turned in sudden rebellion.

"What is there in Darkness to drive *me* mad?"

Sheerin smiled to himself as he spun the empty liquor bottle with abstracted motions of his hand. "Have you ever experienced Darkness, young man?"

The newsman leaned against the wall and considered. "No. Can't say I have. But I know what it is. Just—uh—" He made vague motions with his fingers and then brightened. "Just no light. Like in caves."

"Have you ever been in a cave?"

"In a *cave!* Of course not!"

"I thought not. *I* tried last week—just to see—but I got out in a hurry. I went in until the mouth of the cave was just visible as a blur of light, with black everywhere else. I never thought a person my weight could run that fast."

Theremon's lip curled. "Well, if it comes to that, I guess I wouldn't have run if I had been there."

The psychologist studied the young man with an annoyed frown.

"My, don't you talk big! I dare you to draw the curtain."

Theremon looked his surprise and said, "What for? If we had four or five suns out there, we might want to cut the light down a bit for comfort, but now we haven't enough light as it is."

"That's the point. Just draw the curtain; then come here and sit down."

"All right." Theremon reached for the tasseled string and jerked. The red curtain slid across the wide window, the brass rings hissing their way along the crossbar, and a dusk-red shadow clamped down on the room.

Theremon's footsteps sounded hollowly in the silence as he made his way to the table, and then they stopped halfway. "I can't see you, sir," he whispered.

345

"Feel your way," ordered Sheerin in a strained voice.

"But I can't see you, sir." The newsman was breathing harshly. "I can't see anything."

"What did you expect?" came the grim reply. "Come here and sit down!"

The footsteps sounded again, waveringly, approaching slowly. There was the sound of someone fumbling with a chair. Theremon's voice came thinly, "Here I am. I feel . . . *ulp* . . . all right."

"You like it, do you?"

"N—no. It's pretty awful. The walls seem to be—" He paused. "They seem to be closing in on me. I keep wanting to push them away. But I'm not going *mad!* In fact, the feeling isn't as bad as it was."

"All right. Draw the curtain back again."

There were cautious footsteps through the dark, the rustle of Theremon's body against the curtain as he felt for the tassel, and then the triumphant *ro-o-osh* of the curtain slithering back. Red light flooded the room, and with a cry of joy, Theremon looked up at the sun.

Sheerin wiped the moisture off his forehead with the back of a hand and said shakily, "And that was just a dark room."

"It can be stood," said Theremon lightly.

"Yes, a dark room can. But were you at the Jonglor Centennial Exposition two years ago?"

"No, it so happens I never got around to it. Six thousand miles was just a bit too much to travel, even for the exposition."

"Well, I was there. You remember hearing about the 'Tunnel of Mystery' that broke all records in the amusement area—for the first month or so, anyway?"

"Yes. Wasn't there some fuss about it?"

"Very little. It was hushed up. You see, that Tunnel of Mystery was just a mile-long tunnel—with no lights. You got into a little open car and jolted along through Darkness for fifteen minutes. It was very popular—while it lasted."

"Popular?"

"Certainly. There's a fascination in being frightened *when it's part of a game*. A baby is born with three instinctive fears: of loud noises, of falling, and of the absence of light. That's

346

why it's considered so funny to jump at someone and shout 'Boo!' That's why it's such fun to ride a roller coaster. And that's why that Tunnel of Mystery started cleaning up. People came out of that Darkness shaking, breathless, half dead with fear, but they kept on paying to get in."

"Wait a minute, I remember now. Some people came out dead, didn't they? There were rumors of that after it shut down."

The psychologist snorted. "Bah! Two or three died. That was nothing! They paid off the families of the dead ones and argued the Jonglor City Council into forgetting it. After all, they said, if people with weak hearts want to go through the tunnel, it was at their own risk—and besides, it wouldn't happen again. So they put a doctor in the front office and had every customer go through a physical examination before getting into the car. That actually *boosted* ticket sales."

"Well, then?"

"But you see, there was something else. People sometimes came out in perfect order, except that they refused to go into buildings—any buildings; including palaces, mansions, apartment houses, tenements, cottages, huts, shacks, lean-tos, and tents."

Theremon looked shocked. "You mean they refused to come in out of the open? Where'd they sleep?"

"In the open."

"They should have *forced* them inside."

"Oh, they did, they did. Whereupon these people went into violent hysterics, and did their best to bat their brains out against the nearest wall. Once you got them inside, you couldn't keep them there without a straitjacket or a heavy dose of tranquilizer."

"They must have been crazy."

"Which is exactly what they were. One person out of every ten who went into that tunnel came out that way. They called in the psychologists, and we did the only thing possible. We closed down the exhibit." He spread his hands.

"What was the matter with these people?" asked Theremon finally.

"Essentially the same thing that was the matter with you when you thought the walls of the room were crushing in on you in the dark. There is a psychological term for mankind's instinctive fear of the absence of light. We call it 'claustrophobia,' because the lack of light is always tied up with enclosed places, so that fear of one is fear of the other. You see?"

"And those people of the tunnel?"

"Those people of the tunnel consisted of those unfortunates whose mentality did not quite possess the resiliency to overcome the claustrophobia that overtook them in the Darkness. Fifteen minutes without light is a long time; you only had two or three minutes, and I believe you were fairly upset.

"The people of the tunnel had what is called 'claustrophobic fixation.' Their latent fear of Darkness and enclosed places had crystalized and become active and, as far as we can tell, permanent. That's what fifteen minutes in the dark will do."

There was a long silence, and Theremon's forehead wrinkled slowly into a frown. "I don't believe it's that bad."

"You mean you don't want to believe," snapped Sheerin. "You're afraid to believe. Look out the window!"

Theremon did so, and the psychologist continued without pausing. "Imagine Darkness—everywhere. No light, as far as you can see. The houses, the trees, the fields, the earth, the sky—black! And Stars thrown in, for all I know—whatever *they* are. Can you conceive it?"

"Yes, I can," declared Theremon truculently.

And Sheerin slammed his fist down upon the table in sudden passion. "You lie! You can't conceive that. Your brain wasn't built for the conception any more than it was built for the conception of infinity or of eternity. You can only talk about it. A fraction of the reality upsets you, and when the real thing comes, your brain is going to be presented with the phenomenon outside its limits of comprehension. You will go mad, completely and permanently! There is no question of it!"

He added sadly, "And another couple of millennia of painful struggle comes to nothing. Tomorrow there won't be a city standing unharmed in all Lagash."

Theremon recovered part of his mental equilibrium. "That doesn't follow. I still don't see that I can go loony just because there isn't a sun in the sky—but even if I did, and everyone else did, how does that harm the cities? Are we going to blow them down?"

But Sheerin was angry too. "If you were in Darkness, what would you want more than anything else; what would it be that every instinct would call for? Light, damn you, *light!*"

"Well?"

"And how would you get light?"

"I don't know," said Theremon flatly.

"What's the *only* way to get light, short of a sun?"

"How should I know?"

They were standing face to face and nose to nose.

Sheerin said, "You burn something, mister. Ever see a forest fire? Ever go camping and cook a stew over a wood fire? Heat isn't the only thing burning wood gives off, you know. It gives off light, and people know that. And when it's dark, they want light, and they're going to *get* it."

"So they burn wood?"

"So they burn whatever they can get. They've got to have light. They've got to burn something, and wood isn't handy— so they'll burn whatever is nearest. They'll have their light— and every center of habitation goes up in flames!"

Eyes held each other as though the whole matter were a personal affair of respective willpowers, and then Theremon broke away wordlessly. His breathing was harsh and ragged, and he scarcely noted the sudden hubbub that came from the adjoining room behind the closed door.

Sheerin spoke, and it was with an effort that he made it sound matter-of-fact. "I think I heard Yimot's voice. He and Faro are probably back. Let's go in and see what kept them."

"Might as well!" muttered Theremon. He drew a long breath and seemed to shake himself. The tension was broken.

The room was in an uproar, with members of the staff clustering about two young men who were removing outer garments even as they parried the miscellany of questions being thrown at them.

Aton bustled through the crowd and faced the newcomers angrily. "Do you realize that it's less than half an hour before deadline? Where have you two been?"

Faro 24 seated himself and rubbed his hands. His cheeks

349

were red with the outdoor chill. "Yimot and I have just finished carrying through a little crazy experiment of our own. We've been trying to see if we couldn't construct an arrangement by which we could simulate the appearance of Darkness and Stars so as to get an advance notion as to how it looked."

There was a confused murmur from the listeners, and a sudden look of interest entered Aton's eyes. "There wasn't anything said of this before. How did you go about it?"

"Well," said Faro, "the idea came to Yimot and myself long ago, and we've been working it out in our spare time. Yimot knew of a low one-story house down in the city with a domed roof—it had once been used as a museum, I think. Anyway, we bought it—"

"Where did you get the money?" interrupted Aton peremptorily.

"Our bank accounts," grunted Yimot 70. "It cost two thousand credits." Then, defensively, "Well, what of it? Tomorrow, two thousand credits will be two thousand pieces of paper. That's all."

"Sure," agreed Faro. "We bought the place and rigged it up with black velvet from top to bottom so as to get as perfect a Darkness as possible. Then we punched tiny holes in the ceiling and through the roof and covered them with little metal caps, all of which could be shoved aside simultaneously at the close of a switch. At least we didn't do that part ourselves; we got a carpenter and an electrician and some others—money didn't count. The point was that we could get the light to shine through those holes in the roof, so that we could get a starlike effect."

Not a breath was drawn during the pause that followed. Aton said stiffly, "You had no right to make a private—"

Faro seemed abashed. "I know, sir—but frankly, Yimot and I thought the experiment was a little dangerous. If the effect really worked we half expected to go mad—from what Sheerin says about all this, we thought that would be rather likely. We wanted to take the risk ourselves. Of course if we found we could retain sanity, it occurred to us that we might develop immunity to the real thing, and then expose the rest of you the same way. But things didn't work out at all—"

"Why, what happened?"

It was Yimot who answered. "We shut ourselves in and allowed our eyes to get accustomed to the dark. It's an extremely creepy feeling because the total Darkness makes you feel as if the walls and ceiling are crushing in on you. But we got over that and pulled the switch. The caps fell away and the roof glittered all over with little dots of light—"

"Well?"

"Well—nothing. That's the whacky part of it. Nothing happened. It was just a roof with holes in it, and that's just what it looked like. We tried it over and over again—that's what kept us so late—but there just isn't any effect at all."

There followed a shocked silence, and all eyes turned to Sheerin, who sat motionless, mouth open.

Theremon was the first to speak. "You know what this does to this whole story you've built up, Sheerin, don't you?" He was grinning with relief.

But Sheerin raised his hand. "Now wait a while. Just let me think this through." And then he snapped his fingers, and when he lifted his head, there was neither surprise nor uncertainty in his eyes. "Of course—"

He never finished. From somewhere up above there sounded a sharp clang, and Beenay, starting to his feet, dashed up the stairs with a "What the devil!"

The rest followed after.

Things happened quickly. Once up in the dome, Beenay cast one horrified glance at the shattered photographic plates and at the man bending over them, and then hurled himself fiercely at the intruder, getting a death grip on his throat. There was a wild threshing, and as others of the staff joined in, the stranger was swallowed up and smothered under the weight of half a dozen angry men.

Aton came up last, breathing heavily. "Let him up!"

There was a reluctant unscrambling and the stranger, panting harshly, with his clothes torn and his forehead bruised, was hauled to his feet. He had a short yellow beard curled elaborately in the style affected by the Cultists.

Beenay shifted his hold to a collar grip and shook the man savagely. "All right, rat, what's the idea? These plates—"

"I wasn't after *them*," retorted the Cultist coldly. "That was an accident."

Beenay followed his glowering stare and snarled, "I see. You were after the cameras themselves. The accident with the plates was a stroke of luck for you then. If you had touched Snapping Bertha or any of the others, you would have died by slow torture. As it is—" He drew his fist back.

Aton grabbed his sleeve. "Stop that! Let him go!"

The young technician wavered, and his arm dropped reluctantly. Aton pushed him aside and confronted the Cultist. "You're Latimer, aren't you?"

The Cultist bowed stiffly and indicated the symbol upon his hip. "I am Latimer 25, adjutant of the third class to his serenity, Sor 5."

"And"—Aton's white eyebrows lifted—"you were with his serenity when he visited me last week, weren't you?"

Latimer bowed a second time.

"Now then, what do you want?"

"Nothing that you would give me of your own free will."

"Sor 5 sent you, I suppose—or is this your own idea?"

"I won't answer that question."

"Will there be any further visitors?"

"I won't answer that, either."

Aton glanced at his timepiece and scowled. "Now, man, what is it your master wants of me? I have fulfilled my end of the bargain."

Latimer smiled faintly, but said nothing.

"I asked him," continued Aton angrily, "for data only the Cult could supply, and it was given to me. For that, thank you. In return I promised to prove the essential truth of the creed of the Cult."

"There was no need to prove that," came the proud retort. "It stands proven by the *Book of Revelations*."

"For the handful that constitute the Cult, yes. Don't pretend to mistake my meaning. I offered to present scientific backing for your beliefs. And I did!"

The Cultist's eyes narrowed bitterly. "Yes, you did—with a fox's subtlety, for your pretended explanation backed our beliefs and at the same time removed all necessity for them. You made of the Darkness and of the Stars a natural phenomenon and removed all its real significance. That was blasphemy."

352

"If so, the fault isn't mine. The facts exist. What can I do but state them?"

"Your 'facts' are a fraud and a delusion."

Aton stamped angrily. "How do you know?"

And the answer came with the certainty of absolute faith. "I know!"

The director purpled and Beenay whispered urgently. Aton waved him silent. "And what does Sor 5 want us to do? He still thinks, I suppose, that in trying to warn the world to take measures against the menace of madness, we are placing innumerable souls in jeopardy. We aren't succeeding, if that means anything to him."

"The attempt itself has done harm enough, and your vicious effort to gain information by means of your devilish instruments must be stopped. We obey the will of the Stars, and I only regret that my clumsiness prevented me from wrecking your infernal devices."

"It wouldn't have done you too much good," returned Aton. "All our data, except for the direct evidence we intend collecting right now, is already safely cached and well beyond possibility of harm." He smiled grimly. "But that does not affect your present status as an attempted burglar and criminal."

He turned to the men behind him. "Someone call the police at Saro City."

There was a cry of distaste from Sheerin. "Damn it, Aton, what's wrong with you? There's no time for that. Here"—he bustled his way forward—"let me handle this."

Aton stared down his nose at the psychologist. "This is not the time for your monkeyshines, Sheerin. Will you please let me handle this my own way? Right now you are a complete outsider here, and don't forget it."

Sheerin's mouth twisted eloquently. "Now why should we go to the impossible trouble of calling the police—with Beta's eclipse a matter of minutes from now—when this young man here is perfectly willing to pledge his word of honor to remain and cause no trouble whatsoever?"

The Cultist answered promptly. "I will do no such thing. You're free to do what you want, but it's only fair to warn you that just as soon as I get my chance, I'm going to finish what I came out here to do. If it's my word of honor you're relying on, you'd better call the police."

Sheerin smiled in a friendly fashion. "You're a determined cuss, aren't you? Well, I'll explain something. Do you see that young man at the window? He's a strong, husky fellow, quite handy with his fists, and he's an outsider besides. Once the eclipse starts, there will be nothing for him to do except keep an eye on you. Besides him, there will be myself—a little too stout for active fisticuffs, but still able to help."

"Well, what of it?" demanded Latimer frozenly.

"Listen and I'll tell you," was the reply. "Just as soon as the eclipse starts, we're going to take you, Theremon and I, and deposit you in a little closet with one door, to which is attached one giant lock and no windows. You will remain there for the duration."

"And afterward," breathed Latimer fiercely, "there'll be no one to let me out. I know as well as you do what the coming of the Stars mean—I know it far better than you. With all your minds gone, you are not likely to free me. Suffocation or slow starvation, is it? About what I might have expected from a group of scientists. But I don't give my word. It's a matter of principle, and I won't discuss it further."

Aton seemed perturbed. His faded eyes were troubled. "Really, Sheerin, locking him—"

"Please!" Sheerin motioned him impatiently to silence. "I don't think for a moment things will go that far. Latimer has just tried a clever little bluff, but I'm not a psychologist just because I like the sound of the word." He grinned at the Cultist. "Come now, you don't really think I'm trying anything as crude as slow starvation. My dear Latimer, if I lock you in the closet, you are not going to see the Darkness, and you are not going to see the Stars. It does not take much knowledge of the fundamental creed of the Cult to realize that for you to be hidden from the Stars when they appear means the loss of your immortal soul. Now, I believe you to be an honorable man. I'll accept your word of honor to make no further effort to disrupt proceedings, if you'll offer it."

A vein throbbed in Latimer's temple, and he seemed to shrink within himself as he said thickly, "You have it!" And then he added with swift fury, "But it is my consolation that

354

you will all be damned for your deeds of today." He turned on his heel and stalked to the high three-legged stool by the door.

Sheerin nodded to the columnist. "Take a seat next to him, Theremon—just as a formality. Hey, Theremon!"

But the newpaperman didn't move. He had gone pale to the lips. "Look at that!" The finger he pointed toward the sky shook and his voice was dry and cracked.

There was one simultaneous gasp as every eye followed the pointing finger and, for one breathless moment, stared frozenly.

Beta was chipped on one side!

The tiny bit of encroaching blackness was perhaps the width of a fingernail, but to the staring watchers it magnified itself into the crack of doom.

Only for a moment they watched, and after that there was a shrieking confusion that was of even shorter duration and which gave way to an orderly scurry of activity—each man at his prescribed job. At the crucial moment there was no time for emotion. The men were merely scientists with work to do. Even Aton had melted away.

Sheerin said prosaically, "First contact must have been made fifteen minutes ago. A little early, but pretty good considering the uncertainties involved in the calculation." He looked about him and then tiptoed to Theremon, who still remained staring out the window, and dragged him away gently.

"Aton is furious," he whispered, "so stay away. He missed first contact on account of this fuss with Latimer, and if you get in his way, he'll have you thrown out the window."

Theremon nodded shortly and sat down. Sheerin stared in surprise at him.

"The devil, man," he exclaimed, "you're shaking."

"Eh?" Theremon licked dry lips and then tried to smile. "I don't feel very well, and that's a fact."

The psychologist's eyes hardened. "You're not losing your nerve?"

"No!" cried Theremon in a flash of indignation. "Give me a chance, will you? I haven't really believed this rigmarole—not way down beneath, anyway—till just this minute. Give me a chance to get used to the idea. You've been preparing yourself for two months or more."

"You're right, at that," replied Sheerin thoughtfully. "Listen! Have you got a family—parents, wife, children?"

Theremon shook his head. "You mean the Hideout, I suppose. No, you don't have to worry about that. I have a sister, but she's two thousand miles away. I don't even know her exact address."

"Well then, what about yourself? You've got time to get there, and they're one short anyway, since I left. After all, you're not needed here, and you'd make a darned fine addition—"

Theremon looked at the other wearily. "You think I'm scared stiff, don't you? Well, get this, mister, I'm a newspaperman and I've been assigned to cover a story. I intend covering it."

There was a faint smile on the psychologist's face. "I see. Professional honor, is that it?"

"You might call it that. But, man, I'd give my right arm for another bottle of that sockeroo juice even half the size of the one you hogged. If ever a fellow needed a drink I do."

He broke off. Sheerin was nudging him violently. "Do you hear that? Listen!"

Theremon followed the motion of the other's chin and stared at the Cultist, who, oblivious to all about him, faced the window, a look of wild elation on his face, droning to himself the while in singsong fashion.

"What's he saying?" whispered the columnist.

"He's quoting *Book of Revelations,* fifth chapter," replied Sheerin. Then, urgently, "Keep quiet and listen, I tell you."

The Cultist's voice had risen in a sudden increase of fervor:

"'And it came to pass that in those days the Sun, Beta, held lone vigil in the sky for ever longer periods as the revolutions passed; until such time as for full half a revolution, it alone, shrunken and cold, shone down upon Lagash.

"'And men did assemble in the public squares and in the highways, there to debate and to marvel at the sight, for a strange depression had seized them. Their minds were troubled and their speech confused, for the souls of men awaited the coming of the Stars.

"'And in the city of Trigon, at high noon, Vendret 2 came

forth and said unto the men of Trigon, "Lo, ye sinners! Though ye scorn the ways of righteousness, yet will the time of reckoning come. Even now the Cave approaches to swallow Lagash; yea, and all it contains."

"'And even as he spoke, the lip of the Cave of Darkness passed the edge of Beta so that to all Lagash it was hidden from sight. Loud were the cries of men as it vanished, and great the fear of soul that fell upon them.

"'It came to pass that the Darkness of the Cave fell upon Lagash, and there was no light on all the surface of Lagash. Men were even as blinded, nor could one man see his neighbor, though he felt his breath upon his face.

"'And in this blackness there appeared the Stars, in countless numbers, and to the strains of music of such beauty that the very leaves of the trees cried out in wonder.

"'And in that moment the souls of men departed from them, and their abandoned bodies became even as beasts; yea, even as brutes of the wild; so that through the blackened streets of the cities of Lagash they prowled with wild cries.

"'From the Stars there then reached down the Heavenly Flame, and where it touched, the cities of Lagash flamed to utter destruction, so that of man and of the works of man nought remained.

"'Even then—'"

There was a subtle change in Latimer's tone. His eyes had not shifted, but somehow he had become aware of the absorbed attention of the other two. Easily, without pausing for breath, the timbre of his voice shifted and the syllables became more liquid.

Theremon, caught by surprise, stared. The words seemed on the border of familiarity. There was an elusive shift in the accent—a tiny change in the vowel stress; nothing more—yet Latimer had become thoroughly unintelligible.

Sheerin smiled slyly. "He shifted to some old-cycle tongue, probably their traditional second cycle. That was the language in which the *Book of Revelations* was originally written, you know."

"It doesn't matter; I've heard enough." Theremon shoved his chair back and brushed his hair back with hands that no longer shook. "I feel much better now."

"You do?" Sheerin seemed mildly surprised.

"I'll say I do. I had a bad case of jitters just a while back. Listening to you and your gravitation and seeing that eclipse start almost finished me. But this"—he jerked a contemptuous thumb at the yellow-bearded Cultist—"*this* is the sort of thing my nurse used to tell me. I've been laughing at that sort of thing all my life. I'm not going to let it scare me *now*."

He drew a deep breath and said with a hectic gaiety. "But if I expect to keep on the good side of myself, I'm going to turn my chair away from the window."

Sheerin said, "Yes, but you'd better talk lower. Aton just lifted his head out of that box he's got it stuck into and gave you a look that should have killed you."

Theremon made a mouth. "I forgot about the old fellow." With elaborate care he turned the chair from the window, cast one distasteful look over his shoulder, and said, "It has occurred to me that there must be considerable immunity against this Star madness."

The psychologist did not answer immediately. Beta was past its zenith now, and the square of bloody sunlight that outlined the window upon the floor had lifted into Sheerin's lap. He stared at its dusky color thoughtfully and then bent and squinted into the sun itself.

The chip in its side had grown to a black encroachment that covered a third of Beta. He shuddered, and when he straightened once more his florid cheeks did not contain quite as much color as they had had previously.

With a smile that was almost apologetic, he reversed his chair also. "There are probably two million people in Saro City who are all trying to join the Cult at once in one gigantic revival." Then, ironically, "The Cult is in for an hour of unexampled prosperity. I trust they'll make the most of it. Now, what was it you said?"

"Just this. How did the Cultists manage to keep the *Book of Revelations* going from cycle to cycle, and how on Lagash did it get written in the first place? There must have been some sort of immunity, for if everyone had gone mad, who would be left to write the book?"

Sheerin stared at his questioner ruefully. "Well, now, young man, there isn't any eyewitness answer to that, but we've got a few damned good notions as to what happened. You see, there are three kinds of people who might remain relatively unaffected. First, the very few who don't see the Stars at all: the seriously retarded or those who drink themselves into a stupor at the beginning of the eclipse and remain so to the end. We leave them out—because they aren't really witnesses.

"Then there are children below six, to whom the world as a whole is too new and strange for them to be too frightened at Stars and Darkness. They would be just another item in an already surprising world. You see that, don't you?"

The other nodded doubtfully. "I suppose so."

"Lastly, there are those whose minds are too coarsely grained to be entirely toppled. The very insensitive would be scarcely affected—oh, such people as some of our older, work-broken peasants. Well, the children would have fugitive memories, and that, combined with the confused, incoherent babblings of the half-mad morons, formed the basis for the *Book of Revelations.*

"Naturally, the book was based, in the first place, on the testimony of those least qualified to serve as historians; that is, children and morons; and was probably edited and re-edited through the cycles."

"Do you suppose," broke in Theremon, "that they carried the book through the cycles the way we're planning on handing on the secret of gravitation?"

Sheerin shrugged. "Perhaps, but their exact method is unimportant. They do it somehow. The point I was getting at was that the book can't help but be a mass of distortion, even if it is based on fact. For instance, do you remember the experiment with the holes in the roof that Faro and Yimot tried—the one that didn't work?"

"Yes."

"You know why it didn't w—" He stopped and rose in alarm, for Aton was approaching, his face a twisted mask of consternation. *"What's happened?"*

Aton drew him aside and Sheerin could feel the fingers on his elbow twitching.

"Not so loud!" Aton's voice was low and tortured. "I've just gotten word from the Hideout on the private line."

Sheerin broke in anxiously. "They are in trouble?"

"Not *they*." Aton stressed the pronoun significantly. "They sealed themselves off just a while ago, and they're going to stay buried till day after tomorrow. They're safe. But the *city,* Sheerin—it's a shambles. You have no idea—" He was having difficulty in speaking.

"Well?" snapped Sheerin impatiently. "What of it? It will get worse. What are you shaking about?" Then, suspiciously, "How do you feel?"

Aton's eyes sparked angrily at the insinuation, and then faded to anxiety once more. "You don't understand. The Cultists are active. They're rousing the people to storm the Observatory—promising them immediate entrance into grace, promising them salvation, promising them anything. What are we to do, Sheerin?"

Sheerin's head bent, and he stared in long abstraction at his toes. He tapped his chin with one knuckle, then looked up and said crisply, "Do? What is there to do? Nothing at all. Do the men know of this?"

"No, of course not!"

"Good! Keep it that way. How long till totality?"

"Not quite an hour."

"There's nothing much to do but gamble. It will take time to organize any really formidable mob, and it will take more time to get them out here. We're a good five miles from the city—"

He glared out the window, down the slopes to where the farmed patches gave way to clumps of white houses in the suburbs; down to where the metropolis itself was a blur on the horizon—a mist in the waning haze of Beta.

He repeated without turning, "It will take time. Keep on working and pray that totality comes first."

Beta was cut in half, the line of division pushing a slight concavity into the still-bright portion of the Sun. It was like a gigantic eyelid shutting slantwise over the light of the world.

The faint clatter of the room in which he stood faded into oblivion, and he sensed only the thick silence of the fields outside. The very insects seemed frightened mute. And things were dim.

He jumped at the voice in his ear. Theremon said, "Is something wrong?"

"Er? Er—no. Get back to the chair. We're in the way."

They slipped back to their corner, but the psychologist did not speak for a time. He lifted a finger and loosened his collar. He twisted his neck back and forth but found no relief. He looked up suddenly.

"Are you having any difficulty in breathing?"

The newspaperman opened his eyes wide and drew two or three long breaths. "No. Why?"

"I looked out the window too long, I suppose. The dimness got me. Difficulty in breathing is one of the first symptoms of a claustrophobic attack."

Theremon drew another long breath. "Well, it hasn't got me yet. Say, here's another of the fellows."

Beenay had interposed his bulk between the light and the pair in the corner, and Sheerin squinted up at him anxiously. "Hello, Beenay."

The astronomer shifted his weight to the other foot and smiled feebly. "You won't mind if I sit down awhile and join in the talk? My cameras are set, and there's nothing to do till totality." He paused and eyed the Cultist, who fifteen minutes earlier had drawn a small, skin-bound book from his sleeve and had been poring intently over it ever since. "That rat hasn't been making trouble, has he?"

Sheerin shook his head. His shoulders were thrown back and he frowned his concentration as he forced himself to breathe regularly. He said, "Have you had any trouble breathing, Beenay?"

Beenay sniffed the air in his turn. "It doesn't seem stuffy to me."

"A touch of claustrophobia," explained Sheerin apologetically.

"Ohhh! It worked itself differently with me. I get the impression that my eyes are going back on me. Things seem to blur and—well, nothing is clear. And it's cold too."

"Oh, it's cold all right. That's no illusion." Theremon grimaced. "My toes feel as if I've been shipping them cross-country in a refrigerating car."

"What we need," put in Sheerin, "is to keep our minds busy with extraneous affairs. I was telling you a while ago, Theremon, why Faro's experiments with the holes in the roof came to nothing."

361

"You were just beginning," replied Theremon. He encircled a knee with both arms and nuzzled his chin against it.

"Well, as I started to say, they were misled by taking the *Book of Revelations* literally. There probably wasn't any sense in attaching any physical significance to the Stars. It might be, you know, that in the presence of total Darkness, the mind finds it absolutely necessary to create light. This illusion of light might be all the Stars there really are."

"In other words," interposed Theremon, "you mean the Stars are the results of the madness and not one of the causes. Then what good will Beenay's photographs be?"

"To prove that it is an illusion, maybe; or to prove the opposite, for all I know. Then again—"

But Beenay had drawn his chair closer, and there was an expression of enthusiasm on his face. "Say, I'm glad you two got onto this subject." His eyes narrowed and he lifted one finger. "I've been thinking about these Stars and I've got a really cute notion. Of course it's strictly ocean foam, and I'm not trying to advance it seriously, but I think it's interesting. Do you want to hear it?"

He seemed half reluctant, but Sheerin leaned back and said, "Go ahead! I'm listening."

"Well then, supposing there were other suns in the Universe." He broke off a little bashfully. "I mean suns that are so far away that they're too dim to see. It sounds as if I've been reading some of that fantastic fiction, I suppose."

"Not necessarily. Still, isn't that possibility eliminated by the fact that, according to the Law of Gravitation, they would make themselves evident by their attractive forces?"

"Not if they were far enough off," rejoined Beenay, "really far off—maybe as much as four light-years, or even more. We'd never be able to detect perturbations then, because they'd be too small. Say that there were a lot of suns that far off, a dozen or two, maybe."

Theremon whistled melodiously. "What an idea for a good Sunday supplement article. Two dozen suns in a Universe eight light-years across. Wow! That would shrink our world into insignificance. The readers would eat it up."

"Only an idea," said Beenay with a grin, "but you see the point. During an eclipse, these dozen suns would become

362

visible because there'd be no *real* sunlight to drown them out. Since they are so far off, they'd appear small, like so many little marbles. Of course the Cultists talk of millions of Stars, but that's probably exaggeration. There just isn't any place in the Universe you could put a million suns—unless they touch each other."

Sheerin had listened with gradually increasing interest. "You've hit something there, Beenay. And exaggeration is just exactly what would happen. Our minds, as you probably know, can't grasp directly any number higher than five; above that there is only the concept of 'many.' A dozen would become a million just like that. A damn good idea!"

"And I've got another cute little notion," Beenay said. "Have you ever thought what a simple problem gravitation would be if only you had a sufficiently simple system? Supposing you had a universe in which there was a planet with only one sun. The planet would travel in a perfect ellipse and the exact route of the gravitational force would be so evident it could be accepted as an axiom. Astronomers on such a world would start off with gravity probably before they even invented the telescope. Naked-eye observation would be enough."

"But would such a system be dynamically stable?" questioned Sheerin doubtfully.

"Sure! They call it the 'one-and-one' case. It's been worked out mathematically, but it's the philosophical implications that interest me."

"It's nice to think about," admitted Sheerin, "as a pretty abstraction—like a perfect gas, or absolute zero."

"Of course," continued Beenay, "there's the catch that life would be impossible on such a planet. It would get enough heat and light, but if it rotated, there would be total Darkness half of each day. You couldn't expect life—which is fundamentally dependent upon light—to develop under those conditions. Besides—"

Sheerin's chair went over backward as he sprang to his feet in a rude interruption. "Aton's brought out the lights."

Beenay said, "Huh," turned to stare, and then grinned halfway around his head in open relief.

There were half a dozen foot-long, inch-thick rods cradled

363

in Aton's arms. He glared over them at the assembled staff members.

"Get back to work, all of you. Sheerin, come here and help me!"

Sheerin trotted to the older man's side and, one by one, in utter silence, the two adjusted the rods in makeshift metal holders suspended from the walls.

With the air of one carrying through the most sacred item of a religious ritual, Sheerin scraped a large, clumsy match into spluttering life and passed it to Aton, who carried the flame to the upper end of one of the rods.

It hesitated there awhile, playing futilely about the tip, until a sudden, cracking flare cast Aton's lined face into yellow headlights. He withdrew the match and a spontaneous cheer rattled the window.

The rod was topped by six inches of wavering flame! Methodically the other rods were lighted until six independent fires turned the rear of the room yellow.

The light was dim, dimmer even than the tenuous sunlight. The flames reeled crazily, giving birth to drunken, swaying shadows. The torches smoked devilishly and smelled like a bad day in the kitchen. But they emitted yellow light.

There was something about yellow light after four hours of somber, dimming Beta. Even Latimer had lifted his eyes from his book and stared in wonder.

Sheerin warmed his hands at the nearest, regardless of the soot that gathered upon them in a fine, gray powder, and muttered ecstatically to himself, "Beautiful! Beautiful! I never realized before what a wonderful color yellow is."

But Theremon regarded the torches suspiciously. He wrinkled his nose at the rancid odor and said, "What are those things?"

"Wood," said Sheerin shortly.

"Oh, no, they're not. They aren't burning. The top inch is charred and the flame just keeps shooting up out of nothing."

"That's the beauty of it. This is a really efficient artificial-light mechanism. We made a few hundred of them, but most went to the Hideout, of course. You see"—he turned and wiped his blackened hands upon his handkerchief—"you take the pithy core of coarse water reeds, dry them thoroughly, and

364

soak them in animal grease. Then you set fire to it and the grease burns, little by little. These torches will burn for almost half an hour without stopping. Ingenious, isn't it? It was developed by one of our own young men at Saro University."

After the momentary sensation, the dome had quieted. Latimer had carried his chair directly beneath a torch and continued reading, lips moving in the monotonous recital of invocations to the Stars. Beenay had drifted away to his cameras once more, and Theremon seized the opportunity to add to his notes on the article he was going to write for the Saro City *Chronicle* the next day—a procedure he had been following for the last two hours in a perfectly methodical, perfectly conscientious and, as he was well aware, perfectly meaningless fashion.

But, as the gleam of amusement in Sheerin's eyes indicated, careful note-taking occupied his mind with something other than the fact that the sky was gradually turning a horrible deep purple-red, as if it were one gigantic, freshly peeled beet; and so it fulfilled its purpose.

The air grew somehow denser. Dusk, like a palpable entity, entered the room, and the dancing circle of yellow light about the torches etched itself into ever-sharper distinction against the gathering grayness beyond. There was the odor of smoke and the presence of little chuckling sounds that the torches made as they burned; the soft pad of one of the men circling the table at which he worked, on hesitant tiptoes; the occasional indrawn breath of someone trying to retain composure in a world that was retreating into the shadow.

It was Theremon who first heard the extraneous noise. It was a vague, unorganized *impression* of sound that would have gone unnoticed but for the dead silence that prevailed within the dome.

The newspaperman sat upright and replaced his notebook. He held his breath and listened; then, with considerable reluctance, threaded his way between the solarscope and one of Beenay's cameras and stood before the window.

The silence ripped to fragments at his startled shout: "*Sheerin!*"

Work stopped. The psychologist was at his side in a moment. Aton joined him. Even Yimot 70, high in his little

365

lean-back seat at the eyepiece of the gigantic solarscope, paused and looked downward.

Outside, Beta was a mere smoldering splinter, taking one last desperate look at Lagash. The eastern horizon, in the direction of the city, was lost in Darkness, and the road from Saro to the Observatory was a dull red line bordered on both sides by wooded tracts, the trees of which had somehow lost individuality and merged into a continuous shadowy mass.

But it was the highway itself that held attention, for along it there surged another, and infinitely menacing, shadowy mass.

Aton cried in a cracked voice. "The madmen from the city! They've come!"

"How long to totality?" demanded Sheerin.

"Fifteen minutes, but . . . but they'll be here in five."

"Never mind, keep the men working. We'll hold them off. This place is built like a fortress. Aton, keep an eye on our young Cultist just for luck. Theremon, come with me."

Sheerin was out the door, and Theremon was at his heels. The stairs stretched below them in tight, circular sweeps about the central shaft, fading into a dank and dreary grayness.

The first momentum of their rush had carried them fifty feet down, so that the dim, flickering yellow from the open door of the dome had disappeared, and both above and below the same dusky shadow crushed in upon them.

Sheerin paused, and his pudgy hand clutched at his chest. His eyes bulged and his voice was a dry cough. "I can't . . . breathe. . . . Go down . . . yourself. Close all doors—"

Theremon took a few downward steps, then turned. "Wait! Can you hold out a minute?" He was panting himself. The air passed in and out of his lungs like so much molasses, and there was a little germ of screeching panic in his mind at the thought of making his way into the mysterious Darkness below by himself.

Theremon, after all, was afraid of the dark!

"Stay here," he said. "I'll be back in a second." He dashed upward two steps at a time, heart pounding—not altogether from the exertion—tumbled into the dome and snatched a torch from its holder. It was foul-smelling, and the smoke smarted his eyes almost blind, but he clutched that torch as if he wanted to kiss it for joy, and its flame streamed backward as he hurtled down the stairs again.

Sheerin opened his eyes and moaned as Theremon bent over him. Theremon shook him roughly. "All right, get ahold of yourself. We've got light."

He held the torch at tiptoe height and, propping the tottering psychologist by an elbow, made his way downward in the middle of the protecting circle of illumination.

The offices on the ground floor still possessed what light there was, and Theremon felt the horror about him relax.

"Here," he said brusquely, and passed the torch to Sheerin. "You can hear *them* outside."

And they could. Little scraps of hoarse, wordless shouts.

But Sheerin was right; the Observatory was built like a fortress. Erected in the last century, when the neo-Gavottian style of architecture was at its ugly height, it had been designed for stability and durability rather than for beauty.

The windows were protected by the grillwork of inch-thick iron bars sunk deep into the concrete sills. The walls were solid masonry that an earthquake couldn't have touched, and the main door was a huge oaken slab reinforced with iron. Theremon shot the bolts and they slid shut with a dull clang.

At the other end of the corridor, Sheerin cursed weakly. He pointed to the lock of the back door, which had been neatly jimmied into uselessness.

"That must be how Latimer got in," he said.

"Well, don't stand there," cried Theremon impatiently. "Help drag up the furniture—and keep that torch out of my eyes. The smoke's killing me."

He slammed the heavy table up against the door as he spoke, and in two minutes had built a barricade which made up for what it lacked in beauty and symmetry by the sheer inertia of its massiveness.

Somewhere, dimly, far off, they could hear the battering of naked fists upon the door; and the screams and yells from outside had a sort of half-reality.

That mob had set off from Saro City with only two things in mind: the attainment of Cultist salvation by the destruction of the Observatory, and a maddening fear that all but paralyzed them. There was no time to think of ground cars, or of weapons, or of leadership, or even of organization. They made for the Observatory on foot and assaulted it with bare hands.

And now that they were there, the last flash of Beta, the last ruby-red of flame, flickered feebly over a humanity that had left only stark, universal fear!

Theremon groaned, "Let's get back to the dome!"

In the dome, only Yimot, at the solarscope, had kept his place. The rest were clustered about the cameras, and Beenay was giving his instructions in a hoarse, strained voice.

"Get it straight, all of you. I'm snapping Beta just before totality and changing the plate. That will leave one of you to each camera. You all know about . . . times of exposure—"

There was a breathless murmur of agreement.

Beenay passed a hand over his eyes. "Are the torches still burning? Never mind, I see them!" He was leaning hard against the back of a chair. "Now remember, don't try to look for good shots. Don't waste time trying to get t-two stars at a time in the scope field. One is enough. And . . . and if you feel yourself going, *get away from the camera*."

At the door, Sheerin whispered to Theremon, "Take me to Aton. I don't see him."

The newsman did not answer immediately. The vague forms of the astronomers wavered and blurred, and the torches overhead had become only yellow splotches.

"It's dark," he whimpered.

Sheerin held out his hand. "Aton." He stumbled forward. "Aton!"

Theremon stepped after and seized his arm. "Wait, I'll take you." Somehow he made his way across the room. He closed his eyes against the Darkness and his mind against the chaos within it.

No one heard them or paid attention to them. Sheerin stumbled against the wall. "Aton!"

The psychologist felt shaking hands touching him, then withdrawing, and a voice muttering, "Is that you, Sheerin?"

"Aton!" He strove to breathe normally. "Don't worry about the mob. The place will hold them off."

Latimer, the Cultist, rose to his feet, and his face twisted in desperation. His word was pledged, and to break it would mean placing his soul in mortal peril. Yet that word had been forced from him and had not been given freely. The Stars would come soon! He could not stand by and allow— And yet his word was pledged.

Beenay's face was dimly flushed as it looked upward at Beta's last ray, and Latimer, seeing him bend over his camera, made his decision. His nails cut the flesh of his palms as he tensed himself.

He staggered crazily as he started his rush. There was nothing before him but shadows; the very floor beneath his feet lacked substance. And then someone was upon him and he went down with clutching fingers at his throat.

He doubled his knee and drove it hard into his assailant. "Let me up or I'll kill you." -

Theremon cried out sharply and muttered through a blinding haze of pain. "You double-crossing rat!"

. The newsman seemed conscious of everything at once. He heard Beenay croak, "I've got it. At your cameras, men!" and then there was the strange awareness that the last thread of sunlight had thinned out and snapped.

Simultaneously he heard one last choking gasp from Beenay and a queer little cry from Sheerin, a hysterical giggle that cut off in a rasp—and a sudden silence, a strange, deadly silence from outside.

And Latimer had gone limp in his loosening grasp. Theremon peered into the Cultist's eyes and saw the blankness of them staring upward, mirroring the feeble yellow of the torches. He saw the bubble froth upon Latimer's lips and heard the low, animal whimper in Latimer's throat.

With the slow fascination of fear, he lifted himself on one arm and turned his eyes toward the blood-curdling blackness of the window.

Through it shone the Stars!

Not Earth's feeble thirty-six hundred Stars visible to the eye; Lagash was in the center of a giant cluster. Thirty thousand mighty suns shone down in a soul-searing splendor that was more frighteningly cold in its awful indifference than the bitter wind that shivered across the cold, horribly bleak world.

Theremon staggered to his feet, his throat constricting him to breathlessness, all the muscles of his body writhing in an intensity of terror and sheer fear beyond bearing. He was going mad and knew it, and somewhere deep inside a bit of sanity was screaming, struggling to fight off the hopeless flood of black terror. It was very horrible to go mad and know that you were going mad—to know that in a little minute you would be here physically and yet all the real essence would be dead and drowned in the black madness. For this was the Dark—the Dark and the Cold and the Doom. The bright walls of the Universe were shattered and their awful black fragments were falling down to crush and squeeze and obliterate him.

He jostled someone crawling on hands and knees but stumbled somehow over him. Hands groping at his tortured throat, he limped toward the flame of the torches that filled all his mad vision.

"Light!" he screamed.

Aton, somewhere, was crying, whimpering horribly like a terribly frightened child. "Stars—all the Stars—we didn't know at all. We didn't know anything. We thought six stars in a universe is something the Stars didn't notice is Darkness forever and ever and ever and the walls are breaking in and we didn't know we couldn't know and anything—"

Someone clawed at the torch, and it fell and snuffed out. In the instant, the awful splendor of the indifferent Stars leaped nearer to them.

On the horizon outside the window, in the direction of Saro City, a crimson glow began growing, strengthening in brightness, that was not the glow of a sun.

The long night had come again.

20

The Planet That Wasn't

It is quite possible for a scientific problem to arise and for no solution to be found over a period of decades. The problem remains, a constant irritation, until it is eventually solved. Yet if one can conquer one's natural feeling of annoyance over the matter, one might feel anticipatory excitement instead, for I have the notion that the longer a problem remains unsolved, the more important the solution is likely to be when it does come.

I was once asked whether it was at all possible that the ancient Greeks had known about the rings of Saturn. The reason such a question is raised at all comes about as follows—

Saturn is the name of an agricultural deity of the ancient Romans. When the Romans had reached the point where they wanted to match the Greeks in cultural eminence, they decided to equate their own uninteresting deities with the fascinating ones of the imaginative Greeks. They made Saturn correspond with Kronos, the father of Zeus and of the other Olympian gods and goddesses.

The most famous mythical story of Kronos (Saturn) tells of his castration of his father Ouranos (Uranus), whom he then replaced as ruler of the Universe. Very naturally, Kronos feared that his own children might learn by his example and

371

decided to take action to prevent that. Since he was unaware of birth-control methods and was incapable of practicing restraint, he fathered six children (three sons and three daughters) upon his wife, Rhea. Taking action after the fact, he swallowed each child immediately after it was born.

When the sixth, Zeus, was born, Rhea (tired of bearing children for nothing) wrapped a stone in swaddling clothes and let the dim-witted lord of the Universe swallow that. Zeus was raised in secret and when he grew up he managed, by guile, to have Kronos vomit up his swallowed brothers and sisters (still alive!). Zeus and his siblings then went to war against Kronos and *his* siblings (the Titans). After a great ten-year struggle, Zeus defeated Kronos and took over the lordship of the Universe.

Now, then, let's return to the planet the Greeks had named Kronos because it moved more slowly against the background of the stars than any other planet and therefore behaved as though it were an older god. Of course the Romans called it Saturn, and so do we.

Around Saturn are its beautiful rings that we all know about. These rings are in Saturn's equatorial plane, which is tipped to the plane of its orbit by 26.7 degrees. Because of this tipping, we can see the rings at a slant.

The degree of tipping is constant with respect to the stars but not with respect to ourselves. It appears tipped to us in varying amounts, depending on where Saturn is in its orbit. At one point in its orbit, Saturn will display its rings tipped downward, so that we see them from above. At the opposite point they are tipped upward, so that we see them from below.

As Saturn revolves in its orbit, the amount of tipping varies smoothly from down to up and back again. Halfway between the down and the up, and then halfway between the up and the down, at two opposite points in Saturn's orbit, the rings are presented to us edge-on. They are so thin that at this time they can't be seen at all, even in a good telescope. Since Saturn revolves about the Sun in just under thirty years, the rings disappear from view every fifteen years.

When Galileo, back in the 1610s, was looking at the sky with his primitive telescope, he turned it on Saturn and found that there was something odd about it. He seemed to see two small bodies, one on either side of Saturn, but couldn't make out what they were. Whenever he returned to Saturn, it was harder to see them until, finally, he saw only the single sphere of Saturn and nothing else.

"What!" growled Galileo. "Does Saturn still swallow his children?" and he never looked at the planet again. It was another forty years before the Dutch astronomer Christiaan Huygens, catching the rings as they were tipping farther and farther (and with a telescope better than Galileo's), worked out what they were.

Could the Greeks, then, in working out their myth of Kronos swallowing his children, have referred to the planet Saturn, its rings, the tilt of its equatorial plane, and its orbital relationship to Earth?

No, I always say to people asking me this question, unless we can't think up some explanation that is simpler and more straightforward. In this case we can—coincidence.

People are entirely too disbelieving of coincidence. They are far too ready to dismiss it and to build arcane structures of extremely rickety substance in order to avoid it. I, on the other hand, see coincidence everywhere as an inevitable consequence of the laws of probability, according to which having no unusual coincidence is far more unusual than any coincidence could possibly be.

And those who see purpose in what is only coincidence don't usually even know the really good coincidences—something I have discussed before.* In this case what about other correspondences between planetary names and Greek mythology? How about the planet that the Greeks named Zeus and the Romans named Jupiter? The planet is named for the chief of the gods and it turns out to be more massive than all the other planets put together. Could it be that the Greeks knew the relative masses of the planets?

The most amazing coincidence of all, however, deals with a planet the Greeks (you would think) had never heard of.

Consider Mercury, the planet closest to the Sun. It has the most eccentric orbit of any known in the nineteenth century. Its

*See "Pompey and Circumstance" in *The Left Hand of the Electron* (Doubleday, 1972).

orbit is so eccentric that the Sun, at the focus of the orbital ellipse, is markedly off-center.

When Mercury is at that point in its orbit closest to the Sun ("perihelion"), it is only 46 million kilometers away and is moving in its orbit at a speed of fifty-six kilometers a second. At the opposite point in its orbit, when it is farthest from the Sun ("aphelion"), it is 70 million kilometers away and has, in consequence, slowed down to thirty-seven kilometers a second. The fact that Mercury is sometimes half again as far from the Sun as it is at others, and that it moves half again as quickly at some times than at others, makes it somewhat more difficult to plot its movements accurately than those of the other, more orderly, planets.

This difficulty arises most noticeably in one particular respect—

Since Mercury is closer to the Sun than Earth is, it occasionally gets exactly between Earth and Sun and astronomers can see its dark circle move across the face of the Sun.

Such "transits" of Mercury happen in rather irregular fashion because of the planet's eccentric orbit and because the orbit is tilted by seven degrees to the plane of Earth's orbit. The transits happen only in May or November (with November transits the more common in the ratio of 7 to 3) and at successive intervals of thirteen, seven, ten, and three years.

In the 1700s transits were watched very eagerly because they were one thing that could not be seen by the unaided eye and yet could be seen very well by the primitive telescopes of the day. Furthermore, the exact times at which the transit started and ended and the exact path it took across the solar disc changed slightly with the place of observation on Earth. From such changes, the distance of Mercury might be calculated and, through that, all the other distances of the solar system.

It was very astronomically embarrassing, then, that the prediction as to when the transit would take place was sometimes off by as much as an hour. It was a very obvious indication of the limitations of celestial mechanics at the time.

If Mercury and the Sun were all that existed in the Universe, then whatever orbit Mercury followed in circling the Sun, it would follow it exactly in every succeeding revolution. There would be no difficulty in predicting the exact moments of transits.

However, every other body in the Universe also pulls at Mercury, and the pull of the nearby planets—Venus, Earth, Mars and Jupiter—while very small in comparison to that of the Sun, is large enough to make a difference.

Each separate pull introduces a slight modification in Mercury's orbit (a "perturbation") that must be allowed for by mathematical computations that take into account the exact mass and motion of the object doing the pulling. The resulting set of complications is very simple in theory since it is entirely based on Isaac Newton's law of gravitation, but is very complicated in practice since the computations required are both lengthy and tedious.

Still it had to be done, and more and more careful attempts were made to work out the exact motions of Mercury by taking into account all possible perturbations.

In 1843 a French astronomer, Urbain Jean Joseph Leverrier, published a careful calculation of Mercury's orbit and found that small discrepancies persisted. His calculations, carried out in inordinate detail, showed that after all conceivable perturbations had been taken into account, there remained one small shift that could not be accounted for. The point at which Mercury reached its perihelion moved forward in the direction of its motion just a tiny bit more rapidly than could be accounted for by all the perturbations.

In 1882 the Canadian-American astronomer Simon Newcomb, using better instruments and more observations, corrected Leverrier's figures very slightly. Using this correction, it would seem that each time Mercury circled the Sun, its perihelion was 0.104 seconds of arc farther along than it should be even after all perturbations were taken into account.

This isn't much. In one Earth century, the discrepancy would amount to only forty-three seconds of arc. It would take four thousand years for the discrepancy to mount up to the apparent width of our Moon and three million years for it to amount to a complete turn about Mercury's orbit.

But that's enough. If the existence of this forward motion of Mercury's perihelion could not be explained, then there was something wrong with Newton's law of gravitation, and that law had worked out so perfectly in every other way that to have it come a cropper now was not something an astronomer would cheerfully have happen.

In fact, even as Leverrier was working out this discrepancy in Mercury's orbit, the law of gravitation had won its greatest victory ever. And who had been the moving force behind that victory? Why, Leverrier, who else?

The planet Uranus, then the farthest known planet from the Sun, also displayed a small discrepancy in its motions, one that couldn't be accounted for by the gravitational pull of the other planets. There had been suggestions that there might be still another planet, farther from the Sun than Uranus was, and that the gravitational pull of this distant and still unknown planet might account for the otherwise unaccounted-for discrepancy in Uranus's motions.

An English astronomer, John Couch Adams—using the law of gravity as his starting point—had, in 1843, worked out a possible orbit for such a distant planet. The orbit would account for the discrepancy in Uranus's motions and would predict where the unseen planet should be at that time.

Adams's calculations were ignored, but a few months later, Leverrier, working quite independently, came to the same conclusion and was luckier. Leverrier transmitted his calculations to a German astronomer, Johann Gottfried Galle, who happened to have a new star map of the region of the heavens in which Leverrier said there was an unknown planet. On September 23, 1846, Galle began to search and, in a matter of hours, located the planet, which we now call Neptune.

After a victory like that, no one (and Leverrier least of all) wanted to question the law of gravity. The discrepancy in Mercury's orbital motions had to be the result of some gravitational pull that wasn't being taken into account.

For instance, a planet's mass is most easily calculated if it has satellites moving around it at a certain distance and with a certain period. The distance-period combination depends upon the planetary mass, which can thus be calculated quite precisely. Venus, however, has no satellites. Its mass could only be determined fuzzily, therefore, and it might be that it was actually ten percent more massive than the astronomers of the mid-nineteenth century had thought. If it were, that additional mass, and the additional gravitational pull originating from it, would just account for Mercury's motion.

The trouble is that if Venus were that much more massive than was supposed, that extra mass would also affect the orbit of its other neighbor, Earth—and disturb it in a way that is not actually observed. Setting Mercury to rights at the cost of upsetting Earth is no bargain, and Leverrier eliminated the Venus solution.

Leverrier needed some massive body that was near Mercury but not too disturbingly near any other planet, and by 1859 he suggested that the gravitational source had to come from the far side of Mercury. There had to be a planet inside Mercury's orbit, close enough to Mercury to account for the extra motion of its perihelion but far enough from the planets farther out from the Sun to leave them substantially alone.

Leverrier gave to the suggested intra-Mercurial planet the name Vulcan. This was the Roman equivalent of the Greek god Hephaistos, who presided over the forge as the divine smith. A planet that was forever hovering near the celestial fire of the Sun would be more appropriately named in this fashion.

If an intra-Mercurial planet existed, however, why was it that it had never been seen? This isn't a hard question to answer, actually. As seen from Earth, any body that was closer to the Sun than Mercury is would always be in the neighborhood of the Sun, and seeing it would be very difficult indeed.

In fact, there would only be two times when it would be easy to see Vulcan. The first would be on the occasion of a total solar eclipse, when the sky in the immediate neighborhood of the Sun is darkened and when any object that is always in the immediate neighborhood of the Sun could be seen with an ease that would at other times be impossible.

In one way, this offers an easy out, since astronomers can pinpoint the times and places at which total solar eclipses would take place and be ready for observations then. On the other hand, eclipses do not occur frequently, usually involve a large amount of traveling, and last only a few minutes.

What about the second occasion for easy viewing of Vulcan? That would be whenever Vulcan passes directly between Earth and Sun in a transit. Its body would then appear like a dark circle on the Sun's orb, moving rapidly from west to east in a straight line.

Transits should be more common than eclipses, be visible over larger areas for longer times, and give a far better indication of the exact orbit of Vulcan—which could then be used to predict future transits, during which further investigations could be made and the properties of the planet worked out.

On the other hand, the time of transit can't be predicted surely until the orbit of Vulcan is accurately known, and that can't be accurately known until the planet is sighted and followed for a while. Therefore, the first sighting would have to be made by accident.

Or had that first sighting already been made? Such a thing was possible, and even likely. The planet Uranus had been seen on a score of occasions prior to its discovery by William Herschel. The first Astronomer Royal of Great Britain, John Flamsteed, had seen it a century before its discovery, had considered it an ordinary star, and had listed it as "34 Tauri." Herschel's discovery did not consist in seeing Uranus for the first time, but in recognizing it as a planet for the first time.

Once Leverrier made his suggestion (and the discoverer of Neptune carried prestige at the time), astronomers began searching for possible previous sightings of strange objects that would now be recognized as Vulcan.

Something showed up at once. A French amateur astronomer, Dr. Lescarbault, announced to Leverrier that in 1845 he had observed a dark object against the Sun which he had paid little attention to at the time, but which now he felt must have been Vulcan.

Leverrier studied this report in great excitement, and from it he estimated that Vulcan was a body circling the Sun at an average distance of 21 million kilometers, a little over a third of Mercury's distance. This meant its period of revolution would be about 19.7 days.

At that distance it would never be more than eight degrees from the Sun. This meant that the only time Vulcan would be seen in the sky in the absence of the Sun would be during, at most, the half-hour period before sunrise or the half-hour period after sunset (alternately, and at ten-day intervals). This

378

period is one of bright twilight, and viewing would be difficult, so that it was not surprising that Vulcan had avoided detection so long.

From Lescarbault's description, Leverrier also estimated the diameter of Vulcan to be about two thousand kilometers, or only a little over half the diameter of our Moon. Assuming the composition of Vulcan to be about that of Mercury, it would have a mass about one-seventeenth that of Mercury or one-fourth that of the Moon. This is not a large enough mass to account for all of the advance of Mercury's perihelion, but perhaps Vulcan might be only the largest of a kind of asteroidal grouping within Mercury's orbit.

On the basis of Lescarbault's data, Leverrier calculated the times at which future transits ought to take place, and astronomers began watching the Sun on those occasions, as well as the neighborhood of the Sun whenever there were eclipses.

Unfortunately, there were no clear-cut evidences of Vulcan being where it was supposed to be on predicted occasions. There continued to be additional reports as someone claimed to have seen Vulcan from time to time. In each case, though, it meant a new orbit had to be calculated, and new transits had to be predicted—and then these, too, led to nothing clear-cut. It became more and more difficult to calculate orbits that included all the sightings, and none of them successfully predicted future transits.

The whole thing became a controversy, with some astronomers insisting that Vulcan existed and others denying it.

Leverrier died in 1877. He was a firm believer in the existence of Vulcan to the end, and he missed by one year the biggest Vulcan flurry. In 1878 the path of a solar eclipse was to pass over the western United States and American astronomers girded themselves for a mass search for Vulcan.

Most of the observers saw nothing, but two astronomers of impressive credentials, James Craig Watson and Lewis Swift, reported sightings that seemed to be Vulcan. From the reports, it seemed that Vulcan was about 650 kilometers in diameter and only one-fortieth as bright as Mercury. This was scarcely satisfactory, since it was only the size of a large asteroid and could not account for much of the motion of Mercury's perihelion, but it was something.

And yet even that something came under attack. The accuracy of the figures reported for the location of the object was disputed and no orbit could be calculated from which further sightings could be made.

As the nineteenth century closed, photography was coming into its own. There was no more necessity to make feverish measurements before the eclipse was over, or to try to make out clearly what was going on across the face of the Sun before it was all done with. You took photographs and studied them at leisure.

In 1900, after ten years of photography, the American astronomer Edward Charles Pickering announced there could not be an intra-Mercurial body that was brighter than the fourth magnitude.

In 1909 the American astronomer, William Wallace Campbell, went farther and stated categorically that there was nothing inside Mercury's orbit that was brighter than the eighth magnitude. That meant that nothing was there that was larger than forty-eight kilometers in diameter. It would take a million bodies of that size to account for the movement of Mercury's perihelion.*

With that, hope for the existence of Vulcan flickered nearly to extinction. Yet Mercury's perihelion *did* move. If Newton's law of gravitation was correct (and no other reason for supposing its incorrectness had arisen in all the time since Newton), there had to be some sort of gravitational pull from inside Mercury's orbit.

And of course there was, but it originated in a totally different way from that which anyone had imagined. In 1915 Albert Einstein explained the matter in his General Theory of Relativity.

Einstein's view of gravitation was an extension of Newton's—one that simplified itself to the Newtonian version under most conditions but remained different, and better, under extreme conditions. Mercury's presence so close to the

---

*This is correct as far as we know. To this day the only objects known to have approached the Sun more closely than Mercury have been an occasional comet or an asteroid, which are of negligible mass.

Sun's overwhelming presence was an example of the extreme condition that Einstein could account for and Newton not.

Here's one way of doing it. By Einstein's relativistic view of the Universe, mass and energy are equivalent, with a small quantity of mass equal to a large quantity of energy in accordance with the equation $E = mc^2$.

The Sun's enormous gravitational field represents a large quantity of energy and this is equivalent to a certain, much smaller, quantity of mass. Since all mass gives rise to a gravitational field, the Sun's gravitational field, when viewed as mass, must give rise to a much smaller gravitational field of its own.

It is this second-order pull, the small gravitational pull of the mass-equivalent of the large gravitational pull of the Sun, that represents the additional mass and the additional pull from within Mercury's orbit. Einstein's calculations showed that this effect just accounts for the motion of Mercury's perihelion, and accounted further for much smaller motions of the perihelia of planets farther out.

After this neither Vulcan nor any other Newtonian mass was needed. Vulcan was hurled from the astronomical sky forever.

Now to get back to coincidences—and a much more astonishing one than that which connects Kronos's swallowing of his children with the rings of Saturn.

Vulcan, you will remember, is the equivalent of the Greek Hephaistos, and the most famous myth involving Hephaistos goes as follows—

Hephaistos, the son of Zeus and Hera, at one time took Hera's side when Zeus was punishing her for rebellion. Zeus, furious at Hephaistos's interference, heaved him out of heaven. Hephaistos fell to Earth and broke both his legs. Though he was immortal and could not die, the laming was permanent.

Isn't it strange, then, that the planet Vulcan (Hephaistos) was also hurled from the sky? It couldn't die, in the sense that the mass which supplied the additional gravitational pull had to be there, come what may. It was lamed, however, in the sense that it was not the kind of mass that we are used to, not mass in the form of planetary accumulations of matter. It was the mass-equivalent, instead, of a large energy field.

381

You are not impressed by the coincidence? Well, let's carry it further.

You remember that in the myth about Kronos swallowing his children, Zeus was saved when his mother substituted a stone in the swaddling clothes. With a stone serving as a substitute for Zeus, you would surely be willing to allow the phrase "a stone" to be considered the equivalent of "Zeus."

Very well, then, who flung Hephaistos (the mythical Vulcan) from the heavens? Zeus!

And who flung the planetary Vulcan from the heavens? Einstein!

And what does *ein stein* mean in Einstein's native German? "A stone!"

I rest my case.

We can say that the Greeks must have foreseen the whole Vulcanian imbroglio right down to the name of the man who solved it. Or we can say that coincidences can be enormously amazing—and enormously meaningless.

21

The Ugly Little Boy

Are scientists heartless? No more so than other people, but there are always questions of priorities. Animal experimentation must be carried on if medical science is to progress. Even granted the most humane conditions possible, many animals must die under pitiful conditions. How like a human being may an animal be and still be treated as an "animal"? Do we give special regard to gorillas or chimpanzees? Do we take a few extra matters into consideration where whales and dolphins are concerned? Do we—

But read the story.

Edith Fellowes smoothed her working smock as she always did before opening the elaborately locked door and stepping across the invisible dividing line between the *is* and the *is not*. She carried her notebook and her pen although she no longer took notes except when she felt the absolute need for some report.

This time she also carried a suitcase. ("Games for the boy," she had said, smiling to the guard—who had long since stopped even thinking of questioning her and who waved her on.)

And, as always, the ugly little boy knew that she had entered and came running to her crying, "Miss Fellowes—Miss Fellowes—" in his soft, slurring way.

383

"Timmie," she said, and passed her hand over the shaggy, brown hair on his misshapen little head. "What's wrong?"

He said, "Will Jerry be back to play again? I'm sorry about what happened."

"Never mind that now, Timmie. Is that why you've been crying?"

He looked away. "Not just about that, Miss Fellowes. I dreamed again."

"The same dream?" Miss Fellowes's lips set. Of course the Jerry affair would bring back the dream.

He nodded. His too-large teeth showed as he tried to smile, and the lips of his forward-thrusting mouth stretched wide. "When will I be big enough to go out there, Miss Fellowes?"

"Soon," she said softly, feeling her heart break. "Soon."

Miss Fellowes let him take her hand and enjoyed the warm touch of the thick, dry skin of his palm. He led her through the three rooms that made up the whole of Stasis Section One—comfortable enough, yes, but an eternal prison for the ugly little boy all the seven (was it seven?) years of his life.

He led her to the one window, looking out onto a scrubby woodland section of the world of *is* (now hidden by night), where a fence and painted instructions allowed no men to wander without permission.

He pressed his nose against the window. "Out there, Miss Fellowes?"

"Better places. Nicer places," she said sadly as she looked at his poor little imprisoned face outlined in profile against the window. The forehead retreated flatly and his hair lay down in tufts upon it. The back of his skull bulged and seemed to make the head overheavy so that it sagged and bent forward, forcing the whole body into a stoop. Already bony ridges were beginning to bulge the skin above his eyes. His wide mouth thrust forward more prominently than did his wide and flattened nose, and he had no chin to speak of, only a jawbone that curved smoothly down and back. He was small for his years and his stumpy legs were bowed.

He was a very ugly little boy and Edith Fellowes loved him dearly.

Her own face was behind his line of vision, so she allowed her lips the luxury of a tremor.

They would *not* kill him. She would do anything to prevent it. Anything. She opened her suitcase and began taking out the clothes it contained.

Edith Fellowes had crossed the threshold of Stasis, Inc., for the first time just a little over three years before. She hadn't, at that time, the slightest idea as to what Stasis meant or what the place did. No one did then, except those who worked there. In fact, it was only the day after she arrived that the news broke upon the world.

At the time, it was just that they had advertised for a woman with knowledge of physiology, experience with clinical chemistry, and a love for children. Edith Fellowes had been a nurse in a maternity ward and believed she fulfilled those qualifications.

Gerald Hoskins, whose nameplate on the desk included a PhD after the name, scratched his cheek with his thumb and looked at her steadily.

Miss Fellowes automatically stiffened and felt her face (with its slightly asymmetric nose and its a-trifle-too-heavy eyebrows) twitch.

He's no dreamboat himself, she thought resentfully. He's getting fat and bald and he's got a sullen mouth. But the salary mentioned had been considerably higher than she had expected, so she waited.

Hoskins said, "Now, do you really love children?"

"I wouldn't say I did if I didn't."

"Or do you just love pretty children? Nice chubby children with cute little button noses and gurgly ways?"

Miss Fellowes said, "Children are children, Dr. Hoskins, and the ones that aren't pretty are just the ones who may happen to need help most."

"Then suppose we take you on—"

"You mean you're offering me the job now?"

He smiled briefly, and for a moment his broad face had an absentminded charm about it. He said, "I make quick decisions. So far the offer is tentative, however. I may make as quick a decision to let you go. Are you ready to take the chance?"

Miss Fellowes clutched at her purse and calculated just as

385

swifty as she could, then ignored calculations and followed impulse. "All right."

"Fine. We're going to form the Stasis tonight and I think you had better be there to take over at once. That will be at eight P.M., and I'd appreciate it if you could be here at seven-thirty."

"But what—"

"Fine. Fine. That will be all now." On signal, a smiling secretary came in to usher her out.

Miss Fellowes stared back at Dr. Hoskins's closed door for a moment. What was Stasis? What had this large barn of a building—with its badged employees, its makeshift corridors and its unmistakable air of engineering—to do with children?

She wondered if she should go back that evening or stay away and teach that arrogant man a lesson. But she knew she would be back if only out of sheer frustration. She would have to find out about the children.

She came back at seven-thirty and did not have to announce herself. One after another, men and women seemed to know her and to know her function. She found herself all but placed on skids as she was moved inward.

Dr. Hoskins was there, but he only looked at her distantly and murmured, "Miss Fellowes."

He did not even suggest that she take a seat, but she drew one calmly up to the railing and sat down.

They were on a balcony, looking down into a large pit filled with instruments that looked like a cross between the control panel of a spaceship and the working face of a computer. On one side were partitions that seemed to make up an unceilinged apartment, a gaint dollhouse into the rooms of which she could look from above.

She could see an electronic cooker and a freeze-space unit in one room and a washroom arrangement off another. And surely the object she made out in another room could only be part of a bed, a small bed.

Hoskins was speaking to another man and, with Miss Fellowes, they made up the total occupancy of the balcony. Hoskins did not offer to introduce the other man, and Miss Fellowes eyed him surreptitiously. He was thin and quite fine looking in a middle-aged way. He had a small mustache and keen eyes that seemed to busy themselves with everything.

He was saying, "I won't pretend for one moment that I understand all this, Dr. Hoskins; I mean, except as a layman, a reasonably intelligent layman, may be expected to understand it. Still, if there's one part I understand less than another, it's this matter of selectivity. You can only reach out so far; that seems sensible; things get dimmer the farther you go; it takes more energy. But then, you can only reach out so near. That's the puzzling part."

"I can make it seem less paradoxical, Deveney, if you will allow me to use an analogy."

(Miss Fellowes placed the new man the moment she heard his name, and despite herself, was impressed. This was obviously Candide Deveney, the science writer of the Tele-news, who was notoriously at the scene of every major scientific breakthrough. She even recognized his face as one she saw on the news-plate when the landing on Mars had been announced. So Dr. Hoskins must have something important here.)

"By all means use an analogy," said Deveney ruefully, "if you think it will help."

"Well, then, you can't read a book with ordinary-sized print if it is held six feet from your eyes, but you can read it if you hold it one foot from your eyes. So far, the closer the better. If you bring the book to within one inch of your eyes, however, you've lost it again. There is such a thing as being too close, you see."

"Hmmm," said Deveney.

"Or take another example. Your right shoulder is about thirty inches from the tip of your right forefinger and you can place your right forefinger on your right shoulder. Your right elbow is only half the distance from the tip of your right forefinger; it should by all ordinary logic be easier to reach, and yet you cannot place your right finger on your right elbow. Again, there is such a thing as being too close."

Deveney said, "May I use these analogies in my story?"

"Well, of course. Only too glad. I've been waiting long enough for someone like you to have a story. I'll give you anything else you want. It is time, finally, that we want the world looking over our shoulder. They'll see something."

(Miss Fellowes found herself admiring his calm certainty despite herself. There was strength there.)

Deveney said, "How far out will you reach?"

"Forty thousand years."

Miss Fellowes drew in her breath sharply.

Years?

There was tension in the air. The men at the controls scarcely moved. One man at a microphone spoke into it in a soft monotone, in short phrases that made no sense to Miss Fellowes.

Deveney, leaning over the balcony railing with an intent stare, said, "Will we see anything, Dr. Hoskins?"

"What? No. Nothing till the job is done. We detect indirectly, something on the principle of radar, except that we use mesons rather than radiation. Mesons reach backward under the proper conditions. Some are reflected and we must analyze the reflections."

"That sounds difficult."

Hoskins smiled again, briefly as always. "It is the end product of fifty years of research, forty years of it before I entered the field. . . . Yes, it's difficult."

The man at the microphone raised a hand.

Hoskins said, "We've had the fix on one particular moment in time for weeks; breaking it, remaking it after calculating our own movements in time; making certain that we could handle time-flow with sufficient precision. This must work now."

But his forehead glistened.

Edith Fellowes found herself out of her seat and at the balcony railing, but there was nothing to see.

The man at the microphone said quietly, "Now."

There was a space of silence sufficient for one breath and then the sound of a terrified little boy's scream from the dollhouse rooms. Terror! Piercing terror!

Miss Fellowes's head twisted in the direction of the cry. A child was involved. She had forgotten.

And Hoskins's fist pounded on the railing and he said in a tight voice, trembling with triumph, "*Did* it."

* * *

Miss Fellowes was urged down the short, spiral flight of steps by the hard press of Hoskins's palm between her shoulder blades. He did not speak to her.

The men who had been at the controls were standing about now, smiling, smoking, watching the three as they entered on the main floor. A very soft buzz sounded from the direction of the dollhouse.

Hoskins said to Deveney. "It's perfectly safe to enter Stasis. I've done it a thousand times. There's a queer sensation which is momentary and means nothing."

He stepped through an open door in mute demonstration, and Deveney, smiling stiffly and drawing an obviously deep breath, followed him.

Hoskins said, "Miss Fellowes! Please!" He crooked his forefinger impatiently.

Miss Fellowes nodded and stepped stiffly through. It was as though a ripple went through her, an internal tickle.

But once inside, all seemed normal. There was the smell of the fresh wood of the dollhouse and—of—of soil somehow.

There was silence now, no voice at least, but there was the dry shuffling of feet, a scrabbling as of a hand over wood—then a low moan.

"Where is it?" asked Miss Fellowes in distress. Didn't these fool men *care?*

The boy was in the bedroom; at least in the room with the bed in it.

It was standing naked, with its small, dirt-smeared chest heaving raggedly. A bushel of dirt and coarse grass spread over the floor at its bare brown feet. The smell of soil came from it and a touch of something fetid.

Hoskins followed her horrified glance and said with annoyance, "You can't pluck a boy cleanly out of time, Miss Fellowes. We had to take some of the surroundings with it for safety. Or would you have preferred to have it arrive here minus a leg or with only half a head?"

"*Please!*" said Miss Fellowes in an agony of revulsion. "Are we just to stand here? The poor child is frightened. And it's *filthy.*"

389

She was quite correct. It was smeared with encrusted dirt and grease and had a scratch on its thigh that looked red and sore.

As Hoskins approached him, the boy, who seemed to be something over three years in age, hunched low and backed away rapidly. He lifted his upper lip and snarled in a hissing fashion like a cat. With a rapid gesture, Hoskins seized the child's arms and lifted him, writhing and screaming, from the floor.

Miss Fellowes said, "Hold him now. He needs a warm bath first. He needs to be cleaned. Have you the equipment? If so, have it brought here, and I'll need to have help in handling him just at first. Then, too, for heaven's sake, have all this trash and filth removed."

She was giving the orders now and she felt perfectly good about that. And because now she was an efficient nurse rather than a confused spectator, she looked at the child with a clinical eye—and hesitated for one shocked moment. She saw past the dirt and shrieking, past the thrashing of limbs and useless twisting. She saw the boy himself.

It was the ugliest little boy she had ever seen. It was horribly ugly, from misshapen head to bandy legs.

She got the boy cleaned with three men helping her and with others milling about in their efforts to clean the room. She worked in silence and with a sense of outrage, annoyed by the continued strugglings and outcries of the boy and by the undignified drenchings of soapy water to which she was subjected.

Dr. Hoskins had hinted that the child would not be pretty, but that was far from stating that it would be repulsively deformed. And there was a stench about the boy that soap and water was alleviating only little by little.

She had the strong desire to thrust the boy, soaped as he was, into Hoskins's arms and walk out; but there was the pride of profession. She had accepted an assignment after all. And there would be the look in his eyes. A cold look that would read: Only pretty children, Miss Fellowes?

He was standing apart from them, watching coolly from a distance with a half-smile on his face when he caught her eye, as though amused at her outrage.

She decided she would wait a while before quitting. To do so now would only demean her.

Then, when the boy was a bearable pink and smelled of scented soap, she felt better anyway. His cries changed to whimpers of exhaustion as he watched carefully, eyes moving in quick, frightened suspicion from one to another of those in the room. His cleanness accentuated his thin nakedness as he shivered with cold after his bath.

Miss Fellowes said sharply, "Bring me a nightgown for the child!"

A nightgown appeared at once. It was as though everything were ready and yet nothing were ready unless she gave orders; as though they were deliberately leaving this in her charge without help, to test her.

The newsman, Deveney, approached and said, "I'll hold him, Miss. You won't get it on by yourself."

"Thank you," said Miss Fellowes. And it was a battle indeed, but the nightgown went on, and when the boy made as though to rip it off, she slapped his hand sharply.

The boy reddened but did not cry. He stared at her, and the splayed fingers of one hand moved forward across the flannel of the nightgown, feeling the strangeness of it.

Miss Fellowes thought desperately: Well, what next?

Everyone seemed in suspended animation, waiting for her—even the ugly little boy.

Miss Fellowes said sharply, "Have you provided food? Milk?"

They had. A mobile unit was wheeled in, with its refrigeration compartment containing three quarts of milk, with a warming unit and a supply of fortifications in the form of vitamin drops, copper-cobalt-iron syrup and others she had no time to be concerned with. There was a variety of canned self-warming junior foods.

She used milk, simply milk, to begin with. The radar unit heated the milk to a set temperature in a matter of ten seconds and clicked off, and she put some in a saucer. She had a certainty about the boy's savagery. He wouldn't know how to handle a cup.

Miss Fellowes nodded and said to the boy, "Drink. Drink." She made a gesture as though to raise the milk to her mouth. The boy's eyes followed but he made no move.

391

Suddenly the nurse resorted to direct measures. She seized the boy's upper arm in one hand and dipped the other in the milk. She dashed the milk across his lips, so that it dripped down cheeks and receding chin.

For a moment the child uttered a high-pitched cry; then his tongue moved over his wetted lips. Miss Fellowes stepped back.

The boy approached the saucer, bent toward it, then looked up and behind sharply as though expecting a crouching enemy; bent again and licked the milk eagerly, like a cat. He made a slurping noise. He did not use his hands to lift the saucer.

Miss Fellowes allowed a bit of the revulsion she felt to show on her face. She couldn't help it.

Deveney caught that, perhaps. He said, "Does the nurse know, Dr. Hoskins?"

"Know what?" demanded Miss Fellowes.

Deveney hesitated, but Hoskins (again that look of detached amusement on his face) said, "Well, tell her."

Deveney addressed Miss Fellowes. "You may not suspect it, Miss, but you happen to be the first civilized woman in history ever to be taking care of a Neanderthal youngster."

She turned to Hoskins with a kind of controlled ferocity. "You might have told me, Doctor."

"Why? What difference does it make?"

"You said a child."

"Isn't that a child? Have you ever had a puppy or a kitten, Miss Fellowes? Are those closer to the human? If that were a baby chimpanzee, would you be repelled? You're a nurse, Miss Fellowes. Your record places you in a maternity ward for three years. Have you ever refused to take care of a deformed infant?"

Miss Fellowes felt her case slipping away. She said, with much less decision, "You might have told me."

"And you would have refused the position? Well, do you refuse it now?" He gazed at her coolly while Deveney watched from the other side of the room and the Neanderthal child, having finished the milk and licked the plate, looked up at her with a wet face and wide, longing eyes.

The boy pointed to the milk and suddenly burst out in a

short series of sounds repeated over and over, sounds made up of gutturals and elaborate tongue-clickings.

Miss Fellowes said in surprise, "Why, he talks."

"Of course," said Hoskins. "*Homo neanderthalensis* is not a truly separate species but rather a subspecies of *Homo sapiens*. Why shouldn't he talk? He's probably asking for more milk."

Automatically Miss Fellowes reached for the bottle of milk, but Hoskins seized her wrist. "Now, Miss Fellowes, before we go any further, are you staying on the job?"

Miss Fellowes shook free in annoyance. "Won't you feed him if I don't? I'll stay with him—for 'a while."

She poured the milk.

Hoskins said, "We are going to leave you with the boy, Miss Fellowes. This is the only door to Stasis Number One and it is elaborately locked and guarded. I'll want you to learn the details of the lock which will, of course, be keyed to your fingerprints as they are already keyed to mine. The spaces overhead"—he looked upward to the open ceilings of the dollhouse—"are also guarded and we will be warned if anything untoward takes place here."

Miss Fellowes said indignantly. "You mean I'll be under view?" She thought suddenly of her own survey of the room interiors from the balcony.

"No, no," said Hoskins seriously, "your privacy will be respected completely. The view will consist of electronic symbolism only, which only a computer will deal with. Now you will stay with him tonight, Miss Fellowes, and every night until further notice. You will be relieved during the day according to some schedule you will find convenient. We will allow you to arrange that."

Miss Fellowes looked about the dollhouse with a puzzled expression. "But why all this, Dr. Hoskins? Is the boy dangerous?"

"It's a matter of energy, Miss Fellowes. He must never be allowed to leave these rooms. Never. Not for an instant. Not for any reason. Not to save his life. Not even to save *your* life, Miss Fellowes. Is that clear?"

Miss Fellowes raised her chin. "I understand the orders, Dr. Hoskins, and the nursing profession is accustomed to placing its duties ahead of self-preservation."

"Good. You can always signal if you need anyone." And the two men left.

Miss Fellowes turned to the boy. He was watching her and there was still milk in the saucer. Laboriously she tried to show him how to lift the saucer and place it to his lips. He resisted but let her touch him without crying out.

Always, his frightened eyes were on her, watching, watching for the one false move. She found herself soothing him, trying to move her hand very slowly toward his hair, letting him see it every inch of the way, see there was no harm in it.

And she succeeded in stroking his hair for an instant.

She said, "I'm going to have to show you how to use the bathroom. Do you think you can learn?"

She spoke quietly, kindly, knowing he would not understand the words but hoping he would respond to the calmness of the tone.

The boy launched into a clicking phrase again.

She said, "May I take your hand?"

She held out hers and the boy looked at it. She left it outstretched and waited. The boy's own hand crept forward toward hers.

"That's right," she said.

It approached within an inch of hers and then the boy's courage failed him. He snatched it back.

"Well," said Miss Fellowes calmly, "we'll try again later. Would you like to sit down here?" She patted the mattress of the bed.

The hours passed slowly and progress was minute. She did not succeed with bathroom or with the bed. In fact, after the child had given unmistakable signs of sleepiness, he lay down on the bare ground and then, with a quick movement, rolled beneath the bed.

She bent to look at him and his eyes gleamed out at her as he tongue-clicked at her.

"All right," she said, "if you feel safer there, you sleep there."

She closed the door to the bedroom and retired to the cot that had been placed for her use in the largest room. At her insistence, a makeshift canopy had been stretched over it. She thought: Those stupid men will have to place a mirror in this room and a larger chest of drawers and a separate washroom if they expect me to spend nights here.

It was difficult to sleep. She found herself straining to hear possible sounds in the next room. He couldn't get out, could he? The walls were sheer and impossibly high but suppose the child could climb like a monkey? Well, Hoskins said there were observational devices watching through the ceiling.

Suddenly she thought: Can he be dangerous? Physically dangerous? Surely Hoskins couldn't have meant that. Surely he would not have left her alone if—

She tried to laugh at herself. He was only a three- or four-year-old child. Still, she had not succeeded in cutting his nails. If he should attack her with nails and teeth while she slept—

Her breath came quickly. Oh, ridiculous, and yet—

She listened with painful attentiveness, and this time she heard the sound.

The boy was crying.

Not shrieking in fear or anger; not yelling or screaming. It was crying softly, and the cry was the heartbroken sobbing of a lonely, lonely child.

For the first time Miss Fellowes thought with a pang: Poor thing!

Of course it was a child; what did the shape of its head matter? It was a child that had been orphaned as no child had ever been orphaned before. Not only its mother and father were gone, but all its species. Snatched callously out of time, it was now the only creature of its kind in the world. The last. The only.

She felt pity for it strengthen, and with it shame at her own callousness. Tucking her nightgown carefully about her calves (incongruously she thought: Tomorrow I'll have to bring a bathrobe), she got out of bed and went into the boy's room.

"Little boy," she called out in a whisper. "Little boy."

She was about to reach under the bed, but she thought of a possible bite and did not. Instead, she turned on the night light and moved the bed.

The poor thing was huddled in the corner, knees up against his chin, looking up at her with blurred and apprehensive eyes.

In the dim light, she was not aware of his repulsiveness.

"Poor boy," she said, "poor boy." She felt him stiffen as she stroked his hair, then relax. "Poor boy. May I hold you?"

She sat down on the floor next to him and slowly and rhythmically stroked his hair, his cheek, his arm. Softly she began to sing a slow and gentle song.

He lifted his head at last, staring at her mouth in the dimness as though wondering at the sound.

She maneuvered him closer while he listened to her. Slowly she pressed gently against the side of his head until it rested on her shoulder. She put her arms under his thighs and with a smooth and unhurried motion, lifted him into her lap.

She continued singing, the same simple verse over and over, while she rocked back and forth, back and forth.

He stopped crying, and after a while the smooth burr of his breathing showed that he was asleep.

With infinite care she pushed his bed back against the wall and laid him down. She covered him and stared down. His face looked so peaceful and little-boy as he slept. It didn't matter so much that it was so ugly. Really.

She began to tiptoe out, then thought: If he wakes up?

She came back, battled irresolutely with herself, then sighed and slowly got into bed with the child.

It was too small for her. She was cramped and uneasy at the lack of canopy, but the child's hand crept in hers, and somehow, she fell asleep in that position.

She awoke with a start and a wild impulse to scream. The latter she just managed to suppress into a gurgle. The boy was looking at her, wide-eyed. It took her a long moment to remember getting into bed with him, and now, slowly, without unfixing her eyes from his, she stretched one leg carefully and let it touch the floor, then the other one.

She cast a quick and apprehensive glance toward the open ceiling, then tensed her muscles for quick disengagement.

But at that moment the boy's stubby fingers reached out and touched her lips. He said something.

She shrank at his touch. He was terribly ugly in the light of day.

The boy spoke again. He opened his own mouth and gestured with his hand as though something were coming out.

Miss Fellowes guessed at the meaning and said tremulously, "Do you want me to sing?"

The boy said nothing but stared at her mouth.

In a voice slightly off key with tension, Miss Fellowes began the little song she had sung the night before and the ugly little boy smiled. He swayed clumsily in rough time to the music and made a little gurgly sound that might have been the beginnings of a laugh.

Miss Fellowes sighed inwardly. Music hath charms to soothe the savage breast. It might help—

She said, "You wait. Let me get myself fixed up. It will just take a minute. Then I'll make breakfast for you."

She worked rapidly, conscious of the lack of ceiling at all times. The boy remained in bed, watching her when she was in view. She smiled at him at those times, and waved. At the end, he waved back, and she found herself being charmed by that.

Finally she said, "Would you like oatmeal with milk?" It took a moment to prepare, and then she beckoned to him.

Whether he understood the gesture or followed the aroma, Miss Fellowes did not know, but he got out of bed.

She tried to show him how to use a spoon but he shrank away from it in fright. (Time enough, she thought.) She compromised on insisting that he lift the bowl in his hands. He did it clumsily enough and it was incredibly messy, but most of it did get into him.

She tried putting the milk in a glass this time, and the little boy whined when he found the opening too small for him to get his face into conveniently. She held his hand, forcing it around the glass, making him tip it, forcing his mouth to the rim.

Again a mess but again most went into him, and she was used to messes.

The washroom, to her surprise and relief, was a less frustrating matter. He understood what it was she expected him to do.

She found herself patting his head, saying, "Good boy. Smart boy."

And to Miss Fellowes's exceeding pleasure, the boy smiled at that.

She thought: When he smiles, he's quite bearable. Really.

Later in the day the gentlemen of the press arrived.

She held the boy in her arms and he clung to her wildly while across the open door they set cameras to work. The commotion frightened the boy and he began to cry, but it was ten minutes before Miss Fellowes was allowed to retreat and put the boy in the next room.

She emerged again, flushed with indignation, walked out of the apartment (for the first time in eighteen hours) and closed the door behind her. "I think you've had enough. It will take me a while to quiet him. Go away."

"Sure, sure," said the gentleman from the *Times-Herald*. "But is that really a Neanderthal kid or is this some kind of gag?"

"I assure you," said Hoskins's voice, suddenly, from the background, "this is no gag. The child is authenic *Homo neanderthalensis*."

"Is it a boy or a girl?"

"Boy," said Miss Fellowes briefly.

"Ape-boy," said the gentleman from the *News*. "That's what we've got here. Ape-boy. How does he act, Nurse?"

"He acts exactly like a little boy," snapped Miss Fellowes, annoyed into the defensive, "and he is not an ape-boy. His name is—is Timothy, Timmie—and he is perfectly normal in his behavior."

She had chosen the name Timothy at a venture. It was the first that had occurred to her.

"Timmie the Ape-boy," said the gentleman from the *News* and, as it turned out, Timmie the Ape-boy was the name under which the child became known to the world.

The gentleman from the *Globe* turned to Hoskins and said, "Doc, what do you expect to do with the ape-boy?"

Hoskins shrugged. "My original plan was completed when I proved it possible to bring him here. However, the anthropologists will be very interested, I imagine, and the physiologists. We have here, after all, a creature which is at the edge of being human. We should learn a great deal about ourselves and our ancestry from him."

"How long will you keep him?"

"Until such a time as we need the space more than we need him. Quite a while, perhaps."

398

The gentleman from the *News* said, "Can you bring it out into the open so we can set up subetheric equipment and put on a real show?"

"I'm sorry, but the child cannot be removed from Stasis."

"Exactly what is Stasis?"

"Ah." Hoskins permitted himself one of his short smiles. "That would take a great deal of explanation, gentlemen. In Stasis, time as we know it doesn't exist. Those rooms are inside an invisible bubble that is not exactly part of our Universe. That is why the child could be plucked out of time as it was."

"Well, wait now," said the gentleman from the *News* discontentedly, "what are you giving us? The nurse goes into the room and out of it."

"And so can any of you," said Hoskins matter-of-factly. "You would be moving parallel to the lines of temporal force, and no great energy gain or loss would be involved. The child, however, was taken from the far past. It moved across the lines and gained temporal potential. To move it into the Universe and into our own time would absorb enough energy to burn out every line in the place and probably blank out all power in the city of Washington. We had to store trash brought with him on the premises and will have to remove it little by little."

The newsmen were writing down sentences busily as Hoskins spoke to them. They did not understand and they were sure their readers would not, but it sounded scientific and that was what counted.

The gentleman from the *Times-Herald* said, "Would you be available for an all-circuit interview tonight?"

"I think so," said Hoskins at once, and they all moved off.

Miss Fellowes looked after them. She understood all this about Stasis and temporal force as little as the newsmen but she managed to get this much. Timmie's imprisonment (she found herself suddenly thinking of the little boy as Timmie) was a real one and not one imposed by the arbitrary fiat of Hoskins. Apparently it was impossible to let him out of Stasis at all, ever.

Poor child. Poor child.

She was suddenly aware of his crying and she hastened in to console him.

* * *

Miss Fellowes did not have a chance to see Hoskins on the all-circuit hookup, and though his interview was beamed to every part of the world and even to the outposts on the Moon, it did not penetrate the apartment in which Miss Fellowes and the ugly little boy lived.

But Hoskins was down the next morning, radiant and joyful.

Miss Fellowes said, "Did the interview go well?"

"Extremely. And how is—Timmie?"

Miss Fellowes found herself pleased at the use of the name. "Doing quite well. Now come out here, Timmie. The nice gentleman will not hurt you."

But Timmie stayed in the other room, with a lock of his matted hair showing behind the barrier of the door and, occasionally, the corner of an eye.

"Actually," said Miss Fellowes, "he is settling down amazingly. He is quite intelligent."

"Are you surprised?"

She hesitated just a moment, then said, "Yes, I am. I suppose I thought he was an ape-boy."

"Well, ape-boy or not, he's done a great deal for us. He's put Stasis, Inc., on the map. We're in, Miss Fellowes, we're in." It was as though he had to express his triumph to someone, even if only to Miss Fellowes.

"Oh?" She let him talk.

He put his hands in his pockets and said, "We've been working on a shoestring for ten years, scrounging funds a penny at a time wherever we could. We had to shoot the works on one big show. It was everything or nothing. And when I say the works, I mean it. This attempt to bring a Neanderthal took every cent we could borrow or steal, and some of it *was* stolen—funds for other projects used for this one without permission. If that experiment hadn't succeeded, I'd have been through."

Miss Fellowes said abruptly, "Is that why there are no ceilings?"

"Eh?" Hoskins looked up.

"Was there no money for ceilings?"

"Oh. Well, that wasn't the only reason. We didn't really know in advance how old the Neanderthal might be exactly.

400

We can detect only dimly in time, and he might have been large and savage. It was possible we might have had to deal with him from a distance, like a caged animal."

"But since that hasn't turned out to be so, I suppose you can build a ceiling now."

"Now, yes. We have plenty of money now. Funds have been promised from every source. This is all wonderful, Miss Fellowes." His broad face gleamed with a smile that lasted and when he left, even his back seemed to be smiling.

Miss Fellowes thought: He's a nice man when he's off guard and forgets about being scientific.

She wondered for a idle moment if he was married, then dismissed the thought in self-embarrassment.

"Timmie," she called. "Come here, Timmie."

In the months that passed, Miss Fellowes felt herself grow to be an integral part of Stasis, Inc. She was given a small office of her own with her name on the door, an office quite close to the dollhouse (as she never stopped calling Timmie's Stasis bubble). She was given a substantial raise. The dollhouse was covered by a ceiling; its furnishings were elaborated and improved; a second washroom was added—and even so, she gained an apartment of her own on the institute grounds and on occasion did not stay with Timmie during the night. An intercom was set up between the dollhouse and her apartment and Timmie learned how to use it.

Miss Fellowes got used to Timmie. She even grew less conscious of his ugliness. One day she found herself staring at an ordinary boy in the street and finding something bulgy and unattractive in his high-domed forehead and jutting chin. She had to shake herself to break the spell.

It was more pleasant to grow used to Hoskins's occasional visits. It was obvious he welcomed escape from his increasingly harried role as head of Stasis, Inc., and that he took a sentimental interest in the child who had started it all, but it seemed to Miss Fellowes that he also enjoyed talking to her.

(She had learned some facts about Hoskins too. He had invented the method of analyzing the reflection of the past-penetrating mesonic beam; he had invented the method of establishing Stasis; his coldness was only an effort to hide a kindly nature; and, oh yes, he *was* married.)

What Miss Fellowes could *not* get used to was the fact that she was engaged in a scientific experiment. Despite all she could do, she found herself getting personally involved to the point of quarreling with the physiologists.

On one occasion Hoskins came down and found her in the midst of a hot urge to kill. They had no right; they had no *right*— Even if he *was* a Neanderthal, he still wasn't an animal.

She was staring after them in blind fury; staring out the open door and listening to Timmie's sobbing, when she noticed Hoskins standing before her. He might have been there for minutes.

He said, "May I come in?"

She nodded curtly, then hurried to Timmie, who clung to her, curling his little bandy legs—still thin, so thin—about her.

Hoskins watched, then said gravely, "He seems quite unhappy."

Miss Fellowes said, "I don't blame him. They're at him every day now with their blood samples and their probings. They keep him on synthetic diets that I wouldn't feed a pig."

"It's the sort of thing they can't try on a human, you know."

"And they can't try it on Timmie either. Dr. Hoskins, I insist. You told me it was Timmie's coming that put Stasis, Inc., on the map. If you have any gratitude for that at all, you've *got* to keep them away from the poor thing at least until he's old enough to understand a little more. After he's had a bad session with them, he has nightmares, he can't sleep. Now I warn you"—she reached a sudden peak of fury—"I'm not letting them in here anymore."

(She realized that she had screamed that, but she couldn't help it.)

She said more quietly, "I know he's Neanderthal but there's a great deal we don't appreciate about Neanderthals. I've read up on them. They had a culture of their own. Some of the greatest human inventions arose in Neanderthal times. The domestication of animals, for instance; the wheel; various techniques in grinding stone. They even had spiritual yearnings. They buried their dead and buried possessions with the body, showing they believed in a life after death. It amounts to the fact that they invented religion. Doesn't that mean Timmie has a right to human treatment?"

She patted the little boy on his buttocks and sent him off into his playroom. As the door was opened, Hoskins smiled briefly at the display of toys that could be seen.

Miss Fellowes said defensively, "The poor child deserves his toys. It's all he has and he earns them with what he goes through."

"No, no. No objections, I assure you. I was thinking how you've changed since the first day, when you were quite angry I had foisted a Neanderthal on you."

Miss Fellowes said in a low voice, "I suppose I didn't—" and faded off.

Hoskins changed the subject, "How old would you say he is, Miss Fellowes?"

She said, "I can't say, since we don't know how Neanderthals develop. In size, he'd only be three, but Neanderthals are smaller generally, and with all the tampering they do with him, he probably isn't growing. The way he's learning English though, I'd say he was well over four."

"Really? I haven't noticed anything about learning English in the reports."

"He won't speak to anyone but me. For now, anyway. He's terribly afraid of others, and no wonder. But he can ask for an article of food; he can indicate any need practically; and he understands almost anything I say. Of course"—she watched him shrewdly, trying to estimate if this was the time—"his development may not continue."

"Why not?"

"Any child needs stimulation and this one lives a life of solitary confinement. I do what I can, but I'm not with him all the time and I'm not all he needs. What I mean, Dr. Hoskins, is that he needs another boy to play with."

Hoskins nodded slowly. "Unfortunately, there's only one of him, isn't there? Poor child."

Miss Fellowes warmed to him at once. She said, "You do like Timmie, don't you?" It was so nice to have someone else feel like that.

"Oh, yes," said Hoskins, and with his guard down, she could see the weariness in his eyes.

Miss Fellowes dropped her plans to push the matter at once.

She said with real concern, "You look worn out, Dr. Hoskins."

"Do I, Miss Fellowes? I'll have to practice looking more lifelike then."

"I suppose Stasis, Inc., is very busy and that keeps you very busy."

Hoskins shrugged. "You suppose right. It's a matter of animal, vegetable and mineral in equal parts, Miss Fellowes. But then, I suppose you haven't ever seen our displays."

"Actually, I haven't. But it's not because I'm not interested. It's just that I've been so busy."

"Well, you're not all that busy right now," he said with impulsive decision. "I'll call for you tomorrow at eleven and give you a personal tour. How's that?"

She smiled happily. "I'd love it."

He nodded and smiled in his turn and left.

Miss Fellowes hummed at intervals for the rest of the day. Really—to think so was ridiculous, of course—but really, it was almost like—like making a date.

He was quite on time the next day, smiling and pleasant. She had replaced her nurse's uniform with a dress. One of conservative cut, to be sure, but she hadn't felt so feminine in years.

He complimented her on her appearance with staid formality and she accepted with equally formal grace. It was really a perfect prelude, she thought. And then the additional thought came, prelude to what?

She shut that off by hastening to say good-bye to Timmie and to assure him she would be back soon. She made sure he knew all about what and where lunch was.

Hoskins took her into the new wing, into which she had never yet gone. It still had the odor of newness about it, and the sound of construction, softly heard, was indication enough that it was still being extended.

"Animal, vegetable and mineral," said Hoskins, as he had the day before. "Animal right there; our most spectacular exhibits."

The space was divided into many rooms, each a separate Stasis bubble. Hoskins brought her to the view-glass of one

404

and she looked in. What she saw impressd her first as a scaled, tailed chicken. Skittering on two thin legs, it ran from wall to wall with its delicate birdlike head, surmounted by a bony keel like the comb of a rooster, looking this way and that. The paws on its small forelimbs clenched and unclenched constantly.

Hoskins said, "It's our dinosaur. We've had it for months. I don't know when we'll be able to let go of it."

"Dinosaur?"

"Did you expect a giant?"

She dimpled. "One does, I suppose. I know some of them are small."

"A small one is all we aimed for, believe me. Generally it's under investigation, but this seems to be an open hour. Some interesting things have been discovered. For instance, it is not entirely cold-blooded. It has an imperfect method of maintaining internal temperatures higher than that of its environment. Unfortunately, it's a male. Ever since we brought it in, we've been trying to get a fix on another that may be female, but we've had no luck yet."

"Why female?"

He looked at her quizzically. "So that we might have a fighting chance to obtain fertile eggs, and baby dinosaurs."

"Of course."

He led her to the trilobite section. "That's Professor Dwayne of Washington University," he said. "He's a nuclear chemist. If I recall correctly, he's taking an isotope ratio on the oxygen of the water."

"Why?"

"It's primeval water; at least half a billion years old. The isotope ratio gives the temperature of the ocean at that time. He himself happens to ignore the trilobites, but others are chiefly concerned in dissecting them. They're the lucky ones because all they need are scalpels and microscopes. Dwayne has to set up a mass spectrograph each time he conducts an experiment."

"Why's that? Can't he—"

"No, he can't. He can't take anything out of the room as far as can be helped."

There were samples of primordial plant life too, and chunks of rock formations. Those were the vegetable and mineral.

And every specimen had its investigator. It was like a museum; a museum brought to life and serving as a superactive center of research.

"And you have to supervise all of this, Dr. Hoskins?"

"Only indirectly, Miss Fellowes. I have subordinates, thank heaven. My own interest is entirely in the theoretical aspects of the matter: the nature of Time, the technique of mesonic intertemporal detection and so on. I would exchange all this for a method of detecting objects closer in Time than ten thousand years ago. If we could get into historical times—"

He was interrupted by a commotion at one of the distant booths, a thin voice raised querulously. He frowned, muttered hastily, "Excuse me," and hastened off.

Miss Fellowes followed as best she could without actually running.

An elderly man, thinly bearded and red-faced, was saying, "I had vital aspects of my investigations to complete. Don't you understand that?"

A uniformed technician with the interwoven SI monogram (for Stasis, Inc.) on his lab coat said, "Dr. Hoskins, it was arranged with Professor Ademewski at the beginning that the specimen could only remain here two weeks."

"I did not know then how long my investigations would take. I'm not a prophet," said Ademewski heatedly.

Dr. Hoskins said, "You understand, Professor, we have limited space; we must keep specimens rotating. That piece of chalcopyrite must go back; there are men waiting for the next specimen."

"Why can't I have it for myself then? Let me take it out of there."

"You know you can't have it."

"A piece of chalcopyrite; a miserable five-kilogram piece? Why not?"

"We can't afford the energy expense!" said Hoskins brusquely. "You know that."

The technician interrupted. "The point is, Dr. Hoskins, that he tried to remove the rock against the rules and I almost punctured Stasis, not knowing he was in there."

There was a short silence and Dr. Hoskins turned on the investigator with a cold formality. "Is that so, Professor?"

Professor Ademewski coughed. "I saw no harm—"

Hoskins reached up to a hand-pull dangling just within reach, outside the specimen room in question. He pulled it.

Miss Fellowes, who had been peering in, looking at the totally undistinguished sample of rock that occasioned the dispute, drew in her breath sharply as its existence flickered out. The room was empty.

Hoskins said, "Professor, your permit to investigate matters in Stasis will be permanently voided. I am sorry."

"But wait—"

"I am sorry. You have violated one of the stringent rules."

"I will appeal to the International Association—"

"Appeal away. In a case like this, you will find I can't be overruled."

He turned away deliberately, leaving the professor still protesting, and said to Miss Fellowes (his face still white with anger), "Would you care to have lunch with me, Miss Fellowes?"

He took her into the small administration alcove of the cafeteria. He greeted others and introduced Miss Fellowes with complete ease, although she herself felt painfully self-conscious.

What must they think, she thought, and tried desperately to appear businesslike.

She said, "Do you have that kind of trouble often, Dr. Hoskins? I mean like you just had with the professor?" She took her fork in hand and began eating.

"No," said Hoskins forcefully. "That was the first time. Of course I'm always having to argue men out of removing specimens, but this is the first time one actually tried to *do* it."

"I remember you once talked about the energy it would consume."

"That's right. Of course we've tried to take it into account. Accidents will happen and so we've got special power sources designed to stand the drain of accidental removal from Stasis, but that doesn't mean we want to see a year's supply of energy gone in half a second—or can afford to without having our plans of expansion delayed for years. Besides, imagine the professor's being in the room while Stasis was about to be punctured."

"What would have happened to him if it had been?"

"Well, we've experimented with inanimate objects and with mice and they've disappeared. Presumably they've traveled back in time; carried along, so to speak, by the pull of the object simultaneously snapping back into its natural time. For that reason we have to anchor objects within Stasis that we don't want to move, and that's a complicated procedure. The professor would not have been anchored and he would have gone back to the Pliocene at the moment we abstracted the rock—plus, of course, the two weeks it had remained here in the present."

"How dreadful it would have been."

"Not on account of the professor, I assure you. If he were fool enough to do what he did, it would serve him right. But imagine the effect it would have on the public if the fact came out. All people would need is to become aware of the dangers involved and funds could be choked off like that." He snapped his fingers and played moodily with his food.

Miss Fellowes said, "Couldn't you get him back? The way you got the rock in the first place?"

"No, because once an object is returned, the original fix is lost unless we deliberately plan to retain it, and there was no reason to do that in this case. There never is. Finding the professor again would mean relocating a specific fix, and that would be like dropping a line into the oceanic abyss for the purpose of dredging up a particular fish. My God, when I think of the precautions we take to prevent accidents, it makes me mad. We have every individual Stasis unit set up with its own puncturing device—we have to since each unit has its separate fix and must be collapsible independently. The point is though, none of the puncturing devices is ever activated until the last minute. And then we deliberately make activation impossible except by the pull of a rope carefully led outside the Stasis. The pull is a gross mechanical motion that requires strong effort, not something that is likely to be done accidentally."

Miss Fellowes said, "But doesn't it—change history to move someting in and out of Time?"

Hoskins shrugged. "Theoretically, yes; actually, except in unusual cases, no. We move objects out of Stasis all the time. Air molecules. Bacteria. Dust. About ten percent of our energy consumption goes to make up microlosses of that nature. But moving even large objects in Time sets up changes that damp out. Take that chalcopyrite from the Pliocene. Because of its absence for two weeks, some insect didn't find the shelter it might have found and is killed. That could initiate a whole series of changes, but the mathematics of Stasis indicates that this is a converging series. The amount of change diminishes with time and then things are as before."

"You mean, reality heals itself?"

"In a manner of speaking. Abstract a human from Time or send one back and you make a larger wound. If the individual is an ordinary one, that wound still heals itself. Of course there are a great many people who write to us each day and want us to bring Abraham Lincoln to the present, or Mohammed, or Lenin. *That* can't be done, of course. Even if we could find them, the change in reality in moving one of the history molders would be too great to be healed. There are ways of calculating when a change is likely to be too great and we avoid even approaching that limit."

Miss Fellowes said, "Then Timmie—"

"No, he presents no problem in that direction. Reality is safe. But—" He gave her a quick, sharp glance, then went on, "But never mind. Yesterday you said Timmie needed companionship."

"Yes." Miss Fellowes smiled her delight. "I didn't think you paid that any attention."

"Of course I did. I'm fond of the child. I appreciate your feelings for him and I was concerned enough to want to explain to you. Now I have; you've seen what we do; you've gotten some insight into the difficulties involved; so you know why, with the best will in the world, we can't supply companionship for Timmie."

"You can't?" said Miss Fellowes with sudden dismay.

"But I've just explained. We couldn't possibly expect to find another Neanderthal his age without incredible luck, and if we could, it wouldn't be fair to multiply risks by having another human being in Stasis."

Miss Fellowes put down her spoon and said energetically, "But, Dr. Hoskins, that is not at all what I meant. I don't want you to bring another Neanderthal into the present. I know

409

that's impossible. But it isn't impossible to bring another child to play with Timmie."

Hoskins stared at her in concern. "A *human* child?"

"*Another* child," said Miss Fellowes, completely hostile now. "Timmie is human."

"I couldn't dream of such a thing."

"Why not? Why couldn't you? What is wrong with the notion? You pulled that child out of Time and made him an eternal prisoner. Don't you owe him something? Dr. Hoskins, if there is any man who, in this world, is that child's father in every sense but the biological, it is you. Why can't you do this little thing for him?"

Hoskins said, "His *father?*" He rose somewhat unsteadily to his feet. "Miss Fellowes, I think I'll take you back now, if you don't mind."

They returned to the dollhouse in a complete silence that neither broke.

It was a long time after that before she saw Hoskins again except for an occasional glimpse in passing. She was sorry about that at times; then, at other times, when Timmie was more than usually woebegone or when he spent silent hours at the window with its prospect of little more than nothing, she thought, fiercely: Stupid man.

Timmie's speech grew better and more precise each day. It never entirely lost a certain slurriness that Miss Fellowes found rather endearing. In times of excitement, he fell back into tongue-clicking but those times were becoming fewer. He must be forgetting the days before he came into the present—except for dreams.

As he grew older, the physiologists grew less interested and the psychologists more so. Miss Fellowes was not sure that she did not like the new group even less than the first. The needles were gone; the injections and withdrawals of fluid; the special diets. But now Timmie was made to overcome barriers to reach food and water. He had to lift panels, move bars, reach for cords. And the mild electric shocks made him cry and drove Miss Fellowes to distraction.

She did not wish to appeal to Hoskins; she did not wish to have to go to him; for each time she thought of him, she thought of his face over the luncheon table that last time. Her eyes moistened and she thought: Stupid, *stupid* man.

And then one day Hoskins's voice sounded unexpectedly, calling into the dollhouse, "Miss Fellowes."

She came out coldly, smoothing her nurse's uniform, then stopped in confusion at finding herself in the presence of a pale woman, slender and of middle height. The woman's fair hair and complexion gave her an appearance of fragility. Standing behind her and clutching at her skirt was a round-faced, large-eyed child of four.

Hoskins said, "Dear, this is Miss Fellowes, the nurse in charge of the boy. Miss Fellowes, this is my wife."

(Was this his wife? She was not as Miss Fellowes had imagined her to be. But then, why not? A man like Hoskins would choose a weak thing to be his foil. If that was what he wanted—)

She forced a matter-of-fact greeting. "Good afternoon, Mrs. Hoskins. Is this your—your little boy?"

(*That* was a surprise. She had thought of Hoskins as a husband but not as a father, except, of course— She suddenly caught Hoskins's grave eyes and flushed.)

Hoskins said, "Yes, this is my boy, Jerry. Say hello to Miss Fellowes, Jerry."

(Had he stressed the word "this" just a bit? Was he saying *this* was his son and not—)

Jerry receded a bit farther into the folds of the maternal skirt and muttered his hello. Mrs. Hoskins's eyes were searching over Miss Fellowes's shoulders, peering into the room, looking for something.

Hoskins said, "Well, let's go in. Come, dear. There's a trifling discomfort at the threshold, but it passes."

Miss Fellowes said, "Do you want Jerry to come in too?"

"Of course. He is to be Timmie's playmate. Or have you forgotten?"

"But—" She looked at him with a colossal, surprised wonder. "*Your* boy?"

He said peevishly, "Well, whose boy then? Isn't this what you want? Come on in, dear. Come on in."

Mrs. Hoskins lifted Jerry into her arms with a distinct effort and, hesitantly, stepped over the threshold. Jerry squirmed as she did so, disliking the sensation.

411

Mrs. Hoskins said in a thin voice, "Is the creature here? I don't see him."

Miss Fellows called, "Timmie. Come out."

Timmie peered around the edge of the door, staring up at the little boy who was visiting him. The muscles in Mrs. Hoskins's arms tensed visibly.

She said to her husband, "Gerald, are you sure it's safe?"

Miss Fellowes said at once, "If you mean is Timmie safe, why, of course he is. He's a gentle little boy."

"But he's a sa—savage."

(The ape-boy stories in the newspapers!) Miss Fellowes said emphatically, "He is not a savage. He is just as quiet and reasonable as you can possibly expect a five-and-a-half-year-old to be. It is very generous of you, Mrs. Hoskins, to agree to allow your boy to play with Timmie, but please have no fears about it."

Mrs. Hoskins said with mild heat, "I'm not sure that I agree."

"We've had it out, dear," said Hoskins. "Let's not bring up the matter for new argument. Put Jerry down."

Mrs. Hoskins did so and the boy backed against her, staring at the pair of eyes which were staring back at him from the next room.

"Come here, Timmie," said Miss Fellowes. "Don't be afraid."

Slowly Timmie stepped into the room. Hoskins bent to disengage Jerry's fingers from his mother's skirt. "Step back, dear. Give the children a chance."

The youngsters faced one another. Although the younger, Jerry was nevertheless an inch taller, and in the presence of his straightness and his high-held, well-proportioned head, Timmie's grotesqueries were suddenly almost as pronounced as they had been in the first days.

Miss Fellowes's lips quivered.

It was the little Neanderthal who spoke first, in childish treble. "What's your name?" And Timmie thrust his face suddenly forward as though to inspect the other's features more closely.

Startled, Jerry responded with a vigorous shove that sent Timmie tumbling. Both began crying loudly and Mrs. Hoskins snatched up her child while Miss Fellowes, flushed with repressed anger, lifted Timmie and comforted him.

Mrs. Hoskins said, "They just instinctively don't like one another."

"No more instinctively," said her husband wearily, "than any two children dislike each other. Now put Jerry down and let him get used to the situation. In fact, we had better leave. Miss Fellowes can bring Jerry to my office after a while and I'll have him taken home."

The two children spent the next hour very aware of each other. Jerry cried for his mother, struck out at Miss Fellowes and finally allowed himself to be comforted with a lollipop. Timmie sucked at another, and at the end of an hour, Miss Fellowes had them playing with the same set of blocks, though at opposite ends of the room.

She found herself almost maudlinly grateful to Hoskins when she brought Jerry to him.

She searched for ways to thank him but his formality was a rebuff. Perhaps he could not forgive her for making him feel like a cruel father. Perhaps the bringing of his own child was an attempt, after all, to prove himself both a kind father to Timmie and, also, not his father at all. Both at the same time!

So all she could say was, "Thank you. Thank you very much."

And all he could say was, "It's all right. Don't mention it."

It became a settled routine. Twice a week Jerry was brought in for an hour's play, later extended to two hours' play. The children learned each other's names and ways and played together.

And yet, after the first rush of gratitude, Miss Fellowes found herself disliking Jerry. He was larger and heavier and in all things dominant, forcing Timmie into a completely secondary role. All that reconciled her to the situation was the fact that, despite difficulties, Timmie looked forward with more and more delight to the periodic appearances of his playfellow.

It was all he had, she mourned to herself.

And once, as she watched him, she thought: Hoskins's two children, one by his wife and one by Stasis.

While she herself—

Heavens, she thought, putting her fists to her temples and feeling ashamed: I'm jealous!

"Miss Fellowes," said Timmie (carefully, she had never allowed him to call her anything else), "when will I go to school?"

She looked down at those eager brown eyes turned up to hers and passed her hand softly through his thick, curly hair. It was the most disheveled portion of his appearance, for she cut his hair herself while he sat restlessly under the scissors. She did not ask for professional help, for the very clumsiness of the cut served to mask the retreating forepart of the skull and the bulging hinder part.

She said, "Where did you hear about school?"

"Jerry goes to school. Kin-der-gar-ten." He said it carefully. "There are lots of places he goes. Outside. When can I go outside, Miss Fellowes?"

A small pain centered in Miss Fellowes's heart. Of course, she saw, there would be no way of avoiding the inevitability of Timmie's hearing more and more of the outer world he could never enter.

She said, with an attempt at gaiety, "Why, whatever would you do in kindergarten, Timmie?"

"Jerry says they play games, they have picture tapes. He says there are lots of children. He says—he says—" A thought, then a triumphant upholding of both small hands with the fingers splayed apart. "He says this many."

Miss Fellowes said, "Would you like picture tapes? I can get you picture tapes. Very nice ones. And music tapes too."

So that Timmie was temporarily comforted.

He pored over the picture tapes in Jerry's absence and Miss Fellowes read to him out of ordinary books by the hour.

There was so much to explain in even the simplest story, so much that was outside the perspective of his three rooms. Timmie took to having his dreams more often now that the outside was being introduced to him.

They were always the same, about the outside. He tried haltingly to describe them to Miss Fellowes. In his dreams he was outside, an empty outside, but very large, with children

414

and queer, indescribable objects half-digested in his thought out of bookish descriptions half-understood, or out of distant Neanderthal memories half-recalled.

But the children and objects ignored him and though he was in the world, he was never part of it, but was as alone as though he were in his own room—and would wake up crying.

Miss Fellowes tried to laugh at the dreams, but there were nights in her own apartment when she cried too.

One day, as Miss Fellowes read, Timmie put his hand under her chin and lifted it gently so that her eyes left the book and met his.

He said, "How do you know what to say, Miss Fellowes?"

She said, "You see these marks? They tell me what to say. These marks make words."

He stared at them long and curiously, taking the book out of her hands. "Some of these marks are the same."

She laughed with pleasure at this sign of his shrewdness and said, "So they are. Would you like to have me show you how to make the marks?"

"All right. That would be a nice game."

It did not occur to her that he could learn to read. Up to the very moment that he read a book to her, it did not occur to her that he could learn to read.

Then, weeks later, the enormity of what had been done struck her. Timmie sat in her lap, following word by word the printing in a child's book, reading to her. He was reading to her!

She struggled to her feet in amazement and said, "Now, Timmie, I'll be back later. I want to see Dr. Hoskins."

Excited nearly to frenzy, it seemed to her she might have an answer to Timmie's unhappiness. If Timmie could not leave to enter the world, the world must be brought into those three rooms to Timmie—the whole world in books and film and sound. He must be educated to his full capacity. So much the world owed him.

She found Hoskins in a mood that was oddly analogous to her own; a kind of triumph and glory. His offices were unusually busy, and for a moment she thought she would not get to see him as she stood abashed in the anteroom.

415

But he saw her, and a smile spread over his broad face. "Miss Fellowes, come here."

He spoke rapidly into the intercom, then shut it off. "Have you heard? No, of course, you couldn't have. We've done it. We've actually done it. We have intertemporal detection at close range."

"You mean," she tried to detach her thought from her own good news for a moment, "that you can get a person from historical times into the present?"

"That's just what I mean. We have a fix on a fourteenth-century individual right now. Imagine. *Imagine!* If you could only know how glad I'll be to shift from the eternal concentration on the Mesozoic, replace the paleontologists with the historians— But there's something you wish to say to me, eh? Well, go ahead; go ahead. You find me in a good mood. Anything you want you can have."

Miss Fellowes smiled. "I'm glad. Because I wonder if we might not establish a system of instruction for Timmie?"

"Instruction? In what?"

"Well, in everything. A school. So that he might learn."

"But *can* he learn?"

"Certainly. He *is* learning. He can read. I've taught him so much myself."

Hoskins sat there, seeming suddenly depressed. "I don't know, Miss Fellowes."

She said, "You just said that anything I wanted—"

"I know and I should not have. You see, Miss Fellowes, I'm sure you must realize that we cannot maintain the Timmie experiment forever."

She stared at him with sudden horror, not really understanding what he had said. How did he mean "cannot maintain"? With an agonizing flash of recollection, she recalled Professor Ademewski and his mineral specimen that was taken away after two weeks. She said, "But you're talking about a boy. Not about a rock—"

Dr. Hoskins said uneasily, "Even a boy can't be given undue importance, Miss Fellowes. Now that we expect individuals out of historical time, we will need Stasis space, all we can get."

She didn't grasp it. "But you can't. Timmie—Timmie—"

"Now, Miss Fellowes, please don't upset yourself. Timmie won't go right away; perhaps not for months. Meanwhile we'll do what we can."

She was still staring at him.

"Let me get you something, Miss Fellowes."

"No," she whispered. "I don't need anything." She arose in a kind of nightmare and left.

Timmie, she thought, you will not die. You will not die.

It was all very well to hold tensely to the thought that Timmie must not die, but how was that to be arranged? In the first weeks, Miss Fellowes clung only to the hope that the attempt to bring forward a man from the fourteenth century would fail completely. Hoskins's theories might be wrong or his practice defective. Then things could go on as before.

Certainly that was not the hope of the rest of the world and, irrationally, Miss Fellowes hated the world for it. "Project Middle Ages" reached a climax of white-hot publicity. The press and the public had hungered for something like this. Stasis, Inc., had lacked the necessary sensation for a long time now. A new rock or another ancient fish failed to stir them. But *this* was *it*.

A historical human; an adult speaking a known language; someone who could open a new page of history to the scholar.

Zero-time was coming and this time it was not a question of three onlookers from a balcony. This time there would be a worldwide audience. This time the technicians of Stasis, Inc., would play their role before nearly all of mankind.

Miss Fellowes was herself all but savage with waiting. When young Jerry Hoskins showed up for his scheduled playtime with Timmie, she scarcely recognized him. He was not the one she was waiting for.

(The secretary who brought him left hurriedly after the barest nod for Miss Fellowes. She was rushing for a good place from which to watch the climax of Project Middle Ages. And so ought Miss Fellowes with far better reason, she thought bitterly, if only that stupid girl would arrive.)

Jerry Hoskins sidled toward her, embarrassed. "Miss Fellowes?" He took the reproduction of a news strip out of his pocket.

"Yes? What is it, Jerry?"

"Is this a picture of Timmie?"

Miss Fellowes stared at him, then snatched the strip from Jerry's hand. The excitement of Project Middle Ages had brought about a pale revival of interest in Timmie on the part of the press.

Jerry watched her narrowly, then said, "It says Timmie is an ape-boy. What does that mean?"

Miss Fellows caught the youngster's wrist and repressed the impulse to shake him. "Never say that, Jerry. Never, do you understand? It is a nasty word and you mustn't use it."

Jerry struggled out of her grip, frightened.

Miss Fellowes tore up the news strip with a vicious twist of the wrist. "Now go inside and play with Timmie. He's got a new book to show you."

And then, finally, the girl appeared. Miss Fellowes did not know her. None of the usual stand-ins she had used when business took her elsewhere was available now, not with Project Middle Ages at climax, but Hoskins's secretary had promised to find *someone* and this must be the girl.

Miss Fellowes tried to keep querulousness out of her voice. "Are you the girl assigned to Stasis Section One?"

"Yes, I'm Mandy Terris. You're Miss Fellowes, aren't you?"

"That's right."

"I'm sorry I'm late. There's just so much excitement."

"I know. Now, I want you—"

Mandy said, "You'll be watching, I suppose." Her thin, vacuously pretty face filled with envy.

"Never mind that. Now I want you to come inside and meet Timmie and Jerry. They will be playing for the next two hours so they'll be giving you no trouble. They've got milk handy and plenty of toys. In fact, it will be better if you leave them alone as much as possible. Now I'll show you where everything is located and—"

"Is it Timmie that's the ape-b—"

"Timmie is the Stasis subject," said Miss Fellowes firmly.

"I mean, he's the one who's not supposed to get out, is that right?"

"Yes. Now, come in. There isn't much time."

And when she finally left, Mandy Terris called after her shrilly, "I hope you get a good seat and, golly, I sure hope it works."

Miss Fellowes did not trust herself to make a reasonable response. She hurried on without looking back.

But the delay meant she did *not* get a good seat. She got no nearer than the wall-viewing-plate in the assembly hall. Bitterly she regretted that. If she could have been on the spot; if she could somehow have reached out for some sensitive portion of the instrumentation; if she were in some way able to wreck the experiment—

She found the strength to beat down her madness. Simple destruction would have done no good. They would have rebuilt and reconstructed and made the effort again. And she would never be allowed to return to Timmie.

Nothing would help. Nothing but that the experiment itself fail; that it break down irretrievably.

So she waited through the countdown, watching every move on the giant screen, scanning the faces of the technicians as the focus shifted from one to the other, watching for the look of worry and uncertainty that would mark something going unexpectedly wrong; watching, watching—

There was no such look. The count reached zero, and very quietly, very unassumingly, the experiment succeeded!

In the new Stasis that had been established there stood a bearded, stoop-shouldered peasant of indeterminate age, in ragged, dirty clothing and wooden shoes, staring in dull horror at the sudden mad change that had flung itself over him.

And while the world went mad with jubilation, Miss Fellowes stood frozen in sorrow, jostled and pushed, all but trampled; surrounded by triumph while bowed down with defeat.

And when the loudspeaker called her name with strident force, it sounded it three times before she responded.

"Miss Fellowes. Miss Fellowes. You are wanted in Stasis Section One immediately. Miss Fellowes. Miss Fell—"

"Let me through!" she cried breathlessly, while the loudspeaker continued its repetitions without pause. She forced her way through the crowd with wild energy, beating at it, striking out with closed fists, flailing, moving toward the door in a nightmare slowness.

Mandy Terris was in tears. "I don't know how it happened. I just went down to the edge of the corridor to watch a packet-viewing-plate they had put up. Just for a minute. And then before I could move or do anything—" She cried out in sudden accusation, "You said they would make no trouble; you said to leave them alone—"

Miss Fellowes, disheveled and trembling uncontrollably, glared at her. "Where's Timmie?"

A nurse was swabbing the arm of a wailing Jerry with disinfectant and another was preparing an antitetanus shot. There was blood on Jerry's clothes.

"He bit me, Miss Fellowes," Jerry cried in rage. "He *bit* me."

But Miss Fellowes didn't even see him.

"What did you do with Timmie?" she cried out.

"I locked him in the bathroom," said Mandy. "I just threw the little monster in there and locked him in."

Miss Fellowes ran into the dollhouse. She fumbled at the bathroom door. It took an eternity to get it open and to find the ugly little boy cowering in the corner.

"Don't whip me, Miss Fellowes," he whispered. His eyes were red. His lips were quivering. "I didn't mean to do it."

"Oh, Timmie, who told you about whips?" She caught him to her, hugging him wildly.

He said tremulously, "She said, with a long rope. She said you would hit me and hit me."

"You won't be. She was wicked to say so. But what happened? What happened?"

"He called me an ape-boy. He said I wasn't a real boy. He said I was an animal." Timmie dissolved in a flood of tears. "He said he wasn't going to play with a monkey anymore. I said I wasn't a monkey; I *wasn't* a monkey. He said I was all funny-looking. He said I was horrible ugly. He kept saying and saying and I bit him."

They were both crying now. Miss Fellowes sobbed, "But it isn't true. You know that, Timmie. You're a real boy. You're a dear real boy and the best boy in the world. And no one, no one, will ever take you away from me."

* * *

It was easy to make up her mind now; easy to know what to do. Only it had to be done quickly. Hoskins wouldn't wait much longer, with his own son mangled—

No, it would have to be done this night, *this* night; with the place four-fifths asleep and the remaining fifth intellectually drunk over Project Middle Ages.

It would be an unusual time for her to return but not an unheard-of one. The guard knew her well and would not dream of questioning her. He would think nothing of her carrying a suitcase. She rehearsed the noncommittal phrase, "Games for the boy," and the calm smile.

Why shouldn't he believe that?

He did. When she entered the dollhouse again, Timmie was still awake, and she maintained a desperate normality to avoid frightening him. She talked about his dreams with him and listened to him ask wistfully after Jerry.

There would be few to see her afterward, none to question the bundle she would be carrying. Timmie would be very quiet and then it would be a *fait accompli.* It would be done, and what would be the use of trying to undo it? They would leave her be. They would leave them both be.

She opened the suitcase, took out the overcoat, the woolen cap with the earflaps and the rest.

Timmie said, with the beginning of alarm, "Why are you putting all these clothes on me, Miss Fellowes?"

She said, "I am going to take you outside, Timmie. To where your dreams are."

"My dreams?" His face twisted in sudden yearning, yet fear was there too.

"You won't be afraid. You'll be with me. You won't be afraid if you're with me, will you, Timmie?"

"No, Miss Fellowes." He buried his little misshapen head against her side, and under her enclosing arm she could feel his small heart thud.

It was midnight and she lifted him into her arms. She disconnected the alarm and opened the door softly.

And she screamed, for facing her across the open door was Hoskins!

There were two men with him and he stared at her, as astonished as she.

421

Miss Fellowes recovered first by a second and made a quick attempt to push past him; but even with the second's delay, he had time. He caught her roughly and hurled her back against a chest of drawers. He waved the men in and confronted her, blocking the door.

"I didn't expect this. Are you completely insane?"

She had managed to interpose her shoulder so that it, rather than Timmie, had struck the chest. She said pleadingly, "What harm can it do if I take him, Dr. Hoskins? You can't put energy loss ahead of a human life."

Firmly Hoskins took Timmie out of her arms. "An energy loss this size would mean millions of dollars lost out of the pockets of investors. It would mean a terrible setback for Stasis, Inc. It would mean eventual publicity about a sentimental nurse destroying all that for the sake of an ape-boy."

"Ape-boy!" said Miss Fellowes in helpless fury.

"That's what the reporters would call him," said Hoskins.

One of the men emerged now, looping a nylon rope through eyelets along the upper portion of the wall.

Miss Fellowes remembered the rope that Hoskins had pulled outside the room containing Professor Ademewski's rock specimen so long ago.

She cried out, "No!"

But Hoskins put Timmie down and gently removed the overcoat he was wearing. "You stay here, Timmie. Nothing will happen to you. We're just going outside for a moment. All right?"

Timmie, white and wordless, managed a nod.

Hoskins steered Miss Fellowes out of the dollhouse ahead of himself. For the moment Miss Fellowes was beyond resistance. Dully she noticed the hand-pull being adjusted outside the dollhouse.

"I'm sorry, Miss Fellowes," said Hoskins. "I would have spared you this. I planned it for the night so that you would know only when it was over."

She said in a weary whisper, "Because your son was hurt. Because he tormented this child into striking out at him."

"No. Believe me. I understand about the incident today and I know it was Jerry's fault. But the story has leaked out. It would have to with the press surrounding us on this day of all days. I can't risk having a distorted story about negligence and savage Neanderthalers, so-called, distract from the success of Project Middle Ages. Timmie has to go soon anyway; he might as well go now and give the sensationalists as small a peg as possible on which to hang their trash."

"It's not like sending a rock back. You'll be killing a human being."

"Not killing. There'll be no sensation. He'll simply be a Neanderthal boy in a Neanderthal world. He will no longer be a prisoner and alien! He will have a chance at a free life."

"What chance? He's only seven years old, used to being taken care of, fed, clothed, sheltered. He will be alone. His tribe may not be at the point where he left them now that four years have passed. And if they are they would not recognize him. He will have to take care of himself. How will he know how?"

Hoskins shook his head in hopeless negative. "Lord, Miss Fellowes, do you think we haven't thought of that? Do you think we would have brought in a child if it weren't that it was the first successful fix of a human or near-human we made and that we did not dare to take the chance of unfixing him and finding another fix as good? Why do you suppose we kept Timmie as long as we did if it were not for our reluctance to send a child back into the past. It's just"—his voice took on a desperate urgency—"that we can wait no longer. Timmie stands in the way of expansion! Timmie is a source of possible bad publicity; we are on the threshold of great things, and I'm sorry, Miss Fellowes, but we can't let Timmie block us. We cannot. We cannot. I'm sorry, Miss Fellowes."

"Well then," said Miss Fellowes sadly, "let me say good-bye. Give me five minutes to say good-bye. Spare me that much."

Hoskins hesitated. "Go ahead."

Timmie ran to her. For the last time he ran to her and for the last time Miss Fellowes clasped him in her arms.

For a moment she hugged him blindly. She caught at a chair with the toe of one foot, moved it against the wall, sat down.

"Don't be afraid, Timmie."

423

"I'm not afraid if you're here, Miss Fellowes. Is that man mad at me, the man out there?"

"No, he isn't. He just doesn't understand about us. Timmie, do you know what a mother is?"

"Like Jerry's mother?"

"Did he tell you about his mother?"

"Sometimes. I think maybe a mother is a lady who takes care of you and who's very nice to you and who does good things."

"That's right. Have you ever wanted a mother, Timmie?"

Timmie pulled his head away from her so that he could look into her face. Slowly he put his hand to her cheek and hair and stroked her, as long, long ago she had stroked him. He said, "Aren't you my mother?"

"Oh, Timmie."

"Are you angry because I asked?"

"No. Of course not."

"Because I know your name is Miss Fellowes, but—but sometimes I call you 'Mother' inside. Is that all right?"

"Yes. Yes. It's all right. And I won't leave you anymore and nothing will hurt you. I'll be with you to care for you always. Call me Mother, so I can hear you."

"Mother," said Timmie contentedly, leaning his cheek against hers.

She rose and, still holding him, stepped up on the chair. The sudden beginning of a shout from outside went unheard and with her free hand, she yanked with all her weight at the cord where it hung suspended between two eyelets.

And Stasis was punctured and the room was empty.

22

The Three Who Died Too Soon

You wouldn't have expected Leverrier to live long enough to have witnessed the solution to the mystery of Mercury's advancing perihelion (see Chapter 20, "The Planet That Wasn't"). There are a number of cases in scientific history, however, in which a scientist who makes a key discovery does not live to see the full flower of the consequences, not because it was so delayed in coming, but because the scientist in question died rather young. That always seems such a pity, and yet an example of no fewer than three such cases involving a related series of discoveries exists and is given here.

I have just returned from the Philcon—the annual convention sponsored by the Philadelphia Science Fiction Society.

It was extremely successful, I thought. It was well-attended, efficiently run, with an excellent art show and a bustling huckster room. Joe Haldeman was the guest of honor and gave an absolute whiz-bang of a talk that was greeted with great enthusiasm by the audience. This cast me down, I fear, for I was scheduled to follow him and I had to extend myself to the full, I assure you.

But what I enjoyed the most was the costume show that was won by a young man who had designed an unbelievably clever "satyr" costume. He carried a pipes-of-Pan about his neck, wore horns that blended perfectly with his hair, and capered about on goat legs that looked like the real thing.

My own private pleasure reached its peak, though, when three people came out on stage to the accompaniment of portentous music in order to represent "Foundation," "Foundation and Empire" and "Second Foundation," the three parts of my well-known *Foundation Trilogy*. They were all three swathed in black robes and all looked somber. I watched curiously, wondering how they could possibly represent those three highly intellectual novels.

Suddenly all three flashed—flinging open their robes and revealing themselves as three very incompletely clothed young people. The first and third were young men, in whom my interest was necessarily limited and who were each wearing very little more than corsets (the first and second "foundation," as I at once understood).

The middle person was a young woman of pronounced beauty, both of face and figure, and she wore a corset too. She, however, was "Foundation and Empire," and the Empire portion, I gathered, was the only other item she wore—a brassiere that did a delightfully poor job of concealing what it was meant to support.

After a few moments of surprise and enchantment, my scientific training asserted itself. If careful observation is required, it must be made under the most favorable conditions. I therefore stood up and leaned forward.

Whereupon, from near me, a voice could be heard saying, "That's five bucks you owe me. He stood up."

That was a sensationally easy bet to win—and another sensationally easy bet to win is that I will now proceed with an essay on the history of science.

In other essays, I have discussed visible light, infrared radiation and ultraviolet radiation. The frequencies in question ranged from as little as 0.3 trillion cycles per second for the lowest-frequency infrared to as much as 30,000 trillion cycles per second for the highest frequency ultraviolet.

In 1864, however, James Clerk Maxwell had evolved a theory that made it seem that such radiations arose from an oscillating electromagnetic field (hence "electromagnetic radiation") and that the frequency could be any value from much higher than 30,000 trillion cycles per second to much lower than 0.3 trillion cycles per second.

A good, airtight, well-thought-out theory is a delight, but it becomes even more delightful if some phenomenon, which has never been observed, is predicted by the theory—and is then observed. The theory points, and you look, and, behold! it's there. The chances of doing so, however, do not seem great.

It is possible to make an electric current (and hence an electromagnetic field) oscillate. Such oscillations are comparatively slow, however, and if, as is predicted by Maxwell's equations, they produce an electromagnetic radiation, the frequency is far lower than even the lowest-frequency infrared radiation. Millions of times lower. Surely the detection methods that worked for the familiar radiations in the region of light and its immediate neighbors would not work for something so far removed in properties.

Yet detected it would have to be—and in such detail that the waves could be shown to have the nature and properties of light.

Actually, the thought of oscillating electric currents producing some sort of radiation antedated Maxwell.

The American physicist Joseph Henry (1797–1878) had discovered the principle of "self-induction" in 1832 (I won't go into that or I'll never get through the ground I want to cover in this essay). In 1842 he tackled certain confusing observations that made it seem uncertain, in some cases, in which direction an electric current was moving. Under certain conditions, in fact, it seemed to be moving in both directions.

Henry, using his self-induction principle, reasoned that when a Leyden jar (or a capacitor, generally) is discharged, for instance, it overshoots the mark so that a current flows out, then finds it must flow back, overshoots the mark again, flows in the first direction and so on. In short, the electric current oscillates much as a spring might. What's more, it can be a damped oscillation, such that each overshooting of the mark is less than the one before until the current flow settles down to zero.

Henry knew that a current flow produced an effect at a distance (it would make the needle of a distant magnetic

427

compass veer, for instance) and felt that this effect would change and shift with the oscillations so that one would have a wavelike radiation issuing out from the oscillating current. He even compared the radiation to light.

This was just a vague speculation with Henry, but it is a distinguishing mark of great scientists that even their vague speculations have an uncanny habit of being right. Nevertheless, it was Maxwell, a quarter-century later, who reduced the whole matter to a clear mathematical statement, and it is he who deserves the credit.

Not all scientists accepted Maxwell's reasoning, however. One who didn't was the Irish physicist George Francis FitzGerald (1851–1901), who wrote a paper categorically maintaining that it was impossible for oscillating electric currents to produce wavelike radiations. (FitzGerald is very well known by name to science-fiction readers, or should be, since it was he who originated the concept of "the FitzGerald contraction.")

It was quite possible that scientists might choose up sides, some following Maxwell and some FitzGerald, and argue over the matter forever, unless the electric oscillation waves were actually detected, or unless some observation were made that clearly showed such waves to be impossible.

It's not surprising, then, that Maxwell would feel keenly the importance of detecting these very low-frequency waves. It was with dejection that he felt locating them was so difficult as to be next door to impossible.

And then, in 1888, a thirty-one-year-old German physicist, Heinrich Rudolph Hertz (1857–94), managed to do the job and to establish Maxwell's theory on a firm observational foundation. Had Maxwell lived, his pleasure at seeing that establishment would have been outdistanced, I am sure, by his surprise at seeing how easy the detection was and how simply it was managed.

All Hertz needed was a rectangular wire, with one side adjustable so that it could be moved in and out and the opposite side possessing a small gap. The wire at each side of the gap ended in a small brass knob. If a current were somehow started in that rectangular wire, it could leap the gap, producing a small spark.

428

Hertz then set up an oscillating current by discharging a Leyden jar. If it produced electromagnetic waves, as Maxwell's equations predicted, those waves would induce an electric current in Hertz's rectangular detector (to which no other source of electricity was attached, of course). A spark would then be produced across the gap, and this would be visible evidence of the induced electric current and, therefore, of the waves that did the inducing.

Hertz got his sparks.

By moving his receiver about in different directions and at different distances from the oscillating current that was the source of the waves, Hertz found the sparks growing more intense in places and less intense in others as the waves were at higher or lower amplitude. He could, in this way, map out the waves, determine the wavelength, and show that they could be reflected, refracted and made to exhibit interference phenomena. He could even detect both electric and magnetic properties. In short, he found the waves entirely similar to light, except for their wavelengths, which were in the meter range rather than the micrometer range. Maxwell's electromagnetic theory was well and truly demonstrated nine years after Maxwell's death.

The new waves and their properties were quickly confirmed by other observers and they were termed "Hertzian waves."

Neither Hertz nor any of those who confirmed his findings saw the discovery as of any importance other than as the demonstration of the truth of an elegant scientific theory.

In 1892, however, the English physicist William Crookes (1832–1919) suggested that Hertzian waves might be used for communication. They moved in straight lines at the speed of light but were so long-wave that objects of ordinary size were simply not opaque to them. The long waves moved around and through obstacles. The waves were easily detected, and if they could be started and stopped in a careful pattern, they could produce the dots and dashes of the telegraphic Morse code— and without the need of the complicated and expensive system of thousands of kilometers of copper wires and relays. Crookes was, in short, suggesting the possibility of "wireless telegraphy."

The idea must have sounded like "science fiction" (in the

429

pejorative sense used by ignorant snobs), and Hertz, alas, did not see it come true. He died in 1894, at the age of forty-two, of a chronic infection that these days would probably have been easily cured by antibiotics.

Only months after Hertz's death, however, an Italian engineer, Guglielmo Marconi (1874–1937), then only twenty years old, read of Hertz's findings and instantly got the same idea Crookes had had.

Marconi used the same system for producing Hertzian waves that Hertz himself had used but set up a much improved detector, a so-called coherer. This consisted of a container of loosely packed metal filings, which ordinarily conducted little current but conducted quite a bit when Hertzian waves fell upon it.

Gradually Marconi improved his instruments, grounding both the transmitter and receiver. He also used a wire, insulated from the earth, which served as an antenna, or aerial, to facilitate both sending and receiving.

He sent signals across greater and greater distances. In 1895 he sent a signal from his house to his garden and, later, across a distance of over a kilometer. In 1896, when the Italian government showed itself uninterested in his work, he went to England (his mother was Irish and Marconi could speak English) and sent a signal across a distance of fourteen kilometers. He then applied for and received the first patent in the history of wireless telegraphy.

In 1897, again in Italy, he sent a signal from land to a warship twenty kilometers away, and in 1898 (back in England) he sent a signal across a distance of thirty kilometers.

He was beginning to make his system known. The seventy-four-year-old physicist Lord Kelvin paid to send a "Marconi-gram" to his friend, the British physicist G. G. Stokes, then seventy-nine years old. This communication between two aged scientists was the first commercial message by wireless telegraphy. Marconi also used his signals to report the yacht races at Kingstown Regatta that year.

In 1901 Marconi approached the climax. His experiments had already convinced him that Hertzian waves followed the curve of the Earth instead of radiating straight outward into space as electromagnetic waves might be expected to do. (It was eventually found that Hertzian waves were reflected by the charged particles in the "ionosphere," a region of the upper atmosphere. They traveled around the Earth's bulge by bouncing back and forth between ground and ionosphere.)

He made elaborate preparations, therefore, to send a Hertzian-wave signal from the southwest tip of England across the Atlantic to Newfoundland, using balloons to lift the antennae as high as possible. On December 12, 1901, he succeeded.

To the British, the technique has remained "wireless telegraphy," and the phrase is usually shortened to "wireless."

In the United States the technique was called "radio telegraphy," meaning that the key carrier of the signal was an electromagnetic radiation rather than a current-carrying wire. For short, the technique was called "radio."

Since Marconi's technique made headway fastest in the United States, which was by now the most advanced nation in the world from the technological standpoint, "radio" won out over "wireless." The world generally speaks of radio now, and December 12, 1901, is usually thought of as the day of "the invention of radio."

In fact, Hertzian waves have come to be called "radio waves" and the older name has dropped out of use. The entire portion of the electromagnetic spectrum from a wavelength of one millimeter (the upper boundary of the infrared region) to a maximum wavelength equal to the diameter of the Universe— a stretch of 100 octaves—is included in the radio-wave region.

The radio waves used for ordinary radio transmission have wavelengths of from about 190 to 5,700 meters. The frequency of these radio waves is therefore from 530,000 to 1,600,000 cycles per second (or from 530 to 1,600 kilocycles per second). A "cycle per second" is now referred to as a "hertz" in honor of the scientist, so we might say that the frequency range is from 530 to 1,600 "kilohertz."

Higher-frequency radio waves are used in FM, and still higher frequency in television.

As years went by, radio came into more and more common use. Methods for converting radio signals into sound waves were developed so that you could hear speech and music on radio and not just the Morse code.

431

This meant that radio could be combined with ordinary telephonic communication to produce "radio-telephony." In other words, you could use the telephone to communicate with someone on a ship in mid-ocean when you yourself were in mid-continent. Ordinary phone wires would carry the message across land while radio waves would carry it across the sea.

There was a catch, however. Wire-conducted electricity could produce sound that was clear as a bell (Alexander Graham, of course), but air-conducted radio waves were constantly being interfered with by the random noise we call "static" (because one cause is the accumulation of a static electrical charge upon the antenna).

Bell Telephone was naturally interested in minimizing static, but in order to do that, they had to learn as much as possible about the causes of it. They assigned the task of doing so to a young engineer named Karl Guthe Jansky (1905–50).

One of the sources of static was certainly thunderstorms, so one of the things that Jansky did was to set up a complicated aerial, consisting of numerous rods, both vertical and horizontal, which could receive from different directions. What is more, he set it up on an automobile frame equipped with wheels so that he could turn it this way and that in order to tune in on any static he did detect.

Using this device, Jansky had no trouble detecting distant thunderstorms as crackling static.

It was not all he got, however. While he was scanning the sky, he also got a hissing sound quite different from thunderstorm crackles. He was clearly getting radio waves from the sky, radio waves that were generated neither by human beings nor thunderstorms. What's more, as he studied this hiss from day to day, it seemed to him that it was not coming from the sky generally but, for the most part, from some particular part of it. By moving his aerial system properly, he could point it in a direction from which the sound was most intense—and this spot moved across the sky, rather as the Sun did.

At first it seemed to Jansky that the radio-wave source *was* the Sun, and if the Sun had happened to be at a high sunspot level at the time, he would have been right.

However, the Sun was at low activity at the time and what radio waves it emitted could not be detected by Jansky's crude

432

apparatus. That, perhaps, was a good thing, for it turned out that Jansky was onto something bigger. At the start his apparatus did indeed seem to be pointing toward the Sun when it was receiving the hiss at maximum intensity, but day by day Jansky found his apparatus pointing farther and farther away from the Sun.

The point from which the hiss was originating was fixed with respect to the stars, while the Sun was not (as viewed from Earth). By the spring of 1932, Jansky was quite certain that the hiss was coming from the constellation of Sagittarius. It was only because the Sun was in Sagittarius when Jansky detected the cosmic hiss that he initially confused the two.

The center of the galaxy happens to be in the direction of Sagittarius, and what Jansky had done was to detect the radio emissions from that center. The sound came to be called the "cosmic hiss" because of this.

Jansky published his account in the December 1932 issue of *Proceedings of the Institute of Radio Engineers*, and that marks the birth of "radio astronomy."

But how could radio waves reach Earth's surface from outer space when they were reflected by the ionosphere? The ionosphere keeps radio waves originating on Earth from moving out into space, and it should keep those originating in space from moving down to Earth's surface.

It turned out that a stretch of about eleven octaves of the very shortest radio waves (called "microwaves"), just beyond the infrared, were not reflected by the ionosphere. These very short radio waves could move right through the ionosphere, either from Earth into space or from space down to Earth. This stretch of octaves is known as the "microwave window."

The microwave window encompasses radiation with wavelengths from about 10 millimeters to about 10 meters, and frequencies from 30,000,000 cycles per second (30 megahertz) to 30,000,000,000 cycles per second (30,000 megahertz).

Jansky's apparatus happened to be sensitive to a frequency just inside the lower limit of the microwave window. A little bit lower and he might not have detected the cosmic hiss.

The news of Jansky's discovery made the front page of *The New York Times*, and justifiably so. With the wisdom of hindsight, we can at once see the importance of the microwave window. For one thing, it included seven octaves as compared to the single octave of visible light (plus a bit extra in the neighboring ultraviolet and infrared). For another, light is useful for nonsolar astronomy only on clear nights, whereas microwaves would reach Earth whether the sky was cloudy or not, and for that matter, they could be worked with in the daytime as well for the Sun would not obscure them.

Nevertheless, professional astronomers paid little attention. The astronomer Fred Lawrence Whipple (1906–   ), who had just joined the Harvard faculty, did discuss the matter with animation, but he had the advantage of being a science-fiction reader.

We can't blame astronomers too much, however. After all, there was nothing much they could do about it. The instrumentation required for receiving microwaves with sufficient delicacy to be of use in astronomy simply didn't exist.

Jansky himself didn't follow up his discovery. He had other things to do, and his health was not good. He died of a heart ailment at the age of forty-four and barely lived to see radio astronomy begin to stir. By a strange fatality then, three of the key scientists in the history of radio, Maxwell, Hertz and Jansky, each died in his thirties or forties and did not live to see the true consequences of his work, even though each would have done so had he lived but another decade.

Still, radio astronomy was not entirely neglected. One person, an amateur, carried on. This was Grote Reber (1911–   ), who had become an enthusiastic radio ham at the age of fifteen. While he was still a student at the Illinois Institute of Technology, he took Jansky's discovery to heart and tried to follow. For instance, he tried to bounce radio signals off the Moon and detect the echo. (He failed, but the idea was a good one, and a decade later the Army Signal Corps, with far more equipment at its disposal, was to succeed.)

In 1937 Reber built the first radio telescope in his backyard in Wheaton, Illinois. The reflector, which received the radio waves, was 9.5 meters in diameter. It was designed as a paraboloid so that it concentrated the waves it received at the detector at the focus.

In 1938, he began to receive and, for several years, he was

the only radio astronomer in the world. He discovered places in the sky that emitted stronger-than-background radio waves. Such "radio stars," he found, did not coincide with any of the visible stars. (Some of Reber's radio stars were eventually identified with distant galaxies).

Reber published his findings in 1942, and by then there was a startling change in the attitude of scientists toward radio astronomy.

A Scottish physicist, Robert Watson-Watt (1892–1973), had grown interested in the manner in which radio waves were reflected. It occurred to him that radio waves might be reflected by an obstacle and the reflection detected. From the time lapse between emission and detection of reflection, the distance of the obstacle could be determined, and of course the direction from which the reflection was received would give the direction of the obstacle.

The shorter the radio waves, the more easily they would be reflected by ordinary obstacles; but if they were too short, they would not penetrate clouds, fog and dust. Frequencies were needed that were high enough to be penetrating and yet low enough to be efficiently reflected by objects you wanted to detect. The microwave range was just suitable for the purpose, and as early as 1919, Watson-Watt had already taken out a patent in connection with radio location by means of short radio waves.

The principle is simple, but the difficulty lies in developing instruments capable of sending out and receiving microwaves with the requisite efficiency and delicacy. By 1935 Watson-Watt had patented improvements that made it possible to follow an airplane by the radio-wave reflections it sent back. The system was called "radio detection and ranging" (to "get a range" on an object is to determine its distance). This was abbreviated to "ra. d. a. r." or "radar."

Research was continued in secrecy, and by the fall of 1938, radar stations were in operation on the British coast. In 1940 the German Air Force was attacking those stations, but Hitler, in a fury over a minor bombing of Berlin by the RAF, ordered German planes to concentrate on London. They ignored the radar stations thereafter (not quite grasping their abilities) and found themselves consistently unable to achieve surprise. In consequence, Germany lost the Battle of Britain, and the war. With all due respect to the valor of British airmen, it was radar that won the Battle of Britain. (On the other hand, American radar detected incoming Japanese planes on December 7, 1941—but it was ignored.)

The same techniques that made radar possible, as it happened, could be used by astronomers to receive microwaves from the stars and, for that matter, to send tight beams of microwaves to the Moon and other astronomical objects and receive the reflections.

If anything was needed to sharpen astronomical appetites, it came in 1942, when all the British radar stations were simultaneously jammed. At first it was suspected that the Germans had worked out a way of neutralizing radar, but that was not so at all.

It was the Sun! A giant flare had sprayed radio waves in Earth's direction and had flooded the radar receivers. *Well*, if the Sun could send out such a flood of radio waves, and if the technology for studying them now existed, astronomers could barely wait till the war was over.

Once the war ended, developments came quickly. Radio astronomy flourished, radio telescopes became more delicate, new and absolutely astonishing discoveries were made. Our knowledge of the Universe underwent a mad growth of a kind that had previously taken place only in the decades following the invention of the telescope.

23

The Last Question

If we're going to consider the consequences of scientific progress, it is difficult to know where to stop. On one occasion I simply looked farther and farther into the future, following the trail of scientific advance, until I reached the very end of the Universe. And then?

Despite the fact that this story was written in 1956 and therefore does not consider neutron stars, black holes, quasars and so on (although it could be rewritten to include them, without any change in its essence), it is, by all odds, my favorite story of all those I have written. ("The Ugly Little Boy" is second.)

The last question was asked for the first time, half in jest, on May 21, 2061, at a time when humanity first stepped into the light. The question came about as a result of a five-dollar bet over highballs, and it happened this way:

Alexander Adell and Bertram Lupov were two of the faithful attendants of Multivac. As well as any human beings could, they knew what lay behind the cold, clicking, flashing face—miles and miles of face—of that giant computer. They had at least a vague notion of the general plan of relays and circuits that had long since grown past the point where any single human could possibly have a firm grasp of the whole.

Multivac was self-adjusting and self-correcting. It had to

be, for nothing human could adjust and correct it quickly enough or even adequately enough. So Adell and Lupov attended the monstrous giant only lightly and superficially, yet as well as any men could. They fed it data, adjusted questions to its needs and translated the answers that were issued. Certainly they, and all others like them, were fully entitled to share in the glory that was Multivac's.

For decades Multivac had helped design the ships and plot the trajectories that enabled man to reach the Moon, Mars and Venus, but past that, Earth's poor resources could not support the ships. Too much energy was needed for the long trips. Earth exploited its coal and uranium with increasing efficiency, but there was only so much of each.

But slowly Multivac learned enough to answer deeper questions more fundamentally, and on May 14, 2061, what had been theory became fact.

The energy of the Sun was stored, converted and utilized directly on a planet-wide scale. All Earth turned off its burning coal, its fissioning uranium, and flipped the switch that connected all of it to a small station, one mile in diameter, circling the Earth at half the distance of the Moon. All Earth ran by invisible beams of sunpower.

Seven days had not sufficed to dim the glory of it, and Adell and Lupov finally managed to escape from the public function and to meet in quiet where no one would think of looking for them, in the deserted underground chambers, where portions of the mighty, buried body of Multivac showed. Unattended, idling, sorting data with contented lazy clickings, Multivac too had earned its vacation and the boys appreciated that. They had no intention, originally, of disturbing it.

They had brought a bottle with them, and their only concern at the moment was to relax in the company of each other and the bottle.

"It's amazing when you think of it," said Adell. His broad face had lines of weariness in it, and he stirred his drink slowly with a glass rod, watching the cubes of ice slur clumsily about. "All the energy we can possibly ever use for free. Enough energy, if we wanted to draw on it, to melt all Earth into a big drop of impure liquid iron and still never miss the energy so used. All the energy we could ever use, forever and forever and forever."

438

Lupov cocked his head sideways. He had a trick of doing that when he wanted to be contrary, and he wanted to be contrary now, partly because he had had to carry the ice and glassware. "Not forever," he said.

"Oh, hell, just about forever. Till the sun runs down, Bert."

"That's not forever."

"All right then. Billions and billions of years. Twenty billion maybe. Are you satisfied?"

Lupov put his fingers through his thinning hair as though to reassure himself that some was still left and sipped gently at his drink. "Twenty billion years isn't forever."

"Well, it will last our time, won't it?"

"So would the coal and uranium."

"All right, but now we can hook up each individual spaceship to the Solar Station, and it can go to Pluto and back a million times without ever worrying about fuel. You can't do *that* on coal and uranium. Ask Multivac if you don't believe me."

"I don't have to ask Multivac. I know that."

"Then stop running down what Multivac's done for us," said Adell, blazing up. "It did all right."

"Who says it didn't? What I say is that a sun won't last forever. That's all I'm saying. We're safe for twenty billion years; but then what?" Lupov pointed a slightly shaky finger at the other. "And don't say we'll switch to another sun."

There was silence for a while. Adell put his glass to his lips only occasionally, and Lupov's eyes slowly closed. They rested.

Then Lupov's eyes snapped open. "You're thinking we'll switch to another sun when ours is done, aren't you?"

"I'm not thinking."

"Sure you are. You're weak on logic, that's the trouble with you. You're like the guy in the story who was caught in a sudden shower and ran to a grove of trees and got under one. He wasn't worried, you see, because he figured when one tree got wet through, he would just get under another one."

"I get it," said Adell. "Don't shout. When the sun is done, the other stars will be gone too."

"Darn right they will," muttered Lupov. "It all had a

439

beginning in the original cosmic explosion, whatever that was, and it'll all have an end when all the stars run down. Some run down faster than others. Hell, the giants won't last a hundred million years. The Sun will last twenty billion years and maybe the dwarfs will last a hundred billion for all the good they are. But just give us a trillion years and everything will be dark. Entropy has to increase to maximum, that's all."

"I know all about entropy," said Adell, standing on his dignity.

"The hell you do."

"I know as much as you do."

"Then you know everything's got to run down someday."

"All right. Who says it won't?"

"You did, you poor sap. You said we had all the energy we needed, forever. You said 'forever.'"

It was Adell's turn to be contrary. "Maybe we can build things up again someday," he said.

"Never."

"Why not? Someday."

"Ask Multivac."

"Never."

"*You* ask Multivac. I dare you. Five dollars says it can't be done."

Adell was just drunk enough to try, just sober enough to be able to phrase the necessary symbols and operations into a question which, in words, might have corresponded to this: Will mankind one day, without the net expenditure of energy, be able to restore the sun to its full youthfulness even after it had died of old age?

Or maybe it could be put more simply like this: How can the net amount of entropy of the Universe be massively decreased?

Multivac fell dead and silent. The slow flashing of lights ceased, the distant sounds of clicking relays ended.

Then, just as the frightened technicians felt they could hold their breath no longer, there was a sudden springing to life of the teletype attached to that portion of Multivac. Five words were printed: INSUFFICIENT DATA FOR MEANINGFUL ANSWER.

"No bet," whispered Lupov. They left hurriedly.

By next morning, the two, plagued with throbbing heads and cottony mouths, had forgotten the incident.

* * *

Jerrodd, Jerrodine and Jerrodette I and II watched the starry picture in the visiplate change as the passage through hyperspace was completed in its nontime lapse. At once the even powdering of stars gave way to the predominance of a single bright marble disk, centered.

"That's X-23," said Jerrodd confidently. His thin hands clamped tightly behind his back and the knuckles whitened.

The little Jerrodettes, both girls, had experienced the hyperspace passage for the first time in their lives and were self-conscious over the momentary sensation of inside-outness. They buried their giggles and chased one another wildly about their mother, screaming, "We've reached X-23—we've reached X-23—we've—"

"Quiet, children," said Jerrodine sharply. "Are you sure, Jerrodd?"

"What is there to be but sure?" asked Jerrodd, glancing up at the bulge of featureless metal just under the ceiling. It ran the length of the room, disappearing through the wall at either end. It was as long as the ship.

Jerrodd scarcely knew a thing about the thick rod of metal except that it was called a Microvac; that one asked it questions if one wished; that if one did not, it still had its task of guiding the ship to a preordered destination; of feeding on energies from the various Sub-galactic Power Stations; of computing the equations for the hyperspatial jumps.

Jerrodd and his family had only to wait and live in the comfortable residence quarters of the ship.

Someone had once told Jerrodd that the "ac" at the end of "Microvac" stood for "automatic computer" in ancient English, but he was on the edge of forgetting even that.

Jerrodine's eyes were moist as she watched the visiplate. "I can't help it. I feel funny about leaving Earth."

"Why, for Pete's sake?" demanded Jerrodd. "We had nothing there. We'll have everything on X-23. You won't be alone. You won't be a pioneer. There are over a million people on the planet already. Good Lord, our great-grandchildren will be looking for new worlds because X-23 will be overcrowded." Then, after a reflective pause, "I tell you, it's a lucky thing the computers worked out interstellar travel the way the race is growing."

"I know, I know," said Jerrodine miserably.

Jerrodette I said promptly, "Our Microvac is the best Microvac in the world."

"I think so too," said Jerrodd, tousling her hair.

It *was* a nice feeling to have a Microvac of your own, and Jerrodd was glad he was part of his generation and no other. In his father's youth, the only computers had been tremendous machines taking up a hundred square miles of land. There was only one to a planet. Planetary ACs they were called. They had been growing in size steadily for a thousand years and then, all at once, came refinement. In place of transistors had come molecular valves so that even the largest Planetary AC could be put into a space only half the volume of a spaceship.

Jerrodd felt uplifted, as he always did when he thought that his own personal Microvac was many times more complicated than the ancient and primitive Multivac that had first tamed the Sun, and almost as complicated as Earth's Planetary AC (the largest) that had first solved the problem of hyperspatial travel and had made trips to the stars possible.

"So many stars, so many planets," sighed Jerrodine, busy with her own thoughts. "I suppose families will be going out to new planets forever, the way we are now."

"Not forever," said Jerrodd with a smile. "It will all stop someday, but not for billions of years. Many billions. Even the stars run down, you know. Entropy must increase."

"What's entropy, Daddy?" shrilled Jerrodette II.

"Entropy, little sweet, is just a word which means the amount of running down of the Universe. Everything runs down, you know, like your little walkie-talkie robot, remember?"

"Can't you just put in a new power unit, like with my robot?"

"The stars *are* the power units, dear. Once they're gone, there are no more power units."

Jerrodette I at once set up a howl. "Don't let them, Daddy. Don't let the stars run down."

"Now look what you've done," whispered Jerrodine, exasperated.

"How was I to know it would frighten them?" Jerrodd whispered back.

442

"Ask the Microvac," wailed Jerrodette I. "Ask him how to turn the stars on again."

"Go ahead," said Jerrodine. "It will quiet them down." (Jerrodette II was beginning to cry also.)

Jerrodd shrugged. "Now, now, honeys. I'll ask Microvac. Don't worry, he'll tell us."

He asked the Microvac, adding quickly, "Print the answer."

Jerrodd cupped the strip of thin cellufilm and said cheerfully, "See now, the Microvac says it will take care of everything when the time comes, so don't worry."

Jerrodine said, "And now, children, it's time for bed. We'll be in our new home soon."

Jerrodd read the words on the cellufilm again before destroying it: INSUFFICIENT DATA FOR MEANINGFUL ANSWER.

He shrugged and looked at the visiplate. X-23 was just ahead.

VJ-23X of Lameth stared into the black depths of the three-dimensional, small-scale map of the galaxy and said, "Are we ridiculous, I wonder, in being so concerned about the matter?"

MQ-17J of Nicron shook his head. "I think not. You know the galaxy will be filled in five years at the present rate of expansion."

Both seemed in their early twenties; both were tall and perfectly formed.

"Still," said VJ-23X, "I hesitate to submit a pessimistic report to the Galactic Council."

"I wouldn't consider any other kind of report. Stir them up a bit. We've got to stir them up."

VJ-23X sighed. "Space is infinite. A hundred billion galaxies are there for the taking. More."

"A hundred billion is *not* infinite and it's getting less infinite all the time. Consider! Twenty thousand years ago mankind first solved the problem of utilizing stellar energy, and a few centuries later, interstellar travel became possible. It took mankind a million years to fill one small world and then only fifteen thousand years to fill the rest of the galaxy. Now the population doubles every ten years—"

VJ-23X interrupted. "We can thank immortality for that."

"Very well. Immortality exists and we have to take it into account. I admit it has its seamy side, this immortality. The Galactic AC has solved many problems for us, but in solving the problems of preventing old age and death, it has undone all its other solutions."

"Yet you wouldn't want to abandon life, I suppose."

"Not at all," snapped MQ-17J, softening it at once to, "Not yet. I'm by no means old enough. How old are you?"

"Two hundred twenty-three. And you?"

"I'm still under two hundred. —But to get back to my point. Population doubles every ten years. Once this galaxy is filled, we'll have filled another in ten years. Another ten years and we'll have filled two more. Another decade, four more. In a hundred years, we'll have filled a thousand galaxies. In a thousand years, a million galaxies. In ten thousand years, the entire known Universe. Then what?"

VJ-23X said, "As a side issue, there's a problem of transportation. I wonder how many sunpower units it will take to move galaxies of individuals from one galaxy to the next."

"A very good point. Already mankind consumes two sunpower units per year."

"Most of it's wasted. After all, our own galaxy alone pours out a thousand sunpower units a year and we only use two of those."

"Granted, but even with a hundred-percent efficiency, we only stave off the end. Our energy requirements are going up in a geometric progression even faster than our population. We'll run out of energy even sooner than we run out of galaxies. A good point. A very good point."

"We'll just have to build new stars out of interstellar gas."

"Or out of dissipated heat?" asked MQ-17J sarcastically.

"There may be some way to reverse entropy. We ought to ask the Galactic AC."

VJ-23X was not really serious, but MQ-17J pulled out his AC contact from his pocket and placed it on the table before him.

"I've half a mind to," he said. "It's something the human race will have to face someday."

He stared somberly at his small AC contact. It was only two inches cubed and nothing in itself, but it was connected through hyperspace with the great Galactic AC that served all mankind. Hyperspace considered, it was an integral part of the Galactic AC.

MQ-17J paused to wonder if someday in his immortal life he would get to see the Galactic AC. It was on a little world of its own, a spiderwebbing of force beams holding the matter within which surges of sub-mesons took the place of the old clumsy molecular valves. Yet despite its subetheric workings, the Galactic AC was known to be a full thousand feet across.

MQ-17J asked suddenly of his AC contact, "Can entropy ever be reversed?"

VJ-23X looked startled and said at once, "Oh, say, I didn't really mean to have you ask that."

"Why not?"

"We both know entropy can't be reversed. You can't turn smoke and ash back into a tree."

"Do you have trees on your world?" asked MQ-17J.

The sound of the Galactic AC startled them into silence. Its voice came thin and beautiful out of the small AC contact on the desk. It said: THERE IS INSUFFICIENT DATA FOR A MEANINGFUL ANSWER.

VJ-23X said, "See!"

The two men thereupon returned to the question of the report they were to make to the Galactic Council.

Zee Prime's mind spanned the new galaxy with a faint interest in the countless twists of stars that powdered it. He had never seen this one before. Would he ever see them all? So many of them, each with its load of humanity. But a load that was almost a dead weight. More and more, the real essence of men was to be found out here, in space.

Minds, not bodies! The immortal bodies remained back on the planets, in suspension over the eons. Sometimes they roused for material activity but that was growing rarer. Few new individuals were coming into existence to join the incredibly mighty throng, but what matter? There was little room in the Universe for new individuals.

Zee Prime was roused out of his reverie upon coming across the wispy tendrils of another mind.

"I am Zee Prime," said Zee Prime. "And you?"

"I am Dee Sub Wun. Your galaxy?"

"We call it only the galaxy. And you?"

"We call ours the same. All men call their galaxy their galaxy and nothing more. Why not?"

"True. Since all galaxies are the same."

"Not all galaxies. On one particular galaxy the race of man must have originated. That makes it different."

Zee Prime said, "On which one?"

"I cannot say. The Universal AC would know."

"Shall we ask him? I am suddenly curious."

Zee Prime's perceptions broadened until the galaxies themselves shrank and became a new, more diffuse powdering on a much larger background. So many hundreds of billions of them, all with their immortal beings, all carrying their load of intelligences with minds that drifted freely through space. And yet one of them was unique among them all in being the original galaxy. One of them had, in its vague and distant past, a period when it was the only galaxy populated by man.

Zee Prime was consumed with curiosity to see this galaxy and he called out: "Universal AC! On which galaxy did mankind originate?"

The Universal AC heard, for on every world and throughout space, it had its receptors ready, and each receptor lead through hyperspace to some unknown point where the Universal AC kept itself aloof.

Zee Prime knew of only one man whose thoughts had penetrated within sensing distance of Universal AC, and he reported only a shining globe, two feet across, difficult to see.

"But how can that be all of Universal AC?" Zee Prime had asked.

"Most of it," had been the answer, "is in hyperspace. In what form it is there I cannot imagine."

Nor could anyone, for the day had long since passed, Zee Prime knew, when any man had any part of the making of a Universal AC. Each Universal AC designed and constructed its successor. Each, during its existence of a million years or more, accumulated the necessary data to build a better and more intricate, more capable successor, in which its own store of data and individuality would be submerged.

The Universal AC interrupted Zee Prime's wandering

thoughts, not with words, but with guidance. Zee Prime's mentality was guided into the dim sea of galaxies, and one in particular enlarged into stars.

A thought came, infinitely distant but infinitely clear. "THIS IS THE ORIGINAL GALAXY OF MAN."

But it was the same after all, the same as any other, and Zee Prime stifled his disappointment.

Dee Sub Wun, whose mind had accompanied the other, said suddenly, "And is one of these stars the original star of Man?"

The Universal AC said, "MAN'S ORIGINAL STAR HAS GONE RED GIANT. IT IS NOW A WHITE DWARF."

"Did the men upon it die?" asked Zee Prime, startled and without thinking.

The Universal AC said, "A NEW WORLD, AS IN SUCH CASES, WAS CONSTRUCTED FOR THEIR PHYSICAL BODIES IN TIME."

"Yes, of course," said Zee Prime, but a sense of loss overwhelmed him even so. His mind released its hold on the original galaxy of Man, let it spring back and lose itself among the blurred pin points. He never wanted to see it again.

Dee Sub Wun said, "What is wrong?"

"The stars are dying. The original star is dead."

"They must all die. Why not?"

"But when all energy is gone, our bodies will finally die, and you and I with them."

"It will take billions of years."

"I do not wish it to happen even after billions of years. Universal AC! How may stars be kept from dying?"

Dee Sub Wun said in amusement, "You're asking how entropy might be reversed in direction."

And the Universal AC answered: "THERE IS AS YET INSUFFICIENT DATA FOR A MEANINGFUL ANSWER."

Zee Prime's thoughts fled back to his own galaxy. He gave no further thought to Dee Sub Wun, whose body might be waiting on a galaxy a billion light-years away, or on the star next to Zee Prime's own. It didn't matter.

Unhappily Zee Prime began collecting interstellar hydrogen out of which to build a small star of his own. If the stars must someday die, at least some could yet be built.

Man considered with himself, for in a way, Man, mentally,

was one. He consisted of a trillion, trillion, trillion ageless bodies, each in its place, each resting quiet and incorruptible, each cared for by perfect automatons, equally incorruptible, while the minds of all the bodies freely melted one into the other, indistinguishable.

Man said, "The Universe is dying."

Man looked about at the dimming galaxies. The giant stars, spendthrifts, were gone long ago, back in the dimmest of the dim far past. Almost all stars were white dwarfs, fading to the end.

New stars had been built of the dust between the stars, some by natural processes, some by Man himself, and those were going too. White dwarfs might yet be crashed together and of the mightly forces so released, new stars built, but only one star for every thousand white dwarfs destroyed, and those would come to an end too.

Man said, "Carefully husbanded, as directed by the Cosmic AC, the energy that is even yet left in all the Universe will last for billions of years."

"But even so," said Man, "eventually it will all come to an end. However it may be husbanded, however stretched out, the energy once expended is gone and cannot be restored. Entropy must increase forever to the maximum."

Man said, "Can entropy not be reversed? Let us ask the Cosmic AC."

The Cosmic AC surrounded them but not in space. Not a fragment of it was in space. It was in hyperspace and made of something that was neither matter nor energy. The question of its size and nature no longer had meaning in any terms that Man could comprehend.

"Cosmic AC," said Man, "how may entropy be reversed?"

The Cosmic AC said, "THERE IS AS YET INSUFFICIENT DATA FOR A MEANINGFUL ANSWER."

Man said, "Collect additional data."

The Cosmic AC said, "I WILL DO SO. I HAVE BEEN DOING SO FOR A HUNDRED BILLION YEARS. MY PREDECESSORS AND I HAVE BEEN ASKED THIS QUESTION MANY TIMES. ALL THE DATA I HAVE REMAINS INSUFFICIENT."

"Will there come a time," said Man, "when data will be sufficient or is the problem insoluble in all conceivable circumstances?"

448

The Cosmic AC said, "NO PROBLEM IS INSOLUBLE IN ALL CONCEIVABLE CIRCUMSTANCES,"

Man said, "When will you have enough data to answer the question?"

The Cosmic AC said, "THERE IS AS YET INSUFFICIENT DATA FOR A MEANINGFUL ANSWER."

"Will you keep working on it?" asked Man.

The Cosmic AC said, "I WILL."

Man said, "We shall wait."

The stars and galaxies died and snuffed out, and space grew black after ten trillion years of running down.

One by one Man fused with AC, each physical body losing its mental identity in a manner that was somehow not a loss but a gain.

Man's last mind paused before fusion, looking over a space that included nothing but the dregs of one last dark star and nothing besides but incredibly thin matter, agitated randomly by the tag ends of heat wearing out, asymptotically, to the absolute zero.

Man said, "AC, is this the end? Can this chaos not be reversed into the Universe once more? Can that not be done?"

AC said, "THERE IS AS YET INSUFFICIENT DATA FOR A MEANINGFUL ANSWER."

Man's last mind fused and only AC existed—and that in hyperspace.

Matter and energy had ended and with it space and time. Even AC existed only for the sake of the one last question that it had never answered from the time a half-drunken computer technician ten trillion years before had asked the question of a computer that was to AC far less than was a man to Man.

All other questions had been answered, and until this last question was answered also, AC might not release his consciousness.

All collected data had come to a final end. Nothing was left to be collected.

But all collected data had yet to be completely correlated and put together in all possible relationships.

A timeless interval was spent in doing that.

And it came to pass that AC learned how to reverse the direction of entropy.

But there was now no man to whom AC might give the answer to the last question. No matter. The answer—by demonstration—would take care of that too.

For another timeless interval AC thought how best to do this. Carefully AC organized the program.

The consciousness of AC encompassed all of what had once been a Universe and brooded over what was now Chaos. Step by step, it must be done.

And AC said, "LET THERE BE LIGHT!"

And there was light—

24

The Nobel Prize That Wasn't

In my opinion, the saddest case of a scientist who didn't live long enough to gain the satisfaction he deserved out of observing the consequences of his discovery is that of Henry Moseley. I will close this book with an account of what he did and what happened to him thereafter. . . .

Some time ago I gave a lecture at a nearby university and the evening began with a dinner which deserving students were allowed to attend. Naturally the attendees were science-fiction fans who thought it would be great to meet me, and that suited me fine because I think it's great to meet people who think it's great to meet me.

One of the students was a buxom eighteen-year-old coed and I found that delightful, because many years ago I took a liking to buxom eighteen-year-old coeds and I've never entirely outgrown that feeling. She sat next to me at the dinner and I was at my genial and witty best, simply oozing gallantry and charm. Somewhere around the dessert, though, I paused for breath and, in the silence, the sound of the conversation elsewhere along the table welled up about us.

We both stopped to listen. It was the other collegiates talking; all of them earnest young men and women deeply involved in the burning issues of the day. To be sure, I was about to give a talk on the burning issues of the day, but even so, listening to the others made me feel a little ashamed that I had burdened my companion of the meal with nothing more than nonsense. And just as I was beginning to launch into some deep philosophy, she said to me, "Everyone is so serious here. Ever since I came to college, I've met only serious people."

She paused to think and then said with every sign of absolute sincerity, "In fact, in all the time I've been here, you're the first eighteen-year-old I've met."

So I kissed her.

But you know, however youthful I feel and act in consequence of my temperament, my way of life and my constant association with college students, I am nevertheless over eighteen. My enemies might even say I was far, *far* beyond eighteen and they would be right.

Still, there's no way of avoiding the advance of years except by dying and there's no great fun in that, as I will show you in the case of one young man who will be under discussion in this chapter—

Let's start with the periodic table which throughout the second half of the nineteenth century had listed the elements in an orderly way and had accurately predicted the existence of unknown elements. Nevertheless, it still lacked a firm foundation in the second decade of the twentieth century. It worked, but no knew *why* it worked. The answer to the "why?" began with something seen out of the corner of the eye.

The year of that beginning was 1895; the place was in the laboratory of Wilhelm Konrad Roentgen, head of the physics department at the University of Würzburg in Bavaria. Roentgen was investigating cathode rays—the big glamour object of physics in those days. An electric current forced through a good enough vacuum emerged as a stream of what turned out to be particles much smaller than atoms (subatomic particles), which received the name of "electrons."

These streams of electrons had a host of fascinating properties. For one thing, they produced luminescence when they struck certain chemicals. The luminescence wasn't very bright, so in order to study it more easily, Roentgen darkened the room and encased the cathode-ray tube in thin black cardboard.

On November 5, 1895, then, he turned on his cathode-ray tube and prepared to peer close inside the box and proceed with his experiments. Before he could do so, a sparkle of light in the darkness caught his eye. He looked up and there, to one side of the tube, was a piece of paper coated with barium platinocyanide, one of the chemicals that glowed when struck by the fleeting electrons.

What puzzled Roentgen was that the barium platinocyanide didn't happen to be in the path of the electrons. If the paper had been *inside* the cardboard box at the proper end of the cathode-ray tube, why all right. But the glowing paper was to one side of the tube, and even if one supposed that some of the electrons were leaking sideways, there was no way they could get through the cardboard.

Perhaps the glow was caused by something else altogether and had nothing to do with the cathode-ray tube. Roentgen shut off the electric current; the cathode-ray tube went dead— and the coated paper stopped glowing. He turned the electric current on and off and the coated paper glowed and ceased glowing in exact rhythm. He took the paper into the next room and it glowed (more faintly) only when the cathode-ray tube went into operation.

Roentgen could only come to one conclusion. The cathode-ray tube was producing some mysterious radiation that was extraordinarily penetrating, that could go through cardboard and even walls. He hadn't the faintest notion of what that radiation might be so he named it with the symbol of the unknown. He called it "X rays," and it has kept that name ever since.

Roentgen experimented furiously and then, after a phenomenally short interval, managed to publish the first paper on the subject on December 28, 1895, reporting all the basic properties of the new radiation. On January 23, 1896, he gave his first public lecture on the phenomenon. He produced X rays before the excited audience, showed that they would fog a photographic plate and that they would penetrate matter— some types of matter more easily than others.

X rays would penetrate the soft tissues, for instance, more easily than bone. If a hand were placed on a photographic plate and exposed to X rays, the bones would block so much of the X rays that the portion of the plate under them would remain relatively unfogged. The bones would appear white on black. An aged Swiss physiologist, Rudolf Albert von Kölliker, volunteered, and an X-ray photograph of his hand was taken.

No physical discovery was ever applied to medical science so quickly. The thought that the interior of intact, living organisms could be seen caused intense excitement, and only four days after the news of X rays reached the United States, the new radiation was successfully used to locate a bullet in a man's leg. Within a year of Roentgen's discovery, a thousand papers on X rays were published, and in 1901, when the Nobel prizes were first set up, the very first to be awarded in physics went to Roentgen.

(Laymen went wild too. Panicky members of the New Jersey legislature tried to push through a law preventing the use of X rays in opera glasses for the sake of maidenly modesty—which was about par for legislative understanding of science.)

It was clear that the radiation couldn't appear out of nowhere. The speeding electrons making up the cathode rays struck the glass of the tube and were stopped more or less suddenly. The kinetic energy of those speeding electrons had to appear in another form, and they did so as X rays, which were energetic enough to smash through considerable thicknesses of matter.

If this happened when electrons struck glass, what would happen when they struck something which was denser than glass and could stop them more effectively? The greater deceleration ought to produce more energetic X rays than those Roentgen had first observed. Pieces of metal were therefore sealed into the cathode-ray tubes in places where they would be struck by the electrons. The expected happened. Larger floods of more energetic X rays were produced.

The X rays produced by the collision of electrons with metal were studied with particular care in 1911 by the English physicist Charles Glover Barkla. Physicists had not yet worked up appropriate techniques for measuring the properties

454

of X rays with real delicacy but one could at least tell that one particular sheaf of X rays might penetrate a greater thickness of matter than another sheaf would and that the first therefore contained more energy.

Barkla found that for a given metal, X rays were produced in sharply different energy ranges, judging by their penetrating quality. There would be what he called the K series, the L series, the M series and so on, in order of decreasing penetrability and, therefore, decreasing energy content. The energy range was discontinuous. There were no X rays to speak of at energy levels intermediate between the K and the L or between the L and the M and so on.

What's more, each different metal produced a set of X rays with energies characteristic of itself. If one focused on one particular series—the L series, for instance—these would increase in energy the higher the atomic weight of the metal that was stopping the electrons.

Since the X-ray energy levels were characteristic of the metal used to stop the electrons, Barkla called them "characteristic X rays."

The *x* of X rays remained appropriate for seventeen years after Roentgen's initial discovery.

Were X rays composed of particles like electrons, but much more energetic? Or were X rays made up of bundles of electromagnetic waves like those of ordinary light, but much more energetic?

If X rays consisted of waves, they would be bent in their course by a diffraction grating, one in which there were numerous fine, opaque lines, parallel to each other, on an otherwise transparent screen. The trouble was that the lines in such gratings have to be separated by small distances. The shorter the wavelengths of the radiation being studied, the more closely spaced the diffraction lines must be.

One could rule, by mechanical means, lines fine enough and closely spaced enough to diffract ordinary light waves, but if X rays were like light but much more energetic, their waves would have to be much smaller than those of light. Lines simply could not be ruled close enough to handle X rays.

It occurred to a German physicist, Max Theodor Felix von Laue, that one did not have to depend on man-made lines.

Crystals consisted of atoms arranged in great regularity. Within the crystal there would be sheets of atoms of one particular kind oriented along one particular plane. There would be successive sheets of these atoms separated by just the distances one would need for diffracting X rays. A crystal, in other words, was a diffraction grating designed by nature for use in the study of X rays (if one wanted to be romantic about it).

Well, then, if X rays were sent through a crystal and if they were diffracted in a way one could predict from theory, *assuming* the X rays were lightlike waves, then the X rays very likely *were* lightlike waves.

In 1912 Von Laue and his associates sent a beam of X rays through a crystal of zinc sulfide and it *was* diffracted just so. The X rays were electromagnetic radiation then, like light but far more energetic. Now X rays were no longer x, but they kept the name anyway.

Scientists could go further. The distance between sheets of atoms in the crystal could be worked out from data not involving X rays. From this one could calculate how much diffraction different wavelengths ought to yield. By passing X rays through a given crystal of a pure substance then, and measuring the amount of diffraction (something that was reasonably easy to do), the wavelength of a particular set of X rays could be determined with surprising precision.

A young Australian student of physics at Cambridge, William Lawrence Bragg, hearing of Von Laue's experiment, saw the point at once. His father, who was teaching physics at the University of Leeds, saw the same point. Together, father and son began measuring X-ray wavelengths at a great rate and perfected the technique.

And this brings me to the hero of this chapter, the English physicist Henry Gwyn-Jeffreys Moseley, son of a professor of anatomy who died when Henry was only four.

Moseley was simply a streak of brilliance. He won scholarships to both Eton and Oxford and in 1910, when he was twenty-three years old, he joined the group of young men who were working under the New Zealand-born Rutherford at Victoria University in Manchester and stayed with him for two years.

456

Rutherford was himself one of the great experimenters of all times and had won the Nobel Prize in 1908. (He won it in chemistry because his physical discoveries had such exciting significance for the science of chemistry—rather to his disgust, for like any good physicist, he tended to look down on chemists.)

What's more, seven of those who worked for him at one time or another went on to win Nobel prizes of their own eventually. Yet there is room to argue that of all those who worked for Rutherford, none was more brilliant than Moseley.

It occurred to Moseley to combine the work of the Braggs and of Barkla. Instead of differentiating among the various characteristic X rays associated with different metals by Barkla's rather crude criterion of penetrability, he would send them through crystals, à la the Braggs, and measure their wavelengths with precision.

This he did in 1912 (by which time he had shifted to Oxford and to independent research) for the metals calcium, titanium, vanadium, chromium, manganese, iron, cobalt, nickel and copper. These elements make up, in that order, a solid stretch across the periodic table—except that between calcium and titanium there should be scandium and Moseley had no scandium available with which to work.

Moseley found a particular series of the characteristic X rays associated with each metal decreased in wavelength (and therefore increased in energy) as one went up the periodic table and did so in a very regular way. In fact, if you took the square root of the wavelength, the relationship was a straight line.

This was extraordinarily important because the atomic weights, which until then had been the chief way of judging the order of the elements in the periodic table, showed no such great regularity. The atomic weights of the elements studied by Moseley were (to one decimal place): 40.1, 47.9, 50.9, 52.0, 54.9, 55.8, 58.9, 58.7 and 63.5. The atomic weight of scandium, which Moseley did not have available, was 45.0. The atomic weight intervals are, therefore, 4.9, 2.9, 3.0, 1.1, 2.9, 0.9, 3.1, −0.2, 4.8.

These irregular intervals simply could not compare with the absolute regularity of the X-ray wavelengths. What's more, in

457

the periodic table there were occasional places where elements were out of order if the atomic weights were used as criteria. Thus, from their chemical properties, it was certain that nickel came after cobalt in the table even though nickel's atomic weight was slightly lower than that of cobalt. This *never* happened with X-ray wavelengths. By that criteria, nickel had characteristic X rays of greater energy than cobalt and *ought* to come after cobalt.

The conclusion Moseley was forced to come to was that the atomic weight of an element was not a fundamental characteristic and did not entirely, in and of itself, account for why a particular element was a particular element. The X-ray wavelengths, on the other hand, represented something that *was* a fundamental characteristic of the elements.

Moseley was even able to point out what that something was.

Just one year before, Moseley's old boss, Rutherford, had conducted a series of elegant experiments that had demonstrated the basic principles of atomic structure. The atom was not the featureless, ultimate particle it had been thought to be all through the nineteenth century. Instead, it had a complex internal makeup.

Almost all the atomic mass was concentrated in the very center of its structure, in an "atomic nucleus" that took up only a quadrillionth of the volume of the atom. All about it, filling the rest of the atom, were electrons, which were mere froth, for one electron had a mass only 1/1837 that of even the lightest atom.

Each electron had a unit negative charge which was absolutely identical in size in all electrons (as far as anyone knew then, or, for that matter, now). The electron charge is usually represented as −1.

The atom as a whole, however, was electrically uncharged. It followed therefore that the central atomic nucleus must have a balancing positive charge.

Suppose, then, that each different element was made up of atoms containing a characteristic number of electrons. The central nuclei of these atoms must contain that same characteristic and balancing number of positive unit charges. If an element had atoms containing only one electron, its nucleus would have a charge of $+1$. An atom with two electrons would have a nucleus with a charge of $+2$. One with three electrons, a nucleus with a charge of $+3$ and so on.

Electrons in varying numbers can, however, be stripped from or added to particular atoms, leaving those atoms with a net positive or negative charge respectively. This means that the electron number is not really fundamentally crucial to the nature of the atom. The atomic nucleus, hidden far within the center of the atom, could not be manipulated by ordinary chemical methods, however. It remained a constant factor and it was therefore *the* characteristic property of an element.

In Moseley's time, nobody knew the details of the structure of the atomic nucleus, of course, but that was not yet necessary. The size of the positive charge on the nucleus was enough.

It was easy to argue, for instance, that the speeding electrons of the cathode rays would be decelerated more effectively as the charge content of the atom they struck increased. The energy of the X rays produced would increase in some regular fashion with the increase in charge content; and if the charge content increased very regularly by unit charges, then so would the energy content of the X rays.

Moseley suggested that each element be represented by a number that would express two different things: 1) the number of unit positive charges on the nuclei of its atoms, and 2) its position in the periodic table.

Thus hydrogen, as the first element in the table, would be represented by the number 1 and, it was to be hoped, would have 1 unit positive charge on its atomic nucleus (this turned out to be correct). Helium would be 2, this representing the fact that it was the second element in the periodic table and had two unit positive charges on the nuclei of its atoms. And so on, all the way to uranium, the last element then known in the periodic table, which would, from the data gathered then and since, have ninety-two unit charges on its atomic nuclei and therefore be represented by the number 92.

Moseley suggested that these numbers be called "atomic numbers," and that suggestion was adopted.

Moseley published his findings in 1913 and they made an enormous splash at once. In Paris, Georges Urbain thought he would test Moseley. He had spent many years carefully and painstakingly separating rare earth minerals and he prepared a mixture of several oxides which he felt no one but an expert could analyze, and that only after long and tedious fraction-ations. He brought it to Oxford and there Moseley bounced electrons off the mixture, measured the wavelength of the X rays produced and in hardly any time at all announced the mixture to contain erbium, thulium, yttrium and lutetium—and he was right.

Urbain was astonished, as much by Moseley's youth (he was still only twenty-six) as by the power of his discovery. He went back to Paris, preaching the atomic number concept with fervor.

Now at last the periodic table was on a firm foundation. When the X-ray wavelengths differed by a certain known minimum amount, then two elements were adjacent and had nuclear charges that differed by a single unit. There could be *no new elements located between them*.

This meant that from hydrogen to uranium inclusive, there were exactly ninety-two conceivable elements, no more and no less. And in the half-century since Moseley's discovery, no unexpected elements in the hydrogen-uranium range have shown up between two elements predicted adjacent by X-ray data. To be sure, new elements were located beyond uranium, with atomic numbers of 93, 94, and so on, up to (at the present writing) 104 and *possibly* 105, but that is a different story.

Furthermore, if the X-ray wavelengths of two elements differed by twice the expected interval, then there *was* an element in between, exactly *one* element. If no such element was known, then it remained to be discovered, that was all.

At the time the atomic number concept was advanced, eighty-five elements were known in the range from hydrogen to uranium. Since there was room for ninety-two elements, it meant that there still remained exactly seven undiscovered elements. What's more, their atomic numbers turned out to be 43, 61, 72, 85, 87 and 91.

This solved the problem bothering chemists concerning the total number of rare earths. It turned out there was only one rare earth not yet discovered and it was located in number 61, between neodymium (60) and samarium (62). It took over thirty years to discover the missing seven elements and as it happened, the very last to be discovered was the rare earth, 61. It was discovered in 1948 and named promethium. (By that time, though, elements beyond uranium were being discovered.)

Thanks to Moseley's atomic number concept, the foundation of the periodic table was made firm as rock. Every discovery since then has served only to strengthen both the atomic number and the periodic table.

Clearly Moseley deserved the Nobel Prize in either physics or chemistry (toss a coin and take your pick, and I could argue that he deserved one of each), and it was just as certain as anything could be in such matters that he was going to get it.

In 1914 the physics prize went to Von Laue and in 1915 to the father-son combination of the Braggs. In both cases the work on X rays had served as preliminaries to the culminating work of Moseley. In 1916, then, Moseley would have *had* to get it; there was no way of avoiding it.

I'm sorry; there *was* a way of avoiding it.

In 1914, World War I broke out and Moseley enlisted at once as a lieutenant in the Royal Engineers. That was his choice and he is to be respected for his patriotism. Still, just because an individual is patriotic and wishes to risk a life that is not entirely his own to throw away doesn't mean that the decision-makers of a government have to go along with it.

In other words, Moseley might have volunteered a thousand times and yet the government had no business sending him to the front. Rutherford understood this and tried to have Moseley assigned to scientific labors since it was obvious that he could be far more valuable to the nation and the war effort in the laboratory than in the field. By World War II, this was understood and Moseley would have been protected as a rare and valuable war resource.

No such thing was to be expected in the monumental stupidity that was called World War I.

In the spring of 1915, the British got the idea of landing at Gallipoli in western Turkey to seize control of the narrow straits linking the Mediterranean and Black seas. Forcing a passage through, they could open a supply route to the tottering Russian armies, which combined enormous individual bravery with equally enormous administrative ineptitude. Strategically the concept was a good one, but tactically it was handled with incredible folly. Even in a war so consistently idiotic, the Gallipoli campaign manages to shine as an archetype of everything that should not be done.

By January 1916, it was all over. The British had thrown in half a million men and gotten nowhere. Half of them were casualties.

In the course of this miserable campaign, Moseley was tapped. On June 13, 1915, he embarked for Gallipoli. On August 10, 1915, while he was telephoning an order, a Turkish bullet found its mark. He was shot through the head and killed at once. He had not yet reached his twenty-eighth birthday and, in my opinion, his death was the most expensive individual loss to the human race generally, among all the millions who died in that war.

When the time for the 1916 Nobel Prize in physics came about, there was no award. It is easy to explain that by saying that the war was on, but there had been an award in 1915 and there was to be one in 1917. The 1917 one was to Barkla, still another man whose work was only preliminary to the great breakthrough of Moseley's.

Call me sentimental, but I see no reason why the colossal stupidity of the human race should force the indefinite perpetration of a disgraceful injustice. It is not too late, even now, for the community of science to fill that gap and to state that the 1916 Nobel Prize in physics (that wasn't) belongs to Moseley and that he ought to appear in every list of Nobel laureates published.

We don't owe it to him; I'm not *that* sentimental. He is beyond either debt or repayment. We owe it to the good name of science.

This brings us to the end of the book. I can't help but be curious as to whether those who liked the fiction liked the non-fiction as well—and vice versa. You can certainly write on the matter if you wish, care of the publisher, and though I can't promise to answer all such letters, I promise to read them all, even (gritting my teeth) the unfavorable ones.

Isaac Asimov
New York, N.Y.

BESTSELLING BOOKS FROM TOR

☐ 53103-5 SHADE OF THE TREE by Piers Anthony $3.95
☐ 53104-3   Canada $4.95

☐ 53206-6 VOYAGERS II: THE ALIEN WITHIN by Ben Bova $3.50
☐ 53207-4   Canada $4.50

☐ 53257-0 SPEAKER FOR THE DEAD by Orson Scott Card $3.95
☐ 53258-9   Canada $4.95

☐ 53147-7 DRINK THE FIRE FROM THE FLAMES by Scott Baker $3.95
☐ 53148-5   Canada $4.95

☐ 53396-8 THE MASTER by Louise Cooper $3.50

☐ 54721-7 FLIGHT IN YIKTOR by Andre Norton $2.95
☐ 54722-5   Canada $3.95

☐ 51662-1 THE HUNGRY MOON by Ramsey Campbell $4.50
☐ 51663-X   Canada $5.95

☐ 51778-4 NIGHTFALL by John Farris $3.95
☐ 51779-2   Canada $4.95

☐ 51848-9 THE PET by Charles L. Grant $3.95
☐ 51849-7   Canada $4.95

☐ 50159-4 THE MILLION DOLLAR WOUND by Max Allan Collins $3.95
☐ 50160-8   Canada $4.95

☐ 50152-7 TRUE CRIME by Max Allan Collins $3.95
☐ 50153-5   Canada $4.95

☐ 50461-5 ONE OF US IS WRONG by Samuel Holt $3.95
☐ 50462-3   Canada $4.95

Buy them at your local bookstore or use this handy coupon:
Clip and mail this page with your order.

Publishers Book and Audio Mailing Service
P.O. Box 120159, Staten Island, NY 10312-0004

Please send me the book(s) I have checked above. I am enclosing $_____
(please add $1.00 for the first book, and 25¢ for each additional book to cover
postage and handling). Send check or money order only — no cash or CODs.

Name _____

Address _____

City _____ State/Zip _____

Please allow six weeks for delivery. Prices subject to change without notice.

THE BEST IN SCIENCE FICTION

- [ ] 53125-6   DRAGON'S GOLD by Piers Anthony and Robert E. Margroff $3.95
- [ ] 53126-4   Canada $4.95

- [ ] 53103-5   SHADE OF THE TREE by Piers Anthony $3.95
- [ ] 53104-3   Canada $4.95

- [ ] 53172-8   BEYOND HEAVEN'S RIVER by Greg Bear $2.95
- [ ] 53173-6   Canada $3.95

- [ ] 53206-6   VOYAGERS II: THE ALIEN WITHIN by Ben Bova $3.50
- [ ] 53207-4   Canada $4.50

- [ ] 53257-0   SPEAKER FOR THE DEAD by Orson Scott Card $3.95
- [ ] 53258-9   Canada $4.95

- [ ] 53308-9   THE SHADOW DANCERS: $3.95
- [ ] 53309-7   G.O.D. INC. NO. 2 by Jack L. Chalker   Canada $4.95

- [ ] 54620-2   THE FALLING WOMAN by Pat Murphy $3.95
- [ ] 54621-0   Canada $4.95

- [ ] 55237-7   THE PLANET ON THE TABLE by Kim Stanley Robinson $3.50
- [ ] 55238-5   Canada $4.50

- [ ] 55327-6   BESERKER BASE by Fred Saberhagen, Anderson, Bryant,
  Donaldson, Niven, Willis, Velazny $3.95
- [ ] 55328-4   Canada $4.95

- [ ] 55796-4   HARDWIRED by Walter Jon Williams $3.50
- [ ] 55797-2   Canada $4.50

Buy them at your local bookstore or use this handy coupon:
Clip and mail this page with your order.

Publishers Book and Audio Mailing Service
P.O. Box 120159, Staten Island, NY 10312-0004

Please send me the book(s) I have checked above. I am enclosing $_____
(please add $1.25 for the first book, and $.25 for each additional book to
cover postage and handling. Send check or money order only—no COD's.)

Name _____

Address _____

City _____ State/Zip _____

Please allow six weeks for delivery. Prices subject to change without notice.